I0675671

DESERT SWARM

After his superior officers are killed in action, Corporal Josiah Key assumes command of the 3rd Battalion, Marine Raiders. In the tiny village of Shabhut, Yemen, while trying to put the blast on ISIS forces, an even deadlier enemy emerges: ancient, unreasoning creatures who tear into both U.S. troops and terrorists without mercy, leaving brutally dismembered corpses in their wake.

They are known as the *Idmonarchne Brasieri*, giant prehistoric spiders roused from millennia-long slumber by power-mad terrorists. These aptly-named 'Arachnosaurs' are hungry. They're angry. And they have declared war against all of humanity . . . whose days might just be numbered unless Key and his unit can stop them.

ARACHNOSAUR

Visit us at www.kensingtonbooks.com

ARACHNOSAUR

A Team Cerberus Thriller

Richard Jeffries

LYRICAL UNDERGROUND
Kensington Publishing Corp.
www.kensingtonbooks.com

Heaven wheels above you, displaying to you her eternal glories, and still your eyes are on the ground.
Dante Alighieri

You gotta watch your fuckin' step.
Josiah Key

Prologue

Poised majestically beneath a blazing midday sun, the spotted beast stood half as high as the tall tree, its four spindly legs holding a long and graceful neck directly below the clustered branches. There, its elongated horse-like mouth pulled leaves from those strong limbs, causing the great arms to spring a little with each bite. Sometimes, leaves dropped to the ground. The animal's flat-topped teeth ground the foliage to pulp while the eyes looked ahead at the next bite. The large, flared nostrils handled security for the prehistoric creature, never resting, sniffing for predators— the great cats and wolves, and also the pack-hunters who came from distant caves in the cliff and walked upright and carried pointed sticks that flew through the air with fatal precision.

Other beasts stood with the largest one, ten in the herd. The adults chewed their meals from other trees, not bothering to spit out the grubs and insects that also feasted on the leaves. Now and then a guttural sound would warn one animal not to impinge on the branch of another. If that failed, a head would be lowered and the antlers waggled at the intruder. Invariably, the animals would part and resume their feast as if nothing had happened.

The younger, smaller beasts fed on the fallen leaves or on the less-tasty grasses that were nearly knee-high. Stirred by the cool gentle wind, which also ruffled the short but bristled coat of the mammals, the grasses told the herd which way to move so that the scent of the killers would reach them long before disemboweling claws or crippling teeth did—or those sharpened weapons wielded by the two-legged pack-hunters, their tips dark and painfully hard from the fire-tempering they were given.

Not far away, a river flowed from hills covered with thick layers of ice. It was a new and vital river cutting a new channel, fed by the melting glaciers, and it brought minerals that enriched the plains and allowed the herd to prosper, along with those who fed off them.

The waters also nourished the roots of the trees and those creatures that lived underground, nested among them.

* * * *

Clad in the spotted skins of the very animals they were hunting, their feet covered in viscera that had been pounded into a cushiony softness, three burly men watched the herd from behind boulders that had been left by the retreating ice. By gestures with hands and head, and by rudimentary language—a humming, hissing *mss* for the target, and a blowing, popping expression of *puh* to signal the attack—the trio had been successful in hunting *mss* as well as other big, open targets. As long as the prey did not get much of a head start, the hurled spears could outrace them, wound them so that the men could run forward and gut them with teeth they had wrested from the huge skull of a frightful thing. There were not so many killers like that still alive here. The ice had chased them to the south before living memory and there was still a strong chill in the air so those hunters had not yet returned. The new flowering of the landscape had brought the creatures that fed on plants, however; they were increasingly plentiful. These bipedal hunters, who could retreat to caves for warmth, came with them. Even now, their women and children waited in the cliff-face. The opening had been covered with mist when they left with the rising sun. Now, behind them, it was just a jagged black smudge in the face of a slope.

The men were on the ground, crawling closer but circling round and round so the shifting winds would not carry their scents to the herd. It was especially hard on the knees, which were bleeding; another smell to deal with, as if their matted hair and lice-infested armpits and groins and sweat-coated backs were not enough. Insects buzzed around them, some stirred by their passage, others drawn by their rank odor and blood. The men blew at the pesky *pssts*, named after the sounds they made, and shook their heads to unseat those that landed, but remained focused on their targets.

Mss...puh, whispered one of the men through the tangled whiskers of his beard. He pointed his spear. *This creature, the biggest.*

The others grunted in a mix of sounds that blended assent with excitement. One covered his mouth as the *mss* looked in their direction, sniffing. The three men stopped and remained perfectly still. They heard thumping in their chests and the sound the grasses made when the wind moved over them and the growling of the waters as they raced past them. But they themselves uttered no sound.

And then the shriek of a *mss* at the far end of the herd brought them all to sudden attention. Alert but as yet unafraid, they looked that way, squinting and shielding their eyes from the high sun. So did the other members of the herd, some jerking as if to run but then waiting to make sure there was danger. It could be just a hole in the ground that had swallowed a hoof, or a bite from something that writhed or flew.

Then the creature that had cried out did so again, a far horrible cry that drove its muzzle straight up and wide and had it screaming into the leaves. Its body shook from side to side in jerky moves. The men had seen that kind of movement before, when beasts were caught in the thick, gooey, black pits that pulled food to its death and sometimes spit up furry little dead things.

But there were no such pits here. The men watched and then started as something new was added to the giant's convulsions: sprays of red that shot so far and high and wide the trees and its neighbors were covered with it.

The *mss* went down with a solid *thump* and now the other animals fled but they did not get far. Not quite as one, but close enough: the beasts were moving, then they stopped as if they were stuck, and then they went down in a rain of shrieks and blood.

The men looked from one to another, hooting and huffing and trying to decide what to do. There was easy meat out there, but there was also whatever was pulling them down.

One of the men crept forward very cautiously, looking, listening, sniffing, trying to peer through the thick, moving grasses.

Something came charging toward him. It was a mass of black with spots of blood and what looked like too-many moving limbs and teeth, all of them, and it, growing larger by the moment. The man didn't decide to turn and run, he just *did* it. And on his feet, not his knees, though he never got fully upright. There was a severe burning pain in his ankles and just below his knees, which didn't last long since his ankles and lower legs suddenly vanished. He fell on his face, his hands spread before him, and he began to scream into the cool earth as his legs disappeared up to the hips. The skin itself didn't vanish: it flew up in the air in tiny pieces, like bits of rock from a volcano, streams and beads of blood arcing behind it like lava. He was shuddering violently, then, no longer entirely conscious of being pulled apart and eaten still-alive like the *mss* and, now, like his two companions.

Splats of falling skin and viscera lightly accented the screams that raced through the field like the roaring river. And then, very quickly, there was only the river.

Dismembered bodies of *mss* and men pulsated in the grasses, the dark soil soaking blood and bile as warm-blooded life passed from the plain. The insects, however, did not return to the grasses or alight on the carcasses.

Not yet.

Below them, things still moved, still tore into flesh, still snipped at sinew and bone until the marrow bled out. Things moved around and over the remains, clicking noises rising as they found soft tissue and eyes and aggressively tore back skin that kept them from their morsels. Before the sun had moved too much farther, nothing resembling either of the evolved species remained. It was just a mass of gore that would soon feed the insects and brave little rodents and the seeds that fell from the new, flowering plants that spotted the land.

By the time the sun set, the grasses were once again moving as before, the landscape was quiet, and the killers, having fed, had returned to their nest beneath the ground.

Chapter 1

Lieutenant Colonel Lawrence Goodman's head exploded with such force, and so near Josiah Key's face, that a piece of the commanding officer's helmet smacked the corporal's forehead. It knocked Key unconscious, despite his own strapped-on flack helmet.

Key had no idea how long he was out. It could've been a second, it could've been an eternity. He might even be dead, he couldn't be absolutely sure. What he woke up to certainly seemed like perdition; hell a la Yemen. Sergeant Morton Daniels' contorted face filled his vision, bellowing at him. Then Joe noticed that all around the mans' swarthy, mottled, sweaty head was a halo of fire.

Goodman's brain and body started moving the moment consciousness touched him. Grabbing a fistful of Daniels' curly, black, naturally greasy hair, Key dragged himself up while moving the other man's head out of his field of vision.

Key immediately regretted it. His waking ears and opened eyes were immediately filled by the sound and sight of all-encompassing enemy fire.

At once, releasing the hair of his companion, Goodman's M249 Squad Automatic Weapon was up, seeking targets at the same moment Daniels's M240 machine gun was doing the same in the opposite direction.

Key started barking as soon as he found his voice. "What the hell happ—"

But as usual with the sarge, he was already answering just as loudly. "One sec, nothing, next sec, shit-storm!"

Key could now see that. The dead corporal had warned them things could always get messy as soon as they left base, but not this messy. This messy challenged even Key's well-developed imagination.

"Take cover!" he bellowed, his M249 SAW finding nothing but ricochets, reports, and detonations to target. *Where the hell was the enemy?*

"Copy that!" Daniels yelled back. "Any suggestions *where?*"

Trust Sarge D to crack wise even in a firestorm. Key remembered that was one of the reasons he'd gravitated toward the man in basic, despite his rep of having a bite far worse than his bark. But, strangely, that was just about all Key could remember. As if God was scrunching the edges of his brain, his memories started dissipating like popping soap bubbles.

"Find a friggin' hole and fall into it!" he yelled, getting increasing anxious and annoyed in equal measure.

He felt Morty's huge, rough hand grabbing his arm, and the next thing he knew they were both flat on their backs in a shallow divot created by a tank tread. It was hardly enough to give them cover, but it would have to do.

One question, he thought. *Where's the fucking tank?* Then God started rubbing petroleum jelly around the edges of his eyes as well.

Key tried to focus at the way the front of his boots poked up against the divot's lip, expecting to see his toes blown off at any second. But it didn't take more than another second for him to realize what was happening to him.

"Shit," he said over the whomping going on all around them. "I've been conked."

"What?" Daniels complained as a tree limb shattered above them, scratching their faces with jagged bark. "Not again!"

Yeah, that's right, Key managed to recall. That's where he had heard the "conked" term before. The base doc had said it when he had diagnosed Key's previous, original, concussion. And doc had given him the self-diagnostic list then, too.

"Symptoms check." Key grunted miserably. "I'm nauseous."

"You're nauseous!" Daniels snapped. "*I'm* nauseous! *Anybody'd* be nauseous in this shit!"

There was a vicious whine just above them, and Key could feel a wave of heat make a line from his forehead to his crotch. The thing causing it just missed them before continuing on to smash through an already crumbling wall fifty feet beyond.

FGM-148 Javelin, Joe automatically assumed. Nice that some hard-won memories defied even concussions. But whether the anti-tank missile was fired by the good or the bad guys was anybody's guess.

"Headache, dizzy, ringing in my ears," Key continued, trying to stave off total amnesia.

"Okay, okay!" Daniels grumbled. "You oughta know. What do you want from me?"

"Memory loss growing, need your help."

"Christ, Joe." The honest concern in Daniels voice was music above the cacophony. "Do you even *know* you're Joe?"

"Yeah," Key answered, struggling to be present, feeling stronger already. "Tell me."

"We're 3rd Battalion, Marine Raiders, M Company, eighty-five strong."

"Not anymore," Daniels reported with his usual lack of empathy. "Heavy defensive fire. *Surprisingly* heavy."

That comment let Key know the attack must've been seventh level of hell heavy. Daniels prided himself on taking the worst in stride. "What are we down to?"

"Last time I could check, less than fifty. Sergeant major shot to hell. Lieutenant colonel just blew up in your face."

Key gritted his teeth, then hazarded a quick look around. He returned to his prone position with his cracked skull thankfully still just cracked. But he could still not distinguish enemy from friendly fire. Worse, he couldn't find any human source of the shit-storm. "Where is everybody?"

"Damned if I know," Daniels said.

"Where's comm?"

"No live communication for a coupla minutes now."

"What? So who's commander now?

"Near as I can tell, you," Daniels said. Then he added sarcastically, "God help us."

Key ignored the comment, but couldn't disagree. Finally made it to chief with a nice new concussion as a reward. Even so, he still could remember that his rep was "Joe Cool." According to Daniels, he never lost it. No time to start now.

First things first, he heard the father inside him instruct.

"Where *are* we?" he yelled at Daniels in a tone that broached no sarcasm.

"Outside of Shabhut," Daniels spat back, then couldn't help elaborating. "Well-fucking named. A more miserably shabby mound of huts I've never seen." Then, when Key didn't answer, he felt compelled to add, "Outside of Aden, inside of Yemen!"

Joe remembered where that was. Good sign. "What are we doing here?"

"Orders. Code C3," Daniels reported, then added with just a tinge of doubt, "Do you at least know what that is?"

Clean the town.

"Yeah, I know what that is," Joe answered, struggling to keep misery out of his voice. "But the town seems to be cleaning us."

Key twisted in place, looking in every direction for a sign of anything or anyone who could help. He saw nothing but smoke, dust, and strafing. But, above the wining, sizzling bullet noises, he heard a growing, grinding, thundering sound just as the ground beneath him began to shake.

The tank? He both wondered and hoped. *Had to be a tank. If so, had to be our side. Enemy didn't have...!*

"Fuckaduck!" Daniels bellowed at the same moment the sarge's huge paw dragged Key up. "ASS!"

Within seconds of reaching his feet, Key knew Daniels wasn't referring to their butts, or even suggesting in his usual subtle way that they move theirs. He was using the age-old term for "asset"—one with a lot of firepower.

Sure enough, rumbling and roaring down the tank track was a Marine HMMWV—High Mobility Multipurpose Wheeled Vehicle, or Humvee—that seemed intent on leaving sergeant and corporal jelly beneath their ten-foot-ten-inch wheelbase.

Even though his mental fog, Key could tell that whoever was driving was fully committed to get the hell out of there. The now opaque windshield looked like crimson stained glass, and the doors looked as if they had been pounded by Satan's fists. The big tan Humvee roared by them as Daniels' eyes bulged—first at the retreating vehicle, then at his strangely apathetic friend.

"Fuck," Daniels started as he let his M240 drop, it's strap making it swing behind him. "A," he continued as he grabbed the M32 Multi-shot Grenade Launcher that hung from his other shoulder. "Duck!" he boomed as he aimed it at the back of the diminishing lorry.

Key just stood there, feeling strangely calm amidst the storm. Then, as if his eyes were cameras, they suddenly zoomed in for a close-up on the rear of the Humvee. Strapped to the back of the payload bed was a large rectangular box he didn't recognize.

That's weird, he thought. *We didn't leave base with that.*

"Daniels," he suddenly yelled. "No!"

But it was too late. The sarge had decided that either the enemy had captured the vehicle or some chicken-shit coward was running. Either way they deserved a forty by fifty-one millimeter extended range low pressure high explosive.

Key was jumping onto Daniels as the shell made a grey line toward the back of the barreling Humvee. It hit its target just as Key hit Daniels. The reaction between the two, however, could not have been more different.

The corporal bounced off the sergeant, who had been described more than once, by more than one person—including soldiers too young to know what the expression even meant—as a brick shithouse. The fact that he could carry both a M240 and a M32 at the same time as if they were a messenger bag and a purse gave testament to his size and strength. The grenade, however, did not bounce. It detonated with a cracking bang, followed, as Key feared, with a ground-shaking, Humvee-bouncing, air-quaking ba-boom. The back of the HMMWV was filled with boxed enemy ammo.

Key slammed to the ground just as a sizzling shockwave of heat, dust, sand, and shrapnel swept over him like a scythe. The force was so strong, he didn't even bounce. Instead he was buffeted, shook, and even skidded a little. But this time he was sure he didn't lose consciousness. Which was strange, because a cloud the color of bones settled over him, along with a perplexing sensation of peace.

That's it, he managed to think. *I'm dead.*

The certainty of his demise made it easy for him. If he was dead, the concussion wouldn't matter, nor would anything else. So, he just sat up, rolled to his side, and rose to his feet. He stood there for a few seconds, trying to see or hear anything. Anything: screams, gunfire, Daniels's profanity. But there was nothing. Nothing but the uncanny off-white cloud that seemed to envelope him.

So Key started walking. He thought the mist would soon dissipate, but it didn't. So he just kept moving. He didn't know for how long or in what direction. As long as he was covered in fog he kept moving.

Come on, come on, he thought. *Heaven or hell, make a decision.*

He only paused for a second when he realized that maybe they already had. Maybe this was purgatory. Maybe he was doomed to walk in this for God-knows-how-long.

Key chuckled at the truth of that. *Yeah, only God knew how long. Maybe I shouldn't have taken Your name in vain so often....*

As if in response, the mist finally began to clear. Key stopped dead in his tracks as the smoke retreated—like he was a circular fan. All around him a devastated village began to appear. The whole place looked like a giant lawn mover had been dropped on it. The dwellings didn't look so much detonated as shredded. The foliage didn't look so much cracked or broken as frayed.

Then something else started coming into view. At first Key didn't even recognize them as corpses. The pungent smell—it could've been anything dead. He'd smelled carcasses before, in the mountains of Southern California where he grew up. It wasn't until he realized that the hair, fingernails, and toenails were human in origin that he acknowledged them as more than elaborately slaughtered animals.

The hands and feet of the corpses weren't just sliced open, they seemed inflated until they burst. In fact, all the limbs of the corpses were like that—even the heads. Popped balloons. Balloons popped from the inside, by shattering nails. What sort of weapon did this? What sort of weapon *could* do this?

Key walked slowly around, forcing himself to stare at the devastated bodies—trying to recognize something, anything, about them. Their hair was colored the same dark black by their staggeringly violent deaths, so that was little help. Only the length gave hint of male or female—but not in any convincingly effective manner.

But their remaining, tattered, blood-and-gut-stained clothing held the only real clues. Key could distinguish villager from soldier, but just barely. He dreaded seeing insignia or ID patches, but he looked intently for them just the same.

A young woman's face flashed in his mind's eye. He wasn't proud that he put his hope that Terri Nichols was alive above the rest, but he had felt protective from the moment she joined their squad. She was also from Michigan, like him, and was the youngest, the nicest, and, yes, the prettiest member of the unit. Also the toughest, strongest, smartest girl he had ever met. He was proud to work alongside her, and he wasn't going to blame himself for feeling that way, or for feeling glad that he could find no evidence of her among the corpses.

Then he heard it. And felt it. A foot fall.

Josiah Key looked up, straining to see into the remaining mist, which encircled the ruined village like a net. As he stared, a silhouette began to outline itself in the steamy shroud. He suddenly felt his M249 SAW tight in his hands, but he did not shift his stare a centimeter. He waited until a figure began to emerge from the cloud like a drowning victim surfacing from the sea.

He was not a US soldier. He wore a darkly dyed *thawb*, the traditional long-sleeved, ankle-length garment, only with fatigue pants and army boots. He also wore a turban, but with a gauzy scarf that rippled in the breeze like a flag. But it was not a flag of surrender. Quite the opposite, in fact.

Key would have recognized him even if he was wrapped like a mummy. He had seen his face enough, on screen, on paper, on walls, on desks, and even on flesh in the form of a tattoo. It was Usa Awar, one of the enemy's most wanted terrorists and killers.

He stood twenty feet away from Key, staring back at him with indifference. No, it was more than that. He stared at Key the way a serial killer stares at a victim: not as an animal, but the way a human stares at an animal it is about to kill. As something only worthy of slaughtering.

And he held in his right hand, blood pouring out its neck to spread on the village ground, the decapitated head of Private Terri Nichols.

Key screamed in regret and rage, his forefinger clamping on the trigger of the M249 until its thirty forty-five caliber shells obliterated Awar from his sight. Even then he didn't stop. He instantly replaced the empty weapon with his M9 Beretta sidearm, emptying its fifteen nine millimeter rounds into the same smug face.

It wasn't until a distant beeping distracted him that he finally stopped. He looked down to see a red light flashing inside his pants pocket. The beeping was coming from there.

Like an automaton, Key reached into his pocket to find his personal smartphone flashing and beeping—something he never equipped it to do. He raised it to his numb face to see a small box on the device's screen. The box read: "Military Override. Urgent Incoming Message."

Like so many in the cellphone age, Key's thumb automatically, seemingly involuntarily, responded.

The message appeared, and repeated, again and again. "C5, C5, C5, C5, C5..."

The cleaning had been upgraded. It was now "With Extreme Prejudice."

Josiah Key looked up to see that Awar was gone. There was no sign of Nichols's skull, or any other part of her.

Chapter 2

"You should have seen him," Usa Awar said quietly, even gently, to Private Terri Nichols.

They were in a cave, illuminated by oil lamps and candles, so a glimmering yellow sheen dappled over everything, making her flesh seem to glow. Awar was kneeling before the chair Nichols was tied to. The chair was obviously homemade, from coarse but demonically strong, heavy wood. The rope was also strong and coarse, as well as coiled and thin.

"Obviously in shock, his eyes vacant and unreasoning...."

Her ankles were bent back on either side of her, and lashed to the back slats of the chair seat. The chair did not have arms, but did not require them. Her arms were bent back and slung there by her wrists, which were also noosed around her neck, so if she let them hang naturally, she would strangle herself.

"I was carrying your helmet," Awar said. "You know, the one with your name on it? 'Nichols, T.'"

"He acted as if I was carrying your severed head," Awar continued mildly. "He stared, eyes huge, then started firing wildly." The captor shrugged smugly. "The shooting was easy to evade, as all your attacks are. Apparently I had hit a nerve...."

With that, he diffidently swiped her left breast with the back of his fore and middle fingers. Her nipples were covered by squares of duct tape that he had scraped in the dirt before affixing. Otherwise she was naked, her uniform in a puddle beside her. Nichols cringed, her expression souring.

"Apparently I have hit a nerve of yours as well." Awar smiled. "Please understand that will not be the first or only one I will hit if you do not talk."

Nichols would have loved saying all sorts of things at that moment—
how many others have you captured, how many others have you tortured,
how many others have you killed—but he had taken that choice from her
as well. Her lower face was sealed with swath after swath of duct tape.
Behind it, inside her mouth, was a small light bulb. If she bit down, or they
slapped her, it would shatter, leaving shards behind. If her tongue or jaw
moved, they would cut, filling her mouth with blood until she drowned. If
she swallowed, even involuntarily, slivers would pass through her entire
system, slicing as they went, leaving her to die in continuous, seemingly
endless, agony.

It was the most effective gag she could have imagined—if she had
ever bothered to imagine such things. But, astonishingly, it also gave her
hope. It might mean that there were rescuers nearby her captors didn't
want to hear her.

Even as she thought that, they both heard a sound. They both looked over
to see one of Awar's shrouded men in the cavern opening. His obscured
face was another thing that gave Nichols hope. The fact that they did not
want the underling recognized announced the chance she might be asked
to describe him some day.

The man said something in Arabic, which Awar reacted to with barely
concealed concern. He thought for a moment, looking away from his
prisoner, then nodded slightly before standing. He looked down at Nichols
with an expression that mixed certainty and mercilessness.

"When I return, you will tell me what I want to know. I leave you to
consider the means we will use."

Then he grabbed her uniform and left, along with his underling, leaving
her alone in the small cavern. If Awar expected her to sob, quake, or
despair, he had captured the wrong soldier. As her family had constantly
told her, she could have been anything: a ballerina, a gymnast, a nurse, a
cheerleader. She *chose* to be a marine, and had worked damn hard to attain
it, dealing with obstacles at every turn. Obstacles like Morty Daniels, who
made leeringly clear that she had no business serving in combat units. She
still wasn't sure what she liked least, Sergeant Daniels continually ignoring
her, or his bromance buddy, Corporal Key, continually looking out for her.

At least Key was yet another hope to cling to. He had come looking for
her. That meant he wasn't dead or captured, like so many others. If he had
come looking, he'd still be looking, and others would to.

Nichols forced her eyes to stay dry. She forced her mouth to stay open.
But she couldn't avoid her hands turning into tight fists as the memory of
what had happened threatened to engulf her again.

The emergency orders had been clear: clean a village. That meant make sure that the first and second battalions would not be surprised by the sudden appearance of insurgents who might be occupying the town. No problem; they had trained for this. Marine transport had brought them close, then the drone crew took over. The images that came back were both reassuring and disturbing.

The town was already "clean," in that not a creature was stirring. In fact, the village of Shabhut looked like it had hit by tanks running side-by-side. It was not only seemingly uninhabited, it was flattened. The lieutenant had ordered them in anyway to make certain, and her unit responded with their usual skill and proficiency—until an ambush was sprung on them midway through town.

It was the worst firefight she had ever experienced. Suddenly her comrades had started twitching as if being shot by needles, and, once they hit the ground, started writhing as if the dirt was electrified. She had taken a step, crouching to aid them, then the blasts started.

They were blinding, deafening, and seemingly everywhere. She had staggered away, bringing her M4 Carbine to bear, but there was nothing to shoot. Every target was already contorting, even bursting, before her eyes—her vision already being obscured by a chaotic assault of smoke, dust, and blood.

She spun to find cover, then something hard and heavy hit the back of her skull. When she awoke she was in a cage in this network of caves. Some cowled underlings had taken her to this small cavern, stripped her, then gagged and bound her to the chair. Then Awar had appeared and the "interrogation" had begun.

The memories were just a flash in her brain as she looked in every direction. When she found herself a prisoner, she immediately acted as dumb and numb, while tightening her muscles as subtly, as possible. She wanted them to think she was just a little, terrified, girl. She didn't want them to know what she was capable of.

Sure enough, the underlings judged her book by its cover. As she relaxed her wrist muscles, she felt a little give in the cords. When they wrenched her ankles and arms up, she let her tightened muscles give the impression that this was as high as they could go. Nichols inwardly scoffed.

Yeah, she could have been a gymnast, remember?

When she saw there was another exit opposite where Awar had gone, she worked quickly and efficiently. Her fingers and palm curled into the shape of an empanada at the same second her arms rose up her back into a yoga reverse prayer position. Her arms were free of the choking sling within moments. Despite their numbness, they fell silently upon her ankles on either side of the seat, already scratching at the knots. Her bare feet hit the dirt seconds after that.

Only then did her fingers find the edges of the duct tape on her chest and face. Her Marine training co-eds use to have contests to see how long they could keep uncooked eggs, among other things, intact in their mouths. Political correctness and equality be damned, being female was far from a detriment if you knew how to work it. She was standing, holding the sodden light bulb by its screw-base in front of her, within a minute.

Nichols was not embarrassed or ashamed by her nudity, so she moved silently away from Awar's exit and hazarded a quick look out. The cavern continued down a winding tunnel, illuminated by strung bulbs—much like the one they had put in her mouth—hanging on nails hammered into the rock walls. Incredibly, from this exit to a turn in the cavern, it was empty, with no sounds giving hint of a meeting or eating area beyond.

What, didn't they have LED lights in this godforsaken sandpit? At least if they tried to catch her again, she could do with them, to them, what they wanted to do to her mouth and intestines. If it came to that, she had to admit it would feel great to tear open their flesh that way.

But, as Key had repeatedly told her, first things first. Nichols moved into the low, narrow, rock hallway, intent on being ready for anything. Anything, except for what happened.

Once she had reached the curve in the stone hall, she heard a grinding sound behind her. She whirled to see the opening she had left from being filled by a huge, circular slab—which she had seen, but thought was part of the cavern wall. Apparently, as soon as she left, Awar's people had snuck in and quietly pushed it into position so she was cut off.

What the fuck? Do they want to...

Nichols stopped her recoiling brain. Trying to decide whether they were going to gas, drown, starve, or simply imprison her somewhere else was a waste of time. The lights were still on, and she had yet to turn the corner of the cavern. There was only one thing for sure; they didn't want her to go back, and she was damned if she was going to just stand there.

Nichols started to step forward when a glint in the corner of the cave top caught her eye.

Yeah. They might not have LED lights strung along here, but they definitely had recessed camera lenses stuck deep into the rock.

The whole thing was some sort of insane set-up. But no matter how she racked her prodigious brain, she couldn't figure out why. If they wanted her to go down this hall, why not just throw, or drag, her? And why the hell did they strip her?

Nichols looked at the dim glow at the curve of the cave, feeling something she hadn't felt since joining the Marines, even since waking up in this cave. Dread.

Even so, she looked up at the camera lens with defiance. "Okay, sicko," she said. "You want a show? You'll get a show."

In the cavern that served as his control room, Usa Awar smiled back at Nichol's determined face on the monitor screen. It was just one of many monitor screens, each manned by one of his people, with each person ready to take complete, detailed, notes.

"You see?" he said with a smile. "Look at her. She does not cry." He nodded slowly. "She is the bravest of their soldiers I have yet encountered. Unlike the others, I feel certain we will learn what we need to know from her. We have tried every other variation possible, so watch carefully, my children. Watch carefully, and remember everything."

Back at the curve in the cavern, Nichols turned the corner. She found herself standing in the entrance of a larger, circular cavern. There were no strung lights here. The only illumination came from the lights beside and behind her.

She peered closer. The walls of the space did not seem to be made of rock. They seemed to be made of mossy clay. The clay was tan, like potter's clay, seemingly squeezed on top of the rock beneath it. The moss was white and gauzy, and Nichols immediately noticed it riffled in a wind she did not feel. But that meant that there was an exit somewhere. She could follow the air until escape.

Then something else moved. Her senses knew before she did that it was not human. Every pore on her body went concave. Then whatever moisture was left in her slopped out. Terror widened and sharpened her eyes.

Something was crawling over the lip of a clay-plastered hole. Something as big as a brown bear. Only it wasn't anything as familiar as that.

She saw the legs. She saw the mandibles. She saw the six shining, dead eyes. She saw the bulbous quivering abdomen shuddering like a castanet. She saw the fangs.

Theresa Jane Nichols didn't know she screamed. She didn't realize that she screamed so loudly and piercingly that Usa Awar and his cabal winced and cringed many caverns away.

Then it was on her.

Chapter 3

"You should've seen him!" Morton Daniels laughed. "He was just standing there in the middle of the worst shit-storm ever, looking around like it's a day at the beach. And then he starts walking like he's in candyland or something. Just walking over a bluff like he hasn't got a care in the world—while I'm screaming at him to get the fuck down...."

"Ssh," said a nurse, who, because she wasn't young, pretty, and slim, Daniels ignored.

"You wouldn't believe it," Daniels continued, his eyebrows practically crawling into his hairline. "I'm fighting like a sonuvabitch for what seems like hours only to find him, like, a klick away, staring at nothing, his weapon empty and smoking. Then the next thing you know, he drops into my arms like a fainting debutante." Daniels took a second to grin at Key, who lay, expressionless, in an infirmary bed. "You did, you know," he added pointedly. "You did."

"I told you he was suffering post-concussion trauma and post-detonation deafness," interrupted another, calmer, more professional, voice. Key turned his impassive face to Doctor Stanley Weicholz, who sat on the other side of the bed, away from the leering faces of Daniels' audience, who were other patients at the Camp Lemonnier Hospital.

"Hey, doc, don't be a killjoy." Daniels grinned, hooking a thumb at his listeners. "They seem to be enjoying the story."

"Yeah," said the doctor calmly as he continued to take Key's pulse. "They can. They're not from what's left of your squad."

Daniels's face changed, as if his brain had been yanked out his mouth. He took a second to recover, then patted Key on his other arm. "Yeah, that's right. You take it easy, Joe. Rest and recover, okay? I'll be right outside if you want me."

"Yeah, no wux, as some Aussies say," Key replied, using an old in-joke between the two of them. Even so, his voice was more noncommittal than conciliatory. He waited until Daniels was out the door, and Daniels's audience returned to their own beds and concerns, before turning to Weicholz. "He's just trying to process it, doc. Cut him some slack, would you?"

"Well, there's processing to get better, and then there's processing to get back to where you started," Weicholz commented while filling out Key's chart.

"Hey, it's a miracle he's still alive," Key said. "The blowback from his grenade launcher alone should have perforated him."

Weicholz stood and looked down at his patient with caring concern. "It's a miracle you're both still alive. Honestly, Joe, I don't know why you put up with his, shall I say, somewhat Neanderthal approach to life."

Key nodded knowingly. "Because, as you now know, doc, I wouldn't be here without him. Right?"

Weicholz couldn't argue the point, marveling again at Key's equilibrium, especially after what he had recently been through. He could only attribute it to the calming influence of the post-concussion and detonation response.

"Right," he finally agreed, taking a second to reconsider his reaction. "Okay, I could've done without his crude fairy tale, but his parting advice was solid. Rest and recover, Corporal. That's an order."

Key gave the doctor a mild salute. "Yes, sir," he said, then returned to his recuperation stupor. It was so thick that the doc was almost out the door before Key thought to call out. "Hey, any word on when I can get back to the unit?" But Weicholz was already gone.

Key stared vacantly out the ward's window, trying not to think of anything: not his brush with death, not what now seemed to be "his" unit, and especially not what happened to everyone else in the 3rd. But, try as he might, he couldn't help wondering what he was doing in the Seth Michaud Emergency Medical and Dental Facility at Camp Lemonnier, in Djibouti on the horn of Africa.

Sure, it was directly due west, across the Bab al-Mandab Strait, from Shabhut, Aden, in Yemen, but there had to be at least two aircraft carriers in or near the Strait that were closer, and even better equipped to deal with wounds both physical and psychological. Coming to Lemmonier couldn't have been Daniels's decision. Nothing Morty liked better than hitching a ride on a carrier.

"Corporal Josiah Key?"

He turned his head and instantly guessed that the speaker had something to do with it. Standing in the hospital room doorway was a blonde woman whose blue eyes could be appreciated even from this distance. So could the rest of her, which was amply evidenced by Morty Daniels, who was standing right behind her, much in the way, Key imagined, that the wolf stood behind Little Red Riding Hood.

"Yes," Key replied to her unnecessary question. He had little doubt that the file she was carrying had everything there was to know about him, probably going back to kindergarten.

She nodded, with a small smile of accomplishment, then started walking toward his bed. None of the new gender-neutral uniforms for her. Her service uniform of cap, coat, skirt, and even the one-inch black pumps looked tailored to her with a laser measuring device. But the thing that stood out to Key was the gold second lieutenant bar insignia on her garrison cap and shirt collars. That meant she outranked him, even if the field promotion Daniels had cracked wise about was true.

Only then did Key note the wave of eyes that followed the Second Louie across the room like dandelion seeds following the breeze. They were mirrored by Daniels, who trailed her like a devoted hound, only his eyes were transmitting different information: five-seven, a hundred and twenty pounds; thirty-six, twenty-five, thirty-six...

"Good morning, Corporal," she said, putting out her hand. "I'm Second Lieutenant Barbara Strenkofski. I'll be supervising your debriefing."

She pulled over a metal chair with green seat padding and sat down beside his bed, at the same moment Daniels pulled out the neighboring bed's chair and sat opposite her, with a look of excited expectation on his face. Key looked at him like the endlessly patient owner of a naughty puppy, then turned his calm gaze to the Second Louie.

"I thought I was already debriefed," he told her. "I wrote a thorough report—"

"Which I have right here," she said briskly, holding up the file. "Perhaps debriefing was not a wholly accurate term. Consider this more of a personal follow-up."

"Personal follow-up," they heard Daniels snigger before he leaned in with eager anticipation. "I haven't been debriefed, ma'am. You can debrief me."

There was a moment of silence before Strenkofski slowly looked down and, just as slowly, opened the file. She seemed to be reading, then, without looking up, spoke coolly. "And you are?"

"Sergeant Morton L. Daniels, ma'am."

"Yes. I see you are mentioned in Corporal Key's report."

"Mentioned?" Daniels looked at his bedridden friend with a slight look of hurt on his face.

"Yes," Strenkofski said again, same tone as before, without looking up. She didn't speak until she did look up several moments later. By then the chill of her tone and attitude was just reaching Daniels. "You will be debriefed in good time, Sergeant. Until then, I would appreciate it if you could afford Corporal Key and me a little privacy.

Daniels nodded, smiling, until he processed her actual words. Then, continuing the canine analogies, straightened like a puppy who had been tapped on the nose by a rolled-up newspaper for the first time.

"What? Oh, sure. I mean, yes sir, um, I mean ma'am. Sure." He hastily got up, slid the chair back to the next bed, and started for the door before stopping by the end of the mattress. "I'll be right outside if you need me, Joe."

"Yes," Key said with humorous pity. "I know, Morty. Thanks. I believe I can handle it from here."

Daniels almost got to the door when Strenkofski called out. "Sergeant?"

Daniels stopped on a dime, and made a sharp turn. "Yes, ma'am," he said expectedly.

"What's the 'L' for?"

Daniels looked at her blankly. "'L,' ma'am?"

"In your name," she said patiently, giving him a look that would cool soup.

"My name? Oh. Oh, yeah." Daniels' expression fell a little. "Leonard, ma'am."

Strenkofski turned her head away, as if in disappointment. "I figured it would be something like that. Thank you Sergeant. We'll be in touch shortly."

Daniels left the room with his figurative tail between his literal legs. When the blonde officer's satisfied face returned to Key, he was looking at her with amused disapproval. "I appreciate your, no doubt, hard-earned coping skills, ma'am, but watching a top cat play with a trapped mouse isn't always the most enjoyable thing."

Strenkofski looked at him evenly. "No regrets, Corporal." Her eyes returned to the report. "His kind makes me tired."

Key studied her as she read. Dropping this ice princess into the African horn was the opposite of dropping a cockroach on a wedding cake. Either way, no one would miss the contrast.

"Personal follow-ups can be tiring too, Lieutenant," he said carefully. "What can I do for you?"

She didn't look up, nor react to his mild insubordination—both actions convincing Key that his and her presence here was above and beyond the call of due process. "Your report says something that concerned you about Lieutenant Colonel Goodman's death."

"Yeah," Key said. "It was the last second before the concussion symptoms began taking over. It was the only thing I could be certain of." He waited until she looked back up at him before continuing. "I've spent my life and career distinguishing between flesh and bone exploding from the force of ordnance, and flesh and bone exploding from...other sources."

Suddenly she didn't feel like reading. Apparently, she didn't feel like doing anything except staring intensely into his steel-grey eyes. "What are you suggesting, Corporal Key?"

"I'm not suggesting anything, Lieutenant Strenkofski. Just telling you, or anyone else, what I saw. And what I saw makes me believe that Lieutenant Colonel Goodman's head exploded from the inside."

Chapter 4

Key really didn't want to dislike Captain Patrick Logan, but he also really didn't want to use the wheelchair that Weicholz insisted he have.

Ultimately, he settled for both as means to an end. Besides, even he had to admit it was worth being 'incapacitated' to see the look on Daniels's face as he went by—being pushed by Second Lieutenant Barbara Strenkofski. It gave him a nice opportunity to appreciate Camp Lemonnier's facilities, when he wasn't imagining what the back of Strenkofski looked like pushing him.

The former, like so many of the military bases in this region, was both impressive and makeshift. Lemonnier was five hundred acres of well-meaning intent; an expansive schematic of what were amusingly called "containerized living units," plunked down on the southwest side of the Djibouti-Ambouli International Airport—between the runway overflow and a French military munitions storage facility. It had two recreation centers, a wastewater treatment plant, a Navy Exchange Store, a laundry, a fire department, a Disbursing Office, and even an inflated gymnasium.

Strenkofski wheeled Key into the chapel, a small chamber with six rows of steel pews facing a plain, tan-colored, table before a modest altar. It was empty of people, save for Captain Logan, who sat at the table, seemingly intent on yet another file. Key inwardly smirked at the location and the man.

"Brought me to confession, did you?" he asked the blonde as she rolled him to the table's other side. "Do you think I need it?"

"*Do* you?"

The question was probably rhetorical, definitely unanswerable. In his time, Key had shattered many of the Commandments, often in tandem, frequently in multiples.

There they both waited for Logan to finish reading, acknowledge them in some way, or anything. Key heard Strenkofski's breathing get shorter and shallower, but he just relaxed, letting Logan's tightly wired energy roll over him.

"Do you object to the setting," Logan finally asked, without looking up.

"If God doesn't mind, why should I?"

"All the other camp facilities are stretched thin trying to sort out the Gate of Tears," he continued as if he hadn't heard. Maybe he hadn't. Or, more likely, he didn't care to engage in small talk.

Gate of Tears was the translation of Bab-el-Mandeb, the name of the strait that separated Djibouti and Yemen. But it had come to signify the two-way clusterfuck of refugees fleeing the east's civil war, and smugglers sailing west to take advantage of the conflict. Key had already witnessed the Kafka-esque pit debaters of the situation fell into after two ward-mates took up the issue.

Instead of talking, Key took the time to study Logan. His uniform, like the blonde's, was laser-tailored and the same color as the altar table. That alone gave Key plenty of mental ammo, since it was definitely more than a hundred degrees outside, and here were his friendly neighborhood debriefers in full dress. Although he was given the opportunity to change clothes, Key remained in olive-colored short sleeve, short-pant, hospital scrubs Daniels had found for him.

"Josiah, no-middle-name, Key," the shaved-bald Logan continued quietly, as if reading. "Born 1992 in Murrieta, California. Mother a singer, father a marine and then a USMC recruiter." Logan glanced up to meet Key's eyes for the first time. "Sounds like an interesting recipe. Mom wants an entertainer, dad wants a warrior." When Key continued his silence, Logan's bright, beady, eyes returned to the open file on the table top. "On the basis of your college record, you apparently decided to be both. Wrestling star *and* drama club president. Managed to excel at both."

"You left out the strawberry shaped birthmark on my left buttock and my date for the senior prom," Key finally said.

"I'll make those notations when I give a shit," Logan replied.

Key glanced back at Strenkofski, who looked as if she were molded by a paper-thin coating of ice. "It was Destiny Arnold, by the way," he said pleasantly.

"Sorry?"

"My prom date," Key replied. "Smartest girl I ever met."

Strenkofski looked like she wanted to guess why, but hid behind a small, tight grin.

Key turned back when Logan's voice cut through his bonhomie. "How's your health?"

Key returned the gaze, at half-intensity. "You tell me. You obviously know more than I do, since Doc W wanted me decommissioned, and you, apparently, wouldn't hear of it."

"We have a 'three conks and you're out' rule in the Marines, Corporal."

"Don't I know it," Key retorted. "I was counting on it. De-comm was doc's idea, not mine." He glanced back at Strenkofski again with another pleasantry. "Supposedly that kind of thing is a medico's prerogative but not today, apparently."

"Not today," Strenkofski echoed then waited.

Logan waited until Key returned his attention. "Not here, not now," he agreed. "A supervising commander has full discretion to dictate the service of any active marine."

Key perked up at that piece of the puzzle. "You don't have to quote regs to me, sir. I'm sure you know there's a reason I'm still a corporal at my age. That aberration notwithstanding, I know the regs by heart."

"Yes, I know you do, Corporal Key," Logan said clearly, trying to establish rank without question. But when all Key did was continue to show him his knowing little smile, he went back to studying the file. "And you know how to bend them just to the point of breaking. No reprimands, no blots, no arrests. I can't even find an official warning." He looked back up. "You're still a corporal because the men who could promote you just didn't like you."

"No, sir, I disagree," Key pleasantly, but immediately, responded. "I think they liked me. I think you'll like me too. But I also think that they, like you." He turned quickly to the blonde. "And you."

"Don't trust you," Logan interrupted, again trying to regain control.

Key looked back at him, his smile now dusted with slight resentment. "No, sir, I don't think it's that. Ask anyone I've served with, or under. They trusted me with their lives, sir, and I did my utmost to deserve that trust. No, the people who could promote me didn't like the fact that they couldn't predict what I'd do. And that, in a marine grunt, is not conducive to promotion."

Both men looked up when they heard Strenkofski's quiet realization. "Too smart for a private, too pensive for a sergeant."

Key smiled, nodded, and pointed approvingly at her. "Bingo. You may give Destiny Arnold a run for her money after all, ma'am." Key waited until the blonde reacted to his comment with a hastily-concealed expression of being flattered before turning back to face Logan—who was not even trying to conceal his expression of growing anger for losing control of the debriefing. He resumed flipping through the report.

"I will attribute this borderline insubordination to post-trauma stress," Logan said.

"It isn't, sir," Key informed him.

Logan's impatience was growing. "Oh? What is it, then?"

"Impatience," Key assured him. "We both know why we're all here."

The Captain's look of amazement turned to one of begrudging admiration. He slapped the file closed, leaned back, and crossed his legs. "All right, I'll bite," he announced, clearly deciding that if he couldn't beat him, he'd join him. "Why are we all here?"

Key put his hands up. "You told me so, yourself, sir. 'A supervising commander has full discretion to dictate the service of any active marine.' If you weren't my new supervising commander, you wouldn't have full discretion, now would you, sir?"

Logan just stared at Key, as if he were examining a particularly talented circus monkey. "Go on," he urged.

"So you're here to offer me a new assignment, and I'm here to tell you I'll take it, but with one caveat."

Logan actually laughed. He rose and started walking in a bemused circle. "You'll…take it," he said. "With a caveat."

"Yes, sir."

"What's your caveat, *Corporal*?" He stressed the final rank in a last-ditch attempt to return to normal marine relations.

"Sergeant Daniels has to be included," Key said.

"Why is that?"

"He was there, too, sir. He will be invaluable in this new mission."

Logan stopped and put his hands flat on the altar table. He leaned down to pinion Key with his most challenging stare. "So you already know the mission too, Corporal?"

Key leaned back. "Any Brigadier General could've discounted my report from the safety and comfort of a tropical paradise. They didn't have to send you, and your big guns—" Key had the politically correct grace not to even glance at the blonde behind him "—to the Gate of scorching Tears to read me my life story. But they did. So there's something in my report they want explained, and I'm guessing it's not how I thicken my very fine hair."

By that time, Logan had returned to his seat and reopened the file. "Yes, Corporal, your observations in the field were somewhat contradictory."

"There," Key interrupted, pointing at the file. "That's why you want Sergeant Daniels involved."

Logan looked up in confusion, so Key continued.

"Sergeant Daniels would've said 'contradictory how?' I don't have to. Your case history tells you my IQ, so let's get to the heart of it. You want me to find out how Lieutenant Colonel Goodman died, and I do too."

Logan sat and stared at his new soldier, seemingly trying to decide how to proceed. Finally he sighed, closed the file, stood, and faced the altar. "We can't spare any regular non-comms or officers," he said flatly. "The battalions are stretched too thin. We can't deploy any to investigate this. Not on the word of one Corporal, a corporal no one can—well, no one knows what he'll do."

"But the corporal no one can predict might be the right one for this job," Strenkofski added.

Logan sighed again, and faced him. "You *were* going to be de-commed," Logan admitted. "So, as far as those still in the shit-storm are concerned, you're blameless and at liberty to investigate a possible new weapon. A weapon, if it is a weapon, that we must control at all costs."

"Full discretion, sir?"

Logan looked at Key with renewed exasperation. "You are one piece of work! No, not full discretion, Corporal. You don't spit without clearing it with me, first, is that clear?"

"As a South Pacific sea," Key said without pause or shame. "And my caveat?"

Logan nodded. "You've got your man." The Captain paused. Then, as if trying one final attempt to come out ahead, Logan asked sarcastically, "Anything else you want, Corporal?"

No one was more surprised when Key rose from the wheelchair than Key himself. "Yes, sir," he said. "I need to know what happened to my unit. We went out there a team—a team I've spent two years with. Now they're gone and no one can tell me what happened to them. Are they dead, captured, or what? I need to go out there, find them, or find out what happened, then come back and tell you. I don't know what else I'll need to do that—personnel, tools, intel—but whatever it is, you'll provide it. Yes?"

Logan rose to meet his eyes. For the first time the Captain showed Key something approaching respect.

"Yes, Corporal," Logan said quietly. "If it's within my power, you'll have it."

Chapter 5

If there was a thread that wove its way through Josiah Key's military experience, it was assholes in bars.

No matter what continent, country, city, or town he was in, there they were: darkly brooding or overly friendly, full of bravado or deep in self-pity. He could set his watch by them. If he went into any establishment that served booze, there one would be, a woozy jerk-off looking for a fight.

Key understood, even appreciated, it. When you get up every day with a good chance of getting killed before you went to bed, the need to use your downtime wisely, constructively—get lost in alcohol—becomes a bit more pressing. And, if you went into the military seeking power, only to find out just how powerless you were, even with a big old gun in your hand, those folks you ran into…they tended to get a bit testy.

"Hey," said the latest one. "You don't belong here. This is a military bar." By the slur of his voice, Key estimated he was on his third boilermaker.

They sat in a dark, low-ceilinged, yellow-lit, forty-by-sixty, glorified modular home unit lined with a bar, shelves, and stools that could've been anywhere in the world, but was, in fact, at the edge of the RAFO Thumrait air base in Dhofar Governorate, Oman—a large hop, skip, and jump directly east of Lemonneir and Shabhut.

"We *are* military," Key told him, as he placed a hand on Daniels' chest to keep him from using the drunk's head like a fistful of beer nuts.

"No, you're not," Key heard the drunk slur as he started to turn away. "You don't look it. Where's your uniforms?"

Key took a second to consider their new lightweight, breathable, smooth, odor-eliminating, antibacterial, cool-to-the-touch, slightly shiny black pants, collarless jackets, and dark gray T-shirts.

"These *are* our uniforms," he replied. Then he held open the left side of the jacket to reveal the Sig Sauer 9mm P229 automatic in its shoulder holster. "And these are our side arms. And these are our spanking new badges." He held up his billfold and let it flap down to reveal a gold, blue, and red shield that announced *USMC Criminal Investigation Division, Intelligence Activity.*

"Nice, huh?" Daniels asked the drunk. The drunk suddenly shrunk, then slunk closer to the bar.

Turns out Logan had been as good as his word. Key and Daniels were reassigned and outfitted faster than Weicholz could protest. Key found exactly what kind of pull the Captain had when they waived the CIDSAC Special Agent Course, as well as the normally required six months of on-the-job training.

"This is a special assignment," Logan had insisted, which apparently, was already agreed upon by the powers-that-were even before he arrived at Lemonnier.

"Oh," said the drunk. "Oh, sorry." He started to turn away, but hastily snapped his head back with a final word. "Sir."

"Yeah, you better be sorry, bud." Daniels growled. "We're the military who can lock up drunken, pissant other military, right?

"Yeah, yeah, sorry, *said* I was sorry already," the man muttered before returning to his fourth boilermaker. Key gave the seen-it-all bartender the universal sign of on me, which only added to Daniels's disapproval and increasingly foul mood.

But rather than say what he actually felt, the sergeant groused instead. "Why didn't that second louie assign you herself? Why did she hand you off to the chrome dome?"

"Ah, you know the corps." Key shrugged. "Can't wipe their asses unless the toilet paper's in triplicate. Beside, he had to give Babs something to do or else he wouldn't be able to justify keeping her around."

Daniels stared sourly into his beer. "I want to screw that second louie."

"I know, Morty, I know," Key replied as if Daniels had commented on some bad weather. "But beyond that, you're just pissed we're not in Shabhut yet." Key had wanted to hit Daniels's release valve, and that was all it took.

"Yeah," Daniels exclaimed. "What are we doing in this wasteland? I say screw regs, let's just go. Just two guys, no backup, no ordnance. We'd be in and out before they even knew we were there."

"That's not what intel says," Key reminded him with an edge of misery. "Intel says Usa Awar got Shabhut locked down tighter than a bull's ass in fly season."

"Fuck intel." Daniels growled. "They couldn't keep us out."

Key shook his head sadly. "They couldn't keep *you* out, maybe. I'm not such a great fan of standing on the railroad tracks with my arm out."

"What?"

"It would be an empty heroic gesture, Morty. I told you about it before."

"Remind me."

"Bus of school kids caught on a railroad track. Hero stands there with his arm out as the freight train bears down on him. Everybody will talk about how brave he was, but he's still dead, so are the school kids, and probably most of the folk on the train too. Better to figure out an effective way to save everybody than to make a big show of it."

Daniels stared at Key like he had grown another nose. "Eh, who has time to listen to your shit?" he finally muttered.

He was about to turn his attention back to his beer when Key snapped, "That him?"

"What him?" Daniels snapped back. "Who him?"

"Your friend."

Daniels turned around, looked where Key was looking, and his sour melon almost immediately changed into a sweet persimmon. "Yeah," he said with relief. "Yeah, that's Speedy."

Key raised his hand and opened his mouth to signal him, but Daniels quickly yanked his arm down and hissed a hush. "Naw, naw, you don't spook Speedy," he quietly advised. "Chill out, Joe, just follow my lead."

His lead was right to the bar, where he secured a Jim Beam Black, a pickle, a stalk of celery, a shrimp stick, a beef stick, a boiled egg, four Spanish olives, and a tumbler glass of beer. Then he marched over to where the short, wide-shouldered, young man had sat with his back to the bar, dropped the plate and glasses in front of his face, and announced, "Your Snit, sir?"

Speedy's head snapped up, but when he saw who had served him, he broke into a wide grin. By the time the two had finished bumping fists, chests, and even heads, Key was standing beside them.

"Speedy?" Daniels said, "this is my bud Joe Key. Joe, this is the man who can fly anything, fix anything, and knows everything." Daniels looked at him like a prize bull. "The one they know from America to Asia as the Hispanic Mechanic."

Key's expression was one of sheer disbelief. "Speedy? Really?"

The man laughed. "Yeah, Corporal, no wux as our Aussie brethren say."

Key snorted, acknowledging the clear sign of a connection with Morty

Daniels. "My name is actually Manuel Gonzales," the man continued, "so guess what everybody called me from the school yard 'til now?"

"And guess what?" Daniels laughed. "He made them all eat it, until he started liking it himself."

"Hunh." Key took a chair after Gonzales and Daniels had settled down at the table. "I didn't think anybody still remembered the Speedy Gonzales cartoon."

"I don't know about anybody else," Gonzales said between bites of celery, "but I loved it. Yeah, it might be racist, but it was the only Mexican hero on TV we had. And was he *fast*! *Madre de dios*!"

"Nothing compared to you, Speedy," Daniels said, turning to Key. "He could fix my chopper before I could even completely brake it."

Gonzales took a swig of beer. "But that can't be why you're in this armpit of the Middle East," he said, his voice lowering. "Your message said something about Awar?"

Key nodded. "No one in Bahrain and Djibouti could give us credible, solid, status of where he is now and what he's doing. Morty swore you could."

Gonzales swallowed, then nodded. "This is deep, dark stuff, guys. Sure you want it?"

Daniels nodded with proud defiance. Key was more circumspect. "We were the only ones who got out of the C5 mission to Shabhut."

Gonzales stopped eating and drinking, then sat back. "*Mierda*," he said. "Man, I'm sorry, Corporal. That's rough."

"We're trying to find out what happened, and what is happening now."

Gonzales stood on no ceremony. He leaned over the plate as Daniels and Key joined him. "Word is Awar has claimed it as his. His town. No one in or out without him allowing it."

"He can't cover the whole thing," Daniels maintained, still eager for a clandestine mission.

"The hell he can't," Gonzales stressed. "Awar is *mandamas* in Yemen now."

"Top dog," Key translated for the sergeant.

"Got that from the inflection," Daniels noted.

"He says 'his town,' that means every insurgent, extremist, fanatic, radical, terrorist, even warlord will help out stopping any infidel who tries to set foot in the place. Stopping? Shit. Eradicating. Turning that guy's dust into dust."

Daniels looked obstinate. "What is so important in that shitty little anthill that the brass wanted it wiped, and Awar wants it closed?"

Key leaned back, his face thoughtful. "A weapon that makes people go pop." Then he straightened and gripped the table edge. "Looks like you're right, Morty. We got to get in there."

Daniels acted as if Key had announced every day would be Christmas. "So now you want to stand on the railroad tracks with me, now, huh? Good man, Joe!"

"That's crazy!" Gonzales gaped. "What for? You'll get killed and be no closer to whatever this weapon is."

Key stood up, already hoping for the best and preparing for the rest. "I'm not going in for whatever this so-called weapon is, but I've got to see at least one of the bodies it left behind."

He took a step toward the door, but then froze as Gonzales gripped his arm like a bear trap. He looked down at the man, who was staring up at him like a savior.

"Well, why didn't you say so?" Gonzales said.

"What?" Key demanded. "What do you mean?"

Gonzales was already heading for the door, pulling on his sand storm gear. "You said you were the only ones who got out of Shabhut, but you're wrong," he announced. "In truth, you may be the only ones who got out of Shabhut *alive*."

Key caught up to him at the door, Daniels right behind. "What do you mean, Speedy?"

"I heard that something got out of there *dead*," he announced. "And I know where it is."

Chapter 6

One step out of the bar and the wind slapped them in the face and roared as if Daniels had called her a whore.

Key stepped back instinctively, but saw Gonzales hunker into the tempest and continue toward his pretty remarkable vehicle. It was obviously a personally modified half-track that could run on wheels, treads, or both. There was also something Key had never seen: stiff plastic and rubber flaps hanging outside each door, which allowed Gonzalez to worm inside and grab some shrouded turbans without the cab being filled with blown sand.

He pressed a headcover into each man's arms, and made circular hand movements to indicate how they should be worn, before the sirocco-like conditions filled the orifices of Key and Daniels with silt. Then the newly minted men from the Criminal Investigative Division followed him to the vehicle and crawled into the cab—like astronauts navigating international space station airlocks. Gonzales all but dragged Daniels into the rest area behind the seats, then shoved Key into the passenger bucket, before slamming and locking the driver's portal with a sharp twist of his wrist.

"That was a blast," Daniels cracked.

"Comes in fast—you got to be quick around monsoon season, or they'll still be picking grit out of your ass at your funeral," he said by way of apology. Then he spread his hands as if presenting a birthday cake. "Welcome to the Desert Demon."

Key knew about deserts. He was practically raised in one. He was raised in the mountains of Riverside County, California. His home was located in the town of his birth, Murrieta, on a ridge overlooking the Temecula Valley; the Mount Palomar observatory glistened atop a peak on the opposite side. Wildfires caused by cigarettes or lightning frequently ripped through the adjoining Santa Rosa Plateau or hills covered with brush: there was one burning the day Josiah was brought home from the hospital. It was not wrong to say the boy was born in fire.

Key's father Dan was a marine recruiter who worked out of nearby Fallbrook. Most of the people he signed up were sent to nearby Camp Pendleton. Key's mother Genie, Captain Logan had called her a singer because that was how Key had listed her on all the forms. The truth is she was a former showgirl, complete with boas and fans, who had worked four hours to the east on Interstate 15, Las Vegas. Key was conceived, he later learned, during one of his father's extended leaves. His bastard-conception had never bothered him; Genie could have had an abortion but wanted the child. A paternity test later, Dan did the honorable thing.

Genie still had a lot of friends in Sin City, and she and her son often took weekend trips there. That was when kids could be left alone in a hotel room without child services being called. Along the way, at the behest of her only child, they would pull off the main route and spend a few well-hydrated hours in Death Valley, which was more-or-less on the way.

Living at the edge of the so-called Inland Empire, Key had always watched the massive dust storms blowing by in the distance—the *Bound for Glory*, mountain-high balls of sand that rolled onward over and through everything in its way. Even from a height of more than two thousand feet up, he could see cars pulling off the road as their headlights were obscured by sand. Golden eagles flew wide around the tumult. And the sky, it just vanished, save for just the haziest outline of the sun. It wasn't like one of the rare gully washers, where the wet ground and cleansed air gave the valley a different feel. When the dust storm dissipated, life would start up again as if it had simply gone into hibernation.

So Key respected and loved and feared the desert. But he was not stupidly uninformed about it. He had collected bones from the sands until his mother said it was time to go. The fragile, baked skin of snakes. The burned-to-death tarantulas who had been caught outside when they should have been under a rock. The tiny scorpions that could get in your shoe and sting like a pin. And the dry, miserable heat. At least humid heat gave you warning that you were getting too damn hot: it caused perspiration to dribble hotly down your skin. Desert heat just cooked you, the sweat evaporating before it could even be noticed. And the sunburn: what happened to unprotected skin was probably what it must have been like watching those nuclear tests in the desert without appropriate insulation. It went from normal to painful red in minutes, like the air was a magnifying glass—which, in effect, it was.

So Key knew about deserts and the kind of life that thrived there. That included human life, for there were always those sun-loonies, as his colorful mother used to call them, who loved coming out there, often naked, and becoming one with this perdition.

"They say it's like a snake shedding skin," she'd said when he was nine or ten and they encountered a small group in tents. "You are reborn in the heat and the sun."

His mother could be a philosopher when she wanted to be. Showgirls were like that, which is why Key wasn't like the ordinary straight-ahead killing machines turned out by the USMC. More than once, on leave, Key went back to the desert on his own. His mother had died of cervical cancer when she was young, but she always seemed alive when he came here. Maybe she was, having been reborn in some way he didn't understand. He was always hoping to find a lady sun-loony who he could discuss that with, but it never happened. So like a desert prophet, he ended up camping under the stars surrounded by the creatures that wriggleth and scuttleth in the sand.

All of that was years ago, before Key had turned cynical. Before he had seen war and spilled human blood. Now the desert was an enemy—or at least, he could not assume it was a friend. He was certainly grateful for this ride, especially with the wind as it was. They had hitched from Djibouti on a couple of transports arranged by Daniels's network of macho cronies— another reason Key wanted him as a partner. Being an oddball was great if you yearned to feel special, but not so great if you wanted to get from Djibouti to Thumrait in less than a week. As it was, they had to go from Lemonneir to Bahrain in Saudi Arabia, and only then to Thumrait—just to avoid Yemen airspace.

As per their new no-spitting-without-permission lifestyle, Key let Logan know their plans, but the Captain shrugged it off like an inattentive father. Key wondered, and not for the first time, whether the whole setup was just to keep him out of their hair—or, in Logan's case, scalp—while they concentrated on more immediate, pressing things. No matter, Key saw what he saw.

Now he watched as Gonzales prepped the motor on a semicircular dashboard that rivaled some of the newer jets he had been in. He had little doubt Gonzales had built it all himself. Key recognized some rubber and aluminum attachments that that went way beyond wipers to keep the panoramic windshield clear. Through it, Thumrait Air Base looked like it had been built upon a giant gauze patch that God had personally pressed down on the southwest side of Oman.

The engine didn't so much turn on as come to life, vibrating their organs and very bones. Key grabbed the side of his seat and the top of the dashboard as the thing lurched forward. Key had to yell to be heard over the machine's consistent thunder.

"I'm not even sure how *we* got out of Shabhut," he said directly into Gonzales's right ear. "How did something else get out?"

Gonzales waved the question away as he guided the powerful Desert Demon onto the main camel way. "I know guys who are working on epic raps on how you got out of Shabhut," Gonzales assured them. "You're already a living legend among grunts."

"Did he say epic raps or epic craps?" Daniels asked Key.

Key ignored him. "Okay," he shouted at the driver. "You said something got out of there dead?"

"You know the situation, right?" Gonzales continued, without waiting for an answer. "Oman's the cork on the Arabian Peninsula pressure cooker. Emirates to the left, Saudi Arabia to the right, Yemen down below. Iran and Pakistan right next to the pond."

"The Arabian Sea," Key loudly replied, more for the benefit of Daniels, who, by his wandering eyes and disinterested expression, seemed more intent on searching the growing hillsides for something to punch, shoot or screw.

"So Sultan Qaboos is trying to be friends with everybody," Gonzales went on, keeping his eyes on the wavering road in case one of the bent, shaking palm trees suddenly flew at them, "but doesn't really trust anybody. Yemini the least. So, in the aftermath of the Omani Spring...."

"Protests in twenty-eleven that resulted in promises of reform," Key shouted back.

Gonzales nodded. "An Oman Study Committee was formed, made up of scientists and doctors that the Sultan sends anywhere, with as much diplomatic immunity as they can muster, to study anything he finds interesting."

"And he found Shabhut interesting?"

"Oh yeah. Before Marine HQ did. Apparently the OSC was nearby when you guys showed up."

"How come I never heard about that?"

Gonzales shrugged. "Neighbors quickly figured the OSC was all spies anyway, and didn't look too kindly on their appearances. So over the last few years, they've become more and more low profile and secretive."

"Then how did you know about it?"

Daniels punched Key on the shoulder. "Nothing Speedy don't know," he boasted. "I told you."

"Oh, you were listening?" Key cracked.

"I can multitask up to two," he replied.

Gonzales smirked. "I don't think they're spies. May be used as spies or infiltrated by spies, but anyway, the Study Committee's not going to crow about any of their findings. In fact, they've all but snuck out of the capital to operate where they hope no one will find them."

Like this *armpit*, Key thought. It made sense. Whatever value Thumrait had in the glory days of the frankincense caravan routes was now totally usurped by the capital city of Muscat, which was practically on the opposite end of the country.

"How do *you* know about this?" Key asked, wincing when Daniels punched him in the shoulder again.

"I got a friend," Gonzales said so low that Key nearly didn't catch it. "He rents the Study Committee some space at his place. He told me they left something freaky-deaky with him."

Daniels perked up. "Freaky-deaky how?"

"That's what you're going to find out," Gonzales answered.

"That's where you're taking us?" Key pressed.

"That's where I'm taking you." Daniels's fist appeared between the two men. Gonzales craned around and tapped it with his own fist.

"*No hay bronca. Hoy por ti, manana por mi*," the driver said.

This time Daniels did the translating for Key. "No problem, bro. Today for you, tomorrow for me."

Tumrait had two main thoroughfares—Route 31 and Route 45. Gonzales stayed on 31 until it crossed 45, then took a hard left off road. A residential community sat off to the east, but they were heading southwest into brown, patchy wasteland.

Gonzales kept going until Key started picking out bumps in the landscape that didn't seem quite natural. As he peered closer he realized they could've been Quonset huts painted to look like hills of sand. But soon even those disappeared, until Gonzales seemed to target a rectangular shelter that looked like a cross between a bomb blast bunker and a wild west outpost. It was sitting on the very edge of the habited area, like a lone mole some dermatologist hadn't removed yet.

By the time Gonzales stopped the Desert Demon, the wind had diminished from a steady roar to the occasional spit. Without comment, Gonzales exited the cab, then waited for his passengers to do the same.

Daniels stood, stretched, and squinted in every direction. "What a dump. Where's the town they called the second-best city to visit in the world?"

Gonzales laughed. "You're thinking of Muscat, the capital. And that was back in 2012."

"In a book probably published by the Oman Tourist Agency," Daniels added. "And even those lying sacks couldn't make it number one."

"Where are we?" Key interrupted, studying the structure. Low, but surprisingly long and deceptively ramshackle. As near as Key could tell, it was airtight, soundproof, and made of steel-beam-wire-rope-reinforced concrete. He looked for an industrial air-conditioning unit, but could only spot some sort of recessed, anthill-shaped, skylight on the sloping roof.

"Thumrait Morgue," Gonzales answered. "Or, as we call it, Ayman's Emporium."

Key looked at Gonzales, who was still wearing his shrouded turban. They all were. "That your friend's name? The one who rents space to the OSC?"

"Cool," Daniels said. "Ayman! *Hey* man! Nice name."

Now Gonzales ignored him as they started slogging through the sandy dirt toward the tallest section of the structure. "It means 'Lucky,'" he revealed. "And he has been, till now. Follow my lead. Ayman's easily spooked."

Daniels followed, looking around at the desolate area. "Wonder why." Gonzales gave him a look, and Daniels put up his hands. "Don't worry, don't worry. I'll be as gentle as a fly on a feather duster."

Gonzales and Key shared a look, wondering where Daniels had come up with that, then stopped by the far wall. Key could just make out hair-thin lines in the concrete that created the shape of a door. Gonzales put his hand in a pocket and started pressing buttons on his smartphone without exposing it to the blowing sand.

When nothing happened for a few seconds, Gonzales looked at the others, his eyebrows pinched.

"Siesta time?" Daniels suggested mildly.

Gonzales shrugged, then pressed sharply on the wall where the hair-thin door shape was. There was a click, and a door-shaped section popped open.

"Don't let too much sand in," Gonzales suggested, then slid into an opening only big enough for him. The others followed, stepping into a sauna.

Key looked quickly around. The area consisted of two central rooms—a small one behind them, and a large one in front of them—both illuminated only by a shaft of bright, almost blinding, light coming from the lone circular skylight. But the structure was a large rectangular around a smaller rectangular. All the way across the large room was a freezer door, and lining the walls on either side were small, corpse-size, square, freezer doors. Dotting the floor space was three medical examining tables.

"Hey," said Daniels, looking into the smaller room behind them. "There's Lucky."

Key turned to see what was obviously, and a bit laughingly, the break room. There was a refrigerator, cooler, sink, bathroom, television, video game console, book shelf, sofa, table and chairs. A tall, lanky man in a *dishdasha*—the long-sleeve, floor-length robe that served as the Omani traditional dress—and braided, knotted, shrouded headgear sat, his head resting on his folded arms on the table top. The spotlight from the skylight was near the back of his head covering, causing more shadow than light.

Daniels took a step toward him, but Gonzales put a hand on his arm. "Let our host. The less he knows, the better he likes it."

"OSC rental space in the freezer?" Key asked, nodding in that direction.

"That's what he told me," Gonzales confirmed, already walking in that direction.

"Love me a morgue." Daniels sighed as they went, scanning the square, latched, doors lining the side walls. "But I'm never completely at ease unless I know all the guys who fill the shelves."

"You're never completely happy unless you filled them," Key muttered as Gonzales reached the door.

"Sure, then I know that they're dead."

Gonzales opened it without comment or ceremony, scrutinizing the metal shelves for telltale markings. "There," he said, pointing, then reaching, for a plastic, lidded, oblong box that couldn't have been more than three feet long and two feet wide.

"That's it?" Daniels asked. "That's what we came forty-five hundred miles for?"

"Just wait," Key suggested as he followed Gonzales to the nearest medical examining table. They all faced the freezer, not wanting to have whatever was inside the container thaw too quickly in the morgue's steam bath temperatures. "Any notes on the exterior?"

Gonzales examined the container. "None that I can see. Just a label." Gonzales studied the small sticker, which was on the narrow front side of the container. "That's weird."

"What's weird?" Key snapped, asking almost before Gonzales finished the comment.

"The labels reads *Pawan Sha Bhut sahi bola.*"

"Shabhut?" Daniels interposed. "Ebola?"

"No," Gonzales replied. "Sha bhut," he enunciated carefully. "*Sahi bola.*" He looked at Key with an expression that mixed confusion and concern.

"It translates as 'wind power is very right.'" He shook his head in wonder.
"I think it's a song lyric."

"I'm not surprised," Key said. "If the Study Committee has gotten as careful as you say, it would make sense that they'd use a code. Crude as it is."

"Oh, just take it and let's go," Daniels complained.

"Can't take it," Key snapped at him.

"Why the hell not?"

"One, international law," Key listed with exaggerated ennui. "Two, don't want to alert the Study Committee. Three, prevent contagion."

"Shit!" Daniels exclaimed. "Ebola?"

"No, not Ebola," Key quickly assured him. "Take it easy, Morty. This plastic container is not exactly hermetically sealed, but it's still a good idea not to expose it to too many environments too quickly. I just want to examine it, and maybe take a small sample."

"Okay, okay, already, then just do it, will you?" Daniels moaned. "And let's get out of here. This place is so fucking hot I'm about to go into a coma like Lucky."

Key nodded, then gripped the container top. It snapped and popped off without any worrisome sound of released gas or air.

Inside was what looked like bone fragments, frayed cloth patches, egg shells, wisps of webbing, and a single fingernail.

"Disappointment," Daniels complained. "Always a fucking disappoi...fuck!"

The last syllable was a booming screech. The others jerked in place, then snapped their heads to where Daniels was staring.

Directly between and behind Gonzales and Key was Ayman. From where they were standing his face was now toward them. His mouth was distended into an unnatural chasm, his eyes bulging out of his head like erupting pimples, and his spasming fingers pulsating like a frog's throat—something darker, chunkier, and hotter than blood pumping from every opening.

Chapter 7

"Fuckaduck!" Daniels bellowed, only this time with more anger than surprise than usual. He balled his fist in preparation for a preemptive strike.

"Don't touch him!" Key shouted, scurrying away himself while taking care to keep the container level and secure.

Daniels looked confused, even a little annoyed. "I don't wanna *touch* him, I wanna beat him back to unconsciousness!"

"Back off, Morty, just back off!" Key ordered, keeping his arms out, one in Gonzales's direction, and one pointed at Daniels. "And keep your distance!"

Daniels took a step back, lowering his fist as he went. The three men formed an equilateral triangle around the wretched morgue attendant, who, now that they could focus on him, looked more pathetic than threatening. The shopkeeper twisted and juddered as if a demon puppeteer was yanking on wires attached to every joint, while thick, lumpy, dark liquid burbled out of his nostrils, mouth, and even ears.

"Did Goodman look like that?" Daniels asked Key.

"I don't know," Key answered. "I was a little distracted at the time. What did *you* see? Did anybody else in the unit look like that?"

"I don't know," Daniels answered. "I was busy too!"

Gonzales made a sound that combined shock with revulsion as, while he watched, Ayman's eyes began to split open. The Omani stopped, shuddered, then started violently vibrating.

"*Now* what the fuck?" Daniels complained.

"Take cover!" Key yelled, already charging the freezer.

Daniels fell to the floor and started crawling under the table as Gonzales dove for the break room door. Neither quite made it before Ayman erupted with a flesh-ripping, bone-shattering blast.

Steaming hot liquid splattered the walls, floor, and even ceiling. Shards of bone ricocheted off the morgue doors and tables. Daniels barked in pain and disgust, while Gonzales hit the break room floor and slid into the shelves, bringing down the video games.

Key let the room steam and sizzle for a few seconds before poking his head from the freezer. "Morty, Speedy, you guys okay?"

A few more moments passed before Gonzales moaned. "How do you define 'okay'?"

"Morty?"

"Fuck," Daniels said as he slid out from under the table. "A," he continued as he slowly stood. "Duck," he finished as he looked at the way his hands and head—the two items closest to the detonated attendant—were splashed with brackish, smoking, fluid and pieces of offal. By the look on the sergeant's face, Key wasn't sure what he'd do: go berserk or collapse crying. Instead, he waited until Gonzales slowly started to emerge from the now ironically termed break room, then spoke flatly. "What's the Arabic name for 'Bad Lucky'?"

* * * *

"*Sayiya Ayman*," Gonzales said as he drove the two to his workshop on the southwest corner, just off the grounds, of the Thumrait Air Base.

"What?" Daniels growled.

"Bad Lucky."

Daniels grunted with no pleasure. His skin and hair was already dry from the dousing they gave him at the morgue bathroom. Gonzales had given him his boxers while Key had given him his T-shirt, which was all the sergeant wore now. Key had burned the rest, including Daniels's desert boots.

Daniels, of all people, had wanted to wait for the hazmat team, but Gonzales was all too happy to drive when Key decided they should *vamos*.

They sat silent for a few minutes, digesting what they had just experienced, but, finally, Daniels could take no more.

"Why didn't you just burn *me* too?"

Key, who had been lost in thought, looked at his associate. "What do you mean?"

"I mean, you burned my clothes because you thought they might carry whatever this shit is. You destroyed the samples because they were swimming in this shit too. It doesn't take a fucking genius to figure I'm as good as dead."

Key snorted. "Are you kidding me, Morty? Goodman exploded right next to me, remember? His remains were like an eighth layer of skin for God knows how long. Do I look as good as dead to you?"

Daniels raised an eyebrow. "Not yet," he said cautiously.

Key shook his head. "They did every test on every part of me at Lemonneir," he reminded his partner. "Whatever this thing is, apparently you don't get it by contact with the victim."

Again, by Daniels's expression, they weren't sure whether he was going to start laughing or crying. Ultimately, as per his wont, he settled on anger. "So why the fuck did you burn my clothes?"

"Because," Key said, "you *do* get it somehow. Poor Ayman got it, so I burned on the side of caution."

"Could be in my hair, right? Microscopic particles of shit."

"Possible, but not likely," Key said. "Since boot camp, what were the two things we instinctively covered?"

Daniels grunted. "The fruits—melon and nuts."

Key nodded. Daniels seemed to relax a little.

Gonzales steered his Desert Demon past the Harvest Falcon depot—which housed the Air Force's transportable system of billets, bivouacs, modular equipment, generators, shelters, tents, and vehicles—that stretched off into the distance.

"You're never at a loss of something to repair, are you?" Key asked their driver.

Gonzales shook his head. "Keeps me busy, and informed." He pulled up to what looked like a giant corrugated steel oil tank that had been sliced down the middle and laid on its side. He powered down the Desert Demon, then glanced at Daniels. "I should be able to find you something more suitable to wear inside."

"Good," Daniels said miserably. "Because I don't know what fabric softener you're using, but it ain't working."

"Fabric softener?" Gonzales said with an exaggerated accent as he got out. "We don't need no stinkin' fabric softener."

But even Daniels forgot to keep grousing when they stepped inside the Hispanic Mechanic's Studio. Instead, the sergeant's grin started stretching from ear to ear despite the fact that the trip from the vehicle to the door felt like fire walking to his bare feet. "What did I tell you, Joe? What did I tell you?"

The expansive interior of the crescent moon-shaped space looked like a cut-rate Smithsonian Air and Space Museum combined with Frankenstein's castle laboratory. There were lifts on the floor and hooked chains hanging from the ceiling. There were husks and skeletons of every imaginable land and air craft covering almost every inch—save for eating, sleeping, and toiletry areas.

"What, no videogames?" Key grinned with appreciation.

"What do I need with any media," Gonzales said, his arms out, "when I have this?"

He found Daniels some gym shorts, a pair of sandals they could adjust to his size twelve feet, and an extra-large T-shirt that bore a skull-and-cross-*wrench* pirate symbol above the legend Stay Well Lubricated.

He brought out some MREs—self-contained individual field rations, otherwise known as Meal, Ready-to-Eat—and joined them at a small round table by the kitchen. They started breaking down the kit, but the various packets and bags reminded Gonzales too much of what they had just come from.

"Why did you leave the samples you came so far for?" he asked.

"No point taking them." Key laid out the beef stew bag, crackers, cheese spread, and powdered beverage envelope. "I had to see the stuff to try to figure how this is transmitted." He retrieved the packets of salt, pepper, seasonings, and spoon. "Like I said, definitely not through blood or contact with flesh, so I ruled out the fingernail and the bones."

"What the hell were those egg shells?" Daniels asked, already chewing his packet of pork rib.

"Not egg shells," Key replied. "Too small. Might be eggs, but none like I've ever seen before."

"What came out of them? Birds?"

"Those pea-sized pods are small for birds," Gonzales chimed in. "Bugs, maybe?"

Key sat up straighter. "Bugs maybe." He mused, suddenly distracted.

Daniels didn't seem to notice. "Might be a very aggressive form of lyme disease or malaria or something like that," he suggested, seemingly all but forgetting he had just watched a man messily explode. Then again, it hadn't been the first time.

"Hmph." Gonzales made a chewing noise, deep again in his own thoughts. "If not that, then what?"

"'Wind power is very right....'" Key's tone of voice was both wondrous and self-recriminating.

Both the sergeant and mechanic turned.

"Huh?" Daniels said.

Key suddenly and sharply stood up, scattering his meal all over the floor. "Christ, we have to find the Study Committee, and now."

Chapter 8

"Now that's more like it," Daniels said as he took his first look at Muscat, the big and ancient capital of Oman.

He was wearing a plain white *dishdasha*—though thankfully not what remained of Ayman's *dishdasha*—along with a somewhat sedate turban made of knotted head-cloth, as well as open-toe, open-back sandals. Gonzales had pulled them all out of his workshop's locker before he changed into his own regional garb.

When Daniels complained about the simple footwear, Gonzales had explained, "They're called *nahl*; easy to remove and they keep anything from getting trapped inside."

"'Nahl' kidding," Daniels had drawled. "What could get trapped inside?"

"Everything from sea snakes to the *khanjar* daggers of angry husbands," Gonzales had advised knowingly. "Wear them. You'll thank me."

Key now followed the sergeant out onto dusty tarmac—squinting at the bright blue sky, the sparkling waters of the Oman Gulf, and, in the distance, the copper crags of the Hajar Mountains. It was the tropical opposite of Shabhut; elegance, and even grace, as opposed to oppressive misery.

He turned away from the clean majesty of even this northeastern edge of the city to see Gonzales emerge from his small private jet in full going-native splendor. The Hispanic Mechanic was wearing an authentic *wazar* undergarment beneath his more detailed *dishdasha*, with a long tassel hanging down from the neckline, and subtle, but impressive, embroidery around the wrists, across the shoulder blades, and neckline. On his head was a more ornate *massar* turban. If only given a cursory glance, he could have passed for a native—at least to Key's inexperienced eye.

Key didn't have to ask exactly where they were. Gonzales had gone into detail during the flight. They were at what remained of the Bayt al Falaj airport, which had gone into minimum service once the grander Muscat International Airport opened in 1973. Gonzales had correctly surmised that Key wanted as low a profile as possible, but also didn't want to waste eight hours driving there.

So Gonzales had led them to his prize hobby: a 1991 Cessna Citation light business jet, which he had personally reconditioned after it was simply left behind by an unsatisfied billionaire. That sort of whim had become nearly commonplace in the oil-rich region. Although the Cessna was relatively small, it was certified for operations with a single pilot, and ready to go.

Key had looked at Gonzales incredulously. "Well, what about—" He extednded his arms to encompass the workshop.

Gonzales just grinned as Daniels elbowed Key in the side. "He's a civilian contractor, Joe," the sergeant informed him. "The Corps needs him more than he needs the Corps."

"And I think you need me more than the Corps does at the moment," Gonzales added.

Key's eyebrows had not lowered. "But—"

"Don't worry about any future repairs for the base, Corporal," Gonzales said. "Got some decent assistants. In fact, that drunk who bothered you in the bar was one of them."

That had not exactly put Key's mind at ease. Every few minutes, while Gonzales had filed flight plans and garnered permissions, he offered other reasons why the mechanic should not get involved.

Finally, Gonzales had simply turned on Key with a solemn expression. "Look," he said. "I just watched a guy I know go boom. If he went boom, that means anybody can go boom. So, should I just hang around here or should I take you where you need to go to try stop it from happening again?"

And, according to Gonzales, where they needed to go was Muscat. If they had any chance of cornering anyone from the Study Committee, it would be there.

Key couldn't argue with that, so he had finally shut up and let Gonzales get on with it. Two hours later they were slipping into the edge of Muscat as much as it was possible to do in a country with less than two dozen registered private jets. But, in the interim, Key was informed via text that the Marine hazmat team had locked down Ayman's Emporium, if not what was left of Ayman himself.

Key was half expecting Logan to rip his ear off, but also half expecting what actually happened—a calm, subsequent, text requesting that he keep the Captain informed. Key looked around at the overgrown field and sandy runway, feeling a little exposed.

"You ever get the feeling you're being watched?" he muttered.

"Don't worry, Corporal," Gonzales assured him, misunderstanding the comment. "They know me here. They'll take good care of CJ."

Daniels leaned over and mock-whispered in Key's ear. "That's his plane's name. He names everything."

Already several young men in greasy coveralls, who looked like locals, were walking around the aircraft as if they had done it many times before. Gonzales said something to one of them in Arabic, which sent the man scurrying off.

"So, what now, Corporal?" Gonzales inquired as Key continued to survey the area.

"We need a base of operations," Key reminded him.

"Already done," Gonzales promised. "I arranged it from the cockpit. It's my usual hangout. I wasn't sure you wanted to go there first, though."

Key felt relieved, and not for the first time, that he had finally allowed Gonzales to volunteer for the team. "Good guess," he started, but was then distracted by Daniels giving off a loud moan.

"You have *got* to be kidding me!"

Key turned as a white Toyota Yaris came driving up beside them, and the young man who had scurried away emerged from behind the wheel. He and Gonzales had a rapid conversation.

"He says it's clean, the air conditioning works, and he checked the engine himself," Gonzales told Daniels with only the slightest hint of a smirk. "He wants to know what the problem is."

"As if you didn't know," Daniels complained. "Was that the smallest car you could find? Why not a Yugo?"

"Don't worry, don't worry." Gonzales laughed. "He will take you to where we're staying in his own Jeep."

Key put a hand on Daniels's shoulder. "Didn't think you wanted to go scouring the hospitals with me anyway."

"That's what you're going to do?" the sergeant asked, wincing with anticipated boredom.

"Yeah. And schools. Anyplace we can find out if anybody else"—he looked at Gonzales—"went boom."

"Hospitals and schools?" Daniels echoed. "You think you're going to find out anything there?"

"Got to start someplace," Key told him. "And got to start fast."

Daniels shook his head curtly. "Let me bring our stuff, whatever's left of it, to the hotel, then I'll bring my own prodigious intellect to the problem."

Key had known the sergeant too long to get unduly worried by that statement. Even so, he felt impelled to give Daniels a disclaimer. "Okay, but keep in mind that even with Captain Logan's influence, we don't have much pull here."

"And," Gonzales added, "keep in mind that, according to Arabic laws, women may not be in a room alone with a man who is not a relative."

Daniels shook his head. "Oh, ye of little faith."

Gonzales laughed. "Oh, we of much faith in knowing what you do. And, by the way, it's not a hotel."

"Okay, okay," Daniels said as he waved them away like annoying gnats. "Go off on your wild goose chase, and let the grown-ups get the goods for you."

Key waited until Daniels had gone off with the young scurrying man before getting into the passenger seat of the Yaris.

"You think Morty'll be okay around here?" Key solemnly asked Gonzales, who was in the driver's seat.

"I was just going to ask you the same thing," Gonzales answered, half-jokingly. "Let me tell you something. When Sultan Qaboos took over in 1970, he decided to make Oman accessible to non-Muslims and Westerners—in order that we might 'appreciate the beauty of Islam.' If Morty was anyplace else in the region, we'd probably find him in pieces being eaten by camels when we got back. But here? They don't even allow corporal punishment in the schools anymore. He'll be fine."

"There's a 'but,'" Key observed.

Gonzales sighed a little. "He'll be fine—probably."

Key nodded in hopeful agreement as Gonzales started the Yaris's one-point-five liter, four-cylinder engine.

"Where to, Corporal?"

"Call me Joe," Key finally suggested. "And take me someplace I can find a translator who won't spook the locals, and an expert on communicable diseases." Key looked at the mechanic apologetically. "Preferably both. And step on it."

Chapter 9

Key didn't know whether it was his increasing exhaustion and desperation, or simply the seemingly bottomless, concerned eyes of a new player, an assistant professor, that suddenly turned him very, very honest. Whatever it was, Key felt certain that time was running out. And not just for him.

He didn't think he was just being an alarmist here. That wasn't his nature. But how many times in human history had something unanticipated, like fleas on rodents, caused something unexpected, like the Black Death, that killed around 200 million human beings and came perilously close to wiping us out?

Probably more than I'm aware of, Key thought, wondering how many extinctions had taken a poke at the dinosaurs before *their* clock was punched by an asteroid.

Gonzales had been driving him all over the capital in search of what he had asked for, a universal translator as well as an expert in communicable diseases. They had used up most of the eight hours they had gained by flying here going from hospital to hospital. Muscat had at least five dozen of them, and almost nine hundred clinics, dispensaries, and medical centers.

But Gonzales may have introduced him to both when they finally stepped into an office marked *Professor Basheer Davi* at Oman Medical College—the first private Health Sciences College in Oman—and met the twenty-seven-year-old Esherida Rahal.

"I'm sorry," she said while coming around a lab table covered with equipment, "but the Professor is not in."

To Key's ears, it sounded as if she had been saying that a lot—so much, in fact, that it was beginning to become automatic.

"That's all right," he answered, the weariness in his voice matching her own verbal knee jerk. "My friend here"—he motioned toward Gonzales—"thinks you might be able to help us just as well."

Key watched a variety of reactions flit across her face like a wheel of fortune: it's too late in the day, I'm really too busy, you'll have to make an appointment, and some unformed others. But then her oval head and deep eyes lowered, and he saw a resigned, empathetic smile touch her soft, smooth, dark rose lips.

"Please," she said politely. "Come sit down." She led them into what was obviously Professor Davi's office, which reminded Key of many a professor's office he had seen over the years. Amid piles and piles of papers and books crammed everywhere in the small rectangular room, two simple, inexpensive school chairs flanked a small desk.

"What is the problem?" she asked, her voice the same modulated, lightly accented English it had always been, as she rested against the edge of the desk. Gonzales stood by the door, naturally, and seemingly automatically, assuming the role of a lookout. Key, however, tiredly and gratefully thudded into the chair nearest her.

As Key and Gonzales had come through the halls, they had seen students, both male and female, wearing black pants, white lab coats, and running shoes. There were even coeds without headdresses. But Rahal wore *Omaniya*, the national dress of the country, only hers was a deep red, and her *waqaya* headscarf was dark and beautifully embroidered with what looked like representations of constellations. Despite it covering her from her forehead to the ankle of her five-foot-four-inch frame, he could tell she was a fit, very poised young lady.

"The problem"—Key sighed—"is that something is making people explode." Despite his tiredness, Key carefully noted her reaction of shock. Key's admission was so blunt that the normally reticent Gonzales stepped forward.

"It's true," Gonzales informed her. "I witnessed it. First in Shabhut, and then in Thumrait."

Rahal's mouth opened and closed several times as she blinked. To her added credit in Key's mind, she didn't even suggest the two were joking. "Explode—exactly how, if I might ask?"

Key nodded in satisfaction. "Good question," he answered appreciatively, then plunged ahead without reservation. "It wasn't as if there were a bomb in their chest or anything like that. It didn't explode outward in that pattern. Their entire bodies seemed to be afflicted. Every limb and every joint."

"The eyes bulged, tearing just before the detonation," Gonzales said. "Hot, dark, lumpy liquid came out of every orifice we could see."

"Hot?" she echoed.

"It was smoking," Key added.

"Light or dark smoke?" she asked.

The soldier and mechanic looked to each other for corroboration.

"Not sure," said Gonzales.

"Neither light nor dark," Key decided. "Somewhere in the middle."

That didn't faze her. "Tell me about the detonation," she urged. "How long did they convulse before it happened?"

Key and Gonzales shared another collaborative look.

"Less than a minute," Gonzales offered, and Key didn't dispute him.

"Go on," she advised. "Every detail you can remember."

For the first time since entering the room, Key lowered his gaze from hers. He looked at nothing in particular to see into his memory.

"The first explosion happened in my peripheral vision," he said. "A piece of the skull hit my forehead and knocked me out for a few seconds."

Rahal's luxurious, well-shaped eyebrows rose.

"I had to take cover from the second," Key continued, raising his gaze back to hers. "But I'll never forget the sound."

Her eyes held an equal mix of curiosity and concern. Key went on because she said nothing.

"It was as if every internal part of their body was erupting," he told her.

"Every part?" she asked. "Bones, fingernails, body hair?"

"No," Key said while Gonzales nodded in agreement. "I heard the bones shattering into shards, but I'm certain they weren't exploding. If they were, the skull piece that hit my forehead would've behaved differently."

Rahal nodded, her lips tightening, then she spun off the desk and grabbed a scroll that was wedged atop two piles of files. She spread it on the desk, motioning with her head for the two to join her. Key approached her from the right, and Gonzales from the left, though he kept his eyes mostly on the door.

She was holding open a biological chart of a male anthropoid body. "The human circulatory system consists of three parts," she said intently, her eyes darting around the complex map. "The cardiovascular, pulmonary, and the systemic."

Key remembered it from his mother's teachings. "The heart, lungs, arteries, and veins," he said, following her eyes.

She glanced at him, her look of impressed approval reminding him of his mother. "You missed the coronary and portal vessels," she said, "but yes. The system controls the flow of blood, gasses, hormones, nutrients, oxygen, and other vapors to and from the cells."

"Other vapors?" Key echoed, looking directly at her.

She returned his gaze. "Yes. This system stretches for about ninety-six thousand kilometers."

Gonzales automatically translated it for Key. "Sixty thousand miles."

"So if one of those other vapors turned poisonous—" Key asked.

"Not poisonous," she corrected. "Not even venomous."

"There's a difference?" Gonzales interjected, his mind reeling from all the new information.

"A big difference," she stressed, looking up at him.

"Yes, the unnatural element would have to be volatile," Key said. "As if the blood had been replaced with nitroglycerine."

When he looked back to her, she met his gaze with an expression that mixed concern with growing certainty. "And you want to know how that could have happened?" she asked him directly.

"Yes," he answered just as directly. "But maybe more importantly, whether it's contagious, and if so, how it travels. Because we've been in Shabhut, and then in Thumrait. Now we're here."

The import of his words were not lost on Rahal. Her eyes widened, but she neither recoiled nor became flustered. "How long ago did this last happen?"

"Twelve hours ago."

"Male or female?"

"What?" Gonzales reacted in surprise.

"The victims," Rahal elaborated. "Male, female, or both?"

"Male," Key answered, again glad that Daniels hadn't come along. He probably would have, in his standard operating chauvinism, asked if that was important. Gonzales knew, like Key did, that it might be.

"Do you have any possibilities that—" she started, but then the trio was surprised by a fourth voice.

"Assistant Professor Rahal?"

The three behind the desk looked up, Gonzales cursing himself for not maintaining his self-appointed lookout responsibility. It was a student, holding his books, looking at them all both expectantly as well as regretfully.

Rahal recovered briskly. "Yes, Malik?"

The student looked sheepish. "We had a meeting about my grades," he said. "I'm sorry again that I had to schedule it so late in the day, but my make-up classes—"

"Of course, of course," Rahal said apologetically. She raised her right hand and the chart rolled up to her left hand. "Yes, your graduation depends upon it, doesn't it?"

The comment was for Key and Gonzales's benefit, letting them know that she would not have truncated their talk if it wasn't important. But she seemed to know that a young man's future might be null and void if the problem Key was chasing wasn't solved.

As she started to follow the student out she quickly returned her attention to Key. "Where are you staying?" she whispered urgently.

"The Five Centses Restort," Gonzales answered, having to enunciate the unusual name carefully, and Key didn't miss the way Rahal's eyebrows raised in response. "Staff Suite Two-A."

"I will be there as soon as possible," she assured them. She continued for the student's benefit. "Thank you so much for conferring with me. From what Professor Davi tells me, you can find your way out without problem, yes?"

"Yes," Gonzales assured her, taking a reluctant Key by the crook of his arm. "Thank you, Assistant Professor."

The two made their way out the three-story, rose-colored building flanked by palm trees.

"Everybody speaks English," Key marveled.

"Not everywhere," Gonzales reminded him. "But Oman Medical College is in an academic partnership with West Virginia University. That's why I saved it for last. I thought its rep as something of a *ferenji*—outsider—wouldn't help us as much." He shrugged. "Live and learn."

Once outside, despite everything on his mind, Key was again impressed by Muscat's relaxed, charming, peaceful energy and beautiful surroundings. Gonzales had told him that the Sultan had decreed that new buildings couldn't be more than seven stories, and everything had to be designed beautifully and traditionally, as well as compliment the mountains beyond.

It would be a shame, Key thought, *if all the residents started exploding.*

They stayed silent, that very possibility foremost in their minds, as they neared the parking lot.

"Five Cent-ses Rest-ort?" Key finally repeated, just as carefully as Gonzales had said it to Rahal. "That should come with an automatic 'sic' after every mention. What are they trying to do, attract the hipster, who-gives-a-shit-about-spelling-anymore crowd?"

"Good guess," Gonzales said, "but they're trying to be different. You'll see."

"Assistant Professor Rahal'll be okay there?"

"She'll be fine," Gonzales assured him as they reached the Yaris. "She's everything my contact said."

"And more." Key ruminated as he waited for Gonzales to unlock his door.

The mechanic was struck by the comment, so he just stood for a moment between the driver's side open door and the wheel. "What do you mean?"

Key halted his own descent into the passenger seat then rose and faced him. "You happen to notice her reaction when I first told her?"

Gonzales considered the question. "Yeah," he finally said with a tinge of defensiveness. "Shocked, speechless, maybe even a little scared."

"All of that," Key agreed. "But you missed one 's' word."

"Huh?" Gonzales reacted. "What 's' word?"

"Surprised," Key informed him.

Gonzales reflected on that, shaking his head as he failed to grasp the other man's meaning.

"She was everything but surprised," Key clarified. "My friend, she has heard about this before."

Chapter 10

Key had not intended to take a power nap, but his body had other ideas. He slept for the entirety of the drive from the college to wherever the hell they were staying. He only woke because the vehicle stopped with a lurch.

As always, Key was wide awake and ready for anything, but all he saw was a dark, narrow boardwalk, an iron bar fence, and some shuttered shops facing the Gulf of Oman. According to the dashboard digital clock, only about thirty minutes had passed.

"Where are we?" Key asked mushily, his dry lips sticking together.

"Seeb beach," Gonzales reported as he parked and exited the car. "Fishing village, northwest in Muscat, northeast in Oman. You missed the gardens, palaces, and Royal Stables on the way here. Also, the horned viper I just ran over." He shook his head. "Very venomous."

Key was out the passenger side, breathing deeply of the warm, water-scented air. He was both impressed and concerned by the lack of lighting on the quiet street. It informed him that they were nowhere near tourist traps.

"We're staying where, exactly?" Key asked.

"You're looking in the wrong direction." Gonzales twice-tapped the air to his left.

Key looked in that direction and saw the modest sign, in both Arabic and English, attached to a clay wall. The Arabic words were in black, but the English letters were in blue, red, yellow, and green. They read *Five Centses Restort* above an arrow pointing them around the corner, down a wide alley.

"Oh man." Key nearly groaned as he came around the car. "Google colors, really?"

"Really," Gonzales said, joining him as they approached the alley. "They got two 2010 PCs in the lobby, so they advertise the place as a net-loving paradise. But it's not easy finding a funky joint in Muscat. Even in this fishing village, the rest of the resorts are all four stars."

"I get it now," Key admitted as he walked beside Gonzales up the fifteen-foot-wide alley to the main, side door. "Five cents, as in inexpensive, Five Centses as a play on 'senses,' and Rest-ort, as in a place to rest, not party."

"Right," Gonzales said, passing the simple, but elegant, main door, and walking toward some white stone steps going up a brown stone hill. "But, in reality, out of sight, out of mind, out of the way."

Key remembered the address Gonzales had told Rahal, so naturally figured they were heading to the Staff Suites. He followed the mechanic around the corner to what looked like a cross between a bunker and a prefab motel wedged in the back of the tan, beachfront, stucco structure. Gonzales went to the second door, tapped it three times with his forefinger and once with the back of his pinky, before twisting the latch and stepping in.

"Baby!" Gonzales said. A young woman had leaped onto him.

Key stilled in the doorway until he heard Daniels's memorable bark-laugh.

"That's my Joe." The sergeant laughed from his place on a pile of pillows, holding a beer bottle in one paw. He grinned at Gonzales, who was swinging the girl in his embrace back and forth over the rugs. "Watch him next time he goes into any new room, Speedy." Daniels looked back at Key with approval. "Watch his eyes. They go everywhere, and he won't step in until he knows everything."

Key stepped in, knowing the thickly covered sleeping mats were to the left, the living area took up the rest of the room, the bathroom was to the left in a back hall, and the kitchen was to the right. Rugs covered the floor, drapes covered the walls and ceiling, and pillows were the predominant furniture. The only real sop to the twenty-first century was a flat-screen television in the center of the right wall.

For his part, Daniels didn't seem to mind in the slightest. He wore his biggest shit-eating grin as he reclined near a simple yet ornate table topped with a Turkish coffee set, and, of all things, a hookah.

"Wow." Key sighed. "You sure we're not at the Moroccan exhibit in Epcot?"

Gonzales laughed. "What can I say, Corporal—I mean, Joe. My girl is a real antiques nut. Come on in, close the door, set a spell."

Key followed orders, taking the time to study the girl closer as well. Ironically, she wasn't even Middle Eastern. She was Asian, with a wide, friendly, happy face, and a slim build. He also correctly guessed that she was a hotel staffer, and saw the remnants of her Omani dress uniform lying over the side of one of the sleeping cushions.

At the moment all she wore was the traditional *sarwal* pants, which were loose at the hips and tight at the ankles, and a T-shirt. Since she was inside, her head was uncovered and her black, shining, long hair was loose.

"Joe, this is Chona," Gonzales said, still holding her. "Chona, this is Corporal Josiah Key."

The girl extracted herself from Gonzales's embrace and extended her hand to Key with a smile. "Oh, I know all about you," she said, glancing at Daniels.

Key grinned at the sergeant before returning his attention to the girl and shaking her hand. "Believe half."

"Less!" Daniels barked.

The girl smiled at them both. "You are truly welcome here," she said to Key, before turning her head toward Gonzales as she moved toward the kitchen. "And now I'll prove it."

She disappeared around the corner as Key looked at Gonzales as if he expected an army of dancing girls to appear.

"Just cardamom-scented coffee and sticky dates," Gonzales assured him. "The traditional hotel greeting for weary travelers."

Key nodded and took a second survey of the room. "We're all staying here?"

"Nah," Daniels said as if it were obvious. "We've got our own room and bath next door."

"Temporary quarters for seasonal employees," Gonzales said.

"Better than a brig," Daniels said, "but not by much."

"I thought Professor Rahal would be more comfortable in this apartment, with another woman present," Gonzales continued.

"Probably right," Key agreed. "But I thought women can't stay in a hotel alone."

"There are laws for all Omanis," Gonzales said. "Then there are unwritten laws for Filipinos. They have to watch their steps different ways, but otherwise—" He motioned toward the comfortable, well-appointed, if somewhat dated, room.

"Oh, yes." Chona entered the room with a tray of cups and dishes filled with different colored and shaped dates. "I have more freedom to be a 'loose woman' than natives, as long as I'm not in-your-face about it." She set the tray in the middle of the floor, kneeled there, and motioned for the men to join her.

"And the further you are out in the burbs the looser it can get," Gonzales elaborated. "This place has gotten scruffy enough to be called 'The Two

Centses.'" He smiled happily at the girl. "But that's the way I like it, don't I, *cariño?*"

She smiled back as she poured the savory-smelling coffee. "You do, indeed, *palanggâ.*"

"Oh yeah," Daniels said as they settled in a small circle around the tray, and Chona passed around a plate of dates. "I've been learning all sorts of interesting things from her while you were all out goose-chasing."

Key took a careful bite of the caramel-flavored fruit, then spoke as he brought the small cup to his lips. "All right, Morty, you've been wanting to rub something in since we got here. What is it?"

The sergeant and the maid exchanged conspiratorial glances before Daniels spoke. "One of her friends heard about someone blowing up."

Key and Gonzales's faces jerked toward Chona as if they were robots.

"No, no," she said quickly. "Not blowing up, but—" She stopped, embarrassed.

"But what?" Gonzales pressed. "This is important, baby, so don't hold anything back, no matter how silly it might sound."

"Okay, okay," Chona said, clearly relieved. "Some of my friends work at Club Blue."

"That's in Qurum, the next town over," Daniels explained. "Upperscale burb...mostly."

"That's right," Chona continued. "They're waitresses and hostesses and—"

Daniels took over. "There are whore houses in Muscat, but they're always being shut down by the cops, so they often relocate in suburban hotels owned by Westerners, where they can skirt the laws."

"*Not* whore houses," Chona insisted. "Just, you know, flirting, like in Hong Kong bars."

"Where all the girls are also Filipino," Daniels said, "and they have private lounges with seventy-five dollar sodas and two-hundred-dollar muscatels."

"They say," Chona stammered. "They say that the girls are 'available for any services.'"

"And you know what that means." Daniels winked at Key.

"Enough, Morty," Key grumbled impatiently. "*Someone* tell me about the blowing up stuff."

"I'm sure it's nothing," Chona started, but, after a look from Gonzales, continued more evenly. "A friend of mine said a friend of hers got real sick. She said the poor girl couldn't take any light, and even began to cry blood."

"Dark blood," Daniels added.

Key couldn't help but glance at Gonzales, who only stared at Chona. "Go on," he urged her.

"She said the poor girl then started to have a seizure," Chona elaborated. "They were afraid she was going to collapse until they hustled her into the back room."

Key waited, but that was all Chona said.

"I was going to check it out," Daniels said, "but waited for you. So, let's have a look?"

Key looked to his associate. "Can't yet."

"What, are you kidding?" Daniels complained. "You're the one who said we can't waste time!"

"We got someone coming," Gonzales informed him.

"Then *you* wait for them!" Daniels barked. He turned to the other. "Come on, Joe, let's go."

"Morty," Key said evenly. "Got to wait. This is more important."

"Oh, yeah?" Daniels retorted. "You get a whisper of something and suddenly it's more important! I get a lead, and it's all 'Morty just wants to hang with hookers', right?"

Chona laughed unconvincingly to try to lighten the suddenly contentious mood. "It's just a story from another *pinoy*," she said. "Who knows if it's true?"

"Only one way to find out," Daniels stated as he got up. "I'm going. You coming or not, Joe?"

Key looked up, directly into Daniels's eyes. "Morty, I trust you with my life, you know that. If you can't wait for me, then fine. You go and check it out. If you're not back by the time we're done here, we'll come looking for you. Right?"

Daniels stared back for a few seconds, his expression going from offensive to defensive, but finally softening to appreciation. "Right," he said.

He started to turn toward the door when Gonzales threw the Yaris keys to him. "Chona has her own car," he said.

Daniels nodded in appreciation, then left the room. Assistant Professor Esherida Rahal showed up a few minutes later, seemingly coming directly from her meeting with the student, since she was wearing the same outfit.

Given his mood, Key stood on no ceremony. He quickly closed the door behind her, ushered her into the room, and motioned at the refreshments as he spoke.

"A single young woman going out at night to a remote street in a neighboring village means you think this is important. You weren't in the least bit surprised when I told you the problem, so you already knew about that too. And your superior, Professor Davi, is not absent, he's missing."

Rahal seemed startled for a moment. She recovered quickly. "How did you know?"

Key curtly shook his head and said, "Stay on topic. I'd love to have the time to feel each other out and build a bond of trust, but we don't. I'll tell you flatly now that I am not a spy or double agent or government official. I am a soldier who is trying to find out what happened to his squad and prevent a disaster that could, if it spreads, kill thousands—"

"Millions," she whispered, stopping Key in his verbal tracks.

"Ms. Rahal?" Malik, the very same student who had interrupted them before, stood in the open doorway, wearing the very same outfit, only now with a backpack. "I am so sorry," he said sheepishly, "but I heard the address they gave you, and I forgot to—"

Gonzales clamped the student's right hand in both of his as Key grabbed a pillow off the floor while pulling his Sig Sauer from beneath his light jacket.

Jamming the 9mm automatic's barrel deep into the pillow, he shot Malik right between the eyes.

Chapter 11

At first, Morty Daniels was disappointed by Club Blue.

As he drove there, passing the ocean sparkling in the moonlight on one side and quaint mosques with lush gardens on the other, he had started toying with the idea that Club Blue might be an Omani's idea of a seedy Hong Kong bar, so the actual place, in his mind, would be well appointed and filled with beautiful women—as would befit the clean elegance of the upmarket Muscat suburb. He knew seedy; he'd grown up in it, in Manhattan's Hell's Kitchen. The only thing that kept the crumbling burlesque houses and gay movie theaters from dragging the twenty-three-block area into complete slumdom was its proximity to the glittering theater district on and off Broadway. He had grumped about hookers, but Key had been right. He knew them in both senses of the word, and he loved them. In the same way every good soldier was ready to fight 24/7, a streetwalker was always sexually available, always on the make, always willing. On his way to school each morning, it used to thrill Daniels to walk by the two hookers on Forty-Fifth Street and Eighth Avenue. They would stand outside the corner coffee shop holding paper bags as if they'd just gotten takeout. That way, the police couldn't charge them with loitering or soliciting. They'd accost men with, "You look hot today, honey," or the even less subtle, "I'd like sausage with my muffin." Over the days and weeks, the girls came to recognize him and greet him and stir youthful urges under the worn leather belt that was held together with staples. His printshop owner parents didn't have much money, but they did have stationary supplies. When Daniels was old enough to work at the store on Ninth Avenue, he spent his first wages on one of the girls. She wasn't young and maybe she had a habit and there were cockroaches everywhere in the furnished hotel room that had cost him an extra ten bucks over the sixty he'd paid the black girl who called herself Gigi. Even then he knew the moans and audibles were fake. But he didn't give a shit about any of that. His world and senses had been entirely bound by five foot five of artfully alive flesh and fingers and smell and what his school yard friends called lumpy-bumps.

Daniels smiled as he remembered the phrase. So many expressions from his childhood—nancy-boys, retardo, even fatty—would probably be grounds for suspension these days. But like lumpy-bumps the things they said didn't have a truly disparaging or hateful thought behind them. Not like today, when deeper hate was transmitted in a look or a gesture. Anybody who didn't believe that should spend some time out here.

A pressure cooker like this, he thought, *you could learn to hate your friends as totally as your enemies.*

Back in New York, he had no hate. To the contrary. From that heaven-in-Hell's-Kitchen point forward, Daniels was addicted to love, as the Robert Palmer song went. Low end sex and dives were already in his blood. Everywhere he went in the big, perverse world he hoped for a transfusion.

Once he'd parked on cracked asphalt outside the cramped, tacky place wedged into a copse of Mangrove trees, that dream died, replaced with a sense of "been there, done that, got something that needed shots." Unlike the rest of the country, Club Blue gave him a sense of comfortable familiarity. Once he stepped into the dark bar, decorated in a cheap set designer's idea of the Arabian Knights, he actually felt at ease. Especially since a mirthlessly smiling, slit-eyed, square-faced, surprisingly tall Filipino girl was leaning on his shoulder within seconds.

"You speak *English*?" he asked above the generic thumping music apparently shared by every rundown girlie bar in the world. "You want a *drink*?" He said it slowly, as if emphasizing the words would somehow make them seem more comprehensible.

Those beautifully formed eyes winced a little. "Come on, man," the girl answered. "Are you kidding me?" She slapped him on the chest with a fine, cool, flat hand. "Yes-ee, mister man. I speakee English and I want drinkee. Only now me wantee most expensive drinkee."

Daniels laughed with honest approval, bought her the faux champagne, and was off to the races. Key might not have agreed with his tactics, but that was why Daniels was a sergeant and Key still a corporal. This was far from Daniels's first rodeo, so he jumped through the now familiar hoops, guiding them as much as they guided him.

Three drinks, transfer to private room, bottle planted upside down in the ice bucket, then, right on schedule, an older, squatter, wider, mama-san was at his other shoulder, wondering if he might like to rent a room for a while. And, if he so desired, his companion, whose name was unconvincingly Lailani, was available for any services.

It was "yes" and "yes" from Daniels, who pretended to be drunker than he was, so Lailani "helped" him up narrow stairs and into a small white room with ill-fitting, piss-yellow curtains and a severe, plain, thinly covered bed that looked like it had been bought at a hospital bankruptcy auction.

Daniels was severely certain Key would not have signed off on the next portion of his plan, but it wouldn't do to have Lailani raising a ruckus at any portion of the evening, so Daniels felt his options were limited. The way he figured it, he had only two. Plan B, he could punch her lights out. Seeing Lailani crawl onto the bed made him decide to go with Plan A, screw her clever little brains out. It wasn't her position—flat on her back—that decided him. It certainly wasn't her get-up—a faded lime-colored T-shirt with a gold logo that read *Goochi* over an elastic, blue, polyester tube miniskirt. It wasn't even her body—long and lean, with slightly more pronounced curves than he was used to seeing on Filipino whores. It was her expression.

Clouds seem to dissipate in her flinty black eyes as they wandered the room like it was an old friend. He imagined her replaying many a visit in her mind, but just as that began to annoy him, her eyes returned to him, and her lips widened into an actual, believable, honest smile. Daniels was confused for a second. What did this well-practiced and well-used woman have to smile about? He looked away as he tried to process it, as he mentally scanned all the smiles from all the women he had known.

Not finding a match, his own eyes settled on a small card tacked to the plain, faded, white wall over a tiny metal end table on which sat a pile of condoms and a box of tissues. It was written in both Arabic and Filipino. He met her eyes before nodding to the card.

"What does that say? Check out time is 1:00 a.m.?"

She didn't even look at it. "Mama puts that in all the rooms. She has carried it to every house she goes to. It says, 'Life is too short to make anyone's hour unpleasant.'"

She smiled at him again, and that did it. He recognized the look now. It was a smile of pride, triumph, and possession. He remembered all the other men in the bar—small, sad, furtive, and even ashamed. They couldn't afford the prime Asian and Eastern European prostitutes in the big Western-owned hotel bars. They had to come crawling to Club Blue, and acted like it. Then Morty Daniels had walked in. He may have been many things, but sad, small, furtive, and ashamed were not four of them.

Obviously, every available girl in the place had a momentary, silent wrestling match to see who would claim him. Maybe even the mama-san had decided the match with a nearly imperceptible move of her head. Lailani had gotten the nod, meaning that Lailani was the top cat in the joint. That made Daniels smile back—hard. *Okay, baby,* he thought as he all but ejected his *dishdasha* robe-length shirt from his body. *Top cat, get ready to meet top dog.*

Her eyes widened as he leaned over the bed, reaching for her. Her gaze was focused below his waist line where another big, fat finger was poking up his *wazer* and pointing directly between her eyes. He gripped the hem of the tube skirt and yanked it off her sleek loins like a magician yanking a table cloth away without disturbing the crockery and silverware. He was delighted with the glorious sight of a plush tuft the likes of which he hadn't seen since stealing some of his grandfather's *Playboy* magazines out of the old man's sock drawer way back when.

"Holy cream-pie." He crawled across her. "You hairy little muff-cake you."

She beamed with approval, her spider-leg fingers, with their orange-painted fake nails, crawled and skittered across his shoulders and neck, sending chills down his spine. He could feel her grip change as she molded his muscles with her hands and arms. He saw or felt no fear as she all but clenched him to her. Her entire being all but yelled, "I'll show you. Think you're so tough and strong? I'll show you what we *pinay* are made of."

As far as Daniels was concerned, what she was made of, above the waist, was a little brown sugar, and much more spice. A buddy of his stationed in Japan once bragged about the creaminess of his girl's skin, so Daniels couldn't wait to text him that she had nothing on Leilani. It was like feeling melted caramel.

But now, he thought, *time to see how the bottom half lives.*

He pried and then popped his penis out of his *wazar* while maintaining a one-handed push-up off her. It flopped on her hip before she took a glance toward it—a glance that turned into a stare.

Her eyes snapped back up to his, and in them he saw excitement, anticipation, and even challenge. She looked like a little birthday girl who was given a real bakery cake after years of store-bought brands.

Daniels thought of his brown belt Marine Corps Martial Arts Program training, the one with the advanced bayonet techniques, as he plunged all the way into her. Her flesh was weak but her muscles were strong. And she knew it, immediately compensating for her "used car upholstery" by showing him how durable her engine still was. Her hands shot down to his buttocks, clamping and pushing, all but demanding he go as deep and as hard as he wanted, or could.

Daniels gave her a big fuckaduck-eating grin, with all his teeth on display, as a sign of approval. It was like dipping his wick into a tub of softened margarine. Not butter, margarine, but still. He would have given her a thumbs-up, but his hands were busy seeing if her breasts were of any use. They were sunny-side-up eggs on her chest, decently shaped, with small, oblong aureoles, and even smaller button nipples. Not much to hold on to, but soft and fun to rest on. So Daniels concentrated on his relentless, unflagging, and consistent counterattack.

He watched and waited for any sign of her eyes unfocusing, but they were as clear and sharp as onyx. She stared up at him with a combination of thanks and "is that all you got?" That made Daniels smile all the wider, because he knew exactly what was going on here. Key might have been able to run rings around him on the track or at crossword puzzles, but in here he was king. He knew, but Lailani didn't know he knew, that she was doing everything she could for him—except suggesting he grab a rubber.

There was something she could give him, and there was something he could give her, and, apparently, Lailani was fine with either of them. Daniels, however, was not fine with an STD or an illegitimate kid, so he waited until the girl finally turned her head and closed her eyes before grabbing a condom from the end table, and doing his one-handed trick. He'd seen lots of bar girls tie a knot in a cherry stem with their tongues. His variation was opening the package and sheathing his word with one hand in seconds, like an expert chef cracking eggs.

He did it twice, just in case either prophylactic was defective, and so expertly she hardly knew he had accomplished it between three thrusts. Finally she realized that something was now covering his lance, but, as she started to react, he silently notified her that, perhaps despite her possible presumption, he had not yet truly begun to screw.

She knew now. His approach went from waves-crashing-to-the-shore to tsunami level. He was no longer steady. He was hydraulic, and he pounded into her until her pupils grew soft and her eyelids closed like cherubs were sitting on them.

* * * *

Daniels pocketed both the empty chloral hydrate vial as well as the not-empty condom as he pleasurably glanced over Lailani's long, lean back as she snored, drooling on the thin pillow.

Oh, the things I do for my country, he thought, quelling the urge to write B+ on her spine in lipstick. Instead he pulled up his *wazar* pants and smoothed down his *dishdasha.* He didn't even have to put on his sandals since he hadn't taken them off.

So much for the prologue. Now to the main show.

Unlike the grittier portions of the Middle East and Asia, there was no hulking guard making sure no one caused trouble at the end of each dimly lit hallway. Club Blue was filled with well-mannered, quiet, even respectful natives and tourists who knew better than to risk a good thing in the otherwise strictly principled country. The entitled wealthy hung out at places with registered copyrights after their brand names. Club Blue was for under-the-radar mischief-makers.

Daniels took a second to get his bearings, then headed for the back of the building, keeping an eye out for the rear stairs. Once he found them, he glanced down, just in time to see the mama-san handing a tray off to another female worker. The tray had food and water, and the other worker took the stairs downward. Daniels followed, stopping as long as he had to, wherever he had to, to make sure he got no undue attention.

He stepped down into the basement, which was cheaply paneled and carpeted like a wayward son's makeshift apartment. The only difference was that the only illumination came from dark blue lights. As he moved through the murky space, the female worker who had brought the tray appeared from a door at the end of the hall, sans tray. Daniels walked quickly toward her. So fast, in fact, that she only noticed him when he was practically on top of her.

"*Kamusta ka!*" she blurted but then his paw was on the door latch.

He pushed inside, filling the doorway. By then his eyes had adjusted, so he could dimly see three figures huddled around a card table, upon which the tray sat. He could also just make out six watery, glistening eyes staring at him, their fingers and mouths filled with torn pieces of chicken.

Endless seconds passed and then the three figures scurried into the darkest part of the room while Daniels reached for his smartphone and vaguely felt something tugging his other arm.

"*Walang pakisama!*" she yelled, over and over again, screeching in his ear. "*Walang pakisama!*"

To him, it sounded and felt like a swam of mosquitos. As he brought up his phone, thumbing for the flashlight app, he began to realize that maybe he had drunk a little more than he thought.

"*Walang pakisama! Walang pakisama! Supil! Supil!*"

He thumbed on the flashlight. Suddenly a terrified Filipino girl was staring at him from within the pool of light. She ducked and dodged, but, in his muddled state, he kept following her with the light.

"What? What?" he asked as the woman who had brought the tray all but leaped on his arm. He swung her off, sending her thudding into the wall by the door.

Then they were all on him, scratching, clawing, and screaming. He lurched around the room like a man on fire, the intense flashlight beam bouncing in every direction. It fell to the floor, but, thanks to the phone case, did not break. The beam of light cut from the carpet to the ceiling like a spear.

Morton Daniels started grabbing and throwing, like a man who had stumbled into a giant web of spiders. "Get—*off*—me!" he thundered, stomping, sending the young women to the floor, one after another. "*Get off me!*"

The last one had leaped onto his back, her fingers trying to tear his face. He reached back and grabbed her by her scrawny shoulders and hurled her in front of him, fully intending to smash her into the far wall. Instead, she crashed into two more new arrivals, who collapsed under her.

Then Manuel Gonzales had pinioned his arms and Josiah Key was repeatedly slapping him in the face.

* * * *

"Why didn't you just ask them?" Key demanded.

"Why?" Daniels replied with an implied *duh*. "What, did you think they were going to just *tell* me?"

The three men were sitting in the same room with a groggy Lailani, the mama-san, Esherida, Rahal, and Chona. The latter two had been the inadvertent backstops of the girl Daniels had tried to body-slam. The trio who Daniels had stumbled upon huddled in the darkest corner. They wouldn't leave no matter how their mama-san pleaded with them.

The woman who had brought the chicken to the trio of exiled girls had brought coffee. Lots and lots of coffee, which was managing to cut through Daniels's fog.

"They might have told you," Gonzales maintained. "You never know with these people."

"Talk is for…talkers," Daniels grumbled before turning on Key. "I said you should have come with me!"

"And I should have," Key agreed. "But I had to kill a kid first."

They explained what kept them. As soon as Malik had appeared in the apartment doorway, Gonzales spotted the wires going from his backpack to his jacket, out his sleeve, and to his fist. No one who toiled in this region of the world ignored something like that. Not after the first time a suicide bomber went off in a café. Key had then quickly explained that Usa Awar had seen him in Shabhut. He had taken a good long look, so his entire network probably knew what Key looked like too.

"Shit, really sorry I missed that," Daniels said. He turned back to Gonzales. "I wouldn't have understood them anyway. I couldn't even understand what they were yelling at me when I came in here."

"They were saying, 'no please' and 'stop,'" Chona told him.

Daniels just shook his head miserably at the floor. "How do you know if a hooker is lying?" he muttered. "Her eyes are open."

"All right, Morty, let's just move on," Key suggested, patting him on the back. "Have some more coffee."

"Sure," Daniels replied glumly. "It'll perk me up *and* shut me up."

All the while, Rahal had been in intense conversation with the mama-san. They waited until she was finished.

"What've you got?" Key asked.

"They started getting sick after sleeping with a particular client," the assistant professor said when she rejoined them at the table.

"Chona"—Key asked, "could you get the name of that client?"

"I already have," Rahal said. "It's Fulan Alfulani."

Gonzales snorted. The other men looked at him.

"The Arabic equivalent of John Doe," he explained.

"Should have known." Key sighed. "Go on, Professor."

"Call me Eshe," Rahal replied. Despite being a witness to an execution, and complicit in a brothel near disaster, she was committed to Key's cause, and had said so in the car coming over.

"All right, Eshe," Key said.

"The symptoms quickly worsened. Fever, seizures, even black blood seeping from the nose when one of them tried to tough it out."

"So nobody went boom?" Daniels wondered until a sharp look from Key sent his attention back to the coffee and floor.

"No," Rahal answered. "The one with the nosebleed seemed to recover when she rested in a dark room. In fact, all three quickly realized that the symptoms worsened whenever the light increased."

The mechanic and marines shared a look, all remembering how Ayman was close to the skylight before he died. Key tried to remember if Goodman had come out of the shadows before he went off, but could come to no definitive conclusion.

"So light or warmth might intensify the condition, but how do they get it in the first place?" Key had already told Rahal about the specimens in the morgue freezer.

"And what is it?" Rahal added. "I've asked the—what do you call her?"

"Madame," Key suggested at the same moment Daniels said, "Mama-san."

"I asked the *woman*," Rahal continued, "if I could have blood samples of the three to test." She smiled at Gonzales's girlfriend. "Chona was very helpful in that endeavor."

The Filipino maid shrugged. "It wasn't difficult. Naturally, Club Blue is not exactly friendly with the local police or hospitals. Any report of a sick girl, especially with a possible STD, would quickly result in considerable jail time."

"But what about the kid with the hole in his head?" Daniels asked. "Local law is unlikely to smile on that either."

"Oman has no indigenous terrorist groups," Rahal informed him, "and the authorities work diligently to prevent terrorism within these borders." She looked at Key with concern. "They must want you dead very badly if they were willing to risk—"

The walls, and even the ceiling, started to implode, and intense, all-encompassing, light flooded the room.

Chapter 12

In the aftermath of the blinding, deafening event, Eshe Rahal couldn't see or hear, but she could still feel, and she felt a hand immediately grip her wrist, and pull. She didn't fight it, instantly believing that the fingers belonged to Key, and, since she had no plan of her own, went with him. She hadn't been at Chona's apartment for Daniels' little speech about Key's powers of observation, but she started finding out for herself amidst the sensory chaos of the imploding room.

She heard muffled shouting in Arabic, Spanish, the Filipino language Tagalong, and furious swearing in English above the din of shattering glass, shredding wood, and smashing concrete. But there was not a sound from Key as he pulled her like a banner behind him. Then, after only a few steps, she felt herself being lifted, and suddenly she could see as Key tossed her bodily through a hole made by the makeshift battering ram that had smashed into the front of the club. She landed with her face right beside the huge right front tire of the vehicle that had been weaponized. That, in turn, sat on the edge of the hole it had made with a gigantic pyramid-shaped lance welded to the front. Her head was just below the line of intense forty-five million candlepower spotlights attached to, and powered by, the 360-cubic-inch V8 engine within the snout of the mechanical beast.

Horrible noises arose from behind and below her. She spun her head in that direction, seeing the three Filipino girls—the girls she had so recently scheduled blood samples from—jerking in the light like marionettes controlled by a malicious child throwing a tantrum. She saw the nearest one's bulging eyeballs begin to shear and spit black, lumpy, liquid when she felt herself being lifted again.

Then Rahal found herself standing beside Key, one arm wrapped around her waist, while the other held up his SIG Sauer. She wanted to say, "No, I have to observe what's going on there," but stopped herself. Key was calling the shots and he didn't need to see anything. He had already seen it—twice too often as far as he was concerned. But he knew what she now knew. What was happening here was more than an attack; it was an assassination. The lights were there to make sure she didn't get to draw the victim's blood.

Rahal squinted past the lights and saw cowled figures darting this way and that, all waving AK-47s, seemingly searching for something to shoot. She didn't know how many were out there, but Key did. He had counted four. He also recognized the battering ram. It was a modified Cadillac Gage Commando, which had been supplied to the Saudi Arabians during the Persian Gulf War. He even recognized the spotlights, but their specifics didn't matter at this point.

Key didn't say come on, or anything equally needless. He simply ran for Chona's 2011 Nissan Tiida, pulling Rahal with him. She wanted to shout, "But what about the others?" but once again checked herself. She was certain that Key was not making any decision based on selfishness, or even selflessness. Pragmatic energy came off him like sweat.

At that moment Eshe heard the tearing, cracking, bursting splatter of a human being ripping open from inside from her skull to her toes. Then she heard it again, and again, so quickly the last one sounded like an echo of the second.

Key didn't pause. He kept running, hoping the assassins were too intent on witnessing the deaths they instigated to worry about strays. He was wrong about that. As soon as he heard a shout that came directly at his ears, rather than toward the Club, he twisted his torso and pointed directly at the open mouth the shout came from. In that pointing hand he had his SIG Sauer, with his normally pointing finger wrapping the trigger.

One pull and the shouter folded down to the parking lot, the back of his head a messy crater.

Key knew that wouldn't be it. Still running, he twisted in each direction, and when he couldn't find, or get a clear shot, at the remaining trio, he snapped the automatic back in his shoulder holster, once again grabbed Rahal around the waist but now with both hands, and threw her over the hood of the Nissan.

Rahal couldn't prevent a small shriek of surprise, but then she settled into the slide across the metal, and rolled as expertly as she could to the ground on the other side. She immediately scrambled to the relative safety of the passenger door, staying low, while waiting for Key to continue firing.

He didn't. Rather than risk attracting the divided attention of the other three killers, he ran, crouching, around the trunk of the car, and bumped shoulders with Rahal just in time for her to grab his arm and point away from the Club entrance. Key's eyes darted toward four more cowled figures, holding AK-47s, coming in that direction.

"Shit," he said. *They're not taking any chances*, he thought.

He had ten rounds in his SIG, but doubted he could bring them all down before they unleashed a hail of bullets on them from both directions. The four new assailants were already beginning to trot while raising their weapons, but Key still took a second to look under the Nissan, as well as across the street, before he nudged Rahal.

"Follow me fast," he whispered, then crouched toward the open trunk like a panther sizing distance between himself and his prey. It was the trunk with Malik's corpse, complete with backpack.

"*Neik*," she swore in Arabic, then got ready, knowing what he was going to do.

"Now," he said quickly but calmly, already racing past her across the long, narrow parking lot.

She ran right behind him, seeing him sprint for a small, concrete park wedged between a narrow roadway and a muddy, rundown basin lined with a few cheap motorboats.

Rahal wasn't sure what she heard first; the chatter of small arms fire or the thumping, shattering boom of Malik's suicide knapsack bomb finally going off. The thumping was the actual detonation. The shattering were the nails and broken glass spreading. She may have heard some surprised and pained screams afterwards, but couldn't be sure.

Key was sure he heard them and was content enough that Daniels, Gonzales, and even Chona wouldn't sound that way. Then he heard the leaves of the acacia, palm, ghaf, and mangrove trees rustle with seeming annoyance as a rain of shrapnel doused them.

By then he was across the small, crescent-moon-shaped park. He turned, walking backwards, onto the roadway, one hand bringing the SIG back out, and the other maneuvering Rahal behind him.

Damn it, he thought. *The attackers are not all dead.* At least three of the newer quartet were down and motionless, but the fourth was MIA, while at least two of the original bastards were coming out from the hole they had made in the club.

Of course, he chastised himself, trying to set up a sure shot at either of them. *They had to make sure there were no witnesses.*

At that point he was certain that at least Daniels had gotten away. Two wouldn't have survived if they tried to take down Daniels. And Daniels wouldn't have cared less about having the added distraction of protecting Rahal.

Key immediately judged the odds. Bastards were sure to have body armor, so a head shot was required. Nailing a head shot at this distance on moving targets was tough, especially with the shadowy halo the floodlights were making. He could target the flash of their AKs, but then he chanced one of their rounds hitting him or Rahal before he could return fire. By the looks of their scythe-like magazines, they had a minimum of thirty rounds to his now eight, and both their muzzle velocity and effective range were better than his.

He glanced behind him, studiously ignoring Rahal's fear-stricken, *what-now* face. The road was empty save for one old, nondescript van some ways in the distance. He and the woman might make a break for the boat basin, but the chance of finding an unlocked, fueled motorboat they could steal before being riddled with 7.62 x 39 mm cartridges was slim.

Okay, Key thought. *Showdown time.*

He kept walking backwards, keeping himself between the AKs and the woman, and waited. His gun rose at the same time the others did. The one to his right got off the first burst. Key returned fire with two quick shots, thinking of the rounds more as fists than bullets. If he couldn't kill him, he could at least throw off his aim with some punches to the chest and shoulder. Which is exactly what he did.

He didn't even feel the heat or hear the whine of the AK-47 ammo.

Assholes, he thought. *They think automatic weapons compensate for target practice.*

Then, several things happened at once. The bloodied mamma-san suddenly appeared behind the cowled man to Key's left and rammed a kitchen knife all the way through his neck. It emerged under his chin with a vigorous spray of blood. The man to Key's right recovered from Key's nine-millimeter "punches" and opened up on the woman, making her shriek and twitch violently, spastically, in a collapsing death-throe. Key straightened his aim and pointed directly at the man's face with his gun barrel. But before he could pull the trigger, he heard a screech behind him.

The van was no longer far away. It was right beside Rahal. The side door slammed open and two hands grabbed the assistant professor. Her own two hands reflexively shot out and grabbed Key's hair and jacket. All four arms yanked, and the two beleaguered pedestrians were hauled into the van.

The tires burned noxiously and the van leapt away from what was left of Club Blue and the men who had attacked it.

Chapter 13

Morty Daniels learned a long time ago not to use his instincts in a fight. If he used his instincts, he would just head-butt everybody. And that would do as much damage to his head as to his opponent.

No, he used his training in a fight. Training from his drill sergeant, Key, and even Lieutenant Colonel Goodman. From his drill sergeant he learned Marine hand-to-hand and close quarters combat with knife and fist. From Key he tried to learn how to use his brain as well as his fists. And from Goodman he learned how not to blow up in somebody's face.

But habits die hard. Good or bad.

From Daniels's point of view, it looked like God was grabbing the top of Club Blue's far wall, where it met the center of the ceiling, then made a fist. Following that came a long, crunching, crash—like Satan was eating concrete, glass, and balsawood chili.

And then there was light. Lots of light. Blinding light.

Even Daniels, who would often describe himself as a Tennessee Turkey—because turkeys were so dumb—knew what that was all about. If those sick girls had the black blood fever, they were about to blow up real good. And it was blindingly clear that's what whoever turned on the lights wanted.

The next thing that popped into his head was the suggestion Key gave him after one particularly tough Marine Corps Martial Arts Program training session. "If a gun barrel is there"—Key had pointed between Daniels's eyes—"don't be there." He had just kept pointing between Daniels's eyes. In other words, don't stay a target if you know you're being targeted.

First, Daniels had no intention of being anywhere near exploding bones, blood, and guts. Second, anyone who wanted exploding bones, blood, and guts was likely to continue the favor with anyone else around.

Daniels was already moving while he was thinking all this—back to where he had come from. Since the front wall had caved, and was caving, in, the sergeant double-timed it toward the back wall and the entrance, now exit, door—peering as hard as he could for any sign of his allies.

As soon as he ducked out the door, two things happened. One, he saw the rapidly retreating figure of Gonzales booking it toward the side stairs, all but carrying Chona with him.

Man, Daniels thought, *we don't call him "Speedy" for nothing.*

And two, as he was about to call out to Gonzales, somebody leaped on his back.

Critically, Daniels knew it was somebody, and not something, from experience. He also knew it was a woman for the same reason. He felt at least two more reasons poking into his back. Despite his clinging passenger, Daniels followed Gonzales at essentially full speed. With just a glance, his guess was confirmed. Lailani was all over him.

Daniels didn't feel like talking. Especially when he heard the cracking, tearing, splattering sounds coming from the invaded room, followed by guttural shouts, and the short sizzling spits of automatic weapon fire.

Fuckaduck.

He wished he had his SIG somewhere inside the *dishdasha*, but it was back on the plane since nobody could figure out a way to keep it from being obvious. *That was all right*, he rationalized. The motto of the MCMAP course was "One mind, any weapon."

Now that the shooting had started, he wasn't about to call out to Gonzales, either. No sense drawing the attackers' attention. He started taking the stairs two and three at a time as if Lailani were a backpack, and a nearly empty one at that. He was practically on top of Gonzales and Chona when they all piled out into the first-floor lobby.

There was a split second when the men stopped, and the woman jerked forward, since the battering ram-equipped Cadillac Gage Commando was wedged into the doorway like King Kong's leering face. The men made an instant call, but weren't about to confer and argue about it. For some reason, Gonzales raced left.

If Daniels had thought about it, he might have followed, since Gonzales, and especially Chona, knew the area much better than he did, but he didn't think about it. Instead, he decided not to give whoever was attacking one target, and called upon his vast knowledge of escaping bar room brawls.

In other words, he charged toward the kitchen. There was always a back door in the kitchen. As he was coming in, he tried to use Key's lesson in observation. There was a long silver construction directly in front of him, where waiters picked up meals the cooks made and placed from the other side. Refrigeration bunkers lined the left wall, and stoves lined the right.

At the end of the shoebox-shaped room was the expected, and hoped-for, back door. At the moment he stepped toward it, a cowled, AK-47-carrying a-hole stepped through it.

Lailani made a little sound of fear and panic in his ear. He'd almost forgotten she was there, and continued as if she wasn't.

Lesson two, as MCMAP and Key had taught him. If you want the fight over, don't put distance on it. Get in close and get in close fast.

Daniels charged the man, making no sound. He wasn't out to spook or get the guy's attention, not when he had an AK-47 and Daniels had nothing but the girl on his back.

One mind, any weapon. Daniels grabbed Lailani with both fists, one in her hair and one around her left arm, and hurled her at the cowled a-hole.

To Daniels, it looked, felt, and sounded as if he had thrown a screeching, wet, terrified cat at the guy. Lailani, to her credit, lived up to the role. She landed on the a-hole's head and shoulders—howling, scratching, kicking, and clawing. As she fell, whether she meant to or not, she took his AK-47 with her.

The man reeled in surprise, and was about to wrench the gun back, when Daniels reached him. He wanted to tear the a-hole's head off with his bare hands so badly, but he also wanted to win completely.

"If you do it right," Key had told him, "it's over like that." He had snapped his fingers. "Don't show them how tough you are. Show them how smart you are. It's not how badass you are, it's how effective you are."

Daniels arrived at the a-hole with an iron frying pan in one hand and a butcher's knife in the other. If the sergeant had to make a bet later which he used first, it would be a toss-up. All he was sure of was the pan went as far into the man's skull as he could put it, and the knife was all the way in the a-hole's ear, up to its hilt. Omanis were proud of their knife heritage. Daniels decided they had good reason to be.

Effective enough for you, Joe? He considered thinking about where Key actually was or what he was doing, but he didn't have time for that yet. As Dirty Harry always said, "A man's got to know his limitations."

Even before the a-hole was completely on the floor, Daniels was wrenching the AK-47 up from the twisting bodies. Then, without a word, he sidled out the back door, scanning the area for any more a-holes.

None were obviously apparent. He noted shadows at the edges of the spotlights' bleed-off, but most of his vision was filled with a copse of Ghaf and Mangrove trees, with one big Palm shooting straight up from the middle like a hairy man's erection. The decision what to do next was easy. He sure as hell wasn't going back.

Once in the dense little grove he started toying with regret. And when the shadows he had seen out the corner of his eyes started moving closer to his corneas, he realized the problem. Shooting in here was at least a fifty percent waste of time. Probably more than half his bullets would be sunk in bark, not flesh. And he didn't have that many bullets to waste.

Okay, he thought. *Let's see if these new a-holes know that.*

They didn't. And he really knew they were a-holes because they came at him in a pair, rather than from two sides. That allowed him to use the trees as cover. They didn't even shift to try getting a clear shot. They just sprayed. Daniels let them, getting closer one sharp, careful, step at a time.

Oh, they were so sure their automatic weapons made them all powerful that their expressions didn't even change until he was almost one tree trunk away. They may have been cowled, but their eyes went from sadistic and amused shapes to round and wide open as he sidled to the right, grabbed the nearest man's hot gun barrel with his right hand and put one AK-47 round directly between the furthest one's round and wide-open orbs.

Daniels grinned like a wolf at the pain of his burned palm and fingers as he moved the living a-hole's smoking hot gun barrel far away from his body. "Thanks." He growled as he put a second bullet through the man's chin, his brain, and out the top of this skull. "That's better than coffee."

He found the small, narrow, run-down, concrete boat basin on the other side of the trees. He saw dark figures running toward the small, two-person, boats—untying them, pulling up oars, or trying to start low-power outboard engines. He didn't open fire on them because, even in the moonlight, he could see they weren't armed. Besides, they weren't even looking at him.

But as he watched, one of the fishermen did a herky-jerky dance and slammed across his boat—his head making a hollow thumping sound on the wood. It was quickly followed by the echo of a shot.

Every soldier knew you never heard the sound of the gun killing you, so Daniels took solace in that as he looked in the direction of the weapon's report. Three more cowled, AK-47-toting figures were coming from the trees, and they were mercilessly exterminating the unarmed fishermen who were just trying to get away.

That pissed Daniels off. He turned toward them like a spun top, brought up his purloined AK-47 and quick-marched toward them, carefully targeting and firing as he went.

The first went down, dancing like his victim had. The second altered his aim to try killing someone who had the audacity of being armed and fighting back, but then Daniels's second shot made his dead eyes look to the starry sky before his corpse landed. But then the sergeant's AK was empty.

That *really* pissed Daniels off, because it meant that the a-hole had already used the rest of the bullets to execute innocent bystanders.

Daniels didn't throw the weapon away. That would have been supremely stupid. Just because it was empty of bullets didn't mean it had ceased being a weapon. In fact, what this last a-hole didn't know *could* hurt him.

Daniels wouldn't have reached him in time without the AK. Because as the a-hole shifted his aim to target Daniels, Daniels shifted his aim to target the a-hole. And, because the a-hole didn't know Daniels's gun was empty, he flinched, ducked, and dodged. By the time he realized Daniels hadn't fired yet, the sergeant was on him.

MCMAP had five belts a marine could earn. The tan belt was awarded for learning basic punches, kicks, chokes, locks, holds, throws, and stabs. The gray belt was awarded for intermediate level and basic ground fighting. The green belt came with arm bars, blocking techniques, and enhanced pain compliance. Key and Daniels had stalled at brown belt level because the sergeant was too arrogant, and the corporal was too busy trying to find alternatives to fists and feet of fury. He felt that applying thought rather than muscle would be more effective.

Daniels didn't care about any of that. He just wanted to use the advanced chokes, throws, blades, and firearms to hurt somebody. But now he promised himself that if he survived this, he'd get to black belt level, since that was where he'd be taught rifle versus rifle, short weapon versus rifle, and unarmed versus rifle fighting.

The last a-hole brought his AK-47 around. Daniels blocked its barrel with his, kicking the man in the balls at the same time. The man had expected it, and shifted just enough to take the brunt of the kick on his inner thigh. He used the momentum of Daniels's block and kick to spin around, trying to bring the gun back into play, but all Daniels focused on was the back of the man's head as he spun.

He didn't have time to bring the butt of the rifle up, so he just stabbed the barrel into the man's exposed neck. If he had gotten the man's Adam's apple, that would have ended it. Instead, the man jerked forward, throwing off his own swing. Daniels ducked under the swinging barrel and surveyed his opponent as he stumbled away. He remembered the voice of his instructor when he had a student in a similar position.

"So many ways to kill you, so little time."

As if examining a particularly venomous insect, Daniels punched the a-hole in the kidney, which made the man hiss and bend backwards.

Then Daniels kicked the a-hole in the nearest knee, which made the man unwillingly kneel.

"Tee time." Daniels swung the AK-47 like Barry Bond's best home run shot, steroids or not.

The last a-hole's head erupted like a cantaloupe dropped from a kitchen counter.

Daniels nearly did the same thing to Lailani when she touched his arm a second later. But then he saw it was her. What's more, several of the fishermen were behind her, looking at him with gratitude, relief, and respect. They were also motioning for him to follow them, while Lailani gently tugged his arm in the same direction. He couldn't be sure, but her thankful face gave him the impression she may have forgiven him for all that drugging-her-stuff.

He let them lead him toward the water as he looked back toward the hotel. He heard some gunfire, then the strangled wet scream of someone he didn't recognize.

Sounds like he got it right through the throat. Daniels got a sudden urge to see if it had been Key on the giving end, but quickly decided against it. Key always had better places to put a knife than the throat.

Daniels let Lailani and the fishermen bring him to a small boat. The girl and one man got in with him, then they set off into the wide, blue, calm Gulf of Oman, where, hopefully, there weren't any more a-holes.

Chapter 14

To Key's relief, CJ wasn't in the Bayt al Falaj airport camouflaged hanger Gonzales had left her in. That meant Gonzales had survived the attack on Club Blue as well, and had been here. Key watched the jeep driver talking intensely with Eshe Rahal, and waited patiently. For him to get pushy or panicky at this point would help no one.

"Yes, Speedy came with Chona," Rahal told him as soon as she could. "Faisal said they waited as long as they could, but were convinced to leave." She looked back at Faisal, who owned the Jeep and did look like he was about to get pushy or panicky. "They know the club incident is likely to unleash a lockdown of the city, if not the country. The strengthening of terrorist groups in Yemen has put Oman on high alert. Saudi Arabia and Iran's radical policies have not crossed the border so far, but they fear something like this may lead to a crackdown—"

She stopped, realizing from the subtle shifts in Key's face that something was far more important to him.

"Sergeant Morty wasn't with them," she added sympathetically.

Key cursed under his breath. "Anything else?"

"Yes," Rahal answered. "They want to know who he is." She pointed at the driver of the van.

Key glanced at the middle-aged, mustached man in the Omani traditional dress and lab coat before returning his full attention to the young woman. "And what did you tell them?"

"The truth," she replied. "Professor Basheer Davi."

Key had assumed as much upon first setting eyes on the man, and watched now as he went off with Faisal to choose another car.

"Speedy left his crew here with instructions," she continued, while also watching the process of switching out the van the attackers had seen. "Which boiled down to descriptions of you, me, and Daniels, as well as orders to do whatever we wanted or needed."

"And what is it we want or need?" Key asked as his attention was diverted by so-far unknown members of Gonzales's crew pushing the van to the corner of the hanger, where chop-shop equipment was strewn. By the time he looked back at Rahal, they had already begun expertly dismantling the van.

"Transportation is about all Professor Davi feels comfortable requesting," Rahal said sadly. "As much as we'd love to have another channel of information and communication, the more people involved, the greater the chance he will be found."

"By who?" Key asked pointedly.

Rahal looked him in the eye, her expression rippling with care and regret. "He'll have to tell you that."

Key breathed in deeply and watched as Faisal waved them over to a copper-colored 2015 Nissan Murano. As he and Rahal approached, he saw the narrowing, tinted, windows that were designed to obscure both driver and passenger from outside eyes. Although an adult male Omani driver would draw less attention than an American or woman, Davi motioned for Rahal to get behind the wheel and Key to join him in back. Once there, he motioned for Key to crouch or slide down, so their faces wouldn't be on display. Once again, Key realized, he would kiss all Muscat sightseeing goodbye.

As Rahal began to drive carefully away, having profusely thanked Gonzales's friends, Davi spoke in quiet, calm, perfect English. "I am very sorry to have gotten you, how you say, mixed up in this."

Key shrugged. "I am already very much in this, and mixed up." He locked eyes with the Professor, who looked like he either hadn't slept in quite some time, or had been crying, or both. "But you had no intention of rescuing me, did you?"

"No," Davi somberly admitted. "But Eshe wouldn't have that, would she?"

"Apparently not." Key sighed.

"She has put a great deal of faith in you."

"Repeatedly saving someone's life'll do that," Key informed him. "It's too bad that whatever you're mixed up in required it."

"Yes, too bad," Davi agreed, his expression tight. "We have a saying here. It translates to 'a known mistake is better than an unknown truth.'"

Key nodded. "And I guess that unknown truth is about something that will make people explode. Am I right?"

They heard Rahal's voice from the front seat, saying something in Arabic. Key tensed, thinking it might be a warning about something on the road ahead, but it turned out to be another saying, which Davi translated for him.

"Lying is the disease. Truth is the cure."

Key was already tired of proverbs. They wouldn't help in a firefight. "What are we, and yes, I say *we*, up against? Do you want to tell me, or would you rather I guess so you could agree or disagree?"

Davi hazarded a glance out the bottom of the back window. Key didn't feel the need to follow suit.

When Davi's face returned, he seemed more confident. Something approaching either a grimace or a smile, or both, threatened Davi's lips. "I think the authorities will strive to contain the news of the attack on Club Blue," he said. "Although agitation afflicts all the countries around us, it doesn't effect Oman. Yet. If we needed, I feel certain both Iran and Saudi Arabia would rally to assist us. Oman and Iran are close allies, both economically and diplomatically."

"Afflict," Key echoed. "Interesting choice of words. Do you actually mean infect? Do the Saudis and Iranians know about that?"

Davi sniffed. "You do not even know about that, my friend."

"I'm all ears," Key said, shaking away the image of Davi looking at him. "Okay." He nodded. "Poor choice of idiom. Let's just say I'm very anxious to *know*."

"You will know," Davi assured him. "But I cannot do it here." He made abortive hand motions that looked as if he was trying to magically make the SUV grow larger. "Please wait just a few hours more."

"A few hours? Do we even *have* a few hours?" Key asked.

Davi nodded. "We'll have to make it so. We have no choice."

Key's jaw tightened. There had to be a good reason for Davi to go missing. "Yeah, about that—"

"Please," the Professor interrupted, his head lowering, and his hands making a calming gesture. "I must rest. I do not want to, but I must."

Rahal said, "He had not slept since—"

"No, Eshe," Davi interrupted. "Do not speak. I do not wish any passing motorist to even suspect you might have someone in the vehicle with you." He looked apologetically at Key. "I know this is trying. But it will be rewarded. That I can assure you."

Key exhaled sharply, his lips tight. "Another Arab proverb?"

Surprisingly, that made Davi laugh. "As a matter of fact, yes." He said something in Arabic, then translated. "'Be patient and you will get what you desire.' Now let me rest. And, if you are wise, you will too. Neither of us may get the chance again for quite some time." And the Professor was asleep almost as soon as his head rested upon the seat.

Key shifted to get more comfortable, and was about to say something to Rahal before he remembered Davi's paranoia about passing motorists. That further reminded him that he might, indeed, be more tired than he hoped.

And that was his last thought until the Murano's stopping woke him up. He twitched, then straightened when he saw he was alone in the vehicle. The auto was in a tent the size of a one-car garage. A tent flap was open behind them, and he stepped out.

He blinked into a breathtaking sunrise on a pristine, sweeping desert. Rahal must have driven all night, leaving them at the edge of an astonishing swath of sand dunes. She was standing beside the tent opening, holding a large pile of clothing.

"Welcome to *Rub' Al Khali*," she said, amused by his gaping reaction. Even amidst an attempted suicide bombing, and the purposeful, seemingly malicious, extermination of three infected girls, she had never seen Key be anything but resolute.

"*Rub' Al Khali?*" he repeated for the lack of anything else.

"The Empty Quarter," Rahal translated.

"Well named," he commented, getting some of his equilibrium back. "Where's the Professor?"

Rahal nodded toward the nearest sand dune. "Obtaining for us our next ride."

A man in full Bedouin, desert dweller garb—including a sarong, the ankle length *thobe*, and kimono-shape-sleeved, striped, *aba* sheath—appeared, holding the leashes of three saddled camels.

Key realized it was Davi, then turned back to Rahal, his eyes wide and mouth open. "You have *got* to be kidding me."

"No, we aren't," Davi said as he neared.

Rahal tossed Key the similar Bedouin garb she had been holding. "And you," she told him with the first real smile he had ever seen on her face. "How you say, it? You ain't seen nothing yet."

Chapter 15

It was so well camouflaged even Key didn't see it at first.

One second it was just another sand dune out of millions of sand dunes. As beautiful as they all were, after a couple thousand they got to be a bit monotonous, despite the spectacular skies and landscapes.

The next second the sand shifted just enough to reveal what seemed to be a cloth edge. As the camels ambled forward, the edge became a flap, and suddenly a small section of tent appeared as if by magic.

Sure enough, Professor Davi brought his ungulate to a stop a few feet away, and started the laborious process of dismounting. But then again, everything was laborious where camels were concerned. But Key had ridden in enough military vehicles over ridiculous terrain to have a head start being, as Eshe put it, "comfortable being uncomfortable."

Although Rahal had also informed him that the Rub'al Khali was more than six-hundred-miles long and three-hundred-miles wide—covering parts of Oman as well as Saudi Arabia, the United Arab Emirates, and Yemen—he had no idea where they were despite extensive training in pinpointing his location. But Key supposed that was the whole idea.

Just as he had mounting his camel—the one they jokingly called Alshshaytan, a.k.a. the Devil—he watched Davi and Rahal dismount, and followed suit. They were all wearing full Bedouin garb, including the *maser* hooded headwear, held in place with an *igal* headband of camel wool, so they looked no different than the two men who were suddenly in front of them.

To Key, it appeared as if the desert sand had given birth to them, although he knew they simply had pushed, rolled, or crawled out of a sand-covered tent. They faced Key now, one holding a heavy carbine and the other holding a big, curved, beautifully inlaid and decorated *khanja* knife. Davi said something to them in Arabic, after which they begrudgingly stepped away from the corporal.

"Good timing," Key commented, glancing up at the nearly white sun that stabbed the sky at about the 11:00 a.m. position. "Another few minutes and my head would've been hard boiled."

"After a season in Yemen?" Davi sniffed as he kneeled by the sand-covered cloth. "I doubt that."

"Impressive," Key continued, crouching beside the professor and his assistant. "No way to approach this place without the dwellers knowing."

This time Davi snorted as he buried one hand in the sand. "You don't, how you say, know the half of it. They knew we were coming a mile back."

Key looked over his shoulder to try spotting any lookout. Halfway through the motion, he knew that if he couldn't even make out the tent, he'd never spy a watcher. When he looked back, Davi was already halfway through the tent flap.

Rahal motioned that Key should follow, which he happily did. Once inside, he had another half-expected surprise. It wasn't a constricted hovel, which basic engineering suggested it had to be. Instead, it was an expansive, if low-ceilinged, series of tubular bubbles, strewn with carpets, blankets, pillows, and boxes.

Key blinked and tried to get his head around how they had managed to illuminate the place, as well as air condition it. At any other time he might have questioned Davi about it at length, but not now. The professor had not brought him all the way out here to brag about engineering. In fact, Davi was ignoring the small bowls of rice yogurt and round, unleavened, bread that were being offered to them. Instead, he motioned at Key to follow him deeper into the complex.

"I am descended from the Najdi Tribe," he said as he went. "True Bedouins. When I became a scientist, my father didn't know whether to bless or exile me." Davi stopped in a chamber that looked like a squat version of his college office. "I think he did both."

"Family is family." Key shrugged, stopping just inside the entrance. "You obviously still have friends here."

Rahal joined them.

"Yes," Davi replied. "When they heard of my trouble, they moved quickly to make a haven for me and my findings."

Key found a place to kneel in the center of the area, directly behind a small, low rectangular table amid the piles of papers. He didn't have to ask anything since Davi seemed to have every intention of telling him about his trouble and findings without any prompting.

"As you may have guessed," the professor said, kneeling across from Key and a pile of papers he had placed on the table top, "I am a member of the Oman Study Committee."

"A disgraced member," Rahal stressed, kneeling beside Davi.

Davi gave her a sharp look. "We'll come to that," he admonished her. "First things first."

Key's eyebrows raised at Davi's use of his father's favorite phrase, as well as the way Rahal blushed and lowered her head.

"We found something in Shabhut that has grave consequences for the world," Davi continued.

"And you didn't want to keep silent about it," Key suggested, inwardly kicking himself for trying to support Rahal in some way. Neither chivalry nor machismo was timely in this tent.

"No," Davi retorted. "I would have been satisfied, even delighted, to keep silent about it, if only we had taken immediate, destructive, action."

Key rocked back on his heels. "You had a chance to destroy it?" he marveled with gradually increasing incredulity, "and didn't?"

"Obviously." Davi grunted. "We never would have, should have, or needed to meet each other if we had."

Davi slapped a scroll to the table and rolled it open for Key to see. On it was a series of blueprints, schematics, and pictures of a bulbous, multi-legged fossil, as well as a computerized recreation of it.

"Idmonarachne Brasieri," Davi said sadly. "Their ironstone-preserved remains were three million years old, and found in France."

Key stared at the charts, spotting a measurement bar. According to it, the Idmonarachne Brasieri was about four feet long from its antennae to its multiple legs. Unable to completely comprehend what he was seeing or hearing, he felt an itch that crawled from his skull to his coccyx, then looked up at the professor.

"You mean this is *real*?" he said with open disbelief. "This exists? Now? Here?"

Davi nodded gravely. "The OSC first got wind of a discovery in the bowels of a Shabhut temple, when extremists destroyed it a little too well."

Key translated that for himself. Either ISIS or Awar's gang opened a hole that somehow went back all the way to the dinosaurs, then along came…this.

"I thought I was chasing down a disease," Key retorted. "You mean I'm chasing some sort of prehistoric spider?"

Davi nodded. "Actually yes. It is most similar to the modern arachnid."

"Except it doesn't spin silk," Rahal interjected ominously, rewarded by another glare from Davi, a glare she ignored to finish her statement. "It spins…something else."

Key stared from the woman, to the man, to the fossils. "What?" The professor and his assistant shared a glance, as if they were suddenly reluctant to say more. Key could imagine why. Things were about to get even worse. "What?" he repeated more insistently.

Davi opened his mouth to reply, but before he could, one of the men who greeted them stuck his head into the office. He said one word in Arabic, which made Davi's face go white. Before Key could ask for a translation, both Davi and Rahal had leapt to their feet and were running back to the entrance.

By the time they arrived there, Key was between them. He was practically riding one of the guard's backs as they rolled outside, just as a helicopter shot past them, its struts practically tearing off their heads.

He tried to stop the guard from standing. He failed, and then the man danced as the copter's thirty-millimeter bullets tore into him from turban to sand boot.

Saudi Army Apache, Key immediately identified. *At least five years old. Probably downed by Yemini and somehow refurbished.*

He rolled over and practically kicked Rahal and Davi back into the tent as the helicopter screamed up and around for another pass.

"Chain gun. Maybe anti-tank missiles and rockets!" Key grabbed Davi by the scruff of the neck and propelled him back toward the study. "Talk, and talk fast!"

Davi looked as if a long-delayed execution order was finally being carried out, but he didn't resist. He went with Key back into the tent bowels, and started jabbering as the corporal searched for any decent weapon.

"The authorities want to make peace with Usa Awar. The man even invited the committee to study his new discovery." Davi gasped, trying to catch his breath and order his mind as a large whomping sound shook the tent.

Hydra rocket, Key recognized, gritting his teeth as he kept searching. Direct hit and they wouldn't be able to separate what was left of them from the crystallized sand. "Go on!" he yelled.

"The Idmonarachne Brasieri can excavate any animal carcass," Davi said, slowly backing into a corner, "planting eggs that can gestate in the corpses. We concluded they were sealed in a massive underground mausoleum where seeping groundwater and cannibalism allowed them to survive."

"They? How many?" Key barked.

"We don't know! Awar only allowed us to examine one. But even if it's just two, these arachnosaurs could spread inland like a locust swarm, or send seeded corpses into the Gulf of Aden. It would only be months before they would affect the world."

Another rocket tore a hole through the tent's entryway, exploding some yards off target. But it was enough to make Davi scream and clutch his head. Key grabbed the man by his shoulders and shook him, silently thankful that whoever was manning the copter was a lousy shot.

"Are the eggs making people explode?" Key shouted in Davi's ear.

The question gave the professor something to concentrate on. "No!" he yelled over the din of the swooping copter just a cloth away. "It's their webbing. The webbing! It contains ammonia picrate and picric acid. It's impossible, but if it touches you, or you touch it, the formula enters your bloodstream and somehow intensifies in the light to extreme potency!"

As another explosion sent them staggering, Davi started crying.

Key could've sworn he heard an echo. He turned back to see Rahal had crouched beside Davi, holding him tightly as the professor sobbed.

"What else?" Key yelled at him. "Tell me what else!"

"They want to weaponize them!" Davi yelled back, his face haunted. "They want to weaponize what the webbing makes humans become!"

Key spun around again as the copter made another pass. *There are definitely two copters now*, he realized. *But how did they find us?*

"Can they be stopped?"

"I don't know!"

Davi's hollow answer was not what he wanted to hear.

A gigantic explosion shook the ground. Rahal shrieked and clutched Davi tightly. As shrapnel tore the tent directly over their heads, Key dove atop the professors. As the corporal recovered from the shock wave, he realized he still needed to know one thing. "Why did you run? Who wants you dead?"

His pained eyes locked with the professor's tormented ones.

"They all do," Davi whispered. "I ran because—"

Before he could finish, the tent tore completely open directly in front of them. Rahal screamed in abject horror, her eyes screwed shut. Key leaped forward with the Idmonarachne Brasieri scroll in his hand.

He stopped dead in his tracks as Sergeant Morton Daniels stood in front of him in full tactical gear, with his M240 in one hand and a huge fuckaduck-eating grin plastered on his stupid face.

"Anybody call the cavalry?" he asked.

Key was about to either embrace or slug Daniels when he felt Rahal grab him in a bear hug. He looked down to see an expression of radiant, almost Biblical, reprieve on her face. Before he could look beyond them to see what had actually happened, they all heard Davi's small, resigned voice behind them.

"I ran because—"

Key turned to see the man crumpled in the corner, holding the barrel of a World War Two-era Smith and Western Victory Revolver against his right temple, his finger on the trigger.

"I'm the only one who said they can't be controlled. Remember—"

Key dove at the professor.

"The arachnosaurs can't be controlled." Davi pulled the trigger.

Chapter 16

At first glance, Shabhut looked exactly the same. But at second glance, he actually looked like an Epcot version of Shabhut. The dirty, sandy streets, which were no more than paths, were free of corpses. They were also free of parts of corpses, human or animal. What was left of the dwellings were clean; so clean, in fact, that every surface seemed to glow, as if they had been sprayed with some sort of polymer sealant that glimmered in the moonlight. And, while the structures seemed abandoned, they were not.

When the matte black Mercedes-Benz BMG G83 armored limo rolled slowly down the village's central path, toward what appeared to be a natural, tan-colored bunker, cowled, automatic weapon-carrying figures appeared to its right, left, and behind like spectral wraiths. The three men inside the bulletproof vehicle each looked at the sudden chaperones nearest them.

Saad Al-Abbasi saw that the men seemed to be wearing brand-new clothing. Dale Hood saw that the one nearest him had boots that were unscuffed in any way. Jean-Bernard Toussaint saw that the weapon the one nearest him was holding, a Kel-Tec M45, looked as if it had come straight from its Florida assembly.

The seemingly spectral guards kept their distance as the armored vehicle slowed to a stop alongside one end of the bunker, which, at this angle, looked like the burrow of a giant hedgehog. The trio heard the doors decompress and unlock, cuing them that their trip from the Aden International Airport was at an end.

Al-Abbasi, for one, glanced one final time around the palatial, fine leather and wood veneer interior—taking in the satellite TV, refrigerator, bar, and communication system. He knew that this vehicle had to cost at least a million dollars, and that any part of it was fortified to withstand multiple grenades and a wide array of calibers. It was so well protected that none of them had even seen the chauffeur within his one-way mirrored automotive cockpit.

Al-Abbasi slowly extracted himself from a plush captain's massage chair, and took one last big breath of the limo's recirculated, purified, internal air conditioning system before joining his fellow passengers outside. By that time, their sentinels had positioned themselves like living balustrades, directing the trio unerringly toward the base of the bunker. Hood went first with the stereotypical go-get-'em spirit of an American, while Toussaint diffidently adjusted his gait so he was beside a cautious Al-Abbasi, sometimes a half-step behind, sometimes a half-step ahead. The Arab knew enough to be wary because, in the desert, in this ancient land, djinn and demon birds were once said to dwell.

Al-Abbasi, who wore the traditional Saudi dress of an ankle-length *thobe* shirt, a *bisht* cloak, and a *kufiyyah* skullcap with a *igal* cord circlet, noted that the Frenchman wore a Faconnable sports coat over a Lacoste shirt and Le Coq Sportif slacks, while the American wore a T-shirt and jeans. The T-shirt and jeans had probably cost hundreds of dollars, but they were a T-shirt and jeans nonetheless. The attire seemed to suggest that they were going to a yacht club or barbeque rather than one of the most ominous, dangerous summit meetings Al-Abbasi could imagine.

Although they were three of the world's most wealthy, prominent, and, some might even say, infamous weapons dealers, the American and European seemingly didn't know the reputation of Usa Awar the way the Saudi did. Or perhaps not. Whatever their seeming attitude, Toussaint and Hood still came all this way at this time of night because of a single summons.

If Al-Abbasi were expecting Awar to announce his proud Arabic heritage immediately, he was disappointed. The Saudi was impressed that the man himself was waiting for them, not some flunky underling, but Awar, who stood alone awaiting them, was resplendent in a beautifully tailored, light blue William Westmancott suit, white shirt, and red tie. Al-Abbasi knew that only a few of these were made a year at a cost of seventy-five thousand American dollars.

Awar stood in what looked like the Epcot version of a cave as well. Although the walls and floor were uneven and even sloped, they seemed made of clear polymer-coated rock and sand. They gleamed in soft white and yellow light coming from LED pods that were artfully placed on the walls and ceilings. There was no furniture in this antechamber.

"Gentlemen." Awar spoke first in English, then French, and then Arabic. "Shall we decide upon a language?"

Al-Abbasi was not surprised when English was chosen. He knew that Hood would glower and pout otherwise.

"Please, right this way, gentlemen," Awar told them, motioning, then walking toward the next chamber. "Does anyone need further refreshment above what was in the limousine, or perhaps a rest stop?"

No one took Awar up on his offer, so they simply continued deeper into the expertly engineered catacomb, which got smaller and lower-ceilinged with each chamber. There was no furniture that Al-Abbasi could see, only more cowled, silent, spotless guards with brand-new weapons. None of the visitors was going to show weakness by asking a question, so it was up to their host to take up the conversational slack.

"So," he finally said, stopping in what appeared to be the final chamber, since it seemed to have no egress. "Which of you gentlemen is going to represent me at this year's Special Security and Defense Exhibition?"

All three visitors stilled. The International SADE Conference took place whenever its Dubai masters decided it was time. And they had decided it was to be this year, in just a few weeks, in fact. Everyone in the chamber, probably even the guards as well, knew that, while SADE was famous for the sheer number of attendees, companies, exhibitions, delegates, and countries represented, the real action took place all around the Trade Centre Complex, action that included anything that even the notorious Usa Awar had to offer.

The American spoke first. "Why am I here?"

Awar smiled upon Hood. "You mean, what is in it for you?"

"Isn't that why we came here?" the American shot back.

Awar's smile hadn't wavered. "Why, the same thing that is in it for any of you. Not only a percentage of possibly billions, but a portion of personal power that none of you have yet experienced."

The Westerners shared a doubtful look, but Al-Abbasi, who had heard the Arabian whispers, only stared blankly at Awar.

"*Waladhillik*," he said hollowly, "*faman alssahih?*"

"English!" Hood ordered.

"Yes," Awar said directly to Al-Abbasi. "It is true. I have devised a method to weaponize the creature."

"*M-madha*," Al-Abbasi stammered, then caught himself. "How?"

Awar grinned. "I cannot stand here and explain it to you until morning," he said mildly. "So why don't I just show you?"

Awar turned and signaled a guard, who touched a part of the wall. Before the men's eyes, a large portion of the wall became transparent. All three men gaped at a darkly padded room with a futuristic, cutting-edge, elevated medical table in the center of it. On the table, which could obviously be manipulated to present itself in any direction, at any height, was a young female.

Her nipples were covered by small adhesive squares and her loins covered with the thinnest of bikini bottoms. She was strapped at the wrists, waist, and ankles. But it was her head that drew the most attention. All the visitors had seen multitudes of near-naked women before. Her head was covered by a helmet that seemed to be designed by a team of both science fiction and horror movie directors.

"Gentlemen," Awar said, "may I introduce Private Terri Nichols, United States Marine Corps?" Awar drank in the trio's surprised, amazed, and shocked reactions. "Or, as I like to call her, Idmonphoid Mary."

The American and Frenchman just kept staring, trying to process the meaning of Awar's cryptic pronouncement, but the Saudi stepped back.

Awar turned toward him and said, "But you know all that, don't you, *sadayqaa*?"

The Saudi's mouth dropped open.

Hood looked confused and annoyed. "My friend," Toussaint translated for the American in a whisper.

Awar took another step toward Al-Abbasi. "You know all that because it was you who wanted to capture and interrogate the professor, wasn't it? It was you who wanted to circumvent me, yes?"

"Power." Al-Abbasi took another step back. "Too much power. You wanted it all, as always."

"And I deserve it all, as always," Awar said. "You are too greedy, *sadayqaa*. Selling to both sides at the same time. Drug trafficking, flesh peddling. Your lust I can tolerate; your stupidity I cannot."

"Stupidity?" Al-Abbasi retorted in disbelief. "Is it stupidity to follow the marines, to let them lead me to the professor? I was this close, this close." He held up his hand, showing his first finger and thumb as if he was holding a hair. "One more step and I would've had it all!"

Awar stopped, looked at the floor, and shook his head wistfully. "Yes, *sadayqaa*. With you, it was always just one more step." The man in the seventy-five-thousand-dollar suit took a last step toward the Saudi and simply pushed him into the arms of two guards who had silently come up behind them.

As they dragged the struggling, screeching man out, Awar turned back to the American and Frenchman who were framing the still, quiet, evenly breathing young lady strapped to the table beyond. With another press of the wall, her image disappeared, replaced with another image that inspired even the jaded Westerners to step back.

It was a nest, a hollow, seemingly sealed cavern chamber, covered in what looked like thick, soft, diaphanous cotton instead of carpets and hanging rugs. And within the three-story-high area were dozens of gigantic, ponderous spiders as big as coffee tables.

"Holy shit." Hood grunted, as Toussaint realized that the walls were equipped with digital screens rather than one way glass panels. These images could be coming from anywhere.

"Gentlemen," Awar interrupted. "May I present Idmonphoid Mary's creators? Watch closely and see what the arachnosaur can do."

As Hood narrowed his eyes and Toussaint craned his neck forward, Saad Al-Abbasi appeared, dropping out of the gauze at the top of the chamber.

He must have been put in a doubly sealed antechamber, Toussaint surmised, like a submarine pressure chamber. There was no way Awar would, or should, risk any of these creatures escaping.

Al-Abbasi thudded to the ground, saved from broken bones by thick webbing that covered the floor. He caught his breath and gathered his wits just in time for a final, eardrum-slicing scream as five arachnosaurs scuttled, leaped, and fell upon him from the front, back, sides, and above, their thirty legs piercing, slicing, punching, cutting, and chopping like spears, knives, scalpels, and machetes.

As the Westerners watched, knowing full well that the nest, at least, had to be close by, Al-Abbasi's face was opened like a cracked walnut, his *thobe* and flesh sliced open from his throat to his scrotum, his arms and fingers ripped open and pulled back like pulled pork, and his legs and feet filleted as if by a chandelier of dancing lasers. Each of his organs were popped like helium balloons and his brain unwrapped like removing a turban. Within seconds, all were ingested into the creatures' quivering maws.

The steaming smell of the eviscerated man sent the rest of the creatures into a feeding frenzy. Before their surging, heaving, undulating mass concealed him from sight, wet, unctuous, pulsating eggs erupted from the bulbous spiders' spinnerets, filling Al-Abbasi's torn-open carcass.

Even Hood had to look away, but Toussaint kept watching in abject fascination.

"But what of the American?" he said quietly to Awar, who had slowly moved beside him. "The one who has been tracking you from here to Thumrait and Muscat and back?"

Awar looked at the Frenchmen with growing respect. Although Toussaint did not return his gaze, they both knew who would be representing the man at SADE.

"He is of no concern," Awar said with certainty. Then he joined Toussaint to watch the finale of the arachnosaur feasting. "Because of me," he said, "he suffered a concussion the first time we met."

"But he survived the suicide bomber you sent," Toussaint continued softly. "And the attack on Club Blue. And the attack on Davi's hideout, whoever ordered it."

Awar shook his head. "You are well informed. We will collaborate quite nicely. But do you know what has happened now? Did you hear that this tenacious American suffered yet another concussion in the Professor's company?"

Toussaint finally turned to face Usa Awar, his expression clearly informing the terrorist that, no, he had not known that.

"Yes," Awar told Toussaint with complete certainty. "Corporal Josiah Key is now in a coma."

Chapter 17

Second Lieutenant Barbara Strenkofski found Sergeant Morton Daniels at the Oman Medical College cafeteria.

She had considered seeking him in the bars in the nearby hotels, but didn't have to. She instinctively knew he wouldn't be far from Corporal Key's side. She also knew he was in a really bad way since he didn't look up, even when she purposely placed her right thigh close to his head.

Strenkofski stood patiently, looking down at his miserable, dejected face as he stared into a cup of Turkish coffee, seemingly trying to read the future. But she trusted in his inherent female flesh sensor, since perfume wouldn't clue him. It wasn't allowed here.

Finally, he realized he wasn't alone. He glanced over, then up, at her—immediately snapping to his feet with a salute. Apparently the only thing more powerful than his inner wolf was his military training.

"At ease, Sergeant," she said quietly, placing a hand on his shoulder while looking around to make sure no one would be distracted by their behavior. Thankfully, there was only one or two others at the nearby tables, and they seemed oblivious.

She wore her shirt, tie, long skirt, and flat shoes beneath a lab coat with a white *visitor* tag clipped to the left lapel.

"Please, sit," she told him, joining him in the plastic seat alongside. She studied his worn face as he collected himself.

"With the greatest respect, ma'am," he said, leaning back in his chair and getting at least a little bit of his usual bravado. "What are you doing here? I told Captain Logan all I know."

She waved that away with three fingers and a nod. "Your report was a bit noisy and emotional, Sergeant."

"Well, for-freakin'-give me," he muttered.

She dismissed the apology too, the same way. "Shouting from a copter while rushing your friend to the hospital is not exactly conducive for comprehensive specifics. So the captain felt you might be more forthcoming to, and with, me here. So." She snuggled her rear to the back of the chair, sat straight, crossed her ankles, folded her hands in her lap, and pinioned him with her baby blues. "What happened?"

To his credit, Daniels tried to tell her. His eyes unfocused as the memories flooded back. His mouth opened as he looked away toward the night sky through the cafeteria windows, then his mouth closed. He opened his mouth again, checking to see if looking directly at Strenkofski would get the words flowing. It didn't. Finally, he exhaled and lowered his head before making a decision.

"Come here," he said, standing and making a motion with his right hand as if cupping a floating dandelion leaf. "Follow me."

He took his coffee cup and led her out of the cafeteria into the college's hallways. It was fairly late at night, so only a few teachers and students remained. Since the college was in academic partnership with West Virginia University, they were used to Americans in their midst, so no one gave the blue-eyed blonde and glum giant a second look.

Daniels trudged up two flights of stairs and navigated the halls until they came to the clinic section of the college. Some young doctors and nurses by the entrance desk looked up. One seemed about to inquire into their presence, then he, too, recognized Daniels. They all gave him understanding looks. One even motioned with his head down the hall.

Silently, Daniels brought Strenkofski toward the semiprivate rooms. She looked around, noting that the college clinic looked like many a hospital hallway—no worse, but certainly no better. Same tile floors, same drab walls, same seemingly secondhand medical equipment, and same worn, perforated ceiling tiles.

"Why didn't you bring him to the Muscat Private Hospital instead?" she asked. "It's better equipped than the clinic here, and just a few miles away."

He looked at her, seemed about to speak again, but then held up his forefinger in the universal gesture of "wait a minute." Then they stepped into a darkened room. In the moon and star light coming from the window beyond, Strenkofski saw Key lying in a standard hospital bed, his arm attached to an IV drip, and sensors on his forehead plugged into a biofeedback machine. It indicated that he was stable, but deeply in a world of his own.

"Far more equipped, maybe," Daniels finally said, "but they wouldn't know Joe—I mean Corporal Key—there. Here, they knew, and liked, Professor Davi, and especially assistant professor Rahal. I was convinced they'd take far better care of them."

"Them?" Strenkofski echoed.

Daniels absently motioned to the bed next to Key as he put the coffee cup on an end table and pulled out a chair. Strenkofski's eyebrows raised when she saw the sleeping patient next to the corporal was Esherida Rahal.

"She had to be sedated," Daniels informed the second lieutenant as he sat on one of the chairs between their bedsides. "Deeply sedated. To her credit, she tended to Corporal Key until we were well on our way. When she finally fainted, it took us all by surprise, probably even her. If I hadn't caught her, she probably would've fallen out of the chopper."

Strenkofski sidled into the chair facing Daniels, her eyes glistening with interest. "Must have been shock."

"Fits the bill," Daniels agreed. "She was sweating, cold to the touch, her breathing was irregular, and her pupils were dilated." He looked at the young woman. "I've seen enough soldiers in shock to know." His attention returned to Strenkofski. "After all, she witnessed her mentor blowing his brains out, and survived enough shrapnel showers to perforate a herd of camels."

He looked out the window a second, remembering the sight of the camels the professor, Rahal, and Key had ridden into the desert as the Huey Venom copter he was riding came in for the kill on the refurbished Apache.

"Yes," Strenkofski nodded. "Understandable. Poor girl. But what about Corporal—" She thought better of strict military protocol in these circumstances. "What about Joe?"

"I don't know," Daniels answered, looking at his friend. "No one's sure. He must have hit his head, or something hit him while we weren't looking." He snorted in sour sardonicism. "Maybe even a piece of Davi's skull hit him in the same spot as Lieutenant Colonel Goodman's. All I know is that after he turned from the professor, he went facedown."

They stayed silent for a few seconds as Strenkofski looked from Daniels to Key. "Did the professor say anything to help us trace whatever killed Lieutenant Colonel Goodman? Did Joe?"

Daniels sat up slightly, his brow furrowing. "Hold on. Let me think. The professor said something when he pulled out the Victory." Daniels's eyes pinballed around his sockets. "Where he got that revolver, I'll never know. They were practically showered everywhere but the Middle East under the Lend-Lease Act. They were standard issue for Marine Corps aircrews for decades. Even my dad had one—"

"Sergeant," Strenkofski interrupted. "Did he or Joe say anything that could help us?"

Daniels snapped his mouth shut, then clasped his hands, and put his elbows on his knees in a show of concentration. "Dammit, dammit," he finally said. "I knew they said something, but what was it?" He stared at Strenkofski for a few seconds, then breathed deeply before slumping slightly and hooking a thumb back at the coffee cup. "This junk isn't helping any. You wouldn't happen to have any, you know, Jim, Jack, or Johnnie juice, would you?"

He thought she might frown and read him the riot act, but, to his surprise, she did the opposite. Looking down with a small smile, she subtly started rolling up her skirt hem. Using her hips to block the view of anyone but Daniels, she revealed a plastic flask gartered on her right thigh, and curved so it adhered perfectly to that shapely limb.

"No Bean, Daniels, or Walker," she said softly. "But would Mister Jameson do?" She may have even winked. "Pardon me taking your last name in vain."

"All trespasses forgiven when it comes to my brother from another mother, Jack Daniels," the sergeant said, almost enthused. "How did you get that stuff over the border, let alone in here?"

"A girl's got to have her secrets," she said, slipping him the flask. "But none between us, right? Come on, tell me everything."

Daniels suddenly became circumspect. He looked in every direction, then leaned down conspiratorially. "Look, we can't risk us all getting kicked out of here. They gave me a room in case I wanted to rest. Let's go there, let me use this"—he shook the flask as if he were having tremors—"and when my tongue is nice and loose…"

Strenkofski stood with an inviting smile while rolling down her skirt. "Lead the way, soldier."

Within instants the second lieutenant and sergeant were gone. For more than a minute afterwards, the only thing that happened in the room was the biofeedback graph burping and the patients breathing.

Then Josiah Key opened his eyes. "Okay," he whispered to Eshe Rahal. "Let's go."

Chapter 18

Key and Rahal were skating down the darkened radiology hall in their stocking feet like hospital-scrubs-wearing ninja, doing everything they could not to make a sound other than their hushed voices.

"It's the only thing that makes sense," Key whispered. "They had to know where I was. How else could they have found Professor Davi?"

"But the Saudi copter attacked first," Rahal said.

"The Saudis must've known the desert better," he said, thinking it through. "They figured out the hideout and went after it first. Up until then they must've followed the marines, who were tracking me."

"I still can't believe—"

"Has to be," Key said, his mind racing through possibilities to pinpoint probabilities. "They found Morty too, in the middle of the gulf, for God's sake. Can't be a coincidence. Can't be."

"So why are your superiors tracking you? Don't they trust you?"

Key snorted. "Trust is for the battlefield, not field offices. Make no mistake. It won't be Logan or even Strenkofski spearheading the actual surveillance. They're probably too busy with whoever's pulling their strings. So they passed on the shadowing to locals. The guys who found Morty and me had to be on strict need-to-know duty. No way Logan was going into detail with anyone on something this big."

"So they bugged you, if you'll excuse the term," Rahal said.

"That's my guess," he replied. "Had to be during my recovery at Camp Lemonnier in Djibouti."

"Well, I guess we're about to find out for sure," Rahal replied as they reached the CAT-scan room.

She walked in like this was old home week, but it was all new to Key. He looked at the platform hovering in the middle of a white donut. "Sure a simple X-ray wouldn't do the trick? Or an MRI?"

Rahal snorted as she quickly, and professionally, started the machine. "We don't want to spend all night here, now do we? We can search with X-rays and magnetic resonance imaging, but that's like using a flashlight to find a lost kitten in a forest. Better to just flood you with light to find the potential intruder."

She pointed at the platform, and Key hustled over. "How long will it take to check everything?" he asked while lying down.

"If they're not already listening to every word we're saying," Rahal surmised, "it would have to be a basic tracker put in the least sensitive area. Your back has only a tiny section of the somatosensory cortex devoted to its sensations. And the other parts of the body that are least sensitive are the ventral forearm and the back of your neck. So I'll concentrate on those."

She started the process, and even though she was taking a more direct, pinpointed approach, it was still taking longer than Key would have liked. She could sense his growing disquiet, so thought it would be a good time to both heighten it as well as distract him.

"So," she said quietly while checking the images from his spine, "they must have planted a tracker on Sergeant Daniels as well. When and how do you think they did that?"

Key shrugged. "With the way he saws wood—I mean, sleeps—they probably could've installed a telecommunications tower inside him without him knowing."

"Nothing in your neck or back you weren't born with," she reported. "I'm betting it's in your arm."

"Hope so."

"Stay still."

Key did as he was told as the metal donut hummed from his shoulders to his wrists. As he waited, he heard her voice again. "So why do you think Second Lieutenant Strenkofski came all the way here?"

Key breathed evenly, but his mind was moving quickly through an obstacle course. "Your guess is as good as mine," he finally told her. "And I mean that literally. I'm betting you've got an IQ off the charts. So why do you think a distrustful captain would send his beautiful blonde aide all the way over here to ply Morty with her thigh booze and baby blues?"

Rahal's eyes were intent on the results of the CAT scan, but her mind focused on one conclusion. "Because the captain thinks she can get something from him that they couldn't get from you."

One corner of Key's lower lip turned down as he considered the possibilities. "I guess he, and we, are about to find out."

* * * *

The room the college had loaned Daniels was essentially a windowless broom closet that had been amended into a rest area for exhausted medics. It was shaped like a shoebox, with just enough room for a narrow bunkbed and a coffee table. A lone yellow light was in the middle of the ceiling, yet Strenkofski still looked like a Valkyrie who had escaped from a photo shoot.

Daniels admired her in many ways as she seemingly claimed the room simply by moving into it. As he watched, slowly closing the door behind them, she, unbidden, took off the lab coat, loosened her tie, unbuttoned the top of her shirt, and sat gracefully on the edge of the lower bunk's thin mattress.

"Let me have a shot of that, would you Sergeant?" she said quietly, putting her hand out toward the curved plastic flask he still held.

"Is that an order, sir?" he replied with a growing smile.

"Consider it anything you'd like," she said. "Just give it to me."

"Yes, sir," he said as quietly as she had, handing her the flask as he sat beside her on the bed.

She took an impressive pull, then took her time looking around the room, as she carefully moved her left leg out while drawing her right leg up. Daniels stared, hypnotized, as the move somehow allowed her skirt to drape across her knee. Her shins, not surprisingly, were most impressive.

Although he was sorely tempted to comment, like a well-trained marine, or a well-raised child, Daniels did not speak to superiors until spoken to.

"You know, Sergeant," she said calmly, "I meet a lot of soldiers." Then she purposefully turned her head until her gaze locked onto his like grappling hooks. "But I don't meet a lot of men."

"It's our androgynous society," he said cynically. "Beats the testosterone out of us."

"Out of some," she gently corrected.

He resisted, mightily, the urge to look down when he felt her hand had magically moved to his nearest thigh.

No, you don't meet a lot of men, he thought, *because you eat them.* That's what he thought, but what he said was, "No?"

She took the opportunity to shake her head slightly, smile slightly, and lower her head slightly. "No," she replied. Then he found out why she had lowered her head. She lowered her head so she could raise it again, slightly, and look up at him with eyes that now spat glue. He had met many a woman who used that tact, but none who used it as well as Barbara Strenkofski.

If she had suddenly exploded like Goodman and Ayman, Daniels would not have been surprised. Instead, he felt her right hand—which was, like the other, somehow both warm and cool at the same time—laying flat on his upper right chest. It snaked up slowly until it was behind his neck, while the other five-fingered forward exploratory unit was moving up his thigh. Her pale pink lips parted, but no words emerged. They weren't necessary.

But Daniels was taking no chances. "Permission to come aboard, sir," he asked as her face neared.

"Permission granted," she whispered just before she planted her mouth on his.

God, she was good, Daniels thought as he tasted her delicious lips and her tart tongue darted behind the lines. She was also taking no chances either, her southern hand finding the space between his legs like a homing device.

As he expected, her hunger intensified, but he was undecided what percentage was faked and what percentage was real. Quickly he decided there were more important things than to judge percentages. As she moved in to occupy the territory, he was surprised, and a little delighted, that the seven-part creed of a United States marine, which he was taught at basic training, invaded his mind.

One, this is my rifle. There are many like it, but this one is mine.

She had his rifle between her warm and cool fingers—fingers which were rapidly becoming warmer.

Two, my rifle is my best friend. It is my life. I must master it as I must master my life.

That was no problem, considering the way her mouth was working his, giving his skull no opportunity to retreat, even if he had wanted to.

Three, my rifle, without me, is useless. Without my rifle, I am useless. I must fire my rifle true. I must shoot straighter than my enemy who is trying to kill me. I must shoot him before he shoots me. I will.

It was time to join the dance. Daniels's arms moved to strongly embrace her as he opened his legs and started sitting back.

Four, my rifle and myself know that what counts in this war is not the rounds we fire, the noise of our burst, nor the smoke we make. We know that it is the hits that count. We will hit.

She went with him down toward the mattress, but only so far. She widened her own legs so her skirt rose to her thighs. She straddled him, his unsurprisingly erect member being a Washington's Monument in front of her pristine, dewy, beautifully shaved and waxed Lincoln's Memorial.

If little else, there was one thing Strenkofski and Lailani had in common: they weren't wearing panties.

Five, my rifle is human, even as I, because it is my life. Thus, I will learn it as a brother. I will learn its weaknesses, its strength, its parts, its accessories, its sights, and its barrel. I will ever guard it against the ravages of weather and damage as I will ever guard my legs, my arms, my eyes, and my heart against damage. I will keep my rifle clean and ready. We will become part of each other. We will.

As the blonde gripped his shaft like a detonator switch, and shifted her hips to properly aim it unerringly at her target, Daniels's used both hands to do his condom trick on her shirt buttons.

As much as he would have loved simply tearing it open, letting the buttons ricochet around the room, it simply wouldn't do to have a second lieutenant wandering around the Middle East with an unclose-able shirt. And any disappointment he had about her not servicing him first, with what she had already proved was an amazing mouth, was tempered by his knowledge that she obviously wanted her lips free for other purposes.

Her breasts were extraordinary, dew-dropped water balloons housed in the barest of barely there bras, its spandex lace only just enclosing her pink, circular aureoles and tiny pink button nipples. Her body was equally impressive, his eyes quickly making a now nearly unconscious judgment of thirty-six D, twenty-five, thirty-six. With an easy, casual dropping of his index fingers, her chest bounced free, causing even him to find he was holding his breath.

Then she impaled herself on him.

Six, before God, I swear this creed. My rifle and myself are the defenders of my country. We are the masters of our enemy. We are the saviors of my life.

She grabbed his hands and planted them on her breasts. His hands were not unwilling participants. She started grinding her hips on his with the urgency of an expert bronco buster mixed with a drowning woman. The fact they were locked between bunks in the middle of an Oman college clinic, forcing any noise they made to be discreet, only made it all the more exciting. The sounds that came from her working mouth, like breaths escaping from popping bubbles, only fueled his cannon all the more.

"Sergeant Daniels"—she gasped, grinding—"report."

"Ma'am?" He grunted, squeezing and thrusting rhythmically.

"That's," she mewled, "an—"

He watched her carefully. Her eyes were smoky and unfocused. He saw that she was trying to form the final word, but somehow the road from her brain to her mouth had flooded. Her jaw sank and rose, then sank again. Her head began to droop, her amazing body sagging even further onto him.

"—order," she managed to say before falling into a sedated sleep.

Morty Daniels looked from the beautiful, half-naked, comatose blonde collapsed on his haunches to the plastic flask laying on the floor—the flask he had been holding the entire trip from the patient ward, the flask he had put the remainder of the chloral hydrate he had left over from Club Blue in as she had surveyed the room—and tried to grin. He failed.

"You better pray that saving the fucking world is worth it, Joe," he muttered as he started the careful process of leaving the second lieutenant fully clothed under the covers for a nice, safe, long nap. He had learned his Lailani lesson. Wouldn't do to have the blonde leap on his back as he was trying to escape this place. He had no doubt Strenkofski, unlike Lailani, would leave him headless, above the neck and above the balls.

He took a moment at the door to look on her angelically slumbering form under the thin cover, unavoidably recalling the final line of the Marine creed.

Seven, so be it, until victory is America's and there is no enemy, but peace.

"Amen, brother," Daniels grumbled, then went to find his friend where they had planned to meet.

* * * *

The tracking device was in Key's left arm. Rahal was unsurprised.

"Even if you felt an ache there," she muttered, "you might chalk it up to all the intravenous needles they were using to test blood and nourish you."

"Clever," he admitted.

While they spoke, she used a scalpel and forceps to find and remove the tiny thing. She glued, cotton padded, and taped him back together, resisting the urge to offer him a lollipop. Even that habit had been imported from West Virginia.

They went quickly back to the clinic room, where he put the tracker under his pillow, hoping whoever was manning the surveillance had relaxed since all concerned thought Key was in a coma. It wouldn't do to have been caught leaving the bed, running to radiology, then returning to bed.

As if on cue, Daniels came in quickly and quietly, as they had originally planned. But any happy reunion was quickly and quietly short lived. Rahal immediately started checking Daniels' left arm, praying that whoever installed the things was consistent. As she did, Key surveyed his cohort with a raised eyebrow.

"Even in my coma," he commented, "I had a hard time not rolling my eyes when you started reciting shock symptoms. Why not mention the low urine volume?"

"I had to say something," Daniels cracked back. "I didn't want to start asking how a patrol just happened to be in the Gulf of Oman at the same time Leilani and I were." He smiled at Key and then Rahal. "Ya see, I'm not as dumb as I look, or act."

"Actually, you are," Key answered, but with approval and even regard. "You're just a much better liar than anyone who didn't know you would guess."

Suddenly Rahal stilled, and when Daniels looked at her, he found she was looking at him as well.

"You didn't," she breathed.

"Didn't what?" he asked, the picture of innocence.

"You didn't," Rahal repeated, her thumb feeling an unnatural fleck in his arm, "Leilani her?"

Daniels knew what she was referring to. "The Jameson was right there," he said in his defense. "And I had a little Mickey Finn left over from Club Blue, so—ouch!"

Rahal had taken that moment to slice his skin. "Shush," she warned. "My students can cover for us only so much."

"It's a frigging clinic," Daniels said as Rahal slid the forceps into the cut. "I'm sure everybody on this floor has heard 'ouch' before," he finished with gritted teeth.

They waited as Rahal started extracting the bug they somehow planted on Daniels, until another thought occurred to Key. "Morty," he said, "you didn't give Second Louie Strenkofski the *full* Leilani, did you?"

Daniels gave Key a look that combined utter shock with leering certainty. "A gentleman never tells," he said. "But rest assured that if I did, it was way before Mickey showed up. *Ouch!*"

He looked hurt at Rahal, who had jabbed him again. It was her turn to feign complete innocence. She glued, padded, and taped his cut, then held up the second speck-like transmitter in the forceps. "What should we do with these?"

"Well," Key said, "I was tempted to send Alshshaytan back into the desert with them, but once Babs wakes"—he gave Daniels a cutting glance—"she, and the jig, will be up. Might as well leave them here. Your students, however, should make themselves scarce."

"Already taken care of," Rahal assured them. "I've been planning since our talk in the tent."

Back there, and then, Key had made his concerns clear. His conclusion that he and Daniels were being tracked without their knowledge or permission was not a guess as far as he was concerned. And that, alone, was enough for him to start making extreme alternate plans.

Now, all these hours later, Rahal placed Daniels's bug in what had been her recovery bed, while the sergeant started changing into the scrubs she had secured for him.

"I still don't understand why," she said while tossing them lab coats. "What do they hope to gain?"

Key shrugged on the lab coat. "Don't know yet. It could be they're being careful, or we're some sort of pawns in a bigger game they want to control, or something even more ominous. Any way it's shaking down, I trust myself a lot more than I trust Logan."

Key took Rahal's arm, and the three "Oman Medical College teachers" started for the door. But just as they got there, the tallest, widest one hesitated.

"Sure you want to do this, Joe? Once you go off the reservation, it's hard to get back on."

Key took a second to punch Daniels, directly on the slice Rahal had made. "I know, Morty," he assured him. "You know I know."

Daniels still held back, rubbing his arm. "Come on, Joe, I understand you don't like being screwed with, but maybe this time there's a really good reason. This is big, end of the world big. Logan could be right."

That stopped Key dead in his tracks. But when he turned back to his friend, he had an honest, understanding smile on his face.

"Of course Logan's right, Morty," he said. "If anybody's going to control the weaponized arachnosaurs, it had better be us. But, good and bad news, buddy. Nobody's going to be able to control them. You know it, I know it, even they probably know it. Only difference is that I'm willing to admit it."

He felt Rahal tugging at his sleeve. He held up a finger in the "just a minute" gesture without taking his eyes off Daniels. His expression, body language, and even aura made clear the following words were important, if for nothing else than to keep Daniels from betraying them the way he had betrayed Strenkofski.

"And you know how I know, Morty? Because Professor Davi blew his brains out right in front of us. He preferred to die rather than live in a world where there were idiots who thought they could control weaponized arachnosaurs. Not where there were arachnosaurs…just idiot people who thought they could control them!"

Daniels stared for a minute, and then his smile mirrored Key's. "What, are you kidding? Me? Avoid a chance to fool superiors, maybe earn a charge of treason in the first degree, and have the entire Corps on our ass for the rest of our natural lives? Wouldn't miss it for the world." He joined them at the door to make sure the coast was still clear. "You know Logan's not going to love you anymore after this," he told his friend.

"Oh, sure he will," Key said flippantly. "He has plenty of love left. If he didn't, we'd already be dead."

Chapter 19

"Stay seated," Manuel 'Speedy' Gonzales told them from the front seat of the bronze-colored, 2016 Renault Koleos sport utility vehicle.

Of all of the possible means of transportation Key could imagine sneaking out of Muscat in, this was not one of them. It smelled and looked brand-new, untested, and it had frankly decadent European styling inside and out, setting it apart from the more utilitarian Japanese and Korean SUVs around them.

They were at the Arrival Visa building on the Omani side of the border, a squat, pale, glorified Quonset hut sporting a big blue *Passport Control* sign. Key sat behind Gonzales with Rahal beside him, while Daniels sat behind them in the third row of seats, with, of all people, Lailani beside him.

The men wore the traditional Emirati outfits of the white *kandora* robe, the white *ghutrah* headdress, and the black *agal* rope that affixed the covering to their skulls. The women wore long, loose, black *abaya* dresses, *shayla* scarves, which covered their heads and chests, and, to take no chances, *niqabs*, the face-covering veils.

Gonzales wore the same attire as Key and Daniels, but the driver he nodded to, who turned out to be, not surprisingly, his go-to right-hand-partner-in-crime Faisal, was resplendent in a silk representation of a chauffeur's uniform, complete with cap and driving gloves. Faisal nodded back, took a fistful of passports, and snappily exited the air-conditioned conveyance.

"Standing in line is for peons," Gonzales told them with a somewhat tense grin. "Not for VIPs."

"Like us?" Rahal said from beneath her veil. Her tone was hard to read.

"Like us," Gonzales assured her, and them.

Lailani said something in what sounded like a mix of Arabic and Filipino. But her tone was not hard to read. A healthy heaping of sardonicism, with a touch of bitterness.

Key looked from Gonzales to Rahal for translation. The latter took up the task after a quick conferring look with their host. "It's a bit rhetorical," she explained, "but basically she said, 'here, money talks, tourists walk.'"

Gonzales nodded with approval at her interpretation. "Spoken like a woman in the know," he said.

Once again Key marveled at both Daniels's friend network, and what Gonzales could, and was willing to, do. The corporal had been somewhat grasping at straws when he had reached out, but Gonzales had long ago given him a contact number. When Key dialed it from a cell phone bought from a street peddler—a cell phone that was immediately trashed after that single call—he was initially surprised to hear a fax signal.

Then he wasn't. There was a reason many Government agencies still preferred the fax to the phone. It was because the facsimile machine used the inherently secure Public Switched Telephone Network, which was much harder to hack than email. And even if the hacker could get direct access to the phone line being used, the intercepted file would be indecipherable noise.

Thankfully, Key was able to fashion a succinct message during the nearly frantic search for a fax machine in Muscat. That was when Daniels had suggested they find Lailani where he, and the marine patrol who found them in the Gulf of Oman, had left her. It was in another tacky bar she worked at, a bar so tacky, in fact, that the owner even had a dusty fax machine in the corner of his messy office. So, finally, that set the stage for Gonzales to be surprised when the long unused fax machine in his Thumrait Studio hummed, buzzed, and chattered to life.

"Thank you," Rahal now said to Gonzales many hours after that, "for the compliment, but also for—" She struggled to find a description of all he had done so far: avoiding censure and detection while coming to collect them, as well as supplying clothing and counterfeit documents. "—all this."

Gonzales shrugged. "Told Joe before. I fix things. No world, no things to fix. Besides, it's not like any of you have just been sitting on your *las nalgas* either."

Rahal nodded in realization and acceptance, then looked at the others, stopping to nod directly at Lailani with both apology and respect. She had been surprised when Key had accepted the sergeant's insistence that they collect her without a peep, but now knew that she was not only extremely useful, but Daniels's determination to help her marked great progress in his character.

"Years, maybe even months, if not weeks, ago," Key had told Rahal, "he would have dumped her without a second thought."

"If she hadn't dumped on my ass, then saved it," Daniels had interrupted, "maybe I still would've."

So now they all sat together in the back of a sweet-smelling, air-conditioned SUV as Faisal returned, got behind the steering wheel, and tossed the pile of passports to Gonzales. He said something in Arabic, which Gonzales translatd, "Leaving stamps secured."

* * * *

Unlike Rahal, Key had not been concerned about the forged passports' quality. While Rahal had heard about hard jail time for being caught with fakes at the border, Key had already experienced the first-class Hispanic mechanic service.

"One down, three to go," Rahal said.

"Three?" Daniels echoed. "I thought we're just crossing the border into the United Arab Emirates."

Gonzales nodded. "We are, but the way it works is that we now go to the Emirati border patrol. Then, because of the way the road was built, there's an Omani police checkpoint, followed, finally, by a UAE checkpoint."

"Oh, great." Daniels growled. "Three more chances to risk the joy of anal rape."

Gonzales snorted. "Oh no, Morty," he corrected. "You get nicked, you get three *years* of chances."

The decision to drive four hundred and fifty kilometers northwest was not taken lightly. Key had faxed Gonzales their longitude and latitude, as well as two requests in the form of a single sentence. "Where's Logan/Awar?"

By the time Gonzales had arrived at the landscaper shack at Al-Qurm Park where the quartet of fugitives were holding up, he had the same answer to both.

"Usa Awar has a lot of money," Gonzales informed Key as the Renault continued on its way, "and most of it not from terrorist group support."

"Of course not," Daniels complained. "He gets it like the rest of the towelheads, right? Oil."

"No." Key sighed. "Weapons."

"Right," Gonzales concurred. "And the biggest weapons show in the region is this week."

"And Logan's there, too," Key said. "That's troubling, but not surprising."

"In certain circles," Rahal reminded him, "rumors of some sort of arachnid weapon are rampant."

"And the industrial espionage and infighting that goes on for control of the latest weapon is legion," Gonzales informed them.

It struck Key, thanks to some church sermon long ago, that the use of the word 'legion' was appropriate. It was a New Testament term to describe a clutch of demons. He wondered if Islam had a counterpart to that. Jinn, maybe? Not that it mattered. If they didn't have one, odds were they soon would.

"They're not even seeing these things as monsters," Key said, shaking his head. "Just as possible equipment."

"What?" Daniels sneered. "You want us to just lean back and let Awar have them?"

Key looked at the sergeant evenly and spoke in a slight singsong. "No. I want us to see them as a danger to all humanity and destroy them before it's too late. Right?"

Daniels shut his mouth, folded his arms, and sulked. "Right."

"What are you going to do?" Rahal asked Key as he turned back toward the front.

"Don't know yet," he replied honestly. "But whatever we decide, it couldn't be carried out in Muscat."

The sergeant sniffed, already feeling irritable and hemmed in. He shifted uncomfortably in the comfortable seat to see Lailani looking wistfully out the window, her elbow on the frame, and her chin cupped in her hand.

"What's with you, *pogi*?" he asked, purposely using the subtle Filipino term for someone a cruel person tries to curry favors from in an obviously over-affectionate way. "You act like you're going to miss this dump."

"Shut up, *guwapo*," she retorted diffidently, using the term for handsome men, as well as even handsomer horses. "You couldn't tell flesh from plastic."

Daniels straightened, ready to snap back at her, but Gonzales's laugh distracted him. He looked past Key and Rahal to see Gonzales grinning at him.

"Smart cookie," he told the sergeant. "You should listen to her." He motioned out the windows to the shifting sands all around them. "About three decades ago, almost all of this was just cactuses and scorpions. But in one small village on the coast lived a bunch of divers who found pearls so big that people came from all over to join them. They named their town after a local locust, the *daba*, who ate everything in its reach. Then came the British. They ate everything the locusts had missed."

That elicited another snort from Lailani. When Daniels looked confusedly from her to the others, Key threw him a bone. "The British occupied Manila in 1762."

"In 1762?" Daniels blurted. "That's a long time to hold a grudge."

Rahal cocked her head toward the sergeant. "Don't say anything like that to someone from India or China," she recommended.

"Be that as it may," Gonzales continued, "the grand and glorious British Empire throttled the pearl-rich village fairly thoroughly as late as the nineteen-seventies, but then the town named after a locust ganged up with a half dozen nearby states and created the United Arab Emirates—just in time for Texas tea to be discovered."

"Oil," Daniels said.

"Yes. So what were these pearl divers going to do with all that cash flow?"

"What else?" Key asked. "Invite the world to come on down, tax free."

"And come they did," Gonzales continued. "So many, in fact, that in just thirty or so years, their population outnumbered the pearl divers by ninety-five percent. The place went from seventeen hundred to twenty-one hundred in less time than it took you to grow up."

"Then they still got some ways to go," Daniels said. "I haven't grown up yet."

"I would suggest that it's about time," Gonzales told him.

"Eh? Why spoil a good thing?"

"Because you're off to see the wizard, Morty," Gonzales said. "The wonderful wizard of black gold. So, sit back, relax, and watch how the sand dunes magically turn into skyscrapers."

It was perfect timing. Daniels looked into the distance just as something started rising from the desert, something that looked very much like the Emerald City with sunlight and silver purity and towering spires that rose from atop magical walls. Sometimes the glass reflected sun and rusty sand or other giant structures. At other times the walls just seemed to vanish, as the sky on one side matched exactly the color and clarity of the sky on the other.

"Welcome, Morty," Gonzales said. "Welcome to the city that pride and a ridiculous prime rate bought. Welcome to Dubai."

Chapter 20

Key and Daniels were amused by how the other was trying to adjust to Dubai by acting as if they weren't trying to adjust to Dubai. It had the world's tallest man-made structure, the Burj Khalifa—an icicle of a thing—which had the world's highest restaurant. The city also had the tallest hotel, the highest outdoor observation deck, the loftiest nightclub, and even the uppermost mosque. Given all that height, it was little wonder the marines were having a hard time not being light-headed.

The second stop Gonzales had made was to a secret tailor. The first stop had been to a secret shelter. All the secret shopping could be found within a maze of alleys Gonzales referred to as Souk Land which was, apparently, between the city sections known as Deira and Bar Dubai. From what Key could find out, Deira was once the commercial center of the city, which was now marginalized, much the way Hong Kong had been after the Chinese Government had taken over the lease from the British Government in 1997. Bar Dubai was one of the most historic sections of the city.

Souk Land, wedged between them like a hornet's nest, was a labyrinth of shops ranging from glittering steel and glass warts to stuffed tents. At first, it looked as if Faisal was driving directly into a mound of tent flaps, but he braked just before touching cloth, and Lailani was out of the Renault, grabbing Rahal's wrist. As Daniels reached to complain, Gonzales slapped his hand.

"Women can't go unchaperoned in Dubai," he said casually. "Women can't do a lot of things in Dubai. The sooner they're out of sight, the better for everyone."

"Tsk-tsk," Daniels said. "Compare that to what American women have to put up with—men who don't agree with them."

Daniels looked from Gonzales's heavy-lidded, mirthlessly smiling face, to where Lailani and Rahal had just been, but weren't anymore. He blinked, and ran through a gamut that included confusion, disbelief, then disappointment. Key stifled a laugh. To the leader's eyes—and he had been watching the whole thing, unlike Daniels—it appeared as if the two women had slipped between two tent walls, then simply winked out of existence.

"Damn de damn damn damn," was all Daniels could think to say before he went looking from one tent to the other. The first sold chocolates. The other sold preserved flowers. He looked beyond each. All the rest of the shops there sold nothing like those products. To the east was one spice shop after another. To the west was fish stall after fish stall. "No magic lamps for sale?"

Gonzales moved between him and Daniels, taking them both by the arms. "Come on, you'll find out the secret to the magic trick later," he said.

"Whatever time you think we have left, it's probably less."

Key was impressed how quickly and unerringly Gonzales navigated the web of shops, from open air bazaars and lattice covered gardens to tent hives. Finally, they were in a nest of textiles, crammed inside a warehouse made of intricate wooden lattice. Piles of fabric tumbled against lines of dresses, shoes, and accessories. Shopkeepers and tailors yelled at anyone, but the marines stayed with their host, who ignored them all.

Finally, he came to two tents, similar to where Lailani had taken Rahal. Gonzales slipped between them first, pulling Daniels after him, while Key took up the rear. Had to be that way, Key realized, lest the sergeant start balking like a horse brought to water.

To his impressed amusement, the flaps seemed to wrap them without disturbing their adjoining tents' floor or roof supports. There was only a second or two of disorientation, then the souks revealed their secret. Wedged between them, along the back of parallel, right-angled, and kitty-cornered shops, were spaces occupied by others. Others who were not available to the public or the pretentious. Others who did not wish to serve the spoiled or stupid. Others who only wanted to serve only the ones they chose.

Key felt lucky to be with one, despite Daniels's sour expression. The sergeant didn't like to be out of control. Key patted him on the shoulder and nodded reassuringly as he watched Gonzales talk to an old Arabic man sitting with a sewing machine, surrounded by piles of cloth. The man looked up at the sergeant and corporal with an expression as sour as Daniels's. Key stepped forward, expecting to be measured, but was amused again when, instead, the man merely nodded, and Gonzales came back between them with his hands on their arms once more.

"Okay," he said, "let's go."

They returned the way they had come, Key acknowledging that he would have been lost without Gonzales guiding them, despite some slight pride that he had a good sense of direction. Once they got back to the lone chocolate and preserved flower stall, they repeated the squeezing between trick. This time they emerged into an entrance for a large, circular, tent similar to a small circus enclosure.

Almost every spot of carpeted ground was covered in pillows, mats, straw, and mattresses on which women sat or lay. Key could tell that most of them were South Asian or African. He followed Daniels, who had already spotted Lailani and Rahal all the way across the enclosure, talking to a woman seated on the other side of a very small cafeteria table.

Once they arrived, Rahal turned to Key. Her eyes were haunted. She opened her mouth to speak, but shook her head and closed it instead. Then, to his surprise, she buried her head on his chest and embraced him.

Key looked over her to the faces or Lailani and the Arabic woman with an expression of "what's going on?"

"This is my mama-san here," Lailani told them as Gonzales leaned on the edge of the table, his face blank.

The woman nodded at them, not unkindly. "Call me Hadiyah."

Before Hadiyah could continue, Lailani looked directly at Daniels. "I come here a couple of times a year to work in the big hotels."

Daniels looked as if he wanted to crack, "*In housekeeping*?" but thought better of it.

"She came first as an escort," Hadiyah said when Lailani chose not to go on. "Every hotel bar is full of escorts. It's a hidden culture here."

"My main clients were businessmen from all over the world," Lailani finally added. "The locals don't want Filipinos for anything but maids."

"It was all Filipinos until the recession." Hadiyah scoffed. "Then they were deemed too expensive. Now it's also Ethiopians. Either way, they are paid three-quarters less than Europeans, if they're paid at all."

Gonzales looked at Key. "Like the construction workers, their passports are taken once they arrive."

"Wait a minute," Daniels interrupted. He stared back at Lailani. "You came first as an escort? What do you come as now?"

As her eyes narrowed, Lailani's smile widened, a smile that seemed to infect Hadiyah as well.

"She comes here now as a dominatrix," her Dubai mama-san said. "That's where the real money is."

Gonzales stood up. Key stepped back. They both stared at Daniels in anticipation. But if they were expecting an explosion, they were disappointed. Lailani's and Hadiyah's smiles infected him as well, only his grew even wider and sprouted all his teeth.

"Baby!" he cried, his hand going up. "Now that's the way you do it. High five!"

Lailani slapped his palm with hers, her smile nearly as joyous.

Finally, Rahal looked up, but she did not release her embrace. Key could see her deep brown eyes were glistening wet. "These are all escaped maids," she whispered to him. "They have no place to go. They don't speak Arabic, they don't know the addresses where they worked, and they are at the mercy of their employers—who have no mercy."

Key didn't doubt it. The kind of plastic playground Dubai was would naturally attract people with power issues.

Hadiyah seemed to read his mind. "The government pays for your education up to doctorate level," she said. "There's free health care and no taxes. You even get a free house if you marry."

Lailani's smile stretched wider, but turned mirthless. "In their own countries, they're incompetent, but here everyone tells them they're great. Soon they think they're better than everyone slaving to serve them." Her eyes glittered. "I love whipping them."

Daniels's smile matched hers, and he opened his arms. She jumped into them like a beloved child, or pet.

"And she does it very well," Hadiyah advised him.

"I don't doubt it," the sergeant replied.

Then the mama-san leaned over to speak to Key and Rahal. "Much of the money she earns whipping them goes into helping them." She nodded at the women huddled on the floor.

"If it's any consolation," Gonzales said sardonically, "the construction workers have it worse."

They all turned toward him, seeing that Faisal had returned, carrying some blue coveralls and white hard hats. He laid them across the table as the mama-san motioned them to take up positions around it. Rahal seemed reluctant to let go of Key, but she managed to. She stood next to him, with the sergeant and the dominatrix on the other side. Gonzales stood with Hadiyah on one end, across from Faisal.

"What are these?" Key asked, motioning at the overalls.

"The uniform of the migrant workers," Gonzales told him. "They are ubiquitous throughout the city."

"Mostly from Bangladesh, India, Pakistan and the Philippines," Hadiyah informed them sarcastically. "Many are recruited under what you could call laughingly false pretenses. They pay their recruiter a large fee for the privilege of getting a Dubai job, then find their promises, shall we say, exaggerated?"

Gonzales shrugged. "In the worst cases, passports taken, living conditions ridiculously squalid, working conditions in terrible heat less than ideal."

It was Lailani's turn to shrug. "Things have improved a bit since the economic crash."

"But not so much that when a dark-skinned man puts on this thing, he becomes an invisible man to nearly everyone."

Key nodded, his smile widening. "Just like, I'd imagine, when a white man puts on a thousand-dollar suit, he also, in his own way, becomes invisible too, right?"

Gonzales nodded. "*Si, señor*," he said. "This is a town where women must cover all but the extremities of their arms and legs, extramarital sex is illegal, even if you're engaged—"

Lailani snorted at that.

"Being gay is outlawed," Gonzales continued, "and even PDAs are not allowed."

Rahal looked with confusion at Key.

"Public displays of affection," he explained to her. "Kissing, snuggling—"

"Holding hands," Gonzales added. He pointed at Faisal and the overalls. "But if we put these on, and you put on the suits I just ordered for you, we could move freely throughout the city without anyone raising an eyebrow."

"Even around the Weapons Show exhibition hall," Daniel piped up, "and all its meeting rooms?"

Gonzales beamed at him like a prize student.

"Okay, alright," the sergeant complained. "I get it, I get it. So what do you geniuses have in mind?"

Chapter 21

"This is freakin' ridiculous," Daniels said.

Key thought his companion was referring to the sheer scope of what they were attempting to do, and he may have been, but the way the sergeant stared out the SUV's windows clued the corporal that his comment had at least a double meaning.

They had driven along Mina Road, parallel to the Persian Gulf, past mall after mosque after monument, from the Dubai Museum through the Dubai Zoo to even the Emirates hospital—all of the sights so absurdly pumped-up, over-inflated, and extravagantly accessorized that even the hardened sergeant seemed to be going into sugar shock.

"This place," Daniels stammered on, trying to find a way to comprehend it all. "This place is like Vegas, Disneyland, and a thousand dollar-a-night whore all smooshed together, then drowned in gold."

"When did you ever have a thousand dollar-a-night escort?" Key asked.

"I've heard tell," Daniels shot back.

Gonzales snorted from the front seat. "*Si*," he answered Daniels. "About forty percent of the world's gold is traded in this place. You can even find gold bar vending machines. You see that thing out in the gulf? The one that looks like a giant boat sail?"

"Burj Al Arab hotel," Key said.

"Right," Gonzales continued. "It's got almost two thousand square meters of twenty-four carat gold leaf covering its innards."

"What are you, Speedy?" Daniels complained. "A tour guide—?"

"Yes, and a good one," Key interrupted. "One we really need and are happy to have. Right?"

Daniels grumbled, "To the point of swooning, chief," and turned his eyes back to the passing, pimped-out parade.

Gonzales chuckled. "It's all connected, Morty, I promise you. The tour and the mission. That sailboat-shaped thing showed up in 1999. It's a thousand feet from Jumeirah beach and is connected to the Dubai mainland by its own bridge."

Daniels sniffed a wordless, "*Who cares?*"

"I care," Key clued him. "Just shut up and listen."

"Mouth shut, bowels open, and never volunteer," he said, quoting an old British military saying.

Gonzales nodded back toward the structure he'd been describing. "To make it happen, migrant workers speared hundred and thirty-foot-long concrete pylons into the sand, then surrounded it with seven million tons of rocks and concrete. Two years later, the Palm Islands started to appear miles down the coast." Gonzales pointed past Faisal, who was, as usual, in the driver's seat—only this time wearing a thin robe rather than his chauffeur livery. "That's a migrant worker–made artificial archipelago laboriously tortured into the shape of a gigantic palm tree, complete with a trunk and sixteen frond leaves."

Daniels peered in the direction Gonzales was looking. Off in the distance he could make out some sort of hazy wharf amidst the glittering, seemingly gem-coated, freak shows surrounding it.

"I don't see it," he said. "Anyway, what's an archipelago?"

"A bunch of islands," Key told him.

"And you can only see the palm tree shape from above," Gonzales said. "Way above. The thing took more than five years, millions of rocks, and reportedly a lot of migrant lives."

"So?" Daniels said, not willing to give up his over-stimulated petulance quite yet.

"So," Gonzales replied patiently, "that excited a lot of developers, hot to pump money out of all-too-willing creditors, to start a game of Can You Top This?"

Key raised a finger warningly beside Daniels's frowning face, but that only encouraged the man. "Look, okay. I'm not a statesman and never will be. I'm really trying hard to understand what we're getting into here and why I should care about these things." He looked back at Gonzales. "So I repeat: why?"

Key lowered his finger and just shook his head. Gonzales closed his mouth, smiled, and pointed out the windshield. They all looked to see that Faisal was approaching Wollongong Beach, which looked like a Sim City videogame come to life. The relatively normal sand-scape was crawling with fully dressed people and watercraft of every imaginable variety.

"What are we looking at?" Key inquired.

"Glad you asked," Gonzales replied. "Two years after The Palm came the plan for migrant workers to create The World, *three hundred* islands plopped two and a half miles out that looks, from *way* above, like"—Gonzales was about to have them guess, but decided against it since even he didn't fully believe it himself—"a map of the entire planet."

The interior of the vehicle was silent for a second, until Daniels said the inevitable. "You have got to be shitting me."

"I wish I were," Gonzales answered. "But wait, it gets better. "A year ago, this place was a relative ghost town because 'The World' project had hit a snag."

"That was back in 2008, right?" Key asked.

"Right. The big financial meltdown. Even Dubai wasn't immune. Only two of the planned islands were developed, while the rest of them seemed to be shifting, merging, or even sinking. But now, a decade later, things seem on the uptick, so some genius decided to have migrants make a jumbo jet-shaped island for the next Dubai Air Show."

Daniels perked up. "Now *that* I've heard of," he said, looking at Key. "When was the last one of those?"

"Two years," Key said, leaning toward the front seat, as they got ever closer to the beach. "It's biennial. In 2013, it took in two hundred billion dollars."

"But in 2015," Gonzales reminded him, "that went down to *only* thirty-seven billion." By his expression, Daniels obviously wondered why. Gonzales shrugged. "Things change."

Their nattering was just buzzing in Key's ears as the rampant activity on the beach came increasingly into focus. "It's kind of genius, really," he said. "If you want to get the world to your first major weapons exhibition, why not use 298 artificial, empty, islands to do it?"

"They're only using the lowest, widest, South Pole island, the one nearest the beach," Gonzales reminded him, "but they're still building like crazy to make sure it's suitable for the show, even at this late date." He craned his neck to check out the airspace. "Hadiyah said that it looked like D day for a month with all the ships, planes, and helicopters dropping off and ferrying out stuff."

"It still looks like D-Day...plus one hour," Daniels said, pointing.

As Faisal slowed the vehicle, they all stared at the beach, where mobs of white, black, and blue-covered figures were milling around in organized chaos.

"Shit," Daniels said. "It doesn't look like D-Day. It looks like a gigantic ant, beetle, and maggot farm."

It really did. The blue-wearing workers ran to and from a fleet of smaller boats, as the white-wearing sheikhs chaperoned dark-suited visitors to far fancier vessels. The only thing missing was military uniforms, but Key knew the soldiers were smarter than to make themselves targets.

Even so, everyone was hemmed in by what looked like a fleet of cars that had escaped from a showroom. There were Aston Martins, Bentleys, BMWs, Bugattis, Ferraris, Lamborghinis, McLarens, and Mercedes strewn about the sand, all in a vaguely crescent shape dividing the street from the beach.

"What the eff," Daniels continued. "They having a car show too?"

Gonzales snorted again. "Nope. Those are police cars, Morty. Those are what pass for patrol cars in Dubai."

The sergeant gave a low, hollow, reedy whistle. "I'm not trying any vehicular escape around here anytime soon." He thought a moment then added, "Unless I really have to."

Key blocked all the chatter out to concentrate on the task before them. "At least they're still setting up," he said, regret growing in him as Faisal pulled into the parking lot of a glorified mini-mall that bore a Beach Centre sign. "At least the security won't be impossible yet, since the heavy hitters won't be showing up until later. Even so, it's not like we can just waltz in."

"You can't, maybe," Gonzales said as he and Faisal pulled off their robes to reveal blue worker outfits beneath. They picked up their white hard hats and got out of the car, the morning sun hitting them like a heat lamp.

"Last check," Key suggested, holding up an ancient, handheld, palm-sized walkie-talkie. He clicked its side button. The one in Gonzales's pocket hummed.

Both men wished they could have used more sophisticated communication devices, but, if they were spotted, it would blow the infiltrators' cover. Since they had already seen many a blue-garbed worker carrying the same thing, they thought best to do as the locals did. Especially since they all saw how all the non-blue-wearing pedestrians had acted as if the workers weren't even there.

As Gonzales and Faisal prepared to embark on the risky, but necessary, infiltration, Key felt the urge to say something stupid or stereotypical, but resisted it. Daniels had no such compunction.

"Good luck, suckers," he said. "Better hope everything goes right, because if it doesn't, there's shit-all we can do about it from here."

Gonzales laughed so hard he had to bend over and prop his hands on his thighs. Key laughed too, realizing that was just what was needed to cut the tension. Faisal looked quizzical until Gonzales translated. Then Faisal laughed as well, shaking his head.

The Caucasians watched the Hispanic and Arab walk quickly down to the edge of the largest group of blue-covered men. Neither said anything as they saw Faisal and Gonzales manage to join a group on a boat. The silence continued as that boat started toward what was now deemed SADE Island—and stayed that way until Key brought up small, but very powerful, binoculars.

Through it he saw the new Exhibition Center, which looked like a giant, gleaming, Plexiglas tortoise squatting on SADE island. He exhaled helplessly, and handed the field glasses to the sergeant.

"Shit," Daniels exclaimed. "It looks like Gamera!"

Daniels might well be right, but Key actually rolled his eyes at the mention of the Japanese movie monster, an enormous prehistoric turtle who spit fire from his shell and flew. He wondered if the man were developmentally stunted or just enthusiastic about everything. Key looked back at the Beach Centre's shops and restaurants. "Might as well get something to drink while we're waiting."

Daniels threw up his hands. "At last!" he said. "A beer!"

"This is Dubai," Key reminded him. "Alcohol strictly forbidden. I'll buy you a frosty shake, though. Your choice of flavors."

"What, like Creamy Camel and Frothy Palm Frond?"

"The Arabs were trading vanilla long before there was a United States," Key pointed out.

Daniels' face twisted in displeasure as the two men reluctantly retreated to the air-conditioned safety of the place, which, although spotlessly clean, well-appointed, and relatively upscale, seemed somewhat tacky compared to the glossed-up excess of the rest of the city. Daniels was openly startled by the array of choices: Johnny Rockets, Burger King, Baskin Robbins, or an Arab, Lebanese, and even Chinese eatery.

After a few agonizing moments for the sergeant, they were seated at the former, with Daniels poking a chocolate malt with a straw like he was trying to assassinate it.

"You know I was lying through my teeth before, right?" Daniels muttered as Key sunk his teeth into the best mall hamburger that oil money could buy.

"Which part?" Key inquired.

Around a mouthful of beef and bun he replied, "If anything goes wrong, I'll swim out there if I have to and kill everyone I can get my hands on."

Chapter 22

Outside, while the thing did indeed resemble a massive tortoise. Inside it looked like virtually any convention center Gonzales had ever been in. Even so, he expertly judged it to be at least three hundred thousand square feet, or, about three hundred times bigger than his Thumrait workshop. Given the relative rush and the logistics, he figured no one had time to create anything other than a cavernous, but basic, shell, no matter how much money, or how many migrant workers they had to throw at it.

It was the latter reality that held the mechanic and chauffeur-of-all-trades in good stead. The harried, exhausted, even seasick, blue-garbed workers really didn't have the time, strength, or interest in questioning the appearance of an obviously Arab and Hispanic interloper—no matter how hard they tried to obscure their facial skin with hard hats and scarves. They acted like workers, they dressed like workers, and they looked like workers. In other words, they had darker skin. So, if they were offering help, it would be accepted with only the slightest of raised eyebrows.

Gonzales thought that they might have to pickpocket a pass or two, but the rush to finish the exhibits had obviously gotten so pressing that the door guards were just frantically waving small mobs of workers through with hardly a second glance. By the look on the face of the one Gonzales and Faisal saw from the center of the throng they had sidled into, the previously conscientious safety personnel had, sometime in the recent past, had their asses handed to them by some folk who really knew how to do it.

Nothing like power-mad, glorified party planners to reduce power-mad, glorified drill instructors to quivering masses of yes-people, Gonzales thought as he searched the aisles and skies for any sign of American presence.

It wasn't easy. US companies had dialed back their official attendance at such trade shows in recent years, but the tenacity of Islamic radicals had called for smarter, stronger approaches. Both Gonzales and Faisal peered amongst rows and rows and rows of booths boasting air, ground, and naval armaments, as well as supposedly cutting-edge tech, from more than a thousand companies from every corner of the world.

Yes, Gonzales thought, echoing Key's sentiments, using The World to launch SADE did display a kind of genius. A kind of genius Gonzales would have to channel to accomplish anything useful here. He sought to find it in what he soon realized was about six miles worth of militarized enticements.

As he struggled to deal with the sheer volume of this different kind of input, he felt a tap at his arm. He turned to find Faisal nodding his head toward two exhibitions festooned with very specific iconography. One was red, with dragons and calligraphy. The other was red, with hammers, sickles, and Cyrillic script.

Gonzales placed his hand firmly on Faisal's shoulder. Seems his genius was not only fixing things, but choosing friends. As soon as Gonzales had laid eyes on the massive Chinese and Russian pavilions, the logic galvanized him. If Captain Logan was there, or was coming, to circumvent, or redirect, the sale of arachnosaur-based weaponry, his main competition would be coming from Eastern Europe and the Far East. America certainly had other competitors and enemies, but none with pockets as deep. So it was in, and around, those booths where the most useful intel might be.

Gonzales and Faisal shared a glance, then separated, the former toward the Russian exhibit and the latter to the Chinese. Language would be no greater an issue there than it had ever been, since the only ones they really needed to comprehend were the migrant workers and their angry managers, who spat demands in a bastard mix of Middle and Far Eastern doggerel.

Both men soon found a blue-swathed group slaving on some section of the Soviet and Asian displays who welcomed their assistance. As Gonzales helped his new team assemble a complicated video wall, Faisal aided the men he joined to erect a multi-jointed, flying dragon between the top of the exhibit and the ceiling. It wasn't a weapon, but this show was half-merchandise and half-showmanship.

Despite the pressing schedules and slave-driven commitment to finishing the work, soon everyone within sight was turning to watch the dragon begin its slow rise into the upper airspace of the exhibit hall. Gonzales, however, was immune. He didn't need any undue attention by slacking on the job. But that changed when he felt the walkie-talkie vibrate in his pocket. It was the prearranged signal between the two infiltrators.

He turned his attention in Faisal's direction, and was instantly rewarded by an intense stare from the young man. Gonzales struggled to interpret the look, but came away with only the instinct not to turn. Instead Gonzales saw that Faisal had positioned himself at the head end of the dragon. He was yanking on a wire that brought the slack-jawed monster's fire-breathing skull upward.

Then Faisal twisted his own eyes down and around until Gonzales saw that he was glaring at the dragon team's manager, a swarthy man in dirty khakis and a sweat-stained, short sleeve, sport shirt. He was shouting at the hauling team in an impressive mix of Arabic, Bengali, English, Hindi, and Urdu, urging them to be faster and stronger.

As Gonzales watched, Faisal moved his eyes from the manager to above him. Gonzales followed Faisal's gaze, to see that the man was under the dragon's head—the dragon's head Faisal was controlling.

Gonzales was already running when Faisal cried out, stumbled back, and let go of the rope. The rest of the dragon lifters fell back, but gripped their guidelines tighter. The dragon's ass shot up to nearly smack the ceiling, as the head plummeted directly toward the bellowing manager—who still had no idea he was about to be crushed by a dragon's jaw.

The cries of "look out" in more than six languages seemed to bounce around the floor like dropped tennis balls. The manager finally looked up just in time for the dragon's head to completely fill his vision. He started to screech in fear, but his cries were cut off as Gonzales leaped into him with a flying tackle.

The two men crashed to the floor just as the dragon's head hammered the carpet where the manager had been. Gonzales kept embracing the swarthy man as they finally rolled to a stop under the dragon's haunches. He looked with well-faked concern at the manager's shocked face. The manager looked back in amazement, clearly comprehending what had happened, then twisted his body to pinion whoever had dropped the dragon's head.

Faisal was nowhere to be seen.

"Are you all right?" Gonzales asked, in both Arabic and Hindi. It sounded to him as though the manager's words in those languages had been his strongest.

"Yes," he said, gasping. "Yes, I'm fine."

"No," Gonzales said with certainty and command. "No, you're not." He started to help the man to his feet by pulling the manager's right arm across his shoulders. "You've suffered a shock. Take a moment." He was already walking the manager to the nearest exit. "It will be best," Gonzales assured him. "It will inspire your team. They will not lose time."

The manager opened his mouth, but Gonzales cut him off by snapping at the remaining workers. "You know what to do! Do not fail! Make yourselves proud!"

He continued hustling the manager away. He waited for any resistance, but it did not come. Not even when he nodded at the security guard by the side exit door, who, kindly, opened it for the shaken manager and his noble rescuer.

Gonzales turned into the light so the manager would be first to see the outside, then followed him. But the last thing he noted inside the convention center was that a short, slim, blue-garbed worker had replaced him at the Russian exhibit video wall, a worker who looked and acted just like Faisal.

* * * *

"You will finish on time, I know you will," Gonzales said in the mix of Arabic, Hindi, and English he had rapidly become adept at. He handed the manager a small, warm, plastic bottle of Zamzam, a locally manufactured soft drink, as he hunched down beside him.

SADE Island was beautiful from this vantage point outside the turtle-shaped hall. Surrounded by aqua-jade waters, which were dotted with white-pimple-colored artificial islands, it was all lit by a blue sky and glowing sun.

"In fact," Gonzales said, "I think you will finish early." He held up his own can of Cherry Vimto, another soft drink, like Zamzam, whose company had delivered cases of the stuff since Coke and Pepsi were still kicking their asses in the local markets. "I will even bet you on it." He held up the can, and was pleased when the manager tapped it with his Zamzam bottle in a sort of halfhearted toast.

At first the manager, a half Arabic, half-Indian man named Khalifa Al-Alam, had been reluctant to stay. "I must get back," he kept insisting. But after just a few moments of Gonzales's friendly, seemingly honest, warm, certain approach, he began to relax into a low-level depression that seemed to be his general comfort zone.

Gonzales completely understood as soon as he learned the manager's name. As a *hajin*—half-caste, with a Arab father and Indian mother—he would never be allowed to rise any higher than he already was. Even so, Gonzales continued to use the soothing, calming vocal technique his father had taught him years ago. It was a form of hypnosis that Gonzales had originally rejected, but the more he tried it, the better it worked.

"I know I will," Al-Alam said quietly. "I must. There is no other choice."

"Of course you will," Gonzales assured him, then knowingly added, "No matter how many obstacles they put in front of you."

He was instantly rewarded when Al-Alam silently snorted, his slumped body jerking like a fetal pig. "Yes," he said. "Yes. From the very beginning. After just a few hours, I thought I was working on the French exhibit, not the Chinese."

"French exhibit?" Gonzales echoed. He tried to keep his voice unintrusive as well as encouraging.

Apparently he succeeded, because Al-Alam stared off toward the horizon, shaking his bottle like it was a dice cup. "Yes. Stupid frog. Suggestions, always suggestions. Never to me. Always to the Chink rep. 'Why don't you do it like this? Why don't you try it like that? It will be more attractive this way. You will get more sales that way.'"

Gonzales took up the offence for him. "Who is this *almutataffil*, this *ghusedanevaala*?" he asked with quiet outrage, using the Arabic, then Hindi, word for intruder.

"Some frog." Al-Alam sniffed. "Some frog weapons big shot. The chinks treated him like royalty, like their emperor."

"Ha," Gonzales said dismissively. "What did they call this *ibn il-hommar*?" He used the Arabic phrase for son of a donkey. "I will look out for him. Maybe a dragon's head could fall on him too!"

Al-Alam made a bitter, mocking sound. "Yes," he said, obviously relishing the thought, before carefully making a strange accented sound. "'Zon Baa Nard. Zon Baa Nard,' they called him. 'I am Zon Baa Nard. I know everything. I will make you change and change and change things until you drop.'"

"Insane," Gonzales commiserated. "Unfair—"

He would have said more, but just then the exit door slammed open and an Asian man in a silk suit appeared, his face tight and angry.

"*Mudir!*" he spat, mangling the Arabic word for "manager" with what Gonzales recognized as a thick Shanghai accent. "You do not have break! What—"

Gonzales interrupted by grabbing his own knee and rocking in pain. "Oh thank you, *mudir*," he moaned loudly. "I'm sure I'd be crippled if not for you. Please, go back to work. Thank you for helping me. I, too, shall return soon. Thank you, thank you…"

Al-Alam was already bowing and backing away, kowtowing continually to the Asian, who, stymied but still suspicious, moved back into the exhibit hall. But he continued to chastise Al-Alam even after he slammed the door after them.

Gonzales stopped moaning and rocking, then stabbed at the walkie-talkie in his pocket. Faisal responded with a grunt.

"Anything?" Gonzales inquired tightly.

"*La*," Faisal said. No.

"Then let's go," Gonzales advised tersely, "as fast and in any way we can." Then for Key's benefit he added, "If I know *mudirs*, we don't have much time."

Chapter 23

Gonzales was only partially right. They didn't have *any* time.

"This is what I think happened," he said quickly into the walkie-talkie as the motorized inflatable raft he was clinging to bounced like a rattle swung by an unhappy baby. "Migrant worker managers have notoriously weak spines. As soon as Al-Alam got inside, he told the Chinese what happened. Well, he revealed as much as he could without risking deportation. Which he probably will be anyway, if he doesn't wind up in a landfill. Over."

Key was driving as fast as he could east along Beach Road without drawing a fleet of police super cars on his tail. Daniels was beside him, seemingly doing push-ups off the SUV, his fingers deep in the dashboard, as if trying to shove the Renault faster.

"How close are they now?" Key asked. "Over."

Gonzales turned entirely around to look beyond Faisal, who was manning the outboard motor, to the swath of sea between them and SADE Island. Bobbing on the water, coming fast right at them, was a grey speck.

"About a hundred yards," he reported. "All we could get away with was a four-man inflatable with a eight horsepower motor. By the looks of it, they've got a fiberglass eight-man boat twice as powerful. Over."

"Shit." *And twice as heavy*, Key thought. "Can you see how many are coming after you? Over."

Gonzales wished he had Key's binoculars. He did the best he could with the lurching spray slapping his face. "At least four," he said. "Maybe more. But I'm pretty sure Al-Alam is leading them. Over."

"Who gives a fuck?" Daniels grunted. "There are only two I care about, right?"

Key agreed, but didn't comment directly. "How soon do you think they'll reach you? Over."

"Can't tell yet. Will let you know. Over."

If the walkie-talkie doesn't get water-logged first, Key thought.

"Aim for Jumeirah Beach," Daniels yelled over him, jabbing in that direction. "It's the closest."

Key peered at where Daniels was pointing, recognizing the area from his research during the drive from Muscat. "Go west of the Dubai Offshore Sailing Club," he said. "Your raft won't stick out there. Everybody will think it came loose from one of the cabin cruisers. Over."

"Gotcha," Gonzales answered. "Over and out."

The Hispanic Mechanic had been peeling off his workman's blues when Faisal had appeared out the same exit door Gonzales had taken. He followed his friend's lead by pulling off the blue overalls to reveal the *kandora* beneath. The two hastily had shoved the worker's uniforms under the sand and moved quickly west, around the back side of the tortoise-shaped structure.

By the time they were in eyeshot of the arrivals docks, they had pulled the *ghutrah* head scarves and *agal* headbands out of their pockets and obscured their faces with them as much as possible. Faisal slowed, his expression changing to as much innocence as he could muster, but Gonzales had gripped him by the arm and pulled him along.

"We're not workers anymore," he had reminded Faisal. "We're sheiks now, who don't give a shit about anyone but themselves, right?"

Faisal had nodded, and the two had kept their heads up, noses in the air, until they had spotted a small inflatable, motorized, raft floating far enough away from notice.

"How much time?" Daniels asked Key through clenched teeth.

"Maybe enough," Key replied, scouring the area as he took a hard left, heading toward Jumeria Street. "Maybe not."

"Shit, shit, shit!" Daniels yelled, pounding the dashboard. "They're as good as dead, aren't they?"

"Not yet," Key told him. "Think, Morty. Why send anyone after them at all?"

"*You* think!" the sergeant countered sharply. Then, compelled by a fast, hard glance, he reluctantly did as Key asked. "Why? Why? Because Al-asshole blabbed about some frog, and now they want Speedy dead."

"Maybe, but definitely not in a way that will alert the authorities. They don't want that fleet of super cars after them any more than we do."

Daniels looked out the windshield, his wolf's snarl turned to a wolf's grin. "So we got a chance."

"Always," Key said, nearly squealing the Renault's wheels onto 2C Street. The beach loomed large out their left windows. "They'll want it to look like an accident, not premeditated murder. They'll try to sink or scuttle them, not shoot or even stab them. If Speedy and Faisal can just get to shore—"

"There, there, there!" Daniels interrupted, stabbing at the windshield.

Key followed the sergeant's gaze and saw what he did: a sign at the western egress of the Sailing Club that read *Dubai Ride Jet Ski Rental.*

Daniels was out the passenger door and running almost before Key had even started to slow.

"Morty," he shouted after him, "you need insurance and a license before they'll—" But then he gave up, knowing it was useless from the second he opened his mouth.

Key was thankful that Dubai had plenty of parking as he braked and ran after the sergeant, already planning for what he'd have to do. And the more he planned, the worse it got.

"Morty," he said again, seeing that the sergeant was hurling his *kandora, ghutrah,* and *agal* off to keep running in just his skivvies. "Wait a second. Let me just—"

But then his immediate luck ran out since a class for Jet Ski renters was already well in progress. On the small "Dubai Ride" dock, six Jet Skis were bobbing, topped by a half-dozen tourists being instructed by a sun-glassed, bronze-skinned, copper-haired, beach bum surfer dude. To Daniels's delight, but not Key's, the Jet Skis' engines were on.

"Now, another important thing to remember—" the instructor was saying in Australian-accented English. But that was as far as he got, since Daniels ran by, knocked the youngest, fittest, renter from his seat, and took his place. Before the instructor could even react, Daniels had executed the Jet Ski equivalent of peeling out.

Then Key was there, grabbing the instructor by the arm and jumping into the water with him. As the instructor surfaced, he saw Key making sure the teenager Daniels replaced was safe. Key and the instructor helped the lad back onto the dock as the rest of his family surrounded him.

"Military police emergency," Key kept telling them as he backed away. "Military police emergency. We'll get your water ski back as soon as possible. Thank you for your cooperation."

Then he was back in the car, hearing his own *kandora* squish on the leather interior. He pulled out as quickly as he could, hoping it was fast enough to keep the instructor or any of the family from noting the SUV's license plate.

He drove back to 2C Street, scouring the area for the most logical pick-up point, while planning for any possible outcome. As he did so, he found a grin widening on his mouth. Because every time the odds looked ridiculous, they changed when he factored in the wild card. A wild card called Sergeant Morton 'Fuckaduck' Daniels.

* * * *

"Friggin' Jet Ski," Sergeant Morty Daniels swore repeatedly, trying to make the three-hundred-horsepower Sea-Doo go as fast as the Harley-Davidson V-Rod muscle motorcycle he rode at home. "Come on, come on, you asshole," he urged the machine, judging he was going around forty miles an hour.

At first he couldn't even spot the raft and boat. But he pinointed the center of SADE Island, and headed for it like a radar-controlled missile. In a few intense minutes, he saw some specks in the distance, and corrected his course toward them. Then, less than a minute later, he could make out the raft and boat.

He recognized the latter as a bay boat, designed for use in large shallow bays, like the Persian Gulf. He also saw four men aboard, two holding machetes and two holding hooked poles, the kind used to collect anchor or mooring ropes. Either could also make quick work of an inflatable raft, or human, skin. He leaned forward until his chin was nearly on the handle bars, and opened the throttle as far as it would go.

By the time he got within fifty feet of the two watercraft, the bay boat was bearing down on the raft. He vaguely heard Gonzales shouting, "You don't have to do this, Khalifa!"

"Yeah," Daniels said. "And I don't have to do *this* either."

He targeted the front side of the bay boat, then did his favorite trick. He caught the side of a crest, jerked to attention, and brought the Jet Ski up out of the water.

All he had to do was get above the bay boat's gunwale. He did.

The workmen in the bay boat screeched when the Jet Ski cut diagonally across their bow, sending two men flying, their machete and pole spinning into the gulf.

On shore, Key's walkie-talkie crackled. "Is this your idea? Over."

"Guess!" Key shot back, relief flooding him. "What's your heading, over."

"I see the sign for the Sunset Mall," Gonzales reported. "Over."

"Too far to your left. Go toward your right. West of Jumeira Beach. Look for a half-horseshoe dock. That's the Sailing Club. There's a sandbar to the right of it. Over."

"Gotcha. Thanks for the sea support. Over."

"His pleasure," Key said, keeping an eye out for any angry Australian Jet Ski instructors. "Make sure he brings that thing back. Over."

"Like I'm my Morty's keeper," Gonzales said, tension seeping from his voice. "I'll do my best. Over."

"You always do. Over and out."

By the time Gonzales returned his attention to the attempted water rundowns, Daniels was circling the bay boat threateningly, while Al-Alam stood aboard, desolately holding his hooked pole.

"Bring us near," Gonzales instructed Faisal, who looked skeptical, but did as he was told. Gonzales held up a restraining finger to Daniels, then let the raft float to just outside a hooked pole's reach—all while making sure he saw where the water-treading workers were. Wouldn't be prudent at this late date to have a migrant worker swim behind them with an ever-ready machete. He took a last second to make sure they were out of SADE Island range as well.

"After we leave," Gonzales instructed Al-Alam, "sink the raft. Bring along the deflated shell if you think that will help convince your masters." He motioned for Daniels to come alongside. He knew from experience that the Jet Ski model the sergeant was riding could seat three.

"Tell them we drowned," Gonzales told the bereft manager. He would never forget the look on Al-Alam's face. He recognized surprise, disbelief, suspicion, then, most tragic of all, a despairing hope.

By the time he joined Faisal behind Daniels, all four workers were back in the bay boat. "If they let continue to set up the exhibit," he called to the manager, "finish your shift, then stay with your men. Do not let them separate you from understand. Do you understand?" They might say they want to reward him. They might say they want to promote him. They might say anything to get him alone.

The next second would tell Gonzales the manager's fate. If he nodded, he had a chance. That meant he was thinking, and planning for the worst. If he spoke, he was as good as dead. That meant he had no idea of who he was dealing with, and how they saw him as less than chickpeas they massed into hummus.

"But," Al-Alam said. "But they will think I have followed their orders. There will be no reason to—"

Gonzales didn't hear the rest. Daniels had already gunned the motor, spun the Jet Ski, and was heading toward shore.

Gonzales's lips were thin and tight as he contemplated the manager's fate. Al-Alam was well-trained indeed. The same spinelessness that made him tattle on Gonzales in the first place would see to it that he thought he was going to be respected, even rewarded, for doing as his masters asked. He was wrong.

"I sure as shinola hope this thing had a full tank when I left," Daniels shouted. "Or else we're about to have a helluva swim."

Chapter 24

Even the grateful Australian surfer who taught the Jet Ski class might not have recognized them now. The Key and Daniels who returned the Sea-Doo, none the worse for wear—even filling its fuel tank—looked nothing like the two who'd walked through Burj Park. Gone were the Emirati cloaks and head gear, replaced with perfectly tailored, remarkably lightweight suits.

The suits were waiting for them when they returned to the secreted women's shelter within the souk, as were Rahal and Lailani. The latter tried to act indifferent, but gave Daniels a big hug as soon as he opened his arms. Inspired, Rahal embraced Key as well. Hadiyah smiled on them, and waved them over to the table, which was being covered with small bowls of food by a mix of Filipino and Ethiopian woman.

Gonzales and Faisal dug into the steaming Ethiopian *injera* flatbread, spicy meat stew, slightly wilted greens, rice—both basmati and pilaf—and sweet tea, while the marines, who had eaten before the escape from SADE Island, considered their next move.

"'Zon Baa Nard,'" Daniels said. "Frog, I mean French, weapons guy."

"Jean-Bernard," Key said. "Jean-Bernard Toussaint. Very slick, very friendly, very powerful arms wheeler-dealer." The sergeant looked at the corporal with raised eyebrows, again impressed by the man's depth of knowledge.

"All you have to do is read, Morty," Key said drily.

"I read," Daniels said with mock defensiveness, winking at the others. "Comic books, on the crapper."

Lailani rolled her eyes, while the others just continued in standard-operating-Morty-mode.

"Toussaint could be fronting Awar," Gonzales said around a mouthful of mutton. "He'd need a front. No matter how powerful he is in Yemen, Dubai authorities can't have him just waltzing around tourist traps."

"Is it safe to say the weaponized arachnosaur is the most wanted armament of the SADE show?" Key asked Rahal.

She nodded, her eyebrows making a concerned crown in the middle of her forehead. "So the Chinese would kowtow like crazy for his rep, don't you think?"

Gonzales translated for Faisal, who nodded. Then Gonzales translated for him. "He says Awar is not stupid, but does have balls the size of coconuts. No, he would not walk around anywhere, but yes, he might be in the city, somewhere safe, preparing a demonstration for bidders."

Key leaned back, one hand on his chin, the other on the back of his head. "So how do we find out where that is?"

"Follow Toussaint?" Daniels asked while scooping some stew with a corner of the *injera* he had torn off.

"Sure," Key replied. "How do we find him?"

That stymied them. For a few moments, the only sound was of mastication and tea schlurping, until Hadiyah spoke up.

"I think I might know a few people who could help."

They all looked at her, but she was looking beyond them. They all turned their heads to see a roomful of "invisible women."

"You're not sending them back to the families who abused them?" Lailani reacted incredulously.

"Of course not, dear," Hadiyah answered. "But they know where all the maids gather to gossip and grouse, don't they?"

* * * *

As small groups of fugitive maids went out to collect information—always chaperoned by Hadiyah or Lailani—all covered in *abaya* body sheaths, *shayla* head covering, and *niqab* veils. Gonzales went to work creating new identification cards for the marines, using the network of artisans within the souk land walls. It all came together faster than even Key expected. By the time he and the sergeant held their new Department of Defense IDs, the renegade servants returned with pay dirt.

"Jean-Bernard Toussaint *is* in town," Hadiyah reported, "with his wife and son. While she shops, a Scandinavian nanny takes care of the five-year-old."

"That's not very helpful," Daniels complained.

"Let me finish, *wid kabir*." She smiled. "But also, while she shops, he will occasionally take his son to many of Dubai's child-friendly attractions. They've already been to the water and amusement parks. But one of the maids told us that they're planning to go to the Aquarium today."

"Great job," Key said.

"*Wid kabir*, Daniels said. "You're always calling me *wid kabir* now. What's *wid kabir*?"

Lailani put one arm around his shoulders, and her other hand on his upper chest. "'Big Boy,'" she translated. "Because you're a big boy, aren't you, *wid kabir*?'"

"Oh," Daniels said. "Well, that's all right then."

Key tossed him his new ID, which Daniels caught nimbly. "You're also 'Daniel Morton,' Department of Defense now. Try to remember that, would you?"

"Yes, sir, 'Kenan Josephs,' sir," Daniels replied, using Key's cover name. Gonzales thought best not to get too complex at such short notice.

"Suit up," Key said as Gonzales and Faisal started breaking out their more sophisticated communication devices. "We got an Aquarium to scour."

* * * *

Dubai's aberrations of grandeur didn't make it easy. Like almost everything else in the City of Gold, the Dubai Aquarium and Underwater Zoo was pumped up to almost absurd pretentions. First, it was located in The Dubai Mall, which claimed to be the largest in the world, smackdab in the middle of the downtown area known as Business Bay. Second, the mall was flanked by Burj Khalifa, the tallest building in the world, and Burj Khalifa Lake, a thirty-acre man-made body of water, which, in turn, housed the Dubai Fountain, the largest choreographed water ballet in the world.

At the time they were passing, it was using its twenty-two thousand gallons of water and seven thousand lights to dazzle slack-jawed tourists with a waterlogged interpretation of the *Mission: Impossible* theme.

It was Key's turn to roll his eyes. "Apt," he muttered as Daniels grinned.

Things did not improve once they entered the mall's four levels of excess.

"Ever wanted to know what twelve hundred stores look like?" they heard Gonzales in their ears. "Now you do."

The mechanic was managing the miniature comm-links while Faisal was behind the wheel, backing the marines up from the Renault, which was in one of the lot's fourteen thousand parking spaces. Gonzales felt secure that any passing security attention would be minimal, but, even so, to be on the safe side, he had changed the license plates for this single visit—just in case the mall was in the habit of taking a temporary digi-picture of every vehicle as it entered and exited.

Key stared at the thousands of window-shoppers, tourists, and staff people amid the six million square foot debtor's prison. "Now I know how you felt on SADE Island."

"Yeah, almost too much to take in, huh?" Gonzales said. "Go by the Mediclinic, theme park, movie megaplex, and Ice Rink." He wasn't kidding about any of them. They were all inside the mall, and huge. "Look for the Discovery Zone, or any sign of enclosed water. Even in here it's hard to miss. It's three stories tall."

Daniels tapped Key on the shoulder. The corporal turned to see a huge wall of clear glass, behind which thousands of aquatic creatures swam. Taking up most of his view were dozens of sharks and stingrays, with hundreds of smaller fish serving as a moving mosaic background. He couldn't help wondering which he was, the shark or the stingray. He had the disquieting feeling he was probably a tiny tile in the background mosaic.

"Come on." Daniels sighed, already moving in that direction. "The sooner we make contact the better."

They bought a ticket, accepted a brochure, and checked the information desk for places Toussaint might be with his son. There were many: a Virtual Reality attraction, a King Crocodile exhibit, a Cage Snorkeling Experience, and even a Glass Bottom Boat Ride.

Daniels shook his head at the futility of their task. "What a way to usher in the end of the world." He smirked. "Come on, mister Josephs, let's take 'em one at a time. This should be fun."

They found him, as Key suspected they would, outside the Senior Aquarist Shark Scooter Underwater Experience, the most exclusive and expensive attraction in the place. It lasted four hours and took a VIP guest on a personal behind-the-scenes tour that featured all the above, as well as feedings of both sharks and the rest of the animal kingdom. Toussaint just sat there in the attraction's lounge, wearing a linen suit that must have set his clients back tens of thousands of dollars.

It was a cunning spot. Once the marines had turned the corner, they found there was no window on the swinging door. And once they went through the door, there was no way to retreat that was unnoticeable. To make matters worse, Toussaint was alone in the small, well-appointed, well-lit room. One arm lay along the top of the banquet he sat upon, while his other soft, clean, perfectly manicured hand was in his lap. His legs were crossed at the knees. Key got the errant thought that his loafers might have cost more than his suit.

"Gentlemen," he said in lightly accented English.

"Sir," Key replied, already turning. "Sorry to have bothered you."

"Hardly a bother," he said casually. "Don't leave on my account. Feel free to stay for as long as—"

By then Key was already out the door, with Daniels close behind.

"Joe—" Daniels said, then, remembering their covers, quickly added "—sephs, what the duck?"

But by then he noticed two more men in suits moving smoothly, but swiftly, toward the swinging lounge doors. He also noticed they were looking, with blank faces, directly at them, but by then Key was already moving faster.

To Daniels it looked as if the approaching man was raising his hand to ask a question, and Key was turning so he was facing the same direction as the questioning man. But then the approaching man's face slammed into the floor as if he had been shot from a cannon.

Daniels stared at Key as he slammed the second knuckles of his spearing right hand into the throat of the second approaching man, without looking at him, while kneeing him so hard between the legs that Key would not have been surprised if they found the man's gonads lodged in his throat.

Key did not stop, or wait, to check. Daniels was right behind him as the corporal went as fast as he could without running, looking for any way to go that didn't include the way they had come.

We're fucked, he thought, but said, "Trap," announcing to his entire team that they should defend or kill without pause or question. Since Gonzales didn't respond, Key prayed the Renault would still be there if they managed to get to it.

Too easy. Just the look on Toussaint's placid face told him everything he needed, and didn't want, to know. Information gotten could also mean information given. Key's crew had nothing to offer a desperate runaway. Toussaint's crew had plenty to promise.

Key kept moving, without pausing, his eyes scouring the Aquarium visitors like laser pointers.

"No one," he said to Daniels without looking at him. "Man, woman, *or* child, comes near us. They'll want it to look like an accident. But if they can't, they might try some cellblock shit."

"Oooo," Daniels said just behind and beside him. "Goody."

No one else stumbled or turned toward them in the Aquarium, even by accident. Key nodded sharply, figuring that into his trap conjecture.

"They'll be at every exit," he said like making lunch plans.

"Roger," Daniels said.

Key slammed through the nearest one, crying, "I'm so sorry, I didn't know!" That was enough to get shoppers looking quizzically in his direction, and the two hired killers waiting against the wall on either side of the door to look surprised.

Key stared at the one nearest him—another merc in a suit—with an expression he hoped communicated a simple question. *What's more important to you: your payment or your life?*

As the man's face set and he came at him, Key realized it was the wrong question. Wasn't the payment that was important to this idiot, it was his pride. That's all killers had. That's why they were stupid killers.

Key called it the ninja conundrum. In real life, ninja were miserable wretches with no place on Earth and none in Heaven. All they had was their willingness to do dishonorable things for corrupt masters, which marked them as sad, stupid, and defeatable if you knew what you were doing.

Key worked very hard to keep learning what he was doing.

Given the parameters, Key felt certain these hirelings were working under, it was likely that the man would try to *accidentally* stumble, slam Key against the wall, and, with his body covering Key from view, shove a pin under his sternum or up his nose. Anywhere else, like his ear or eye, would be witnessed.

The combination defense and counterattack was therefore obvious. Key waited for the man to stumble, then turned, shifted, and slipped just outside the man's spreading arms, so close, in fact, that the man's fingerprints slid along Key's jacket, and then he let the man's head collide with the mall wall.

Of course, it didn't hurt that Key's right ankle had somehow crossed the man's right ankle, and Key's left hand, in his attempt to *help* the man, had actually vaulted him harder and faster. It didn't hurt Key, at any rate.

With a quick glance out his peripheral vision to make sure Daniels wasn't still dancing with his assassin, Key kept moving. They were on the first floor. They needed to get up to the second where Faisal had parked the Renault.

Daniels wasn't still dancing. He was back just behind and beside Key.

"What did you do to him?" Key muttered.

"I stumbled first," Daniels said into Key's ear. "The pin went into his own thigh. Pretty much down to his knee. These guys are either well paid, well trained, or both. He didn't make a peep. You should've seen his face, though."

The sergeant considered asking escalator or stairs but realized the answer before speaking. They would stay in public view, because that limited their enemy's options. Causing a public scene, and risking innocent bystanders, would shift all that oil money from construction to bringing the wrath of heaven down on whoever dared disturb Dubai's tourism.

"The closer we get to escaping, the more desperate they'll get," Key said as he hopped on the escalator.

"Tell me about it," Daniels retorted, right behind him. They each stood, with one leg bent on a higher step, so each took up two escalator stairs, giving them more room to move, and less room for anyone to attack. "Don't I know it. Cellblock shit at twelve o'clock."

They both saw one, two, three, and then four suited men congregating at the top of the escalator, waiting for them. They were spread far enough apart that the people exiting in front of the marines didn't think twice about them, but, as Key and Daniels neared, the quartet got tighter, leaving them nowhere to go. Or so the killers thought.

"Alley oop?" Key queried.

"Of course alley oop," Daniels replied with exaggerated certainty. "Alley—" he said as he webbed his fingers together and held them down at his crotch.

"—Oop," Key responded as he put his hands on Daniels's shoulders, and his foot in Daniels's palm stirrup. Daniels threw his hands skyward as Key dove upward.

The suited men at the top of the escalator stepped back, their mouths agape, as Key was vaulted into the air over them.

Daniels almost laughed as he saw them struggle to figure out what to do. They may have been well-trained, but not well-trained enough to instantly decide who would handle Key and who would handle Daniels.

Especially when Daniels cried out, "Oh! I'm so sorry," as he *accidentally* sent a woman into the suited men nearest him.

Key enjoyed watching the confusion, even panic, on the men's faces before he delivered the final blow.

"Look out!" he cried, pointing frantically. "A knife! Help, help, they've got knives!"

Daniels *accidentally* slammed the nearest suited man's hand between his hip and the escalator wall, while keeping his balance by sinking his fingers into the man's hair, then yanking as if pulling a parachute's ripcord.

People were screaming and scurrying as security guards came running, while a suited man tumbled down the metal escalator stairs, the shiv hidden up his sleeve spinning out for all to see.

By then Key stood far away from the action, moving quickly backwards to make sure none of the remaining suited men pursued him. One was cracking his skull on the escalator stairs, one was beneath a writhing, shrieking female shopper, the third was sidling along the balustrade in the opposite direction, while the last stood amongst the chaos, staring in shock and anger at Key as he was backing away.

The fourth man took an impotent step toward the corporal, but stopped when he saw Key stop as well, lower his chin, and shake his head sadly. One second afterwards, the fourth man grimaced, teeth grinding, then fell to his knees, and, finally, to his face. Daniels came out from behind the man and joined Key at the garage entrance.

"Poor guy," he said, "He fall down, go boom."

"Roger that," Gonzales said, to their great relief, in their ears. "They tried to surprise me with silencers, coming from two sides. But they should have wondered why the driver's seat was empty."

"Details later," Key interrupted, hurrying toward the parking space. "We've got to get back."

"What's up?" Daniels asked, still just behind and beside him. "Looks like we got things under control."

Up ahead, Key saw Faisal slithering out from his lookout spot beneath the SUV, and jumping back behind the wheel. Daniels saw Gonzales open the side door for them, revealing two motionless bodies on the floor of the vehicle.

"The trap was set by Toussaint and Awar." Key seethed as he ran the last few yards to the Renault. "But it was on information supplied by—"

"Shit!" Faisal cried as he gunned the motor to life, then tromped the accelerator almost before Daniels and Key had leapt in.

Chapter 25

The man who had dropped Saad Al-Abbasi to his death prayed for death.

Not his own. He prayed for death to all the infidels who disagreed with him, and he prayed for death for everyone who opposed his master and leader Usa Awar. He prayed for death to all the non-believers. He prayed for death to any one he wanted to die.

The man who prayed for others' deaths no longer had the name forced upon him at birth. In actuality, he had the same name as all his brothers who shared the responsibility to protect this nest. His name was Malud Bin Awar, which meant born the son of Awar. They were all Malud Bin Awar.

This Malud Bin Awar savored the feeling of power his prayers for others' deaths gave him. He fed on the feeling that his dedication to his leader's cause bestowed upon him. He had done, and would do, whatever his abu, father, asked of him.

For years, he'd felt unhappy because his abu had not yet asked him to give his life for the cause. Every time another was sent out with a knife, gun, or bomb, never to return, he'd felt regret because it hadn't been him.

But the reward was worth it. When Master Awar found this nest and created this cave, he blessed his dedicated servant with one of the most important posts and positions. Malud had witnessed the creation of the Holy Gate he guarded. He had nearly even helped construct it until master Awar insisted it be touched only by the most proficient engineers.

"It has to be secure beyond secure," Usa Awar Abu Jmye, father of all, had said. "It must be fail-safe beyond fail-safe, foolproof beyond foolproof." And it was. The father of them all had seen to it. Why else would he have left his beloved, honored, children behind to protect the nest if it were not?

But the Holy Gate's perfection did not diminish this Malud's watchfulness. The Holy Cavern had no seats, but it did not require any. This Malud gained strength from letting the holy energy of the nest fill him. To this moment, he marveled at the technology within this place. The suddenly transparent walls, the magically appearing images fed from miles around.

Even so, these things were not his concern. His concern was only to ensure that the seal of the Holy Gate remain intact. That those bringers of justice within remain content and secure.

This Malud Bin Awar was certain of that indisputable fact. So certain that he would spend minutes, even hours, kneeling in prayer for his master's success and his enemies' deaths. Hours facing the entrance to the Holy Gate, his powerful, protecting back to the seal.

He was so certain he didn't even open his eyes when he heard a click from behind him that he had never heard before. He knew there was no reason for concern. His brothers were assigned to continually study the security cameras' video screens. If anything was unusual within the nest, they would have alerted him.

So this Malud Bin Awar was slow to turn toward the Holy Gate. But when he did he sprang to his feet, clutching at the AK-47 Master Awar had entrusted to him.

The seal was not broken, but it was sprung, and trying to crawl out of the air lock was an Idmonarachne Brasieri. This Malud had never seen one before. They hadn't even let him watch what happened to Al-Abbasi after he had forced the traitor into the rubber-raft-like interior of the Gate and slammed the air lock door upon him.

This Malud told himself he should not be frightened of the thing his master called arachnosaur. They were merely tools of his divine vengeance. But he was. It was even bigger than he imagined. The four moist, stubbled tubes that made up its face quivered in an unnatural way, and its many black, dead, marbleized eyes seemed to tear into the guard's brain. One of its eight long spider legs was already tapping the cavern floor. As this Malud watched, another leg came springing into view, as if pulling itself from a net.

This Malud gripped his automatic weapon, his flesh already crawling and covered in sweat, but he did not pull the trigger.

"Brothers!" he cried in his native tongue. "Brothers! The seal is broken! The Holy Gate is breached! What should I do? Stop, or protect the master's instruments of righteousness? What should I do?"

When the thing's third leg scratched out of the opening, this Malud stepped back, unnatural, unwanted, unexpected fear freezing him. It wasn't the sight or sound of the creature that did it. It was its unnatural, inhuman, incompatible energy, throbbing from it in invisible waves.

This Malud started to scream "brothers" again, but the word ended in a cry of childlike terror as his fingers spastically clenched. The AK-47 barked in his hands, its bullets splattering the Plasticine-covered sand, ricocheting off the metal lip of the gate, and splattering against the wall.

Then the arachnosaur was free. It both leaped and scurried forward, its eight spider legs traveling in a terrible rhythm. This Malud only had a second to feel the literal creepiness of its suprahuman movement, as if it was progressing between reality rather than in it, before its first foreleg stabbed into his stomach.

Then, in far less than a second, all the legs were in him, ripping, cutting, tearing, and scrambling. His scream would have shaken the cavern had the thing's first leg not split him from navel to chin in one smooth, uninterrupted slice, rendering his larynx useless.

But his brothers had heard his earlier cries. Two who guarded the outside entrance to the Holy Gate came running in, their weapons at the ready. They stopped, confused, when they saw the arachnosaur standing in what looked like a dissected life raft. But then they realized it was a life raft with a human skull.

In the instant they were watching, the thing's pincer-like legs punctured Malud's eyes like squeezed grapes, and flayed open his face as if it were a rubber mask.

They opened fire, but the thing was already moving, spraying blood and guts like Silly String and confetti as it scurried. It came at the first one on the right, but just as the terrified second man started shooting without aiming, it darted toward the second. That made the first man swing too fast and too far, just missing the arachnosaur, but spraying the second man's hips and stomach with bullets.

He staggered, screaming, his own AK-47 swinging from ceiling to floor as the creature leaped onto the first man, its legs opening like a maw, turning the guard's torso into a blood splattered, bone-spinning, gut-erupting blossom.

By then many other Malud Bin Awars had spilled into the Holy Gate antechamber, skidding to a stop from all the screams and blood that splashed the entrance frame and puddled on the floor. Without a word, the half-dozen cavern guards gathered in the far entrance like a panic-stricken firing squad, their weapons aimed and ready.

The screaming just within the far chamber stopped, and the blood stilled. The men waited, for what seemed like minutes. Finally, the one nearest the chamber stepped forward, lowering his head to try peering beyond the wall. Naturally, it was at that moment that the arachnosaur sped out.

All six men opened fire. For a brain-freezing moment, they misjudged the creature's expected speed, and all their rounds ripped up the floor just beyond the monster. It seemed as if a spider's leg would pierce the first man, but then the fourth pulled his aim back and down, and his bullets pounded into the beast's bulbous, pulsating, upraised abdomen.

They all winced at the sound of an unnatural screeching, but drowned it out by adjusting their aim and pouring all the bullets all six weapons had left into the pulverized body of the thing. Black blood spat out as it shuddered and danced in the veritable cloud of lead. But finally the guns were empty and the thing was still.

By then more men had gathered, virtually from every department of the enclave.

"What should we do?" asked the one who operated communications. "What should we tell his holiness?"

The first guard, who had nearly been punctured, dared to poke at the arachnosaur carcass with the barrel of his AK-47.

It was just a spider, he thought. *Nothing but a big spider.* Emboldened, he spoke directly to the communications man.

"Report the truth! There has been a momentary breach of security, but it has been corrected.All is in readiness for the master leader's return."

Satisfied, the men began returning to their posts. The first guard instructed several nearby guards to clean up the Holy Gate guard's remains. When one asked who should replace the fallen martyr, the first guard replied with certainty.

"I shall. I am the only one worthy."

No one argued the point, so the first guard went to reload his weapon before taking up his new position. As he went he saw the communications man returning to his own post, but, while doing so, behaving strangely. He waved next to his head as if shooing an insect.

The first guard thought nothing of it until, during his walk back to the Holy Gate chamber, he saw a few other guards doing the same thing.

The incident must have effected their nerves, he thought. *I shall inform the master upon his return. We of true faith need fear no nerves. We need fear nothing, for we are blessed in the light of our leader.*

The first guard continued on his righteous path, until he felt something light and thin brush his hair. Instinctively he waved his hand at it, then realized what he'd just done. He stopped dead in his tracks. He turned to look at the others nearby, but before he could see if they were doing it too, he felt another filmy strand touch his cheek.

He quickly pinched at it, then looked down to where his forefinger and thumb met. At first he saw nothing, but then the unnatural light of the cave's LED fixtures caught some sort of clear, diaphanous, gossamer hair.

He felt a chill, but then heat. He looked up.

The arachnosaur nearest him—one of many—dropped down from where they were crawling upside-down on the cavern ceiling.

They had, over a span of days, camouflaged the edge of the nest's security camera lens nearest the ceiling air-lock opening, then spun finer and finer webs to force the supposedly unbreachable lower seal wider and wider until their bulbous bodies could fit within it. Then an ever-rotating series of creatures started constructing another wedge in the plastic and steel mechanism of the upper lock. It took time, but they had plenty of it. And when the first freed arachnosaur created a diversion, the others had also crawled out.

The first guard may have screamed. But the horrid noise that resulted also could have been part of the sounds the creature atop him made when spiking open his skull. Ultimately, it was irrelevant because those sounds were quickly overwhelmed by the symphony of wholesale slaughter combined with the thudding detonations of human circulatory systems.

Chapter 26

The man started shooting as soon as he entered the shelter.

He was dressed as any Emirate, in *kandora* robe, *ghutrah* head scarf, *agal* headband, and *bisht* cloak, but with an extra gauzy black scarf to obscure most of his face. He also gripped a silenced Glock 19 compact automatic and was using it, although far from indiscriminately.

So, Eshe Rahal thought in a strange, almost unnatural, calm. *He expects to leave survivors and escape safely.*

As soon as he had come in, Rahal had looked up from the table, where she had been intently scribbling formulas. She was expecting, hoping for, and even praying that it was Josiah Key, but froze as soon as she saw the gun. Key didn't carry his gun in Dubai, nor even a smartphone, to avoid detection.

Then, for the first time since the attack on the desert tent, everything seemed to decelerate. The doctor within Rahal understood it as the mental state called slow motion perception, where massive amounts of sensory input caused rapid saccadic eye movement, which altered the brain's perception of time.

So she watched the assassin carefully survey the area with both his eyes and the gun barrel until it centered on the face of a young Ethiopian who was already on her knees, waving her arms and screeching in Arabic.

"Not me, not me, they promised!" Rahal's brain slowly translated through the girl's accent. "I did as you—"

The assassin pumped a nine-millimeter round into her face.

That was why he was here, Rahal realized. The frightened, desperate girl had betrayed them. Then the assistant professor watched calmly as the killer started walking across the room toward her. He held the gun slightly down and to the right as he came steadily closer.

From the left, another girl leaped at him, screeching and clawing. He smoothly pulled the gun up and over and shot her in the chest. Rahal suddenly understood where the term shoot her down came from, as the poor girl was punched to the floor rugs by the bullet. A third shrieking girl charged him from behind.

Stop screaming, stop screaming, Rahal's mind begged them, but she stayed silent and still, watching it all like an analytic scientist. As she feared, the killer simply twisted, brought the gun behind him, and shot her in the head—without slowing his steady pace.

Then, as Rahal watched dispassionately, no longer hearing the screams of fear or really noticing the others crawling, scrambling, and running away, he turned toward her, still steadily striding. When he finally stopped, ten feet away from her, and pointed the gun at her face, Rahal closed her eyes and prayed.

In the name of Allah, the Gracious, the Merciful, I seek refuge with Allah from Satan, the accursed.

She did not expect to open them again. When she heard a different sort of scream, a deeper, masculine one, Rahal opened her eyes to see that everything was back at normal speed. The killer's right wrist was cleaved open and gutting blood, while his left hand was tight over his right eye, and even more blood was seeping through his fingers there.

Hadiyah, who was holding the kitchen knife in one hand, grabbed the fallen Glock with the other and scuttled back. Lailani, who was across from the mama-san, was holding her dominatrix whip at the ready. She had already split the man's eye open with her first strike.

The two had attacked at the same time. And neither had made a sound while doing it.

The man screeched in Arabic, unsure as to who to attack now. Seeing only with his one remaining good eye, he realized that the older woman had the gun, and the Filipino had the whip. So he painfully focused on Rahal, then, face twisted in pain and rage, he charged the unarmed woman.

Or, more accurately, the woman who seemed unarmed. Because she had already learned from Key that anything could be a weapon, and the more unexpected, the better. The assistant professor stood and brought the chair she'd been sitting on up and around in one strong arc. It smashed into the assassin's face like a coarse wooden scythe.

He staggered, miraculously managing to stay upright, then slammed face first into a roaring SUV grill that came ripping through the canvas wall, filling the space with the sound of screeching tires.

Everyone but the driver was out of the Renault before it had even completely stopped. Gonzales leaped to Hadiyah's side, and claimed the Glock with her approval and gratitude.

"Typical chauvinistic arrogance," the mama-san seethed, breathing deeply. "If they had used a woman with a knife, Eshe would already be dead."

Daniels ran toward Lailani, but, as he picked up on what had happened, his pace slowed and his grin widened. But it was Rahal who ran to Key. Rather than the other way around, as he carefully studied the situation.

"We've got to go," he told the others urgently as Rahal clung to him. He had already informed them that the enemy already knew everything. "Now."

They would remember that "now," in retrospect, as a cue. Because the moment he said it, the rest of the secret shelter's carpet walls and canvas ceiling came down, torn and trodden by the boots of a fully equipped assault unit, whose armaments and uniform color they recognized. In the next second, the three men and three women who remained were surrounded by an arena-shaped phalanx of M4 carbines.

"Belay that," Captain Patrick Logan said harshly as he stepped up to within an inch of Daniels's face. "And what the hell is a corporal doing giving orders to a sergeant anyway, dammit!"

* * * *

Rahal finally broke the silence. "Where are we?"

"Glad you asked," Daniels said with a mirthless smirk. "You want to tell her, Joe?"

Key exhaled strongly as he continued to rest his cheek on one fist. "'Undisclosed location, Eshe." He sighed. "You can always tell from the handcuffs and hoods they used on us."

"And the lovely décor of the place they brought us to," Daniels added, spreading his arms to encompass the severe plainness of the rectangular room, a room equipped with only a bolted down table and five non-bolted-down chairs. It could have been any interview room in any headquarters anywhere in the world.

Key sat up, swiveled, and looked at her. "But, in case you didn't count off the amount of time we were being driven, I'm guessing the American consulate, close to the shores of Dubai Creek." He smiled at the little, dark surveillance balls wedged six different places along the ceiling. "Got that right?"

His insolence had the effect he wanted. The single door in the corner slammed open, and Captain Logan stormed in, carrying a thick file. He stomped to the table, yanked out a chair, and slammed the file down.

Daniels's eyebrows rose when he realized the captain was alone, but that didn't surprise Key. He imagined the captain had even switched off the video and audio recorders just before he entered. The subject of their inevitable discussion would be highly sensitive indeed.

Daniels's eyebrows rose even farther when Second Lieutenant Barbara Strenkofski reached in and gripped the outside door handle before slowly and quietly closing it. Rahal saw the sergeant and second louie's eyes meet before the blonde sealed the door with herself outside, but, try as she might, the professor couldn't read it. But when Daniels's returned his attention to the table, he couldn't hide a small smile.

Logan either ignored or didn't see it. His eyes tried to bore into Key's as the corporal pulled himself closer to the table directly across from the captain. On the basis of all the American movies she'd seen, Rahal expected Key to start making strong, logical demands like, "Have you arrested Jean-Bernard Toussaint? You should be searching for Usa Awar rather than us!"

But, instead, Key just sat silently and calmly waiting. He even crossed his arms and leaned back.

Logan was forced to speak first. "You think you're so goddamned smart, don't you, Corporal?"

Key seemed to consider that question, then put his hands on the table and leaned in. "No, sir," he said honestly. "I'm just trying to do what I think is best. I know you are too, sir."

At first, Logan reacted as if his bear trap had snapped onto Key's ankles, but, when he spoke, his mouth moved as if he was sucking something bitter. "You know what I see, Corporal? I see one soldier who follows orders, and another soldier who doesn't. And we both know what happens to a marine who doesn't follow orders, don't we?"

Key seemed to be considering that as well. He didn't have to say, "He doesn't get promoted," because everyone in the room was loudly thinking it. Neither did he say what Daniels wanted him to, something along the lines of, "What about planting tracking devices without our knowledge, or collaborating with the enemy instead of stealing from him," or other such nonsense. Instead Key just sat there, thinking.

Rahal realized she was holding her breath.

Finally Key opened his mouth. "Yes, sir," he said, motioning to the thick file Logan was holding like a life preserver. "But I'm already in so deep, I really got nothing to lose, so let's face it." He stared calmly and deeply into Logan's icy stare. "I know, and you know. Now tell me how you're convincing yourself you're doing the right thing."

The two men held the stare for five long seconds. Daniels watched Logan's lips to see if he was mentally counting it off. But, as far as he could tell, the captain's lips only got thinner.

"I don't have to tell you shit-all, *Private* Key," their commanding officer finally said, nearly snarling. He slapped open the file and gave it a sheet-metal glance. "I'd read off the charges against you but we'd be here all day, and I got far more important things to do." He slapped the file closed and stood, his fists on the table, staring down at Key. "Suffice it to say that your coconspirators will be detained for indefinite debriefing, and, if I have my way, you'll be sunk so far and so deep for so long that—"

The trio were spared from whatever agonized metaphor the captain was about to trot out by the door. It snapped open, swung in, and slammed against the wall so sharply that Rahal gave out a surprised squeal, and even Logan grimaced.

Framed in the doorway was a tall, chiseled, older man in what Key recognized as the uniform of a full three-star retired general. "Then you better not have your way, Captain," he said in a voice that sounded like gravel being smeared on a bass drum.

Key didn't know who he was. Daniels did.

Holy shit, the sergeant thought in disbelief, praying that he wasn't talking aloud. *Lionheart Lancaster.*

Logan gaped for a moment, then instantly snapped to attention and gave the intruder a stiff salute.

"At ease, Captain," said General Charles L. Lancaster, retired, as he stepped into the room with his own very thin file. He turned and smiled and nodded with understanding at the stunned blonde outside. "You too, Second Lieutenant." Then he closed the door on her shaken, disbelieving face.

"Sir, what, to what do I—" Logan stammered, and stepped back.

"I said 'at ease, Captain,'" Lancaster said affably, putting his arm around Logan's shoulder and slowly moving him back toward the chair. "No need to get up on my account." Logan sat, looking as if he had just been slapped in the face with a fish, as the retired general surveyed the others with a shrewd smile. "Sorry to interrupt, but I couldn't stand idly by to a miscarriage of military justice."

That brought Logan back to his previous height. "Sir, with all due respect, this is none of your concern, or, if I may say, business. This is strictly marine protocol, and you gave up that right when you—"

But the captain's defensive diatribe withered when Lancaster made mild swatting motions with his hands, while smiling even wider, as if the whole thing was just a misunderstanding. "I'm afraid it is both my concern and my business, Captain, since these men, and, as you called them, their coconspirators, have just been assigned to the Cerberus Unit."

"The Cerberus—" Logan blurted. "I've never heard of the—" But by then Lancaster had presented him the lone piece of paper from his file, and again, with just a guiding hand on his shoulder and the power of his personality, urged the captain to sit back down.

Daniels, especially, was vastly entertained by the tumbling expressions of shock and awe on Logan's face, and by the way his eyes pinballed around his sockets as he read.

"All charges dropped? Immediate assignment overriding all others? Complete discretion to investigate national and international threats beyond those of normal military protocol?" He looked up from the order like he was having a heart attack. "But, but—" he struggled, hurriedly searching through his own thick file. "I have a direct order from the secretary of defense to do whatever necessary to secure—"

"Did you note my letter's signature?" Lancaster asked gently.

Rahal could hear the kindness in the general's voice, but also recognized the steel sword serving as its spine. And Daniels thought that, by the way Logan's eyes bulged, he might be about to go the way Goodman and Ayman had.

Although Retired General Charles Leonidas Lancaster was nominally speaking to Logan, he was looking directly at the other seated man. "I'd say an order from the commander-in-chief trumps one from the secretary of defense," he concluded with a smile that might have contained slivers of Logan's soul. "Wouldn't you, *Sergeant Major* Key?"

Chapter 27

What many called hardship, Cala Haza called life. She knew no other way of living, so, for her, walking along mountain paths to get water, spending the day milking the cow, tending sheep, grinding flour, keeping bees, picking corn, raising wheat, preparing food, and then filling the evening weaving or embroidering, was normal. Sometimes she watched the village boys play soccer in the dirt as the sun went down, bathing the mountain in swaths of gold.

Once a month a traveling teacher gathered all the children of her Yemeni mountain village to tell them of the rest of the country and the outside world. Today was that day, so Cala hurried along to the one-room brick schoolhouse.

"Yemen," the teacher said, "is an impoverished nation on the southwestern end of the Arabian Peninsula. It is alongside *Bab-el-Mandeb*, a slender channel that divides the country from the Horn of Africa, where it joins the Red Sea on one side and the Indian Ocean on the other."

Cala accepted that, but didn't truly understand his use of the word impoverished. She had shelter. It may have been simple and made of bricks and cement born of the mountain, like all the others in Wuyan village, but it kept her dry and warm. She had clothing, a bright *Sana'ani* dress made of multicolored *Al-Masoon* cloth she dyed herself. She had even knitted her own *Al-Momq* head cover, paying particular attention to the red and white decorations. And there was food, goat and lamb as well as plentiful herbs and vegetables.

"Yemen," the teacher elaborated, "has four main regions: eastern highlands, coastal plains, western highlands, and the *Rub al Khali* desert. You are near all of them."

That was good. Thanks to him, Cala knew where she was in the world. Those words were helpful, but the teacher had even more words, words that sounded like a fable. "Here," the teacher had said, "there is a war. A war between the government, Houthi rebels, fanatics, and even foreign countries."

That, Cala truly couldn't understand. She thought that fights were between two people, not four. The teacher tried to clarify the situation, but his explanations became more and more confusing. Thankfully, it got better when the teacher finally revealed that the snipers, tanks, and air raids were far away, in the southwestern cities. She and all her fellow villagers were actually part of the huge majority in Yemen, the ones who lived in the country, or on the mountainsides. Here, life stayed much as it had been for generations, so the end of the teacher's lesson also puzzled her.

"Estimates state that more than three million Yemenis have been displaced," he said. Cala asked what that meant, so the teacher answered that they had been forced to leave their homes. Cala thought that was awful until the teacher said that Yemen had a total population of twenty-five million. That made Cala feel better because that meant many more people weren't displaced.

For some reason, that seemed to upset the teacher, who then said that, of those twenty-five million, twenty-one million needed something called humanitarian assistance. When the teacher couldn't explain that to Cala's satisfaction, he finished the day's lesson by saying at least ten thousand people had been killed in the war.

"The cities' wars?" Cala asked. The teacher had not answered that, and soon left Wuyan to continue his teaching in the nearby villages. Cala walked slowly out of the schoolhouse with the other children, who ran to the fields or home. Cala watched the teacher make his way down the grassy rocks until he reached some concrete steps the villagers had forced into the hillsides to help the pack donkeys navigate, as well as for the occasional visitor.

Cala let her eyes wander from the teacher to the mountainsides all around him; mountainsides filled with green trees veined by brown rocks, and dotted with concrete squares of housing. Above it all were blue skies splashed with cottony white clouds. She recognized everyone in the village as they carried food and firewood, wearing their flowing outfits of black, blue, orange, pink, and yellow.

When she looked back, the teacher was gone. Soon she knew his teachings would be gone too. Even though she knew of no other, she was certain that her life in Wuyan was a good life, and she was content.

Cala Haza then looked down because she felt something under her feet. A vibration shivered the woven sandals she had made herself. It was almost nothing, as if the Earth had hummed, but it was something she had never felt before. It didn't feel like an earthquake.

She kept looking as the ground beneath her kept humming, and would have stayed that way for a while longer if she had not felt something on her head. She reached up and pulled from her brown hair a strand of gold, as if sunlight had taken form. She used her other hand to stretch it. Like the ground shivering didn't feel like an earthquake, the strand didn't feel like silk.

But as she stared at it, more golden strands, glimmering in the sunlight, floated down into her vision. Cala raised her head to see shimmering strands raining down from over the hill, like white bubbles at the end of a breaking ocean wave. They rolled over each like lace taking shape on a loom. As they grew, the shivering beneath her feet grew as well, until it felt like a cat's purr.

Cala looked around in confusion, seeing her fellow villagers doing the same. She met one's eyes, and then the other, and then the next. It was like looking into her own eyes. Everyone in the village knew each other, so there were no strangers and no secrets. But then she looked at one of her schoolmates. He was a boy she liked, a boy she would often watch play soccer.

As she watched he began to shake. Not shiver, not hum, not vibrate, but really shake. Then something black started oozing out of his eyes, nose, mouth, and even ears.

Cala looked away, quickly, her own eyes wet. Banging sounds were coming over the hill, and getting louder. Sickening, cracking, wet bangs, one after another. And then came a wave of different noises. Women's screams.

She screamed herself when the boy she liked tore open right in front of her. Cala couldn't think anymore. An unreasoning, unknowing terror had clamped into her. She spun and ran. She didn't know where she was going, and she didn't care. The screams were getting louder now, and closer. So were the thumping, cracking, and banging noises.

The golden lace was showering down on her like netting. She tore at it, swinging her clawing fingers, as her feet and the ground slapped each other with every step. Her eyes were huge and unseeing, vaguely registering colors and shapes as muscle memory and instinct took over.

She felt showers of slivers pinching her, and sharp wetness splash her, as she realized she was trying to run home. She finally got to the gate of her family's house, and reached agonizingly for it. But just before her fingers clenched on the latch, it swung open.

Cala slid to a stop directly in front of her father. His face was contorting, his eyes shredding. Lumpy, steaming, black blood pumped out every orifice. His fingernails cracked and steaming black blood poured out of them as well.

Cala's mother ran up behind him, hysterically crying his name, and reaching desperately for him. She had just touched him when he ripped open.

The detonation sent Cala back four feet. She slammed onto the ground, and slid two feet more, covered in her father's blood, guts, and bone. To her astonishment, she did not lose consciousness. She blinked up to the blue sky, its white cotton clouds knitted into golden doilies floating over her.

She waited until she heard no more noises, not realizing that her father's death had deafened her. She slowly managed to get to her feet, and saw that pieces of her father's bones had pierced her mother's throat and chest.

Again Cala looked away. She tried to find solace in the beautiful countryside, but now the mountains and valleys were dotted with fast-moving things, all pouring over the hilltops and scuttling, scurrying, scampering down toward her.

She had seen spiders before. She knew what spiders were. These were not spiders.

All the women of her village were wailing, begging, and pleading as their husbands, brothers, and sons shredded open all around them. As she watched, the eight-legged things reached them.

It was a curse that Cala was already deep in shock. It was the only way she could have witnessed the torn-open male corpses being pounced upon by the things while lumpy, pulsating, mucous was pumped into their steaming cavities while the screaming women were being eviscerated by swirling, lightning-fast, pincers.

And the things just kept moving. They laid their venomous eggs in the males, exenterated the females, then went on to the next. Dozens and dozens of them swarmed nearing her.

The first pincer stabbed into her stomach, but not the others. She had no idea her body was flayed open because she was already down, her skull hitting the dirt. For some reason the arachnosaur that reached her didn't bother with destroying her head. Perhaps the thing's appetite was slacked. Perhaps it saw a more attractive target beyond her.

Whatever the reason, Cala lived on for a few seconds more, staring in the opposite direction, at the valley and the brooks and the villages beyond. What had the teacher once said? Oh yes. That Wuyan was very well positioned in the country. To the north was Shabhut and Dabuh. To the south was Medmahdah, Fusai, and finally the Gulf of Aden, which spread into the Red Sea, the Arabian Sea, and the Indian Ocean. After that, no part of the world was out of reach. No part.

Cala Haza died three weeks shy of her twelfth birthday.

Chapter 28

West of the Jumeirah Golf Estate, south of the Jebel Ali Village's Lost City, east of the Medical & Hazardous Waste Treatment Plant, and near the Abu Dhabi border was Dubai Industrial City—an ominous-looking maze waiting for a figurative minotaur.

It squatted on the edge of the city on steroids like a warning. *This*, it seemed to silently say, *is what happens when the fun times, and financial credit, run out.* It was the skeleton of another grand idea, with no soul to complete it.

Deep within the skeletal labyrinth was another monstrosity that looked like a deserted industrial park, all pipes, concrete, unfinished walls, and construction cranes. At any given time, at least twenty percent of the world's cranes were operating, or awaiting operation, in Dubai. Tourists were well known to complain that it was hard to get a good photo of the city's skyline because of all the cranes slicing through it. Here, close to the edge of the Dubai Investment Park's Steel Mill, was what looked like the crane cemetery.

But, if like a small caravan of dark, bulletproof SUVs, you got closer, you could see a cunning design. A cunning design that had not been there a month before. Opaque, reflective walls, created to camouflage, hemmed in a ballroom-sized space deep in the heart of the park, complete with an innocuous entry hall, also cunningly disguised to blend in with the rest of the complex.

It was more of that demented SADE Island genius, taking advantage of Dubai's crazily conceived developments that were officially still under construction,. In reality, they were abandoned and vulnerable, making them prime targets for trespassers, or a top-secret presentation far away from the rest of the city's glitz, glamor, and prying paparazzi eyes.

Captain Patrick Logan was expected. He took not a single unprotected, unsecured, or even unobscured step from the private limo pick-up chamber of the Jumeirah Bab Al Shams Desert resort to this undisclosed, specially made, viewing compartment within the essentially invisible construction.

More shrewdness, Logan thought. He was certain that the few other SUVs he had spotted in their short caravan had contained high-ranking representatives from China, Russia, Jordan, and Saudi Arabia, but it was wise not to let any participant know exactly who. Logan thought he would have to wait as each representative was personally shown to their private viewing box, but even that was handled smoothly and efficiently in such a way that it seemed as if he was the only guest.

His chaperone was a beautifully dressed Omani, but one whose head-covering *ghutrah* had an extra flap to obscure their face. He showed Logan into the ten-by-six soundproofed chamber, then silently closed the door behind him. Despite the state-of-the-art viewing screen and luxurious five-thousand-dollar Osaki OS-PRO recliner, complete with attached tablet, Logan couldn't help feeling he was back in a video peep show room from his college days.

He quickly shook off that feeling, and settled in to the perfectly padded cushions and noted that the tablet was already loaded with cutting-edge software that would allow him to bid while namelessly seeing the other bids. It even gave bidders the option to include anonymous, distant, representatives to pool their resources in real time.

Smart, Logan marveled again. This way no one had to know who the other bidder was in order to become even more competitive. Just as he was settling in, numbers in English started appearing on the seventy-inch, high-definition screen, six feet in front of him.

Five, four, three, two, one—

A stark image appeared of two people in a simple, darkened room. One was a clearly frightened, naked, handcuffed man. The other was a young, fit, red-haired woman who was also nude except for a face-molding eye shield.

Logan, being Logan, recognized neither Terri Nichols nor Khalifa Al-Alam.

The man started tried to pull away, but his handcuffs were attached to a thin, almost indiscernible cable. The woman's eye-shield became transparent while unseen, recessed lights shone around them.

The girl's eyes glowed green, and vibrated. The man started shrieking as thin streams of black liquid came from the girl's nostrils, eye ducts, and even out of her mouth. That was when the cable slowly, inexorably, pulled him toward the woman.

Logan was almost out of his chair, opening his mouth to complain. No one had told him that it would be a live demonstration, with unwilling participants. But his conscience immediately chastised him. *What did you expect?*

Apparently, the other attendees had no misgivings. The bidding on the tablet screen started popping like fireworks. Logan fell back into the chair, and gaped at the prices which went from six to seven digits within a second, and the weaponizing hadn't even been revealed yet.

I can't let anyone else have this, he reprimanded himself. *I have my orders!*

His finger hovered over the tablet's number pad as the shrieking man got closer and closer to the quivering woman, as well as the liquid, which now looked like black veins etching her pale, freckled skin.

It was just a few centimeters more. Just a few, and then the man and woman would unavoidably touch. Logan's fingers hovered the same distance above the number pad. He would wait, he would see, and then he would outbid them all.

Two millimeters away, one—

Suddenly the ceiling and a wall of the room the man and woman were in collapsed. For a split-second Logan saw the jib of a construction crane poking in the wall like God's forefinger. But that astonishing sight was bypassed by another crane's trolley hook dropping in from the ceiling.

Logan gaped in amazement. Attached to it was a metal coffin. And he could have sworn, on a stack of whatever holy book were handy, that there were men riding the crane jib and hook, one burly and one slim. Then their own human arms swung down, and Logan was blinded.

When he could see again, the room on the screen was empty of people, but out the holes in the ceiling and wall he could see beautifully dressed, cowled men shooting at something above them. Logan leapt from the chair and kicked open the door.

He charged down the hall, past bodyguards scurrying to protect their paychecks. He vaguely recognized an Arabic defense minister and a Chinese People's Liberation Army general as he went, but he didn't care. Logan burst into the open to see a small mob of bodyguards and security men firing a wide range of Glocks and Heckler & Kochs above their heads as Jean-Bernard Toussaint ran among them, waving his arms and screeching *"Cessez-le! Cessez-le!"*

Dubai authorities frowned on discharging a firearm in public, especially by a foreign national. So much so, in fact, that their frowns could mean life imprisonment for any of these idiots.

Logan looked toward the sky, his jaw tight, at two bullet-ridden cranes seemingly giving them all the middle finger, as a small, apparently homemade helicopter grew smaller and smaller in the distance.

* * * *

"How the hell—"

Captain Logan was at something of a loss for words when he burst into the clinic of the American consulate.

"What the—" He managed no better on his second try, standing amid the ample and various activities going on in what he always thought would be a small, simple room.

In the far corner, Esherida Rahal was standing between two beds that lay beside several tables full of scientific equipment. On one lay a comatose Terri Nichols, only this time without her eye covering. On the other lay Josiah Key. They were attached by blood transfusion tubing. Standing beside him was a protective, encouraging Morton Daniels.

"Is that the best you can do?" Logan heard in his ear. He spun to look up at General Charles Lancaster, retired.

"Well, after what you've been through, I can't say I'm surprised." Lancaster, still wearing his uniform, walked by him. As he went, he called out to the beds, "You'll be happy to know the bird is stowed."

The men nodded with appreciation and relief.

"What bird?" Logan asked suspiciously.

"As if you didn't know." Lancaster sat at a simple metal desk in the opposite corner, then motioned for Logan to join him. "A remarkable flying machine designed and piloted by the mechanic who created the crane yo-yo we also required. And all with remarkable speed. All with proper airspace permissions, I assure you. I believe you've already met the man in question. But no matter. He'll be here presently."

Logan just stared at the retired general, trying to regain his moral equilibrium. "How did you do it?" he finally asked. "How did you even know?"

"Despite appearances, we've been working on this project for some time." Lancaster sniffed, looking at Key and Daniel. "But we couldn't have done this particular operation without two great Americans," he said flatly. "The first is a man named Dale Hood. He supplied intel he acquired at great personal risk." Lancaster locked eyes with Logan. "Lost his way for a while, and may do so again, but when it came right down to it, he was a true American patriot."

Logan thought he got the message, but was about to find out he hadn't quite. "And who was the second?" he asked resentfully.

"You," Lancaster said with a knowing smile.

"Me?" Logan was flabbergasted as he thought about the secrecy and security he had gone through to attend the weapons auction. "How did you even know where I was?"

Lancaster snorted. "Easy, we bugged you like you bugged them." He motioned toward the soldiers. "But nothing so crude as injected trackers. Remember when I was so chummy with you before? I rubbed an odorless liquid on your neck that could be traced." Lancaster looked at Rahal. "The Cerberus labs are far more advanced than the Marines'. But even we need to pool resources every now and again."

"It has to be in her chromosomes," Rahal interrupted. "I've been working on this since Dr. Davi first collected samples in Shabhut. Infected men became explosive, but not women."

"Wait a minute," Daniels said. "What about the women at Club Blue?"

Key looked over with a placid expression. "Those were transvestites," he told his friend. "Didn't you see that?"

Daniels looked at him with skepticism.

Key shrugged. "I thought it was obvious."

Logan, finally unable to control the abuse on his ego, slammed his hand on the desk.

Everyone except Lancaster flinched.

"I've had it with your smartass attitude, Corporal." Logan stood. The man's cavalier attitude was infuriating, especially after he rode a hundred and eighty-foot crane sheave to pull off a magic trick amidst some of the most severe security possible. "Where do you get off being so smug in this mess?"

Key looked up in all seriousness and opened his mouth to answer, but Lancaster beat him to it. "That's sergeant major, Logan. I wasn't joking about that. He's with Cerberus now, and if I have to promote him to full major, I will."

Logan looked around the room as if it were a madhouse. "Cerberus? What the hell is Cerberus anyway?"

"Dog who guarded the gates of hell, I think," Key offered.

Lancaster was about to elaborate in no uncertain terms when another, lightly accented, voice came from the door.

"Excuse me, sir." They all turned to see Manuel Gonzales. "You too, Captain. Think you both better come see this." The man's expression and tone cut through even Logan's outrage.

Leaving Rahal, Key, and Nichols behind, they marched down the consulate hall toward the communications center. Lancaster was striding with such certainty that he soon passed even Gonzales, allowing Daniels to catch up with his old friend.

"What's up?" he whispered.

"Faisal and I were clued in as we were coming back from the garage," Gonzales whispered in return. "Surveillance satellite picked up something in south Yemen."

"Something bad?" Daniels asked blankly, trying to get his head around it. He was still trying to get his head around everything.

"Something very bad," Gonzales said as Lancaster and Logan went into the comm center. "Something end-of-the-world bad."

Chapter 29

Tell me what I need to know.

Key didn't actually say that as he stood in the doorway of the briefing room onboard the USS *Leon Amphibious* Transport Dock. It would have been too limiting. After all, why leave it up to his listeners to determine what was important or not? Even if they told the truth, it would inevitably be interpretive, subjective.

He did, however, hold up a forefinger to let Eshe Rahal and General Lancaster know when he wanted to listen to what Captain Logan was saying to the expeditionary warfare unit and rapid deployment force commanders gathered within.

"I know this is even a more sudden notice than usual," Logan said, "but we have no choice."

Key decided the captain wasn't bending the truth even a little. The mission had come together quickly after Lancaster had seen the satellite video. Even in radiant imaging, the moving pictures were unmistakable. It was a horde of literally uncountable creatures sweeping across the Yemen countryside, laying waste to whatever was in their way.

Within seconds, the general was communicating with his contacts, making Logan feel impelled to do the same. Cerberus apparently had great clout to convince normally cagey politicians of the urgency. Whatever the protocol and chain of command, the order came back to do what was necessary to halt, contain, or even eradicate the threat.

Key pointed at the general.

"I tapped into the comm noise throughout the country," Logan said.

He, too, wanted to hear what Logan ordered. The man might be an overly ambitious bureaucrat at heart, but he was Operation Arachnosaur's commander, simply by being in the right place at the wrong time. In other words, no one in authority could get anyone of higher rank or greater experience there in a timely fashion.

"Usual extremist bullcrap in the north," Lancaster said, once more inwardly cursing that he had retired, and couldn't lead the attack himself, "but the south was full of hysterical radio calls about monsters that gutted everyone." The general was both regretful and relieved that Yemen was not a more modern country. The word would have gone out faster if the mountain villages had smartphones, but it would have started an international panic, and the sociopolitical clusterfuck that always engendered.

Key held up his finger. Logan was talking again. "We are dealing with a force of spider-like creatures, who, according to reports, are as large as wolves, but fast and vicious. Their eight legs end, apparently, in razor-sharp pincers that have been reported to be able to dissect a human or animal within seconds."

The landing force commanders couldn't stay silent at that. As they buzzed amongst each other, Key pointed at Rahal.

"Most spiders are solitary or even aggressive toward each other," she said, "but not these. They've developed, evolved."

"'Evolved,'" he said. "From *what*?"

"We don't know," she admitted. "Most likely, whatever root produced the familiar spiders people know and don't love so much."

"How many?" Key returned to more urgent matters.

Rahal was unfazed by his rapid shifts, his desire to pin this down in his own brain. She, better than anyone alive, knew the urgency of the situation. "Studies have counted certain colonies of modern spiders numbering as many as fifty thousand—"

Lancaster cursed under his breath.

"Yes," she said. "A formidable number. But these were restricted to a cave hollow, and must have cannibalized each other to survive. I estimate—hope—no more than two hundred."

"Two hundred or two hundred *thousand*?"

"The former," she reassured him.

Key held up his forefinger again.

"It is vital for you to know," Logan said, "that these spider things do not create standard webbing. Instead they emit thin strands that can—" The captain paused, scarcely believing what he was about to say. "That can cause male blood to boil and detonate if you come into contact with it."

"Detonate," Key repeated carefully. "Explode?"

"Violently," the captain answered. "Think of it as the obscene bloat that comes from the venom of a lethal creature like the coral snake, only accelerated, with greater inflation and beyond the point of bursting."

The buzz that ensued after that bombshell put the first to shame. Key knew what was coming next, so he pointed at Rahal again.

"I still don't know enough because Private Nichols is the only survivor," she said. "She's awake, but confused. Apparently her captors thought they could control her through the light in her eyes. Tests on her transfused blood suggest that she could transmit the toxicity with a touch." Key raised his finger.

"We will do everything possible not to come into contact with these creatures," Logan said, "but it should be obvious that our frontal force should consist of as many females as possible."

Key grimaced a mirthless, sympathetic, grin for poor Logan. His mind unavoidably went back to the days when African Americans were used as cannon fodder as recently as the Korean War. His pointing at Rahal now took on an ironic edge.

"Has to be the double-X chromosome," she stressed. "Men have an X and Y chromosome—women have two X chromosomes. It's a difference of only seventy-eight genes, but one of those has to be a corrective component for the ammonia picrate and picric acid."

Key nodded, almost unconsciously, his forefinger drooping to a forty-five-degree angle as he thought about all the obsessive research he had been doing about spiders since discovering his adversary.

"It is an absolute imperative," Logan said, "that we stop these things before they reach the coast." He did not need to say why. Everyone knew that if they could move underwater, remain near the surface where the pressure wouldn't crush them, they could spread throughout the world with virtually no possible opposition. For that matter, their exoskeletons could make it possible for them to withstand the seabed. Certain species of crab did.

"Any progress?" Lancaster asked Rahal.

Rahal gave Key a meaningful look, which he missed, before returning the general's stare. "Only the most rudimentary," she admitted, "but I'm truly doing the best I can."

"I know you are," Lancaster assured her, his hand on her shoulder. "If you join Cerberus, I assure you the finest facilities possible—"

"If there's any Cerberus left to join." Logan was suddenly at their shoulders in the doorway, trying to sidle past as the commanding officers behind them fell out to find female volunteers in their units. "You'll be happy to know, I suppose, that we've found and arrested Jean Bernard Toussaint."

"Great work, Captain." Lancaster grunted, stepping away so Logan could get past. "We need the ventriloquist; you got the dummy."

That snapped Key out of his reverie. He and Lancaster shared a silent glance. Both knew, but neither needed to say, that Usa Awar was still in the wind, and, for all they knew, could have been in Timbuktu by now. Instead of checking on the terrorist weapon dealer's whereabouts, the Captain had spent all his free time trying to deny Cerberus's influence. As Logan sourly went, double-time, back to his command center, Key and Rahal followed Lancaster up the stairs toward the deck of the Leon.

They emerged into bright ocean sunlight where the Arabian Sea met the Gulf of Aden. Normally the Leon stayed in the southern Red Sea, many nautical miles to the west, but extraordinary times called for extraordinary locations. One thing it had in common with its usual location was proximity to the Arleigh Burke class destroyer, the USS Nexus. Both had been ordered into position off the coast of Yemen as soon as the threat had been discovered.

They did not have far to go. US Navy ships had been a common sight in the waters off Yemen, to prevent any threat to the three million barrels of oil that cruised by every day. The entire area of Yemen, Oman, and the United Arab Emirates were about as large as the east coast of the United States, so travel time was not a desperate concern, especially with the jets and helicopters available to the Marines and Cerberus.

As soon as Key, Lancaster, and Rahal appeared, Gonzales and Daniels flanked them, all heading for CJ-the-jet, where Faisal awaited in the cockpit. It was parked on the corner edge of the Leon's flight deck. Luckily, the LPD—landing platform/dock—had already been at full alert, so it incorporated a hanger facility as well as a flight deck for planes and copters, and a well deck for landing craft and amphibious vehicles. They were going to need all of them if they were going to pull this off.

Lancaster stopped Key before he started up the jet's steps. Key turned back to the general without reluctance. He knew if Lancaster had something to say it would be important. And it wouldn't be about the immediate mission. They both already knew that, while the newly dubbed sergeant major was not part of Logan's attack force, he was reluctantly allowed to serve as observer and consultant.

Daniels was just behind Key, listening intently, but all the preparations for the assault was drowning out the words, even though he was only inches away.

"I thought you should know that I was the reason you went to Shabhut in the first place," Lancaster said in Key's ear. "Davi was a double agent, so we've known about, and been working on, the situation for some time.

But powers that were made a deal with the Awar devil when he contained these monsters. I kept pushing until the order went out to clean Shabhut. That's when FUBAR took over."

Every soldier knew that acronym. Fucked Up Beyond All Reason.

"Your unit went in ignorant," Lancaster confessed, "inadvertently empowering Awar. Now you got to correct my mistake. Got it?"

Key turned his head and looked directly at Lancaster. The expression on the general's leathery, lined face was one of conviction and faith. He had been looking to recruit the ex-corporal ever since he saw Key's battlefield report.

All the sergeant major did now was nod, then look at Rahal as she stood beside the tall, tough, old war bird. Her expression held the same concern it had since they returned with Nichols inside the steel coffin. She impulsively grabbed his hand, jumped up, and kissed him full on the mouth.

She was the first to turn and head toward the Leon's control tower. With raised eyebrows, Lancaster shrugged and followed. Key stepped back into Gonzales's private jet, finding she had left a note in his hand. As Daniels stood beside him, watching the scientist and military man go, Key read.

Be aware.

He looked up from the two simple words, back to where Rahal was nearing the pilot house bridge. As she took the first step onto the steel ladder leading to it, she turned her head and looked back at him. Even from fifty yards away, he could see the concern in those deep eyes of hers. He knew she had wanted to question his decision to be part of the operation, especially so soon after the transfusion, but he also knew she knew it would be useless, even foolish, to do so. Key could no sooner stay behind, even if he had given more blood, than she could stop caring.

Their gaze was ended only by Faisal closing the jet door. Key turned, slipping the paper into the pocket of his gear, and strode toward his seat. He sat down and buckled up next to Daniels as the sergeant leaned back and spoke to the ceiling.

"I've been meaning to ask Lionheart all along," he said with exaggerated casualness. "What does Cerberus mean, anyway? Monsters of North America Really Come Hither? The Monsters of North America part works okay. After all, he came up with it to 'investigate national and international threats beyond those of normal military protocol,' right? But I've been having a hell of a time with the rest." He was silent, but only for a moment. "Or *maybe* it's not an acronym, eh? Maybe it just means king, like in the old movie *King Dinosaur* about just the biggest goddamn—"

"Shut up, Sergeant," Key said evenly, preparing for a fight unlike any other he had ever experienced. Then suddenly he knew. Not what Cerberus meant, but why Lancaster had promoted him to sergeant major rather than the six ranks between, including sergeant and corporal. "And that's an order from a superior officer."

Chapter 30

The command center on the USS *Nexus* looked almost the same as the one on the USS *Leon*. They were both dark enclosures with a wall of monitors that curved around a communications console which was manned by four Navy specialists.

Captain Patrick Logan sat just behind the quartet in the center of the one on Nexus. Lancaster and Rahal stood behind the men in the one on Leon. The captain was planning to refuse the general's and scientist's presence on the destroyer, but Lancaster hadn't even asked. To the general, Logan looked like Captain Kirk on the bridge of the starship *Enterprise*, and, to the Cerberus man's mind, he was trying to act like him too.

Logan is no Kirk, Lancaster thought. That go-get-'em quality in *Star Trek* was missing. In its place was calculation, the man's eyes moving like little machines.

On all the screens were images from the forward formation of drones. They had swept inland, and had started picking up the movement of the monsters within minutes.

"We were just in time," Lancaster rumbled. "Even an hour more and we would have been too late."

The men in Gonzales's jet heard everything. All communications were patched into CJ, and anything they said in the air could also be heard by Lancaster and Rahal on the sea. Gonzales had all the jet's outside lenses focused on the ground as he repeatedly came in low. The creatures showed the same disinterest in the jet as they would any bird.

"Wish we were outfitted with napalm," Gonzales muttered. "Or, at least bombs."

"We're observation, consulting, noncombatants," Key grumbled. "But let's see if we can give them something to consult about."

Gonzales came around for another pass, careful not to block the sightline of any drone below them.

"Do we have a count?" Logan asked flatly.

A Navy man at the console used recognition software to seek out anything of spider shape. "One hundred eighty-three, sir."

"Are they all here?" Rahal asked.

They could hear everything from the Lexus command post, but Logan could hear nothing from the Leon, unless a control board sailor contacted him directly. To Lancaster's growing disgust, the captain had cited something about not wanting any unnecessary distractions.

"Let's hope so," the general answered the scientist.

Rahal leaned closer, her face troubled. "Why haven't any Houthi, Hadi Government, or even Al-Qaeda forces taken these creatures on?"

"They're almost exclusively in the cities to the west—" Lancaster began, but was interrupted by one of the control board men.

"Ma'am," he said, pointing. "Ma'am?"

Lancaster and Rahal looked to where the sailor was pointing, a screen on the far right. A drone had spotted a group of three locals with rifles, crawling on top of a bluff, above the arachnosaurs which were pouring down the valley below.

"It's like an *Old Testament* plague," Rahal remarked. Then she said, "Maybe they were."

"Good men," Lancaster said, interested right now only in results, not context or philosophy. "This will help us estimate the creature's vulnerabilities."

The men took positions, aimed, and started firing.

"They've hit one, sir," reported a sailor, pointing. As they shifted their gazes to that screen, they all saw a creature rear up on its hind legs and start to shake.

"They got him." Lancaster smiled. But Rahal was not so easily convinced.

"Wait," she said. "I recognize that movement. Widen your focus," she instructed the sailor, then remembered who and where she was. "Please."

But even before she said the magic word, he was already pulling back the lens so they could see around the area more fully. The creatures had stopped swarming and appeared to be maneuvering.

"Can it be?" Rahal asked.

"Can it be what?" Lancaster demanded.

"It's mimicking!" Rahal exclaimed. When she saw the perplexed expressions around her, she quickly continued. "Look, look, at what the others are doing!" She pointed at the screen, to where several other creatures were racing up the bluffs from the side and back.

"The bastards are ambushing our guys!" Lancaster seethed.

Rahal peered even closer at the screen, her troubled expression now also amazed. "They're displaying cooperative division of labor, like ants, but with greater mobility...agility."

"Stop admiring them," Lancaster snapped.

Rahal was taken aback but apologized under her breath. He was right, in his brusque way; she was learning, but he was fighting. She'd forgotten her place.

No one had to ask if the creatures' new skills were bad, for, in the next moment, the three encircling arachnosaurs pounced. The humans all watched in dismay and disgust as the three villagers were clutched by black claws, held firm, penetrated, and burst open like erupting stove-top popcorn. Then all the attacking monsters pumped bulbous, thick sputum into the torn-open cavities, before speeding down to rejoin the main throng.

"I need to see those eggs," Rahal cried. "We have to get samples of those things!"

"We'll do our best." Lancaster growled as a sailor passed on the request to the Lexus. "But first things first."

Obviously the Nexus had seen enough. They all heard the thundering boom of the destroyer's Tomahawk missile launchers, and watched as Gonzales's jet retreated before the thousand-pound high explosives smashed into the countryside. The valley erupted into yellow-orange flame and grey-white smoke that sent the drone cameras spinning.

When the smoke cleared, everyone in the Leon control room could hear everyone in the Nexus control room cheering. When the drone views came back into focus the valley looked like scorched, empty, earth.

Lancaster straightened, his smile growing, but Rahal all but put her face onto the nearest screen. "No, no, look!"

One arachnosaur after another reemerged from what appeared to be organic trapdoors in the dirt.

"They were burrowing," she cried. "The missiles may have gotten some, but not nearly enough."

"Jesus Christ on a crutch!" the general boomed. "What else can these things do?" He looked at Rahal. "Awright. *Now* I'm listening."

Rahal turned to Lancaster, her face haunted. "Have you ever stepped on a spider?" she asked pointedly.

"Of course."

"Multiply that by a thousand or more."

"That doesn't help me," he said. It was almost an accusation.

"No, and this won't either," she said. "These spiders can step back. They can grab your foot and kill you with just that."

"So what do we *do*?"

"Shit," Key muttered in their ears. "We'll have to attack."

"No," Lancaster said. "They will."

And, as he said it, they started. The Nexus's two Sea Hawk helicopters, and the Leon's two Sea Dragon helicopters, took off from their decks and sped inland. Gonzales's jet stayed far out of the way, as the choppers came in fast and low before unloading all their Hellfire missiles directly at the front line of scurrying creatures.

The missiles lived up to their names. The already pounded countryside exploded again as the copters soared away to avoid shrapnel. Then, even before the dust settled, all four choppers came back to strafe the area with their door-loaded M60 machine guns and GAU-17 miniguns.

"Not so low!" Rahal cried. "Tell them not to come in so low!"

But, incredibly, one of the sailors, apparently high on hope, faced her with an assured expression. "Don't worry, ma'am, our boys know what—"

Lancaster furiously grabbed the man's swivel chair and spun it around to face the screen, just as an arachnosaur leaped from the smoke like a demon from the pit and slammed into the side of a Sea Hawk.

"Holy shit," the sailor shouted, scrambling for the send switch of his comm. But it was too late. Everyone on the Nexus already knew.

"I'm a fool," Rahal gasped hollowly. "Of course they can perform every basic function *any* spider can do. All modern spiders evolved from them."

Before Lancaster could question what that meant, Key's voice was in their ears. "They can hunt on land or water. They can jump."

He stopped when the helicopters started flying in a specific pattern of alternating teamwork, each targeting specific creatures and pumping bullets at them.

"No, get them away," Rahal yelled. "We haven't seen the worst yet."

The sailor who had turned spoke intently into his mike, then fell silent, listening. When he turned back to them, his face was haggard. "Captain Logan said 'Stand down. Stand down and shut up.' He says, 'they know what they're doing.'"

General Lancaster went very still as tears dropped slowly out of Rahal's eyes.

"My God," she said. It was a realization.

"What?" Lancaster snapped.

"The webs," she said. "We haven't seen the webs yet."

They didn't have to wait long. Just as the dust settled again, a silky, gleaming strand shot out into the sky and slapped onto the circular rotor compartment of one of the copters. It suddenly became the end of a swinging club.

"'Capture blob,'" Key said miserably. "Bola spiders hunt by snagging prey with—"

He was cut off by the searing, shredding sound of the helicopter crashing into the ground. Its rotors shredded, tearing into the arachnosaur that downed it.

But no one celebrated. Landing craft was already belching from the Leon's gut, the forward sections filled with female soldiers.

"Fall back," Rahal choked. "Retreat."

"We can't," Lancaster said quietly. "No matter what, we can't let them reach the sea."

They watched in silence as the remaining helicopters landed at the beachhead, and a small unit jumped out to await the others. As soon as the humans appeared, the inland arachnosaurs began to congregate.

"They have enhanced eyesight," Key informed them.

"What are they doing?" One sailor gaped.

"I recognize it," Lancaster said grimly. "They're getting into formation."

"They're displaying hive mentality again." Rahal groaned as if she were intoning a death knell.

A long row of creatures at the back turned, and, almost as one, their opisthosoma rose.

"I...I believe they're going to shoot their webbing," Rahal said.

"From that distance?" The sailor moaned.

Rahal didn't need to answer. The monsters lifted their abdomens higher. Since the weight of the webbing was greater than that of a normal spider, it would have to travel farther, with greater propulsive force. The display was something vile and dark, confident, contemptuous of any other life-form.

"Like tanks getting ready to fire," Lancaster said with fear and awe.

A spreading mesh of webbing erupted into the air, creating a lace roof over the countryside. It drifted upward like spray from a lawn sprinkler, then began to descend like a net.

They watched as, obviously on orders, the women soldiers ran forward, bringing their M249 SAWs, fifty-caliber machine guns, eighty-one millimeter mortars; and M203, MK19, and M32 grenade launchers to bear.

"Flamethrowers," Rahal whispered. "Don't they have flamethrowers?"

"They were phased out in 1978," Key said gently.

They all fell silent again. Logan smugly ordered, "Unleash hell."

Lancaster closed his eyes and shook his head.

The landing force opened fire, and, again, the countryside near the sea exploded with lead, explosions, and flames. The rear line of monsters remained, but the rest, as if they had nothing else to lose, charged at top speed toward the firepower. But they did not go directly. They dodged and weaved faster than the assault troops thought possible.

The Cerberus unit watched from the air and sea as the creatures, as well as their webbing, got nearer and nearer the troops. Soon, the men didn't care about their orders. They refused to stay behind. They joined the women on the front line, targeting and firing fiercely. As the pincers and mesh got ever closer, they, too, seemed to feel they had nothing left to lose.

Lancaster had experienced defeat before. Then, as now, he saw what was going to happen. Here, the women would be ripped open while the men would explode apart. The enemy would reach the water, floating on a bridge of blood.

"Leon!" Key blurted. "General, you're on the Leon?"

"Of course I'm on the Leon," Lancaster bellowed. "What are you—"

Key was already telling Gonzales, "Fly directly into the web net from the side. Like clearing a doily from a table."

Lancaster was opening and closing his mouth in confusion when the sergeant major returned his attention to him. "General," he barked. "LaWS!"

Lancaster was stunned by the revelation. "Yes!" he barked back, and was already racing for the door. "Of course!"

"What?" Rahal asked as Gonzales's jet began to come around the edge of the beachhead. "What?"

"The Leon field-tested the AN/SEQ-3 Laser Weapon System three years ago," Key all but yelled. He pronounced it "Ann-sec-three."

"The US Navy reported that it worked perfectly." Lancaster ran onto the deck, scouring it for the telltale planetarium-shaped turret. "There," he boomed, spotting it at the crown of the bridge, and racing toward it.

"But how can it help us now?" Rahal demanded helplessly.

"Light, Eshe, it's concentrated light. We've all seen the webbing. We all saw what it can do. Even fire might not destroy it, but—"

"Light," Rahal said. "Yes, it could work!"

"No time for chain of command," Key said. "Have flight traffic control ready 'cause we're about to be flying blind."

Rahal was initially confused by Key's last comment, but then Gonzales's plane flew into the east side of the canopy of webbing, and pulled it along like a pole sliding aside a curtain.

CJ couldn't clear it all. Some strands broke off and floated down just as the first few arachnosaurs reached the front line.

Rahal had to look away as even some soldiers who managed to unload their weapons directly in the faces of the creatures were flayed open. More soldiers pumped lead into the monsters, but the beasts seemed to compartmentalize the damage, like a stricken ship closing off compartments. Their legs still swung and spasmed, ripping open flesh with every twitch. And unlike the humans, there was no sign that these creatures felt pain. There was just the punch and brief delay of the gunfire and then they moved again.

"Now hear this, now hear this." The announcement went through every inch of the Leon. "All LaWS personnel report to your stations immediately."

Rahal couldn't tell whether it was the retired general's voice or the ship's commander. It didn't matter. She turned back to the screens just in time to see some of the male soldiers start to shake uncontrollably.

"Sergeant Major," Lancaster said. "Order or no order, we're ready here. What do we target?"

"Wait," Key said tightly, trying to find any place on the jet's windshield that wasn't completely obscured by the webbing.

"If that shit gets in the engine—" Gonzales whispered to Faisal. "Prep the parachutes."

"Don't bother," Daniels said from the cockpit door. He was wearing one and holding three others.

On the beach, the first soldier's head exploded.

"Wait for what?" Lancaster demanded.

"Look!" Rahal pointed at the screen. "The back line of beasts is preparing to shoot more webbing!"

"Of course," Lancaster said through a wide wolf's grin. "Hive mentality. You got rid of their last net, so—"

"Wait until all their webs first intersect," Key said, standing between the pilot and copilot's seats. "As soon as they do, light the fuse."

Lancaster looked down at the lone man in the overalls that bore an octagonal LaWS patch. He sat in a cushioned office chair before three computer monitors, holding a joystick in his lap, his right thumb on the top of it.

"Can you do that?" Lancaster asked the young sailor. The sailor just smiled like a kid who had just set a new videogame's high score.

Two more soldiers on the beach tore open from within themselves. They looked like they were being ripped inside out by unseen claws. Rahal wanted to turn away again, but could not, as more soldiers, both men and women, blasted at the creatures while their flesh was shredded.

"Come on." She fumed at the back row of arachnosaurs with their rear abdomens in the air. "Come on!"

As one, the rear row started spraying webbing. The organic lattice coursed into the sky and then, at a uniform high point, their ends started to spread and interweave.

"What is it, sentient fucking web?" Lancaster boomed.

Inside the small LaWS control box, Lancaster found he was holding his breath as the laser sights tracked the infrared movement of the webbing—each entwining from left to right, one after another.

"Come on," Lancaster joined Rahal's underbreath chant. "Come on!"

The last web linked. The LaWS tech's left thumb tapped once.

Everyone who could looked skyward as the entire web lit up, then, like individual lightning bolts, lanced back to their sources. The entire line of arachnosaurs—a hundred strong—exploded as if they were humans touched by their own webbing.

Chapter 31

Gonzales landed blind.

He had a choice: ditch the jet and parachute out, or land it on the rocking deck of the USS *Leon* by instruments alone. Actually, not quite alone. Virtually every pilot onboard the amphibious transport dock was willing to talk him in after what he and the others had done. Even General Lancaster was on his way to air traffic control to lead the way.

"I know CJ better than I know myself," he had said. "After all, I haven't stuck my face or fingers into my own guts. So guess what I'm doing?"

Key, Daniels, and Faisal stayed onboard with him, although the sergeant looked at the parachutes with just a touch of disappointment. Daniels would have bungee-jumped into hell just for the, well, hell of it.

Once they landed on the abbreviated flight deck of the Leon—Gonzales having made it look easy, although they all knew how hairy it actually was—the four stepped out into a mop-up confrontation. After the bulk of the arachnosaurs had been destroyed by the web-igniting laser weapon, the remaining creatures were digitally targeted and physically hunted down with a vengeance. Logan practically exulted in every image of a bullet-ridden creature dancing its death throes. After a hard-fought half-hour, the situation seemed to be under such firm control that the captain was hurrying to a surviving chopper to supervise the remainder of the rout himself.

But not alone. Lancaster was snapping at his heels, his set expression informing Key that the retired general was ready to bite the heads off wickets. Once the jet quartet neared, they could even hear the men's combative conversation.

"You have no right to ask anything of me," Logan yelled over his shoulder. "I keep telling you that you have absolutely no authority here. You keep not hearing me! You gave that up when you retired, remember? But even that's not the important thing. You're lucky I don't have you thrown in the brig for the illegal seizure and use of military property."

The words might as well have been sea spray for all the effect they had on Lancaster. "*I'm* lucky?" he snapped, not slowing a bit. "Without that seizure and use, the only thing you'd have authority over would be the worst disaster in human history. Now are you giving us"—he motioned at Rahal behind him and the four men from the jet who were approaching from the other direction—"a ride to the beach or not?"

Logan stopped in his tracks and faced the retired general. "One thing is debatable and one isn't," he said. "Worst disaster? I, for one, have and had, supreme faith in my troops to turn the tide, with or without your self-proclaimed, illegal, help. As for hitching a ride on an official US Navy transport?" He stuck his forefinger in Lancaster's face. "You are not official US Navy personnel. You are not official US military anything." He looked at all of them. "None of you are. Not anymore."

"We'll see about that," Lancaster said, looking at Logan's finger like it was a corn dog.

"Yes, I'm sure you will," Logan replied defiantly. "But not today, and not now. So if you'll excuse me, civilian, I have an operation to complete." Logan hopped aboard the Sea Dragon, and all but gave them the finger.

Every other soldier and sailor onboard looked at them with expressions that shouted, "We would if we could but we can't," as well as other things that were just too profane to translate.

The copter lifted off.

When the rotor noise finally subsided, Daniels said, "What. An. Asshole."

The general shook his head and turned back toward the bridge, the others right behind him. "Just misguided," he said almost sadly.

"Ambitious." Gonzales sighed.

"Frightened," Rahal suggested.

"Insecure," Key added.

At the base of the bridge ladder, Lancaster stopped and faced them. "We're on the same side, but have different goals." He looked off as the Sea Dragon swept down toward the still active beachhead. "He wants to get ahead. I just want to save my country."

"Yeah." Daniels summed it up for them. "He wants to kiss ass, and you want to kick ass."

Lancaster chuckled, despite the situation, then turned to Gonzales. "You still got that whirly thing you patched together to airlift Private Nichols out?"

The mechanic shared a look with Faisal, who nodded conspiratorially. "Yeah, we hid it below decks, with, I might add, the enthusiastic cooperation of the crew."

"Then what are we waiting for?" Lancaster demanded.

They were airborne within minutes. There was no problem getting permission. Logan may have been commander of the attack force, but the USS *Leon*'s commander wanted to give Lancaster a medal. Since Gonzales had created the heli-thing to transport four men and the captive private as well as a metal coffin, carrying the six-person Cerberus team was not an issue.

They landed off-site of the main battleground, at about the place the jet would have ditched if the mechanic had decided to do that. Before they hopped out, Faisal opened a long metal box behind the seats and handed each man a M240, and gave Rahal, in deference to her size, a Glock 26 automatic. She accepted it without a word of protest.

"The spider has a central nervous system made up of two cords that run below their abdomens," she told them as they started along the water's edge. "With nerve cell clusters as control centers in all their limbs. Their brain is made up of several nerve cell clumps set both ahead and behind their mouths."

"So avoid the legs if they come at you," Key added, "but aim at, and eradicate, their snouts."

"But we're not here for bloody revenge," Lancaster said over his shoulder. "We're here for intel."

"And eggs," Rahal said.

"Yeah, those fucking eggs," Daniels said. "That shit they dump into the bodies of whoever they tear open."

"Logan will definitely try to get all of them," Lancaster warned. "He still wants to have his DoD cake and eat it too." By then they all knew Logan's main goal was to make sure any weaponized creature would be Department of Defense property. "So do what you have to, short of getting arrested. We still need all of you, no matter what happens here."

They soon saw the bulk of the assault team cleaning up the beach head. If their professional behavior was any evidence, the heat of battle was over. But the crowning clue was Logan, who stood amongst them, beaming like Patton on the Western Front. Lancaster even saw him trying to arrange a picture with him putting one foot on a fallen arachnosaur, until saner heads convinced him it would be a mistake.

The four men and one woman scoured the area, but could find no untended arachnosaur, or human, corpses.

"Well, I'll give the son of a bitch one thing." Lancaster growled. "He came prepared."

Already there were more hazmat-suited figures on the beach, and across the countryside, than there were soldiers in tactical gear.

Rahal found she was biting her lower lip as her eyes focused on the landing crafts being filled with the wounded. To her dismay, and building anger, the hazmatted figures far outnumbered the medical staff. She felt a reassuring hand on her shoulder, but was surprised when she turned, to find it was Gonzales.

"No, no," he assured her. "That's a good sign. More dead monsters, less dead us."

She nodded, then stopped looking for unguarded arachnosaurs, and started looking for a missing member of the Cerberus team.

"Where's Joe?" she asked.

Her question seemed to reach each Cerberus man like a mosquito flitting from ear to ear. One by one they, too, started looking around for something other than Logan, his people, and prehistoric spiders.

"Here," Key said over the comm-links. Gonzales's comm-links were so small and comfortable, they had nearly forgotten that they still had them in their aural cannels. Key gave them his longitude and latitude. "Come on up," he invited, "but try not to be obvious doing it."

The experienced soldiers and mechanics knew exactly where Key was, but they put on a fairly convincing, as well as subtle, show of frustration that the beachhead was locked down tight. They wandered back the way they came, seemingly in resignation, but once they were out of sight of the captain and his core crew, they moved north into the hills.

They found Key kneeling by four corpses, three human and one arachnosaur, on the bluff where three brave villagers had their last stand against a mimicking monster.

"This one gave its life so these three could be ambushed," Lancaster said, pointing at the fallen arachnosaur, then the gutted trio.

"I guess the search software only homes in on living creatures," Gonzales said.

"Like us?" Daniels asked.

"They're not programmed for 'us' shapes," Key informed him. "Just spider shapes."

Only he and Lancaster didn't grimace when Rahal immediately fell to her knees and shoved her arms, up to her elbows, into the soupy gunk inside the nearest human corpse.

"Don't you need a hazmat suit or gloves or something?" Daniels said with distaste.

"Got any?" Rahal snapped. "I guess we'll see if I do." She pulled out, and held up, one of the lumpy globs the creatures had pumped into every victim. "Did any of you sons of bitches come prepared, or do I have to carry this all the way back myself?"

Faisal was already pulling a extra-thick, lock-topped, plastic bag from his pocket. As he helped Rahal secure the sample, Lancaster turned to the others. "Get the arachnosaur back to the copter," he ordered Daniels and Gonzales. "We've got to get all of this to the best, nearest, safest, lab ASAP."

The two started back toward their transport, but stopped when Key spoke up.

"I'm not going."

Rahal stared at him in disbelief. "Why not?"

"It's not over," Key told her, then, before anyone else could complain or inquire, he spoke directly to the scientist. "You said they were displaying hive mind."

Rahal nodded.

"Who's mind?" he asked. "What's mind?" Key turned his attention to Lancaster. "After LaWS took out the bulk of them, the rest kept attacking. If the mind they were taking orders from was amongst them, they would have been confused and disorganized. Did they look confused or disorganized to you?"

Lancaster thought back carefully, then answered just as carefully. "No."

Key stood, looking at the others. "Best intel then said they all escaped from the home hive, and swept toward the sea. Best intel now says that all the escapees are here. No stragglers." He glanced at the dead thing in Daniels and Gonzales's hands. "No living stragglers, at any rate." He returned his gaze to Rahal. "What's the operative word in my lecture?"

Lancaster rolled his eyes. "Sergeant Major, this is no time for rid—"

"Home." Rahal's quiet answer cut through the retired general's frustration.

Key nodded, not at all happily. "Home," he repeated. "There's no place like the home hive." He stood at attention in front of Lancaster. "Permission to return to Shabhut," he said. "Sir."

Chapter 32

"No."

That's what it came down to. Lancaster would have loved to have contacted anyone else to get Key military backup for his return to Shabhut, but time was of the essence.

When Lancaster approached the C-130 Hercules cargo jet on the USS *Nexus*, where Logan was supervising the loading of his arachnosaur samples, the captain clearly had visions of major, colonel, or even brigadier general bars dancing in his brain. So no request, no matter how logical, was going to distract him from his planned presentation of total triumph to his superiors.

The weasel, being a weasel, intrinsically knew that Lancaster would only show his face again if he needed something, something even eating a whole murder of crows wouldn't convince the gloating Logan to grant.

"Can't you get it through your armor-plated skull that we've won?" He practically spat in Lancaster's face, although he nearly had to stand on his tiptoes to do it.

"Not yet," Lancaster replied, trying to kick-start Logan's self-preservation instincts. "Stopping here, stopping now, could come back to bite you on the ass, Pat."

Logan almost turned his back on the man, clearly thinking furiously. When he turned back, he had practically built a mental moat against him. He pointed at the sealed hazmat containers being loaded into the C-130's belly.

"We stopped these things from getting to the sea, *Chuck*," he blustered. "Those were my orders, and I carried them out to the letter!"

Lancaster opened his mouth to reply, but Logan beat him to it, turning tail and dismissing him with a wave. "Present intel clearly indicates

Shabhut is a ghost town." The captain sneered in parting. "A ghost town surrounded by insurgents, radicals, fanatics, and terrorists just waiting to take the head off of anyone stupid enough to show up."

Getting an idea of a good parting shot, Logan turned around, faced Lancaster and rooted himself on the *Nexus* deck. "If your people are stupid enough, have fun," he said insolently. "But my people have done their job beautifully and bravely. I'm not going to waste them on a fool's errand." With that, he finally turned heel and marched up the ramp into the *Hercules*.

Lancaster sighed and walked past Gonzales, who had been waiting a respectful distance away. "Some people are good at doing their jobs," he muttered as he fell into step beside the retired general. "Others are better at keeping theirs." When Lancaster didn't respond, Gonzales tried again in a resigned, slightly sarcastic, tone. "Well, at least he had the brains to check present intel,"

"Did he?" Lancaster asked. "How soon can you get clearance for takeoff?"

Gonzales raised his eyebrows. "The captains and commanders of these ships would kiss your ring, if you wore one. Say when."

Lancaster didn't say when. He said, "Now." And he said it in a tone that had Gonzales running to alert the others.

* * * *

Gonzales didn't say now. He said, "Wow," when he took the first look at what had happened to his Thumrait workshop.

His first surprise was when Lancaster informed him and Faisal of that destination. Given the mere seven hundred and fifty kilometers they had to traverse, CJ got them there in less than an hour.

"I hope you don't mind that I ordered some…enhancements to your place," Lancaster commented quietly as he shouldered past the mechanic. Key and Daniels wedged in the doorway on either side of Gonzales, so they all marveled at the change. Now Gonzales's projects looked like art installations dotted amongst some of the most modern, advanced tech the trio had ever seen. There was a new engineering section, a weapons armory, a communications hub, a research center with the latest computers, and a scientific/medical/laboratory area where Rahal was already poring over her samples.

Key and Gonzales stared in amazement at Lancaster, continuing to comprehend the gist of Cerberus's influence and funding.

Daniels, meanwhile, had forced his way past, and was searching, with growing irritation, for something. "What?" he complained. "No gym?"

Lancaster laughed drily. "It'll be here when you get back," he promised.

Daniels looked at him pointedly for just a second. "*If* we get back," he answered quietly, then flopped down on the shabby sofa that was left over from Gonzales's original floor plan.

His comment elicited a sharp look from Rahal, before she quickly returned to her dissecting. Key had not missed the glance, but was now distracted by Gonzales's stunned stumbling through what had been his sanctuary, and was now his wonderland.

"How—" he stammered. "I know I was gone for a while, but still—"

Lancaster approached him with a grim, yet still generous, smile. "As I believe you said to these gentlemen, you have some 'decent assistants.' You had told them of your hopes for this place, so I just supplemented them with Cerberus's needs." He looked around with satisfaction. "I knew we'd need an outpost away from Logan-ville and other pockets like it."

"Very nice," Key said honestly as he approached. "But we're only, what, eight hundred kilometers closer to Shabhut?"

Lancaster leveled him with a look. "You can't just walk in, Sergeant Major."

"Bet you that's exactly what we wind up doing," Daniels said with a ravenous grin.

Key looked from the sergeant to the retired general pointedly. Lancaster was unfazed.

"Give me a few minutes," Lancaster said evenly. "Meanwhile, take the time to rest. You're going to need it."

Key couldn't argue with that. As Daniels went to scour the weapons section, Gonzales approached the new engineering garage while motioning with his head toward the swinging door to his quarters. Key gratefully took the hint.

Apparently that had been upgraded as well. The lighting and air conditioning were equally advanced, sealing the immediate, comfortable area off from not only the workshop and the nearby airbase, but the rest of the world. The king-size platform bed had the latest in mattress and pillow advancements, and the sheets were cool to the touch.

Key was asleep almost even before his head touched them, and stayed that way until someone sat beside him. As was his wont, he was immediately awake and alert, looking up at Eshe Rahal.

She sat, one foot on the floor, the other tucked beneath her thigh, her knee pointing at him. She was wearing short-sleeve, V-neck scrubs, while her face wore an expression of respect, concern, compassion, and something else. Something he couldn't quite put his finger on.

"You're not much for small talk, are you?" she asked fondly. She laughed softly when he didn't answer, thereby answering her. Her sweet, deep laugh both itched and scratched something inside him. "Well then," she said as she slowly pulled off the scrubs top, revealing a formfitting T-shirt.

Prior to that she had always been in *abayas* or something like it. But even those robes hadn't completely submerged her youthful, womanly shape, but now her vitality was clearly partnered with her body. Whatever was left to his imagination was soon gone as she pulled the T-shirt over her head as well.

Her skin was the color of café au lait and her breasts were two of the most perfect he could imagine—not too large, small, or misshaped—as they jiggled and settled high on her chest. They were firm, yet soft, which he discovered as she slid beside him, pulling off her pants as she went. The next moment her breasts, with their nearly perfectly circular brown aureoles and nipples, were squeezed against his chest, while her elegant hands and shapely legs snaked around him.

She reached up and pulled off her headcloth, shaking loose her thick, silky, glistening, black hair. Then her deep eyes opened and sought his as her arms and legs closed. Her eyes held caring but also fear, a fear he recognized. It was the fear of losing someone before you even really found them.

"I have been waiting for this," she said tenderly. "I think you have too."

He smiled and cocked his head slightly as if considering it. "I've been *aware*," he replied kindly.

Her eyes flashed. Then her smile widened as his arms and legs wrapped around hers. "Remind me about that," she said, moving her mouth toward his. "Later." Then their lips met.

He hoped the soundproofing was as advanced as the air conditioning and lighting. It was. Within moments, he realized what the other thing that had been in her initial expression. It was not only respect, concern, and compassion, it was also passion. A passion he returned until they were moving in harmonious rhythm, locked together as a single pleasure-giving animal.

Every touch, of everything, everywhere, set off bliss in their brains until they were nearly drowning in it. He was so hard and she so soft, tight, wet, and warm that neither could completely comprehend it.

The pain of his concussion had shut down his mind. This opened it until both were clamping onto each other, hoping against hope that the sensations wouldn't diminish until they were done.

The last thing he remembered was groaning. The next thing he knew, there was a hand on his shoulder, shaking him awake. He stared up at Lancaster, Daniels, and a fully clothed Rahal by the bed, staring down at him.

"Look alive, Soldier," the retired general said. "Briefing time."

Thankfully Lancaster then turned and marched out because, on the basis of Daniels's sudden, disdainful, bewildered expression, Key's expression must've been one for the ages.

But, as the sergeant turned, Rahal took pity and shot the major an empathetic, grateful glance that told him it hadn't been a dream. Just to make sure, she waited until just before he passed her before speaking. "Yes, Joe. Time to be aware."

The four gathered around Gonzales's table, as Key and Daniels had after the infamous visit to Ayman's morgue. Although the appliances had been upgraded, thanks to Lancaster's largess, the welcoming mood was unchanged. Once everyone had the beverage of their choice, Rahal got down to business.

"They're not eggs," she reported.

"Thank God," Lancaster said.

"Maybe not," she continued. "They're arachnosaur excrement."

"What?" Daniels exploded. "Are you kidding? That stuff's spider shit?"

"Shut up, Sergeant," Key said. "Think about it. If the webbing comes out of their ass, and that makes men explode—"

Daniels frowned and looked dubiously toward the lab.

Rahal nodded. "I've found much of the same components as the webbing," she told them. "Dunnite and picric acid, but also other items I haven't completely identified yet. But yes, they could have an explosive component that we need to pinpoint and protect ourselves against."

"Christ," Key muttered. "We got organic grenades, but we don't know what the pins look like."

Rahal nodded regretfully, then turned to Lancaster. "I've gone as far as I can with this equipment, sir. You said something about a fully equipped lab?"

"Yes." The retired general grunted. "But it's not near, and we don't have the time."

"Oh, we might have plenty of time," Daniels reminded them. "We got plenty of questions, and even some answers, but we're not a step closer to Shabhut, and, with no air or ground support, who knows when we will be?"

"I do," said Gonzales, who was approaching from the new engineering section, with Faisal right behind him. "Correct me if I'm wrong, General, but the more noise they make going in, the more trouble they'll be attracting, right?" Lancaster nodded.

"Told you we'd be walking in, Joe." Daniels laughed, but with anticipation.

"Isn't that what you've wanted all along, Morty?" Key asked before turning to Lancaster. "A stealth force, in and out, right?" He couldn't help noticing Rahal blushing at that description and looking at the floor.

"That's right, Sergeant Major," Lancaster agreed. "But not a suicide squad. You've got to have at least a few people to watch your back. People we're in short supply of, I'm afraid."

"Maybe not," Rahal walked to the door of the medical clinic. "There's someone I think you should know. Someone who wants to say something to you."

She opened the door. Private Terri Nichols stood there smiling, in full uniform, her green eyes clear.

Chapter 33

Nobody, and everybody, wanted her along.

Everyone wanted Nichols to take it easy, recover completely, and use the time to revel in her second chance. But no one was going to disagree with her when she spoke.

"What's the point?" she asked, her voice strong, even, and with just a hint of an ageless Irish lilt. "Why should I revel in a second chance when there may not be one for thousands, or millions, or even no one?"

Gonzales beamed at her. It was just the way he felt. No one in this workshop did what they did looking for a recess reward or the key to a playground.

"This fucker killed my friends," she continued. "He fucked with me in the worst way, trying to make me a mindless killing machine. Well, I'm not going back looking for him, but I sure as hell will cover your ass if you do." She looked directly at Key. "And, by the way, Sergeant Major, if I do happen to run into him, I'll show him how good a killing machine I was *before* he fucked with me."

Daniels flashed a twisted, Popeye-like *she yam what she yam* grin for anyone who happened to look at him. He made as if he were about to verbalize something when Key held up a warning finger. Daniels's mouth clapped shut before he had a chance to say, *"And boy, here's a redhead who'd give a certain blonde second louie I know a run for it."* It was obvious from his expression that was suddenly what he was thinking.

"Besides," she said. "My bunkmates said we were the last ones standing when the smoke cleared. So that makes you my commanding officer, doesn't it?"

Lancaster stood. "It does. And, as the sole survivor of the unit that originally went into Shabhut, you are free to do as you please."

Key looked to Rahal with raised eyebrows. "She seems completely *compos mentis*," the scientist informed them. "The doctors of the airbase clinic and I can find no ill, or lasting effects from her ordeal at the hands of Awar's captivity, or the legs of the arachnosaur infection."

Daniels snorted with appreciation at her play-on-limbs.

"If anything, her instincts and reactions, both physical and mental, seem sharper."

Daniels pumped his fist and gave a low whistle. "Whoa," he said. "You mean we wound up with Spider Woman?"

Rahal shook her head at the sergeant. "Not quite, but it will do until we can get to that more extensive lab the general keeps alluding to."

"Retired general," Lancaster added, nodding with promise. "And not dead yet."

Rahal returned her attention to Nichols and Key. "But I'd ask you—ask you both—to be aware of not only what's happening around you, but also inside you. Be very conscious of anything your body is trying to tell you."

Key's eyebrows were getting a workout. He motioned toward Nichols, and then himself, with a shrug.

"You were connected to her via the transfusion," Rahal reminded him. "You were the first and last to give her blood once we emptied her own virulent supply. Something may have happened during the transference."

The look on her face gave Key the distinct impression that not only was there no "if" involved, but, in fact, Rahal may have seen to it. But before he could question her further, Lancaster waved them all over to a table in the engineering section. There, Gonzales and Faisal were already poring over detailed charts.

"We're using that thing Speedy made to snatch Private Nichols in the first place," Lancaster said.

When Daniels looked dubious, the mechanic reassured him. "Pieced together from the best," he explained, pointing at the thing Faisal had landed just outside. "AugustaWestland body and engine, Boeing tech, Leonardo-Finmeccanica modifications. I call her FB Law."

"What does the FB stand for?" Daniels asked.

"'Fuck Bastards,'" Gonzales answered.

"How did I miss that?"

"Right, I mean, what else? By the way, her external video cameras can sweep three hundred and sixty degrees with 4K density and even infrared."

As he spoke, Key collected two M110 SASS rifles, then handed one to the sergeant and one to the private.

"Okay." Daniels hefted the weapon in one paw. "So we can spot 'em and swat 'em one at a time, but what if there's a horde?"

Faisal took that moment to walk past, holding an M32 grenade launcher in one hand, and an M203 grenade launcher attached to an M16 assault rifle in the other. As he passed, he tossed one of the grenade canisters to Lancaster. The retired general caught it with ease.

"Modified to use the most powerful, far-reaching, and fast-spreading incapacitating agents imaginable," he said, and, after seeing Daniels's disdainful reaction, he added, "Or, if the swarm has too many stingers, the most powerful, far-reaching, and fast-spreading toxin."

"To only be used in case we need to commit suicide," Key added pointedly. "Don't want the mission fucked on a whim of the wind."

Daniels handed out the latest gas masks, which looked like a lightweight, silicon-padded cross between a jet pilot and scuba diver's head covering.

"Okay." Key sighed. "Shut up, gear up, mount up. Let's go."

They all did as he bid, except, of course, for Rahal. As they left, she approached. Not caring if anyone noticed or not, she put her right hand gently on his chest.

"Come back," she whispered.

Key was trying to formulate a reply that wasn't a stupid cliché, a hopeful lie, or impossible clairvoyance. Ultimately he settled for a smile, shrugged, and simply said the only truth he could come up with. "I'll see you. Soon."

* * * *

It was a slow, intense, hour.

Gonzales came in as low as he could, but high enough not to speed directly into any errant portable ground-to-air missile. Although he had made as many modifications as he could to protect and diminish the noise of the rotors, they still sounded like a bee swarm sizzling overhead.

Daniels and Nichols were strapped in elastic harnesses in the opposite doors, ready to use the M110s on Key's word from the video feeds at the navigator station. Gonzales and Faisal kept a sharp eye out from the pilot and copilot seats.

The difference between the Marines and Cerberus was evident in what they all wore. In addition to their toxin masks and protective helmets, Cerberus wore a tan base layer from ankle to chin, and wrist to wrist, that was the latest in air-wicking technology. Over that went a desert-camouflaged coverall that zipped and belted for an amazing fit. Key had never felt anything like it. The outfits even had their own matching, jointed, second-skin gloves, and waterproof, insulated, laceless boots.

"Cali-brake," Lancaster had informed them. "Most comfortable, effective bullet-proofing ever invented. Cerberus bought the proprietary rights. Trademarked, registered, copyrighted. Amazing what you can get if you're not trying to protect a corporate industry from competition…or extinction."

Even so, they were still lucky. The ground they rapidly covered was devoid of resistance. Key had not wanted to share his suspicions, lest he dull his team's vigilance, but he was hoping this would happen. They were making a beeline up the very same ground the arachnosaurs had swept down. It didn't take a genius to surmise that the latter occurrence probably ensured that this particular landscape would be devoid of even insurgent intruders for quite some time. Logan's supposed factual chant of "radicals, fanatics, and terrorists, oh my" be damned.

"Border of Shabhut in three minutes," Gonzales said via comm-link. Faisal had already gotten up, holding a video camera-equipped drone in his hands.

"Let it fly," Key said, keeping his eyes on the surveillance screens. Despite the power of the copter's cameras, Key wanted an even closer look.

It looked the way Dale Hood had described it to Lancaster. Abandoned, deserted, slightly shiny, clean, devoid of even Awar's guards. They had mopped up the marine corpses Key, Daniels, and Nichols had left behind, and whatever Plasticine treatment Awar had coated the structures with was still in effect.

Gonzales didn't have to ask where to land. After as thorough an examination as all of them could make by camera or eye, he brought FB Law down right next to the bunker-like burrow the American arms dealer had entered. The wheels hadn't even completely settled before Key was up, Daniels right behind him. The sergeant had switched out the M110 for his M249 SAW, while Key had a Beretta M9 at his hip and a M4 carbine in his hands.

He shared a meaningful look with Nichols before handing the private the carbine. The three stepped out, taking a second look at the village which had changed their lives. It was, thankfully, desolate, but full of bad memories. None of them showed on any of the ex-marines' faces, however.

"Test the helmet-cams," Key instructed. The trio pressed a small button at their temples, then waited for the pilot to give them the okay.

"Reading, hearing, and seeing what you are loud and clear," Gonzales told them.

Key turned back and took a bulbous pack Faisal handed him. "You know the deal," he told the pilots. "No heroic bullshit. Anything happens, *anything*, and you take the matching pack, prime it, toss it in, and take off. Got it?"

"Got it," Gonzales said, then took a position opposite Faisal to better secure their position.

Key looked from Daniels to Nichols for a second, then headed toward the bunker entrance. The sergeant thought he might have caught an oh-shit expression shooting across Key's face, but couldn't be sure.

The three clicked on their helmet headlights, and stepped into the entry hall. They heard Nichols hiss, but she didn't retreat. The shellacked cavern was the same one Dale Hood had entered, only now the guards he saw at attention were littering the floors with their vivisected, spider-shit-pumped, corpses. Thankfully the trio's gas masks handled the smell, but the sight was bad enough.

Key stiffened, alerting Daniels. "What?" the sergeant asked, then snapped his tongue. "Sir."

Key ignored the jape. "No flies. There should be flies."

"That means you were right," Rahal said in their ears. "There's probably a queen. The flies are what she's feeding on. But she herself would not be collecting them."

"Queen's consorts," Lancaster said. "How many, doctor?"

"At least two," said Rahal. "Maybe more, if she felt the need to have an attendant to cannibalize if the flies ran out."

Daniels tightened his grip on his M249. "Now I bet you're glad I brought grenades."

"I'd cite you for disrespect, if I weren't so glad," Key said as he crouched slightly. "Speedy, send in the drone." Within seconds, the small, square, four-rotored thing came swooping into the cavern. "Send it ahead."

The team watched the video images as the drone soared through the cavern halls, checking every wall and ceiling. The roaming white light indicated that they were all clear. Finally it thoroughly searched the Holy Gate chamber. It too, was clear.

"All right then, go," Key ordered, already leading the way, not stopping or turning until he entered the room with the modified airlock on the floor.

"Careful," Rahal said. "Consorts would likely be stationed in, around, or just inside the entry."

"Got it," Key said, turning toward Daniels. "You ready?"

Daniels nodded, bringing his SAW to bear. "I'm ready."

Nichols was in the process of joining him when Key stopped her. "You're the most important person in this forward unit," he told her. "You stay safe until it's time."

She looked about to complain, but then nodded submissively and stepped back behind Daniels. She didn't lower her M4, however.

Key moved quickly to the other side of the air lock, and gripped the round handle-wheel. He looked back toward Daniels, who nodded again.

"Both ahead and behind their mouths," Rahal said, then Key yanked up and back.

The arachnosaur came leaping from the air lock on astonishingly springy legs. For a frozen second the enemy was pinioned in three intersecting helmet lights, and then it raced in its hideous scuttle and took off again, directly at Daniels.

If the sergeant was fazed he didn't show it. Coolly, and with a short burst, he practically drew a dotted line around its insectoid face, that essentially punched it out with bullets. The consort dropped from the sky and slammed to the floor.

Before its legs had even stopped bouncing, Key was over it, pointing at the thing with every order. "Stuff it with grenades and use it to plug the entry hole! Kick it through just before detonation!"

Nichols thought Daniels's understanding grin would split the sergeant's face as he shoved grenades into the creature's bullet-ravaged maw, while simultaneously helping Key drag the carcass back to the Holy Gate.

"Yes, excellent!" Rahal cheered. "At least one consort, this one, would have been waiting on the ceiling just inside. Another one, likely waiting to attack whatever got past it!"

Key and Daniels slammed the creature down on the hole. Daniels moved to jump on it, but Key pushed him back. "You can hold me better than I could hold you!"

The sergeant couldn't argue, so he jumped over to the maw. Modern grenades had exact fuses, so there was no longer any second delay one way or the other. He didn't even say ready, just flicked open the pins.

"One, two, three—" they counted in unison, then Key leaped into the air.

He slammed his entire weight onto the carcass on "four." The creature fell down and through the gate on "five." Daniels grabbed Key before he tumbled in after the beast and threw himself on the ground alongside Nichols just as the grenades erupted.

Even before the last of the debris had fallen, Key was back up grabbing the drone in one hand while intensely motioning Nichols up with the other.

"Stick the camera lens just below the air lock surface," he instructed. "Keep all your digits above the lip. Speedy, can you turn the camera three-sixty?"

"Yes, sir," Gonzales responded in their ears.

"Okay," Key continued to Nichols. "Then just cram it down there."

Nichols responded in kind, grabbing the drone at the same moment she fell to her knees by the gate, quickly making sure where the camera was.

"*Hunh.*" Daniels grunted, looking at the rubberized maw of the gate. "Looks like a fucking muff."

As Nichols stuffed the thing through, careful to keep even her gloved fingers clear, Key didn't bother saying anything like "not now" or "not helping" to his friend. Keeping his eyes intent on the video feed in the corner of his goggles, he just quickly and lightly back-fisted the sergeant in the nuts.

Daniels did a quick, involuntary, seemingly German-military bow, his expression communicating that he got the message loud and clear. Then he, like the others, saw that the booby-trapped consort had done its job. Its carcass lay splattered all over the place while two more creatures lay on the web-padded floor directly under either side of the opening. One's belly was torn open, while the other had at least three ruined legs.

Daniels snatched the M4 Key had given Nichols out of her hands and shoved his M249 into her arms instead, anticipating Key's orders. "Finish them."

Without pausing, Nichols used the barrel of the SAW as a syringe directly in the center of the soiled va-jay-jay, then followed it. Both Daniels and Key grabbed her hips and legs as her top half disappeared.

From her vantage point, she saw the wounded pair bathed in her helmet light, then pounded their heads with bullets, directly in the space ahead and behind their mouths, one after another.

"Done," she reported, and, to her surprise, was immediately yanked up. "Hey," she added, "I thought I'd get a closer examination."

"Not going to risk you when we have the drone," Key snapped. "No telling what the bitch queen might do with her guards gone."

"Yes," Rahal said. "You weren't at the beach, Private. You didn't see how they could leap or lasso."

Nichols remained silent, but she may have swallowed.

"Speedy," Key said. "Study, analyze, report on the camera's input."

"We're both doing it now, Sergeant Major," Gonzales said. "Being thorough."

"Good. Anything?"

"Webs padding everywhere," Gonzales answered, "but the biggest concentration is in the farther corner, away from the ceiling opening."

"Not surprising," said Rahal. "Fairly standard arachnid camouflage behavior."

Key nodded at Daniels, who uncoiled elastic rope from his pack and knelt before Nichols. "All right, Private, you know the deal. Given your previous exposure to the webbing, and your recovery, the odds are that you're far more, if not totally, resistant to it. So it has been decided by majority rule that you go in solo."

"Not by me," Daniels grumbled as he attached a harness to Nichols.

Key ignored him. "Don't try marksmanship practice," he warned, handing her the matching pack to the one he left at the copter. "Use the SAW only if you need it to make a clear path to the target. Then prime it and toss it. We'll see that it's on target and yank you up. Right?"

"Yes, sir," she said.

"Okay." Key sighed, helping her to her feet. "Let's finish the job and get the hell out of here."

The sergeant and major took their positions on either side of the entrance. Without hesitation or even a look back, Nichols hopped onto the center of the rubberized maw, and started sinking through it.

"I am not going to say what that looks like," Daniels commented as he expertly handled the rope.

"I knew you wouldn't." Key sighed. If he hadn't been so sure of Daniels's dependability, he would have buried his foot between the man's legs for even attempting to relieve the tension.

By then Nichols was through and being lowered to the nest floor. Six pairs of eyes scrutinized the images from her helmet-cam. They all, Nichols included, made careful note of the carcasses she landed between, making sure they didn't, like in some bad slasher flick, suddenly spring back to life. They didn't, so after making a quick survey of the entire space, Nichols stepped toward the opposite end of the cavern, toward the predominance of webbed padding.

"Shit, it even looks like a web-padded throne," Daniels muttered.

"Shut up, shut up, shut up," Key ordered, concentrating everything he had on the images. He even found himself leaning forward, although he knew that would have no effect on the image size. Something twitched inside the center of the webbing.

Rahal gasped.

"Open it up," Key said, even as Nichols's M249 was up and tearing a jagged hole right where the twitch had come.

Shit, Key seethed to himself. *Knew it was the damn pedipalp antennae.* He should have ordered Nichols to shoot just below it. But even he paused for a second as they all stared into the torn, wet, quivering, maw of the arachnosaur queen, its crimson-onyx eyes burning with pain and hate.

But that was all they had time to do, because, even before Nichols had a chance to prime the explosives, Usa Awar appeared directly behind the queen. He stood, pushed forward a gold-plated, fifty-caliber Desert Eagle automatic and shot Private Terri Nichols in the head.

Chapter 34

Daniels yanked Nichols back and up, while Key dove directly into the maw, Beretta M9 first. It happened so fast no one had a chance to do or say anything about it.

Daniels swore a blue streak behind him, but Key didn't care. As soon as his eyes cleared the bottom lip, he was firing at the arachnosaur queen and Awar, whatever came first.

He had the gratifying sight of seeing his bullets plow into the creature's gigantic head, as well as ricochet off the Desert Eagle's gleaming barrel in a shower of sparks that sent the heavy handgun lurching to the side.

But then he had to concentrate on flipping his feet around, so he landed without breaking his skull or neck, as well as keeping whatever exposed flesh he had away from the webbing. Nichols's limp body soared past him, and then his boots hit the padded floor.

He managed to get another shot off, which he hoped hit the queen or Awar, then his knees bent and he was in a tight, fast, somersault. He came up firing again, moving forward as fast as he could. No way was he going to retreat or hide. The last thing he wanted was an extended shootout in this poisonous space.

One more step was all it took to make him fully realize what was going on. Awar was using the queen as cover, which meant that the man knew the creature could take care of herself. He was basically forcing Key to all but jump into the monster's maw. And it was quite the maw. Now that he was close, and the creature had shaken off most of its camouflage, Key could see just how big it was. It had to be at least six times the size of the largest arachnosaur any of them had seen.

Key dove to the left, trying to find Awar behind the creature. But Awar was compensating for every move Key made, keeping the queen between them. She was so big, neither man had any room to maneuver. There was nothing for it. Key stepped on the joint of the queen's second left leg, using it as a step. Before the other legs could stab at him, he vaulted up, twisted around, and rolled across the creature's back.

Awar jumped up in retaliation, trying to bring the Desert Eagle to bear. But the almost five-pound, ostentatious weapon was a beacon for Key's boot. He tried kicking it back into Awar's enraged face as he scrambled across the queen's right side. Key grabbed at Awar's gun wrist with his free hand, as Awar grabbed Key's gunhand.

Key landed against him, sending them both into the curved cave wall behind the queen's left flank. They held each other's arms up, their faces nearly touching. The weapon dealer's expression, as well as weapon, told Key all he needed to know. The man was incensed to the point of mania, but also so arrogant he thought the Desert Eagle was his golden scepter. The overblown thing could only hold seven fifty-caliber rounds to the Beretta's fifteen.

It hardly mattered, because Awar had the strength of a madman. Maybe he wanted to scream obscenities and threats, but he remained silent, all but spitting as he tried taking Key down. The terrorist attempted to gain leverage. Key didn't bother. He ignored his hands. Keeping Awar's gun away, at the same time Awar held his own gun wrist, rendered his arms void. And Awar was so intent on kneeing Key's groin that he forgot his feet.

Key didn't. He kicked under Awar's left knee. If Awar had been able to take a step, the knee would fail and he would go down, but he couldn't take a step. They were both wedged against the wall by the back of the queen's bulbous abdomen. So Key lifted his left foot and stepped on a very specific spot on Awar's shin. The terrorist's face twisted in pain, then his eyes and mouth popped open as the pain changed.

It was an acupressure point that Daniels once described as rebooting your existence. It went beyond any pain a human could experience. It wasn't like a broken bone, a knife stab, or even a gunshot. It overwhelmed the senses in a way that was blinding, indescribable, and even personality-changing.

Awar went down like a howling demon, but he didn't let go of his gun or Key's wrist. As the queen lurched outward, the two men slammed to the web-covered ground—sending up shards of the toxic strands.

"God damn it," Key yelled. "What the fuck are you doing?"

"What I should have," Awar said in perfect English. "Making sure you die!"

Key supposed he should have demanded to know how the terrorist survived in the queen's chambers, how he weaponized Nichols, or what he thought he was doing here, but there just wasn't time, especially after the queen jerked forward, pounced on the explosive pack Nichols had dropped, and ingested it like an vitamin.

Awar laughed. "She is feeding her young! Her new brood will be even more virulent than the last!"

"*Neik*," Rahal swore in his ear. "She can lay thousands of eggs!"

With the creature no longer wedging them, Key tried to bring his leg up, but just as he was about to tromp on Awar's knees, something like a truck fell on him. He was slammed atop Awar so tightly that neither man could bring his gun to bear.

"What is going on?" Lancaster asked. "We can't see anything."

"The fucking queen crawled on top of us," Key said in disbelief. "It's grinding!"

"It's trying to mate!" Rahal cried. "Find the *epigyne* on the underside of her abdomen! It's near the joint between the front and back sections!"

Key let his fingers scramble across the weight on top of him until he found a hole. Not even waiting for further instructions, he plunged his fist into it, digging around until his arm was in the arachnosaur all the way up to his shoulder.

Then, finally, he felt what seemed to be the queen's equivalent of the crap the others had pumped into the corpses they had vivisected.

"Eshe!" he howled. "Have you found a catalyst for the spider shit yet?"

There was a microsecond's hesitation before she cried back. "We haven't been able to test it yet!"

"I don't give a—"

She yelled, "Salt!"

The sea, he realized. They had been heading for the sea, where their excrement could have been depth charges for any ship that tried to stop them. And human hands, collecting the corpses, could have turned them all into land mines. What did arachnosaurs know of coroner's rubber gloves or hazmat suits?

He jerked his arm, pulling his glove free of his sleeve. Then he squeezed and punched with all his might.

The queen made a sound that caused everyone listening to wince in pain. Then she vaulted herself off the humans, leaping almost as high as Daniels had elevated Nichols. Key scrambled to his feet, all but spitting out webbing that had crammed into the openings of his helmet and mask. He faced the queen, which had twisted to face him.

The thing was gigantic, and extremely unhappy. Its legs chopped through the thick carpet of webbing that covered the floor, edging toward him. He looked up to see where his bullets had plowed harmlessly into its face. Now its eyes had turned almost entirely scarlet, with pumping veins of black coursing through it. It opened its maw, revealing its acidic, salivating rage. It quivered, ready to pounce.

Key felt a blinding pain at his neck. He staggered forward, closer to the creature, who reared onto its back four legs in response. He managed to twist his head around to see Usa Awar. The weapons dealer and terrorist had hit him with his Desert Eagle, and was now pointing it directly between Key's eyes.

"You are the lucky one," he said, a look of consummate triumph on his face. "You will die at my hands, not hers."

Awar pulled the trigger. The fifty-caliber bullet thudded into the queen's maw, because Key was flying. Daniels had used Gonzales's bungee-yo-yo, the same device they used to spring Nichols from Toussaint's exhibit, to grab and lift him. Daniels threw Key into the ceiling's maw so hard that Key practically speared all the way through.

Daniels had grabbed the bottom lips of the maw, and hung there, looking back at a stunned Awar.

"Fuckaduck, huh?" he said as Awar brought the gun up to target him.

But then Gonzales, Faisal, and even Nichols yanked Daniels up, and out just before the pack of explosives the fifty-caliber bullet had inadvertently primed detonated.

Key, Daniels, Gonzales, Faisal, and Nichols were already running, and were catapulted out of the entire burrow when the first detonation set off the queen's egg sacs, the ones that Key's sweat had primed. A second later, it immolated the entire cavern as if it had been painted with napalm.

Key did not know how long he was out, nor how long he just lay there, staring at the Shabhut sky. All he could wonder was why he wasn't dead. Not just from what he had escaped from, but the webbing's toxic infection.

All he knew for sure was that the first human thing he heard was Daniels's voice.

"Heroic bullshit reporting for duty," Morty drawled from where he lay beside him. "Sir."

Epilogue

"So," Morty Daniels said, leaning back in his Thumrait clinic bed. "Raped by a spider. That's new for you, isn't it?"

Josiah Key looked at the sergeant from his own bed, trying to keep his expression blank. He failed. So, instead, he looked at Eshe Rahal, who stood in scrubs and lab coat, holding a clipboard, next to Lancaster.

They were all in a large, isolated, sunlight-infused ward. If Key had thought the examinations after his concussion were thorough, they were nothing compared to what Rahal had just finished putting them through. Lancaster had wanted a clean bill of health for the survivors, and he got it.

"How is Private Nichols?" Key asked, looking at the sleeping redhead across the aisle. "And why isn't she dead?"

The scientist shared a glance with Lancaster which expressed their appreciation that the man asked about her first rather than himself.

"No longer a private if she takes my offer to join Cerberus," Lancaster answered. He considered that statement for a moment. "Actually she's probably going to be promoted whether she takes my offer or not." Then he got back to Key's question. "I told you about Cali-brake, Sergeant Major."

"But that was in the uniform, wasn't it?" Key countered. When Lancaster merely smiled, Key continued. "All right, even if it was in her helmet, a fifty-caliber round fired point-blank at her head?"

"It may have been fired directly at her head," Rahal said, "but it didn't hit there. I told you about her enhanced reactions, remember?"

Daniels made an apologetic face on Key's behalf. "Forgive him, doc," he said with mock sympathy. "Spider-raped." Daniels made a circular motion with his forefinger beside his ear. "Must've scrambled his brain."

He then looked at the retired general, simultaneously jerking a thumb at Key. "And you meant Sergeant Major, right?"

Lancaster continued to just smile.

Daniels gaped. "You've got to be kidding me!"

Lancaster shrugged philosophically. "I got tired of saying the entire rank, so I shortened it, Master Sergeant."

"Huh?" Daniels replied, pointing at himself.

It took a second for that to sink in, but when it finally did, Daniels beamed. "Call me MS," he told Key.

"With pleasure," he answered before returning his attention to the others. "So. She dodged a bullet."

"Not exactly," Lancaster chuckled. "It hit her, but not head on. There was a second when Awar basked in his power, which allowed her to start moving out of the way. You can review the video. The bullet struck the protective gear, then glanced off. Still, it *was* like a punch from a giant." He glanced at her with sympathy, and then back at Key with irony. "Now *she's* the one with the concussion."

"Shit," Daniels said. "But I guess it's better than a fifty-caliber hole in the head, huh?" He looked at Key. "What are you always telling me, Joe? Watch the guy holding the gun, not just the gun, right?"

Key couldn't disagree. "So, okay, now tell me. Why aren't *I* dead?"

Daniels sat up. "Yeah," said the newly promoted master sergeant. "I kept far away from the webbing, but Joe's face was smooshed in it."

Rahal and Lancaster shared a conspiratorial glance. The former opened her mouth to speak, but Key interrupted.

"Let me guess," he said with a tired smile. "You've hinted often enough. Something about an extra X and two-way transfusion?"

Rahal blushed—making all the men smile—but only for only a moment. "Like a number of you have said," she explained, looking deeply into Key's eyes, "with the fate of the world at stake, I couldn't just stand there and try nothing." Then she straightened. "I felt certain that any possible harm would be overwhelmingly compensated by the curative effect."

Daniels leaned over to punch Key on the arm. "Ooo, you've got girl chromosomes, Joe, and you notice she only gave it to you, right?"

"Yes," Rahal countered sharply. "Because I knew, of the two of you, which one was more likely to be selfless."

"Hey!" Daniels retorted with mock hurt, tinged with real hurt. Then they all saw him thinking about it. "Well," he confessed to Key, "I did watch you down in the pit for awhile, waiting for just the right moment to pull you out. I wanted to shoot the crap out of those two monsters, but you kept getting in the way."

Key slapped him on the arm in return. "You handled it right. Amazingly right. I thought I had suddenly gotten the power to fly."

Now it was Daniels turn to turn a little embarrassed. "It's just what you taught me. Be smart, not badass. Well, not *just* badass."

"With your help, we've nearly developed a complete antidote at Cerberus Labs," Lancaster assured them. "Just in case there's still a straggler or two out there somewhere."

"Ah, the infamous Cerberus Labs," Key grinned, grateful for the chance to change the subject. "Will Eshe ever actually get to see it, or is it like your imaginary girlfriend?"

The change of subject was short-lived. Key's humor faded as Lancaster's face grew serious. "Sooner than either you, or I, might prefer," he answered, then tapped his ear with a forefinger. "Gentlemen, please report to M Ward immediately."

Both Key and Daniels sat up in their beds despite their bruises and exhaustion.

Before the remaining team members arrived, Lancaster continued. "After the destruction of the arachnosaur queen, the same hazmat team that served Captain Logan at the beachhead was ordered to make sure Shabhut was truly clean and Usa Awar was truly dead. Thankfully, it, and he, were. The only one who was initially left unhappy was the captain himself, who had crowed far and wide that it was he who had saved the day just hours before."

"Initially?" Key inquired.

Lancaster nodded philosophically. "I let him have the credit for Shabhut, too."

"What?" Daniels exploded. "Oh, come on!"

"Shut up," Key told Daniels, then added as a respectful afterthought, "Master Sergeant."

Manuel Gonzales entered the room with Faisal behind him. They were both wearing outfits similar to the light, airy ones Key and Daniels had as CID men. They took up positions on either side of the beds.

"Gunnery Sergeant Gonzales and Corporal Safar reporting, sir," Faisal said quietly. His quietness was counterbalanced by the loudness of Daniels's reaction.

"You speak English?" he exclaimed. "How long have you spoken English?"

Faisal couldn't help but smile at the look of surprise on the bedridden soldiers' faces. He looked meaningfully at Lancaster, who nodded permission.

"The entirety of my life, *aamirika albukm*," he told Daniels, using the Arab term for stupid American. "Ever since I was born in Dearborn, Michigan, and long before I was recruited by Cerberus."

"Corporal Faisal Safar, people," Lancaster said, cutting through the surprise. "One of the pioneer Cerberus agents. He joined shortly after its inception." Lancaster's gaze went from one to the next. "I may have retired from the military, but I've never retired from why I joined the military. I try to make the world safe, but I soon found, to my chagrin, that even the greatest army can't make the world completely safe."

He locked eyes with Key. "You know Logan. All too often, the military is like him. Hammers ordered to pound nails. And once they do, they stop, awaiting orders to pound the next one. But as long as it's a nail, or something like it, our forces can handle anything."

"Anything," Key echoed, "except things they don't believe exist."

Lancaster nodded, with a widening smile. "Exactly. You see? That's why I wanted you with us. And I knew you would bring like minds along." He looked at each person gathered in the hospital ward. "I discovered that the dangers that threaten our world are much more than nails."

"Things like the arachnosaurs," Safar explained.

"Things?" Daniels said, suddenly catching on. "Plural?"

Lancaster nodded again. "I'm afraid so, and I don't use the word 'afraid' euphemistically. Many modern men wouldn't believe that the arachnosaurs actually existed as far back as tens of millions of years ago, so they certainly couldn't believe they returned just a few months ago. But, over my long career, I have acquired and established influence, so I used that influence to convince powerful people that these different kinds of nails were real and would not be stopped by conventional hammers."

"Cerberus," Key said quietly.

"Cerberus," Lancaster agreed. "A well-funded, well-trained, versatile organization created to hunt down the threats that prey on people's disbelief in order to survive and subjugate."

"And to hunt in an open-minded way that is tailored to, and effective for, each threat," Safar elaborated.

It was like the hallelujah chorus to Key's ears. "That's why Logan gets the credit, Morty. Hard to be versatile and effective if everyone knows about you." He returned his attention to Lancaster. "So we may be seeing your imaginary girlfriend sooner rather than later because we've tripped over another nail?"

"Like your use of 'we,' Soldier," Lancaster replied. "Yes, Major. It has taken quite some time, but the pattern has become increasingly apparent."

He nodded at Gonzales and Safar before turning. "I'll let Speedy and Faisal fill you in while I prepare for our departure." He headed for the exit.

The gunnery sergeant didn't keep them waiting. "Corpses are multiplying in the border towns between Pakistan and India."

Daniels snorted. "Well that's nothing new!"

This time Key said it aloud. "Wait for it."

"Corpses that have been totally drained of blood," Safar elaborated.

Daniels immediately turned his head and shouted after Lancaster. "I'll take care of this on one condition! What the hell does Cerberus mean anyway?"

But the door was already closed and the general was already gone. The master sergeant didn't seem to mind. In fact, he turned to the others with a huge duck-eating grin and said two words with consummate anticipation. "Hammer time."

About the Author

Richard Jeffries holds a degree in creative writing, obtained before he went to work for American intelligence. He has seen the world—and things in it—which inspired the writing of these novels. Now retired from covert ops, Jeffries divides his time between rural Connecticut and London. In his spare time he pursues his lifelong interest in Kung Fu and classical piano.

Prologue

Craven knew his master was serious. He knew it in the most abhorrent way conceivable

Craven had moved to Veranesi to become an acolyte, and had been serving the master for years. He had become this slum's *taaboot* in order to best perform this function. When someone died in this warren of fetid stones, it was Craven who came to take the corpse away—often leaving the site filthier than when he entered.

In truth, he could have only become a "caretaker of corpses" in these bowels of the village, since the rest of Veranesi would not have allowed him anywhere near their deceased. Veranesi was a place that studied, embraced, and even venerated death, and anyone who did not have to beg Craven's services prayed he did not exist.

His name was not Craven, but he did not remember, or even know, his birth name. Craven was his death name—the name his mother gave him as she died of dysentery in his arms, telling him feverish stories of his past and future lives on the Night of Demons.

Craven could not remember how old he had been then. He might have just become a teenager, but he doubted it. He could only judge by his memories of being strong enough to hold his mother on a muddy bank of the Ganges, keeping her torso above the water line as she clutched and screeched at him.

He could have been as young as five, he decided, since, by then, his mother was little more than a skeleton covered in parched, paper-thin flesh. As she contorted and writhed in his spasming arms—pumping blood, mucous, water, and feces into the blessedly dirty river from her submerged lower half—she vomited out her hysterical demands and dire warnings.

His father was *Mahasona*, she swore—the most feared demon, the one whose very name meant vileness.

"That is your fate, that is your destiny, that is your calling," she babbled at him. "You cannot escape it, you cannot avoid it, you cannot deny it."

When she had finally become very quiet, still clutching at him with claws that seemed sculpted by the gods upon him, he simply loosed his muscles until the Ganges mighty current pulled her away. The scratches her broken nails left in his flesh festered for what seemed like months.

The woman had been right. For a pitifully short time, Craven had tried to find a way out of his doom, but each time it seemed as if he might make a human connection, the internal and external disease his parents had infected him with made him a source of revulsion at best, shame at worst. All too soon, he embraced his fate and went in search of his father.

To his surprise, and then quickly his fear, it did not take long. In the cramped recesses of every town and village he was forced to hide in, the name of the "Great Demon" could be heard. To Craven's addled mind, it was as if he was following whispers that floated in the fusty air like stinging nettles.

By the time he had reached Veranesi, their meeting seemed preordained. Even before then, Craven accepted that he was seeking his master, not his father. And his master was the first man he set eyes upon once he stepped onto the stones of the rocky graveyard on the outskirts of the city. As the legends said, his master was a fierce giant with the head of a bear and the eyes of a tiger. From deep within his cowled robe, Craven heard him say but a single instruction.

"Serve me well."

Then he walked away, deep into Veranesi, bringing the souls, skins, and skulls of his victims behind him like the folds of a draping cape.

Every year since then, Craven brought his master an offering on the Night of the Demon. At first it was the freshest corpse he had collected. Initially, he had tried sneaking into the hovels of the recently deceased and stealing the bodies, but the family members who caught him—rather than have him beaten or arrested—had begged him to complete his task, with their repulsed consent.

Eventually, emboldened by his master's acceptance of his offerings, Craven dared make one request: "Free me."

It seemed as if his master ignored him, but Craven knew he did not. Each year, on the Night of the Demon, he gave his offering and made his request. But, as the years wore on, his master grew bored.

"Fresher, stronger, younger," Craven had heard him say. Or maybe he heard the master *think* it—he was never sure.

Soon, Craven began experimenting in preservation, trying to keep the youngest bodies fresher, longer, littering his abattoir with his experiments in different stages of decomposition.

The results satisfied his master for a time—too short a time—but then the demand for more potent offerings returned.

As horrified as the other slum-dwellers were, none dared approach Craven. Yet none rebuffed him when he appeared to take their deceased from them. Eventually, however, a young doctor dared visit, emboldened by the whispers that had reached him. Other doctors came later, amazed at the tales told by the first man.

All seemed impressed by Craven's skills, if not his appearance and rancid odor. There were no complaints about his demeanor, however. In stories told around café tables, Craven's manners were always described as unfailingly humble, soft-spoken, and polite. Soon, the doctors, too, were giving the man tasks they found too distasteful to complete.

So that year, on the Night of the Demon, Craven had brought his master a fresh fetus, taken from the corpse of a pregnant girl. For the first time his master had met his eyes, and, self-aware of his own accomplishment, Craven had taken that moment to elucidate his traditional request.

"Free me of my pain."

His master had not answered in thoughts or spoken words, but his eyes had glimmered with understanding, and his expression had set in acknowledgement.

That had been the year before this, and, as the seasons had passed, and the Night of the Demon had approached, Craven felt as if he were about to be truly born. He had no idea what year it was, or how old that made him. He knew from how the heat and rain was diminishing that the time was coming. Then, he knew from the full moon that it was the very night.

He stood in his worn, permanently stained, robes. His feet, as always, were unshod. He took a thin canvas sack and pulled it over his shoulder—its contents across his dark, sinewy back. He didn't bother looking around the long, thin, narrow, stone room that had seemingly been constructed around him by necessity—straw mats in one corner, stone tables in another, drains in the dirt floor that emptied fluid into the Ganges, and discolored buckets of steel and wood everywhere.

One way or another he knew he would not return to it.

When he stepped into the night, he did not see his neighbors, and they struggled not to see him. That was especially true on the Night of the Demon, when forgotten souls are remembered and charity is done though prayer. Those who were not hiding would be at Mass or doing vigilance at family graves.

Craven trudged a path that was not well worn, but one he knew well. It was a path that stank of offal, flowers, muslin, silk, and ivory. It was a trudge through excrement, food scraps and rubbish. But the aromas and obstructions grew few and then gave way to nature. It took him out of the residences and into the hills.

At a place where three paths met he came to a mass of seemingly impassable rocks, but, as he had many times before, found a place that left just enough room for a human to twist themselves through a fissure. Inside was another path that seemed to grow in length and height as he stepped. There was a pulsating glow from around a corner that led him, as it always had.

As Craven stepped around the outcropping, his master's inner sanctum lay before him. The foul scent came first, long before he laid eyes on the place. In the triangular-shaped space, the walls were etched with images of an elephant, deer, goat, horse, and sheep. His master sat amid them, on a throne of stone, eating pig flesh and drinking buffalo blood with red hands painted upon his own hands, and red eyes painted above his own eyes.

He sat behind a bonfire that made the shadows of his inner circle dance. But Craven could only see the shadows. The inner circle was veiled from his still human eyes. The only other human he could actually perceive was his master's companion for the evening.

Each year, there had been another—always the most vital, always the most lovely—stretched out at his feet, as if in a living coma. Craven was certain that others also presented his master an offering on this night—an offering that was far out of his ability to attain.

But this year, even Craven paused, his pained eyes widening in acknowledgement. The dark haired girl who was curled between his master's feet and the fire was the most beautiful he had ever seen—as if her face, shape, and even her essence had been fashioned from his innermost desires.

"Yes."

Craven could not tell whether his master's voice appeared in his ear or in his mind. It made no difference. By causing him to form it, Craven may have cursed himself to many more years of abject servitude. He quickly and expressionlessly laid his burden down on the other side of the fire, and pulled the sack from around it with no hesitation.

A thin, young, dead girl was revealed. A thin, young, dead, pregnant girl.

His master lurched in the seat, one hand reaching for her, but then he froze, his expression changing. It was not distaste, but it was clearly a memory of a flavor he had tasted from Craven's previous offerings.

"Fresh," Craven said softly. "No preservatives."

His master's eyes locked on his for the second time. "Tonight?"

Craven nodded. "Tonight," he echoed. "Her blood may still be--." But, by the time he said it, his master was already on his offering.

Craven looked away. He always had when his master fed, and since his master had never corrected him, he didn't dare change, no matter how impressive the offering. As he waited, however, he did dare something. He dared to dream.

He, and certainly his master, knew that he could hardly do better than this. Yes, he could bring live offerings, but his would never compare to those of the others, simply by nature of his environment. Certainly he could take younger and richer prey, and, while their terror might make them more exciting to his master, they also both knew that sort of prize would not be long in coming. As long as Craven remained in the bowels, any authority might look the other way. But once he set foot above his station, he risked exposure to everyone. And exposure was the one thing his master would not tolerate.

But now, tonight, his master might contemplate finally fulfilling his request. Tonight would be the perfect time, when Craven was certain all the circle knew that this was his crowning offering. From here it would only be repetition, or attempts to recapture previous tastes.

So Craven waited for acknowledgement, even long after the sounds of feeding had diminished—sounds that, to Craven's ears, included both the carrier and her unborn passenger. He waited, hoping and daring, until all that remained was the crackling of the fire and the moaning of the wind.

Finally he dared to look back toward the flames. He looked back just in time to see his master feeding on his offering's bowels.

His mother's words returned to him. *Watch! Watch, for when they devour the still living offal, they devour the life essence!*

His master had never done that before—not in front of him. Now was truly the time to dare more than dream.

"Master, please," Craven pleaded in agony. "Fulfill my request. Fulfill it now!"

Craven found that his eyes had closed in supplication. When he opened them again, he was alone with a dying fire.

Craven did not know anything else until he found himself standing by the roaring Ganges, directly above the spot where his mother had died. Here, the fifteen hundred mile long river seemed to boil with its own angry life, like the pulsating back of a serpent coiling to strike. As he looked into the broiling current, it seemed to form the face of his mother—both mocking and entreating him.

He took a step to join her, but stopped when he heard another voice in his mind's ear. A deep, soft, soothing, female voice—one that was nothing like his mother's, even before the disease gripped her.

"What did you want?"

Craven turned to see his master's companion—the one who had laid at his feet—standing a yard away from him. She wore a thin robe, belted at her waist—a robe that revealed both her shapely legs and astonishing cleavage.

"From your master," she continued as if the roar of the river was nonexistent. "What did you want?"

All he could do was stare. Her beauty was cathartic, even hormonal.

She smiled, making him feel even weaker. "Do you think I am a dream?" she asked. "Do you think all of this is a dream?" She motioned gracefully at the surroundings. "Do you think it has all been a dream since the moment you became aware?"

When she glanced away, it gave him the power to answer, despite the gasping weakness of his reply. "A nightmare."

Her smile widened and became more believable. "For you, I'm sure it was." She lowered, and shook, her head demurely. "But I can assure you it is not." When she raised her head again, her eyes locked on his. "When your master was beheaded eons ago, a deity took pity on him, for he was once a proud warrior. The deity quickly replaced it with the first head that could be found." She shrugged sadly. "But what do gods know, or care, of mortals? The result was grotesque and people became ill and terrified at the sight. So he took refuge in graveyards—"

"Like me," Craven realized.

The woman's smile became tender and knowing. "Like you. So tell me. You have told him, so now tell me. What is it you want?"

Craven was not intimidated by her question. In fact, quite the opposite. He suddenly felt superior to her. *She must be tajabana*, he realized. *Freshly made. Her awakening hunger must be enormous*. It had to be the only reason she would dally with him.

"Power," he answered, perhaps being truthful for the first time in his life. But not insightful.

She laughed. Although he reacted at first as if she was mocking him, he immediately realized that her laughter was honest.

"Oh, my dear fellow," she said sympathetically as she took her first step toward him. "You'll have to do better than that. Now really, what is it that you truly want?"

"Power," he repeated as her lovely, elegant, hand reached for his scalp. "Over innocence."

The forefinger of her other hand caressed his cheek, turning his face from hers. "That's better," she assured him, her fragrant breath making his flesh crawl. "Although I cannot guarantee you that, there's one thing I can do—"

He was tempted to inquire further, but then her tongue was at the back of his head, at the exact spot where his skull met his spine. Then, there, on the banks of the Ganges River where his mother had died, Craven was set free.

Chapter One

Mount Rushmore National Memorial Superintendent Bernard Gensler would never forget the little girl's face.

Normally he'd never remember it. He had seen so many faces, every day, since taking the job to manage the Black Hills of South Dakota Tourist Attraction—in fact, around three million faces a year. But it was the strangest thing. As this blonde girl, who he judged to be about three years old, made her way through the crowds, flanked by her mother and father, no one seemed to notice her.

Instead, if anyone looked down from the awe-inspiring sight of the Presidential faces carved into the mountain above them, their eyes seemed to glance off the twelve-ounce orange juice carton she held in both hands in front of her as if she were a flower girl at a citrus wedding. They seemed to focus on that, and not see the angelic face behind it at all.

But Gensler's eyes had become sharper in the eight months since he took over the job. His gaze now almost always went to any weak link in a pattern of movement. And while there were always many children at the park, even now when the weather was getting cooler, most were in strollers or their parents' arms. This little blonde child was walking steadily and serenely, the juice carton like a shield.

Gensler fought the urge to approach the trio, because he also learned it was never wise to make suggestions to parents on how to treat their offspring. That was one of the reasons he had gotten the job in the first place. The previous superintendent had always erred on the side of over-caution, until the pile of complaint emails and letters had toppled over onto her.

Instead, he paused in his own walk to study the trio's progress. Other sightseers seem to flow around them, like drops of oil in water. Fairly certain that there were no impending collisions for the moment, Gensler's gaze shifted back to the child's beatific face.

It truly was amazing, as if fashioned from every movie, painting, cartoon, and picture he had ever admired. It was so striking and serene that it was only after he managed to move on that he realized he had not even bothered to look at her parents' faces. At the time, he had shrugged. It wasn't as if he didn't have things to do.

He was proud of the changes he had made that allowed this child to fully enjoy the stirring, even awe-inspiring, attraction he was now responsible for—from the Memorial Grounds, Information Center, Visitor Center,

Sculptor's Studio, Evening Lighting Ceremony Amphitheater, and Rushmore Plaza Civic Center, to the paths, trails, restrooms, parking spaces, exhibits, and even scenic roads that all came under the aegis of the National Park Service. He may not have been serving the Marine Corps in an official capacity any longer, but he was honored to be a part of the Department of the Interior—no matter how his old "few and proud" buddies kidded him about the "step down."

Gensler continued his unofficial rounds along the Avenue of Flags Walkway, as ever enjoying the fifty-six flags that represented the fifty states, one district, three territories, and two commonwealths of the United States—arranged in alphabetical order with the A's near the concession building and the W's near the Visitor Center and Museum. And they all seemed to be waving at the beautiful, grand sculptures of George Washington, Thomas Jefferson, Theodore Roosevelt, and Abraham Lincoln that artist Gutzon Borglum had begun in 1927, and his son Lincoln Borglum had finished in 1941.

Gensler truly enjoyed taking the long way round to the park café, rather than huddling in his office. To be among the people he had done this all for was his best reward. After 2001 and the World Trade Center attack, the security had tightened like disapproving lips all over the country. But here they focused on improving public buildings and viewing area safety rather than restricting access to the mountain itself.

But that wasn't as bad as the over-reaction in 2009, when a group of Greenpeace protestors had managed to make it to the top of the Presidential heads to drape an anti-global warming banner there. Following that was years of limiting access and clamping down on the circulation of images of the top. National Park Service officials believed distribution of these images constituted an unjustifiable security threat.

Even then Gensler had come across the report from the U.S. Government Accountability Office that read "Preventing individuals seeking to climb to the top of the monument for nefarious purposes is difficult." But he had found that the real problem was the lack of funds needed to man those surveillance feeds and police the summit.

The superintendents before him had struggled to balance the visitors' freedom with park security, but they had neglected to incorporate the human factor. Upon his hiring, he almost immediately realized the key was using their limited funds to their best advantage, as well as steward training.

These forest rangers were more comfortable with trees than they were with other people, and had to have an attitude adjustment to change their preconceptions about "the annoying interlopers." Once he made it clear that every visitor should be treated like a possible nature lover, and led by example, the mood slowly but steadily changed.

They all worked to make any visit so enjoyable that few seemed to notice Gensler's steps to make sure the Presidential sculptures themselves were well and truly off limits. Nobody could get up there, but he did everything in his power to make sure they didn't even think about wanting to.

Gensler breathed deeply of the fresh, crisp, autumn air. They were in the weather sweet spot where the southern Chinook winds took on cold Canada air trying to permeate the area, leaving them in a pocket of peace. As he straightened at the crest of his breath, he unavoidably glanced upwards. His eyes, sharpened by years of training, narrowed. His brain, sharpened by the same training, slammed down the sudden panic that filled it.

There were three specks in his vision, where they couldn't be, moving along the crest between the stone coiffures of Teddy Roosevelt and Abraham Lincoln. Two black specks, and one blonde one.

Not possible, Bernard Gensler thought. He blinked, praying they were shadows of soaring birds or clouds. But when he looked again, they were still there, and still moving—getting ever closer to the edge of the precipice.

Not possible. They couldn't get up there. There was no way they could've gotten past security.

Gensler's arms moved while his gaze didn't falter. Up came both his hands—in one his smartphone, in the other the Sunagor Super Zoom Compact Binoculars he always kept in his jacket pocket. Without looking, he thumbed the universal code on the cellphone's digital buttons, linking him with every ranger and staff member, and stuck it against his ear.

"Code green," he said quietly. "S, L, X, T and A." As he was giving the message meaning "scalp-line between Teddy Roosevelt and Abe Lincoln," he brought the most powerful compact zoom binoculars available to his eyes as calmly as he could.

"Not possible," he heard someone gasp from the monitor room.

Not possible, Gensler heard echoed in his own mind as he thumbed the Sunagor up to its full hundred and ten times magnification. It was as he feared. Somehow, it was the little girl he had fixated on, or her twin. But even if she were a twin, the people who had flanked her before were flanking her now.

But his fear was not just because they had somehow gotten past all the security measures, but because he knew there was no conceivable way they could have gotten up there that fast—not unless they were all, somehow, twins. Another blonde twin who was still holding a twin juice carton in front of her like an offering to the gods.

Above the buzzing in his head and the ambient sounds from the tourists all around him, Gensler became aware of other voices in his ear. Babbling coming from ranger stations all around the back and top of the mountain stridently maintaining that they had seen nothing and no one had passed, mingling with desperate questions and even accusations.

"R.S.," he said strongly as he watched the three figures stop at the lip of the cliff. *Radio silence*. It was an antiquated code, but still effective. "Move," he ordered the rangers nearest the spot. "Secure, safeguard." Those were meant for both the location and the trio.

All the while, he never took his eyes off the three specks. His breath caught in his throat as the blonde girl seemed to lurch forward, but he breathed again when the man beside her suddenly gripped her shoulder. He watched as the man and woman leaned down. The girl looked up at them.

"What are they doing?" Gensler may have whispered. *Are they talking? What are they talking about*? "Move, move, move!" he snapped, the word becoming more urgent with each repetition.

As he did so, he started becoming aware of nearby tourist voices also become more urgent and strident. Others had binoculars too.

Gensler's head craned forward on his neck, desperately hoping that somehow might help. But as he did, the three atop the monument stopped talking, the girl turned back to face him, and the adults flanking her each gripped her elbows and ankles.

"No," the superintendent said, the word seemingly torn from him by talons. But his building dread prevented nothing. The two adults swung the girl back and forth as if they were aerialists about to launch their youngest member to the top of a circus tent.

"No," Gensler breathed with each swing. "No!"

As two park rangers appeared at the far side of both Washington and Lincoln's heads, the two adults hurled the little girl off the cliff. Gensler watched as she swung out in a huge, diving, arc, holding the juice carton out over her head.

He didn't even stop watching when a loud explosion—it sounded like a firecracker in a metal trash can—engulfed the carton and her. The shock wave blew off massive, ugly chunks of Roosevelt and Lincoln, while scarring Jefferson and even Washington. The biggest pieces struck outcroppings and shattered into smaller chunks, like an obscene asteroid entering Earth's atmosphere. More facial curves and details were ripped off, small chunks that were no longer identifiable as other than what they were: rock. The *crack-crack-snap* of each strike arrived a moment after the visual, the sound traveling slower, the cloud of the explosion and the dust setting up a haze in the air. It was like a scrim to mute the pain of the vignette being played out.

But it didn't. It couldn't. Nothing could. And the distant sounds couldn't blot the nearby screams and shrieks and guttural roars and swearing and orders to *run, run, move!* that everyone seemed to be shouting at everyone else.

It was the longest and yet most viciously scarring few seconds Gensler could remember having lived through....

* * * *

"They threw her because she wouldn't have done as much damage if she had merely jumped," Bernard Gensler muttered.

"What?"

Gensler looked up as the harried, incredulous Pennington County Sheriff tried to encompass all the activity of the Mount Rushmore security office, while local police, Highway Patrol, Park Police, rangers, emergency medical personnel, and even officers from the local Air Force base struggled to proceed.

"Nothing," Gensler told the sheriff. "Just trying to collect my thoughts. Christ, I'm just trying to *think* thoughts."

The minutes following the attack were chaos, as tourists screamed and ran in fear of further explosions. Thankfully there were none, and there was protocol to follow, which Gensler had his staff practice monthly. But others had protocol to follow as well, and the park was locked down within the half hour—state police interviewing every visitor while those injured in the panic were tended to.

C.I.A. and F.B.I. agents were on their way, but Larry Michaels from the National Security Agency's Q Directorate was already on scene. When Gensler had asked how he had arrived so quickly, he admitted to be on vacation with his family.

"Yeah, you'll have to have your thoughts collected," Michaels said. "These monsters not only used a child to carry a bomb but they stained this—what did Franklin Roosevelt call it?"

"The Shrine of Democracy," Gensler reminded him. "When he officially opened it." The man must've paid some attention during his vacationing tour.

"Yeah," Michaels drawled, trying, like everyone else, to get his head around it. "The same year the Second World War started, right?"

Gensler nodded absently.

"Well…no matter what your thoughts, you'll probably get shit-canned for this."

Gensler looked at the NSA man sharply, but his words belied his angry gaze. "I probably *should* get shit-canned for this," the former Marine snapped. "My watch, my fault."

"Bernie," Pamela Chinoa interrupted. She had been the one on duty at the surveillance screens when it happened. She had been the one who gasped. "We checked and rechecked the footage from every possible approach. No one got by. No one even appeared."

Gensler couldn't disagree. He had pored over the footage himself, as many times as he could once he felt certain his staff had the turmoil under control. "But still somehow they got up there," he said bitterly. "And two are still missing while two of our own are still dead."

Chinoa's mouth shut and grew tight, her eyes watering. The two rangers who had appeared at the last second were the victims, their fronts torn apart—seemingly from the explosion's shrapnel.

"How could they have gotten up there?" Gensler seethed. "Why weren't they killed by the explosion too? Worse, how could they get out again?"

"Worse?" Michaels snorted. "How is that worse?"

"Because," Gensler snarled at him, "this time we were on alert."

Michaels shrugged and sniffed. "They must've slipped out in the panic."

"We were locked down," Gensler said almost to himself. "No one was getting in, yet they somehow got out. And no one saw them either way."

"We sure as hell saw what they did," Michaels said, looking at his cellphone screen. "The visitors might not be able to get to their cars yet, but even with the Wi-Fi shut down, tourists videos of the explosion are already all over the net."

Gensler looked up abruptly. If there was enough coverage that videos could get out, any call he needed to make might go out as well. It might be picked up by any manner of surveillance device, but that didn't bother the former Marine in the slightest.

"Pam," he said, all but snapping to attention, "I'll be in my office. Let me know if anyone needs me."

"Yes, sir," she said, but he was already on his way out of the security room, his thumb already dancing on his phone screen.

As he strode down the hall, surveying the activity outside, he felt a swell of pride mingling with his misery. His staff and the local authorities were working together at prime efficiency. Something terrible, inexplicably terrible, had happened, but the response was more than he could have hoped, or asked, for. He prayed that it continued.

A good sign was that the person he was calling answered on the first ring.

"Chuck," Gensler said. "You've heard?"

"I've heard," retired General Charles Leonidas Lancaster replied. Unbeknownst to Gensler, he was replying from Tashkurgan, Kashgar, Xinjiang, China. "I'm watching the video now."

"Chuck," Gensler continued with immediate confidence born of long experience. "I've checked our surveillance footage closely and I can't tell if it was the juice carton or not."

Lancaster paused a microsecond longer than normal. "Well," he said evenly, "if the explosive wasn't in the juice carton—"

Gensler interrupted. "Didn't you tell me about a report you read where a soldier swore his superior officer wasn't shot, but exploded from the inside? It was in Syria, I think."

"Yemen," Lancaster corrected. "Yes, I did. And I know just the man to talk to about it."

"Good," Gensler replied, feeling more hopeful than he had since setting eyes on the angelic blonde girl.

"I'll need a full report, Bernie."

"You'll get it," Gensler promised. "N.S.A. be damned, you'll get it. But one more thing for now, before this place is overrun—"

"What?" Lancaster asked quickly, knowing how these things went.

"Chuck," his fellow former Marine said, his voice tight and unbelieving. "There was no blood. A little girl blew up from the inside, and I saw flesh and bone, and even muscle, but no blood. I may be going mad, but I tell you. To my dying day, I'll swear on a tall stack on Bibles. There was no blood."

Chapter Two

Josiah Key learned all he needed to know about Sujanpur, Punjab, India, one smoggy afternoon. It was the afternoon when no one seemed surprised to see a naked man run through their festival market carrying a child's corpse.

The former Marine Corporal had come to this village after being assigned to investigate reports of bloodless bodies. He and his Cerberus team had been following the rumors all along the India/Pakistan border—from Attari to Amritsar to Dera Baba Nanak, then finally, to this smallest, humblest, most northern town, which was also closest to the border.

The problem was that they just kept missing the corpses because all the previous cities were quick to get rid of their dead. It wasn't like Attari, which was the last Indian stop on the Trans-Asian Railway, or Amritsar, the spiritual center of the Sikh religion, or Dera Baba Nanak, which was one of the most sacred Sikh centers, would let any corpse, bloodless or bloodfull, gather dust.

By the time Key and his team arrived, the possible evidence had already been cremated. India hardly had time, or room, for the living, let alone the dead. But the mortician at the last stop shared, as all the previous ones had, word of another such body. Thankfully, like many morticians everywhere, the ones in India prided themselves on their English proficiency.

Not surprisingly, a bloodless corpse was quite the conversation starter, especially among dealers in dead bodies. And the chance to talk to living people who weren't grieving was also something that loosened tongues, especially when the ones not-grieving were a placid, handsome man, his tall, muscular associate, and a lithe, green-eyed, redheaded young woman—all wearing slightly shimmering, thin, light, grey T-shirts, slacks, loafers, and open, zip-up jackets.

"You're in luck with this one," the Dera Baba Nanak mortician had said, obviously having a different standard for 'luck' than the average citizen. "My Sujanpur colleague says it is a child's corpse."

"Not so lucky for the kid," Morton Daniels—Key's tall, muscular, shameless right hand man—commented.

"No, no," said the mortician. "Traditionally all Hindus are cremated, except saints and children. The body should be washed in a mixture of milk, yogurt, butter, and honey while mantras are being—"

The team didn't hear the rest since they were already out the door and into the Ford Ecosport Ecoboost—the fastest sports utility vehicle they could readily find in India. Terri Nichols, Key's lithe, redheaded, right-hand woman, had floored it and made the sixty-nine kilometers in record time, despite the habitual traffic on these Punjab roads. The vehicle's interactive map showed her exactly where the small local constabulary was, but they all studied the area as they neared.

It was a humble, unimpressive town that seemed to be stuck between the 1950s and 1970s, wedged between canals of the Ravi River. The air was heavy with moisture, with the colors of green and brown seemingly coated on everything from wood to marble to metal. Off in the distance they heard calliope music and saw what looked like cheap Christmas lights.

"Place is supposed to have a big garment market," Nichols murmured, having let the Ecosport's onboard computer feed her information along the way. "Probably means most townies are good with English too."

She, like Key, had wanted to get familiar with the local language, until they both quickly discovered that India had more than a hundred major languages, as well as nearly sixteen hundred minor ones.

Nichols pulled in front of the small police department, and Key and Daniels were out the door almost before she had stopped the vehicle. But they all reached the front desk at the same time.

The cooperative constable on duty, who was, indeed, conversant in English, directed them to a cement hut out back, where unclaimed, unidentified corpses were stored. All it took was one look at Key's impressive International Crime Investigation Department ID. It was so much more effective than any explanation Key could give about the Cerberus organization he ostensibly worked for. No matter how he tried to describe that, even to himself, it hardly sounded credible.

So, although the Sujanpur constable on duty had no way of knowing it, the Cerberus team's support unit had made sure the hunters were supplied with effective identification cards, and even badges, tailored to whatever location they were sent. Meanwhile, unbeknownst to the Cerberus support unit, *CID* was the name of India's most popular, longest-running TV series, with more than a thousand episodes to its credit—all of which had been seen by the Sujanpur constable on duty.

"Lucky for us there's only a couple of thousand people in this backwater," Nichols murmured as they walked out the rear door of the small station, crossed the worn, muddy, rectangular yard, and stepped into the bunker that housed the bodies.

"We spend way too much time in morgues," Daniels complained as they all surveyed the depressing enclosure. "Look familiar, Joe?"

There was a low, dirty ceiling with two strips of yellowing, flickering fluorescent lights, two stained metal tables with rusting legs, and a meat locker on the far wall. Naturally Key couldn't help but recall a similar one in Thumrait, Oman, where they had first seen the devastating effects of their previous, prehistoric, adversaries.

"What, we're supposed to just rummage around until we find the girl?" Nichols asked, staying close to the entrance.

"Better that than to have a suspicious chaperone," Key reminded her.

"Aw, just take a look," Daniels grinned as he ambled toward the meat locker's freezer door. "Smaller than a woman, bigger than a baby, not breathing—you can't miss her."

"Shut up, Morty," Key sighed as he moved beside Daniels.

"Okay," the big man snorted as he pulled open the heavy vault door. "Say we got here in time. Say the kid is in here and actually bloodless. So what? What are we looking for?"

"I think it's one of those 'we'll know it when we see it,' right?" Nichols offered from the door.

Key nodded, stepping into the meat locker. "First things first," he quoted his father as he surveyed the wooden shelves along the freezer walls. "We claim the body and bring it to Professor Rahal."

There were two body bags on one side and a naked man on the other. Key stepped toward the smaller of the body bags as Daniels eyed the unclad man across the aisle.

"Fresh meat," he said drily, then joined Key as the former Corporal unzipped the smaller bag.

He looked down into the face of an angelic child, who couldn't have been more than three years old when she died. He then nearly twitched when a voice popped into his ear.

"I guess they all look like that when they're at peace," he heard Nichols say gently before looking over his shoulder to see her at his side. The men had known the young lady long enough not to be surprised by her enhanced reflexes anymore. Not after what she, and they, had been through. But they were, constantly.

By then Daniels had checked the other bag, making sure it wasn't also a child. "Okay," he said. "We just take it and take off, or are we stopping to check with Barney Fife first—"

That was as far as the former Sergeant got when the naked man suddenly appeared, grabbed the child, and ran.

To the agents' amazement and annoyance, the man had done it so quickly, powerfully, and silently that even Nichols was taken by surprise. Daniels was so startled he didn't even blurt profanity. They froze an unwanted moment, each chastising themselves in their own way, then took off after him.

Nichols was first out of the bunker, and probably would have been even if her reflexes hadn't been heightened by an *Idmonarchne Brasieri* infection and Professor Rahal's subsequent treatment. Daniels was next, just by dint of his size taking up the entire doorway as he lumbered after her. That was fine by Key, who knew it was best that he get the big picture, focusing in on what had been vague details before.

He was tempted to jump into the SUV, just to keep up with Nichols, but the first thing he realized was that the streets were too narrow and haphazard to make the Ecosport any advantage. The second thing he noted was how fast the naked man was going. He had looked every inch a corpse—haggard, emaciated, aged—but now he was running like a teenage shoplifter. Thankfully Nichols was going after him like a gazelle.

Key saw that Daniels was already drifting to the west. Smart cookie: he was automatically finding another path that would narrow the naked man's escape routes. So Key moved quickly to the east, to create a trident of pursuit. The naked man was sprinting south, directly toward the calliope music and Christmas lights.

They all ran into thickening crowds. It seemed that everyone in town was at, or going to, the garment market, which was either always like this, or celebrating some special festival. Either way, to the westerners' eyes, it still seemed like a minor flea market, transient street fair, and rinky-dink traveling amusement park in some lower-middle-class suburban town.

Nichols was just steps behind the naked man when he burst into a patchy, compact fair ground between tent-like booths, bent, discolored, miniature, ancient rides, and a makeshift stage from which a local band played classic catchy, danceable, Indian pop music. None of that was a problem. In fact, it effectively hemmed in the naked man. What the problem was were all the young men in out of fashion jeans and shirts acting like it was their own personal mosh pit.

They were jumping, kicking, and thrusting their arms in the air to the live music, while the few women present were off to the sides. The latter were the ones who started reacting to both the naked man and redhead first. Their little shrieks and cries acted like a wave, catching the attention of the dancers like a pond ripple. The result was the naked man turning toward Nichols on the far side of a human circle, while the path was closed off behind the redhead by curious, concerned, festival-goers.

Nichols slowed, letting her peripheral vision take in all the confused faces. But she concentrated on the man, who was now holding the corpse like a sleeping child while babbling something in Punjabi, the local dialect.

"What is he saying?" she asked no one in particular. But her sharp tone elicited a reaction from a nearby co-ed.

"He says you are a demon, a redheaded demon, who attacked his family."

Nichols didn't look away from the man as she quickly responded. "Tell them he is a child molester who stole that girl. I'm trying to stop him!"

To the co-ed's credit, she tried translating for the crowd, but the naked man was louder, and already speaking in their language. Nichols tried taking a step forward, but suddenly she was confronted by several angry, suspicious, young men beginning to advance on her. She recognized the look of distrusting amazement. She had seen it wherever redheads were not the norm—which made up most of the world.

She heard the co-ed's shrill admonitions suddenly cut off, then found out why. Daniels was right beside her, his back bent, his fists clenched, and a ravenous grin on his otherwise mirthless face.

"What's Punjabi for 'bring it on'?" he growled.

Nichols didn't want a riot, but left that to Daniels. She took another step toward the naked man, who started shoving the nearest young men in front of him, all while still babbling in despair and fear. She could see exactly what he was doing, but was nearly powerless to stop him. Even with her heightened speed, she saw no way to get to him without becoming entangled in the encroaching crowd.

As Daniels looked ready to take them all on, Nichols kept her gaze locked onto the child snatcher. To her angry despair she saw him take the final step toward the fairground's northmost exit, all while looking directly back at her with a triumphant, knowing grin on his face. That's when she saw Josiah Key appear behind him.

To her regret, she let her relief and pleasure infuse her own face, alerting the man. He ducked, crouched, and scrambled like a wet pig, shaking off Key's hands, and started running again. Infuriated at herself, Nichols stepped before Daniels while pulling her Sig Sauer P239 from its shoulder holster. As she saw Key go after the naked man, she pointed it straight up and fired.

"Make way for the redheaded demon with a gun," she cried, and used the crowd's momentary shock to race through them.

She heard Daniels following suit, accompanied by the exclamations of a foolhardy few who tried to stop him, but by then she was already out the fairground's other side – hardly noticing that it led to a stony, root-veined, vine-covered path. If the information she had gleaned on the drive here was to be trusted, this had to be the trail to the temple fort, which stood between the town and the river.

A second later she was past Key, wishing she also had the time to take a shot at the naked man, but knowing that she couldn't risk hitting the child. Dead or not, that was why they were here, and any further damage to her might negate the whole mission. Her speed was being turbo-charged by her anger and resentment, so she no longer had time to question anything because she was on the guy.

His surprise was almost gratifying as she grabbed his neck with one hand and brought the gun butt down on his head with the other. They both went down on mossy ground in front of three stories of crumbling brickwork surrounded by leafy shade tress. Nichols mirrored the man's triumphant, knowing, grin as she landed across his back, but then also mirrored his surprised expression when, rather than stay down, rendered unconscious by her blow, he rolled, twisting, and came up in a crouch, still holding the child.

Nichols was so shocked she didn't take the moment to just shoot him in the face, and then lost her chance as Daniels cannoned by her and brought his fist directly toward the naked man's nose, point-blank, with all the force he had gathered from wanting to take on an entire festival crowd.

He missed.

Daniels was stunned when he found his target was no longer directly in front of him, and was aghast when his momentum and lack of balance sent him flying forward like a hurled javelin. Nichols, who was directly behind him, was so confused by the big man's collapse that, once again, her gun remained unused.

Finally, both westerners managed to catch sight of the naked man, who was scrambling toward the main archway, which framed the sparkling, dirty, roiling river beyond. They hadn't even started to regain their footing to continue the chase when Key stepped out from a rocky brush to block the naked man's escape.

He didn't rush the man, try to tackle him, or even shoot him. He just stepped out, far enough in front to go in any direction the man might choose, but also essentially cornering him within the small hall of the archway, since Daniels and Nichols were still blocking any retreat. Key's expression was not antagonistic in the slightest. If anything, it was curiously interested.

"We must've caught you within seconds of your entry," he said mildly. "You probably just threw your robe under the shelves and lay there, right?" Key shrugged, appreciating the naked man's blank face. "Who would have thought that whoever followed you in there would be after the same thing you were? Bad luck, yes?"

Key continued to stand still, casually surveying the man, and waited. The naked man didn't move for several seconds, but then they all saw his back curve and heard a strange animal sound. Key's eyebrows rose and his head shifted back on his neck.

"Are you snarling at me?" he asked in mock incredulity, before making a tsking noise and shaking his head sadly. "You shouldn't be growling at me. Not when you're so close to fulfilling your assignment." Key jutted his chin at the man. "Are you the only one sent to collect these corpses? Or did you go, on your own, by yourself, to clean up your mess? I mean, why else would you do it? Why not just leave well enough alone?" Key let his expression change to one of realization, then he smiled sadly and nodded with sympathetic understanding. "Or did you hear about some people—" He motioned to the strongman and redhead behind them. "—who were showing interest?"

The naked man's lips came off his teeth, and the growl snapped off as both he and Key charged.

But to the surprise of all the others, Key did not leap toward the naked man. He leaped to the left of the naked man. Nichols and Daniels had hardly started to react when the big man felt disappointment that his superior had so blatantly missed the mark. The child snatcher would clearly get away, having made them all look like fools.

The naked man seemed to think that too, if his renewed expression of cunning triumph was any evidence. He all but dove past Key, his eyes filling with the hills, woods, and water beyond.

But that expression winked off like a snuffed candle when the child snapped out of his grip. The naked man stumbled a few feet down the rocky path, then twisted to see Key standing placidly behind him, holding the corpse child like a crafty cornerback who had intercepted the game-winning touchdown pass. He waited a second until Daniels and Nichols flanked him, their guns at the ready, before commenting.

"Keep your eye on the prize, asshole," he said.

That was all he got to say before the temple fort grounds were invaded by a screeching assault team in military gear. "Down, down! Hands up, get down! Now, now!"

Key did not get down. He watched the naked man scurry off toward the river even faster than he had before, then turned to pinpoint the commanding officer of this bunch of stupid interlopers. To Daniels's surprise, Nichols's chagrin, and Key's presumption, it was the man they had known as Captain Patrick Logan.

"You have *got* to be kidding me," Key complained as he raised his hands, holding the child corpse to the sky like an offering.